THE LAZARUS COVENANT

JOHN FENZEL

THE LAZARUS COVENANT

BREATHE PRESS

Published by BREATHE Press

BREATHE Press is a registered trademark of BREATHE.

This is a work of fiction. Names, characters, places, and incidents
either are the product of the author's imagination or are used
fictitiously, and any resemblance to actual persons, living or dead,
business establishments, events, or locales is entirely coincidental.

Printed in the United States of America

Design by Wildfire
Title Page Illustration by Mike Wade
Chapter Graphic by Chad Burkey (adapted)
CIA Memo Font: F25 Executive by Volker Busse

Library of Congress Cataloging-in-Publication Data
Fenzel, John
The Lazarus Covenant / John Fenzel.—ed.
I. Title

ISBN 978-0-9822379-0-8 (acid-free paper)
Library of Congress Control Number: 2009901671
1. Former Yugoslavia—Fiction. 2. War—Fiction.
3. Religious Extremism—Fiction. 4. Nuclear Terrorism—Fiction.
6. Vatican—Fiction. 7. Special Operations—Fiction
8. Northern Ireland—Fiction. 9. Ethnic Conflict—Fiction.
10. United Nations—Fiction.

10 9 8 7 6 5 4 3 2 1

First Edition

To Ciri, Anna, Erin, and Luke
for making everything possible

ACKNOWLEDGMENTS

My heartfelt thanks to…

Kelly Moore, without whose friendship and invaluable insights, this novel would not have been possible.

Colonel (Ret.) Tom Rendall, whose demonstrated leadership and courage in the Balkans have been matched only by his friendship and tremendous support through the years.

Colonel Michael Fenzel, Gail Maiorana, Pat and Ed Weaver—the best editors and proof readers an author could ask for.

Gary Heidt, literary agent and friend. For having the faith to take on an unpublished author and a different kind of novel.

John and Muriel Fenzel—my Mom and Dad. The finest people I know.

Dr. Joan Murnane, for sharing her extensive knowledge of plants, poisons and human physiology, and for making the most complex concepts understandable.

Ann Tyson for her invaluable professional perspectives and suggestions.

Steve Veyera, good friend and FBI agent, for lending his superb expertise.

Donatella Lorch, a remarkable wartime journalist and friend, for her insights on the "expose" and its construct.

KP, for providing an insider's view of our nation's special mission units, equipment, and tactics.

Captain (USN) Pat Hall, for the insider's "Flag Bridge" view of USS Enterprise and her truly impressive capabilities.

My partners and friends in the Immediate Office of the Secretary of Defense: Colonel Kevin Vest (USMC), Colonel (USAF, Ret.) Bill Erikson, Colonel Greg Schwab (USAF) and Captain (USN) Brian Helmer, for guiding me through the intricacies of tactical flight and naval operations.

For the U.S. Army Special Forces NCOs and Officers with whom I have had the privilege to serve through the years. For the example they provided and, most of all, for their service. Heroes, all.

Lisa and Mike Zehring, Mark Fenzel, Steve Delonga—for their extraordinary, selfless support.

My wife, Ciri, for always being there, assisting me, in every way—through it all.

THE LAZARUS COVENANT

THE DIRECTOR OF CENTRAL INTELLIGENCE
Washington, D.C. 20505

INFORMATION MEMO

April 15, 1977, 12:00 PM

FOR: THE PRESIDENT OF THE UNITED STATES
FROM: Stansfield Turner, Director of Central Intelligence

SUBJECT: Sources of Future Balkan Conflict-Yugoslavia After Tito

(C) You asked for our best analysis of the worsening situation in Yugoslavia and what the future holds for its president, Josep Broz Tito. This memorandum addresses those issues.

Background:
(U) Notwithstanding the common Slavic ancestry of the Balkan people, the renewed conflict between the Serbs, Croats and Bosniaks (Slavic converts to Islam) is deeply rooted in past centuries of conquest and subjugation. Historically, Yugoslavs have been divided by history, geography, language and culture. The Ottoman Empire's victory over the Serbs at Kosovo Polje ("Field of Blackbirds") in 1389 marked the beginning of eventual Ottoman domination over the region and mass conversions to Islam.

(S) The Balkan wars of the early 20th century and World War I strongly influenced the ultimate formation of Yugoslavia-- "the Land of the South Slavs." In 1929, Yugoslavia's creation as a unitary state, while favored by many South Slav intellectuals, largely ignored known entrenched divisions within its diverse populace, contributing to ethnic hatred, religious enmity, cultural clashes and language barriers. In 1941, Nazi Germany invaded Yugoslavia, partitioning the state into zones of occupation and annexed territories. The predominantly Roman Catholic Independent State of Croatia was created and ruled by the Ustashe--a fascist puppet regime. During World War II, a bloody civil war erupted between the Ustashe, the Bosniaks, the Serb Royalist "Chetniks," and Josep Broz Tito's communist partisans. With U.S. Office of Strategic Services (OSS) assistance, Tito emerged from World War II as Yugoslavia's sole leader. In short order, Tito transitioned himself as Yugoslavia's dictator.

(S) Tito sought to eliminate sectarian nationalism in favor of socialist unity in Yugoslavia by creating six federal republics. Included among these were: Bosnia and Herzegovina, Croatia, and Serbia. Despite OSS/CIA warnings, Tito refused to closely align his governmental boundaries with Yugoslavia's diverse ethnic divisions.

(TS-**WNINTEL**) In an effort to stabilize the resulting domestic volatility in Yugoslavia, Tito is now resorting to mass arrests of suspected spies, dissidents and intellectuals. CIA HUMINT sources (LAZARUS) confirm, through eye witness accounts, that these prisoners are being executed *en masse,* and buried in unmarked mass graves around the country. Tito's purges have produced an illusion of peace and harmony within Yugoslavia, but a strong undercurrent of nationalistic strife remains.

Analysis:
(TS) Tito's remaining life expectancy is estimated to be no more than three years. In the absence of a chosen or natural successor to Tito, a power vacuum in Yugoslavia is viewed as certain. Nationalistic fervor will feed demands for greater autonomy and political reform among all six republics. These movements could splinter Yugoslavia and will likely result in civil war closely drawn along ethnic and religious lines. Religious animosity among the three major denominations--Eastern Orthodox (Serbs), Roman Catholic (Croats), and Islam (Bosniaks)--will remain the dominant divisive cultural factors in the Yugoslavia; and if exploited effectively, would contribute to armed unrest between ethnic factions extending beyond the 20th Century.

CLASSIFIED BY: DCI - Stansfield Turner
REASONS: X2
DECLASSIFY ON: April 15, 2009

Indeed, it is true that in these acts of revenge on others, men take it upon themselves to begin the process of repealing those general laws of humanity which are there to give a hope of salvation to all who are in distress, instead of leaving those laws in existence, remembering that there may come a time when they, too, will be in danger and will need their protection.

Thucydides

Only part of us is sane: only part of us loves pleasure and the longer day of happiness, wants to live to our nineties and die in peace, in a house that we built, that shall shelter those who come after us. The other half of us is nearly mad. It prefers the disagreeable to the agreeable, loves pain and its darker night despair, and wants to die in a catastrophe that will set back life to its beginnings and leave nothing of our house save its blackened foundations.

Rebecca West

PART I

SEPARATION

CHAPTER 1

THE WORLD CHANGED the afternoon they were released early from school. The rain began in March, more of a drizzle at first, but then it became heavier, the clouds darker and more ominous. One Sunday morning, the heavens opened and the rain hammered down in torrents, continuing through the spring. In April, the Drina River spilled over its banks and flooded surrounding fields. The farmers warned of catastrophe, claiming they could smell more rain on the way, but that afternoon when a plumbing malfunction caused school to let out early, only a few drops wet the youthful faces of cousins Marko and Celo Mescic.

Twelve-year-old boys with the rest of the day now free, they jumped over fences and ran through fields of wet, shoulder-high weeds, their chests heaving. Along the way, they could smell the smoke drifting from fireplaces and wood-burning stoves. Passing between the engorged Drina and the sprawling Zvornik aluminum plant, they stepped into a recently plowed field and found themselves suddenly mired in dark, thick mud, slogging their way through. Their shoes made loud sucking sounds like the croaking of bullfrogs in a vast swamp. When one of Celo's shoes was pulled off by the muck he cursed a stream of obscenities. Marko howled, amused at their predicament and at Celo's heated reaction. Some of the words, Marko had never heard before—at least, not in those combinations. After yanking and pulling on one another, they finally extricated themselves from the muddy field and rushed down the long, grassy trail that skirted Dulici village, lungs and legs pumping.

By the time they arrived home, the rain had stopped altogether; the air was cold and the skies clear. Their dripping clothes clung to their bodies; mud still covered their shoes. Once inside, steam rose from them and they laughed as they watched each other shiver uncontrollably. Goosebumps covered their bodies. They quickly changed into dry clothes, leaving their wet ones on the pine-planked floor along with the gobs of mud they'd tracked inside.

Concerned that no one would be home for several hours, and just so Celo wouldn't forget, Marko complained for the hundredth time that he was hungry and that it was lunchtime. And for the hundredth time, Celo told him to shut up. When Celo was dressed, he marched into his parents' room.

He reemerged, holding his father's shotgun boldly in one hand and an old Makarov pistol in the other, smiling ear to ear. He looked like a lanky, long-legged urban gangster. Marko looked at his cousin with wide eyes, but before he could say anything, Celo grinned, motioned him toward the door with the pistol in his hand and announced matter-of-factly, "There's nothing for us to eat here, so we'll hunt it down ourselves!"

Marko was fixated on the weapons in Celo's hands. "But, what will your papa say?" he whispered.

"He won't know, because you won't tell him. You scared?"

"I'm not scared!"

"Then why are your knees shaking?"

"But . . . where . . . and what is there to hunt?"

"Just shut up," Celo shoved the pistol under his belt. "I know a place, by the dam."

Marko pointed at the grey wooden floor where they'd tracked in large clumps of mud. "We should clean—"

Celo gave him an angry glare. "I said shut up! We'll be back before Mama and Papa come home. We'll clean everything up then."

"But—"

"Let's go."

Soon they were walking uphill, on a trail that meandered along a ridge, winding north, east, and then north again. The trail led up to the pumiced ruins of a past era—either Roman or Turkish—that overlooked the Drina River to the east, and the deep ravines that surrounded it. To their right, the Drina cut a jagged edge along the provincial border between Bosnia-Herzegovina and Serbia. On the opposite bank, the terrain was an undulating green. On its western bank, their side of the river, the city of Zvornik was contained by the Banat Mountains—striking peaks of limestone, earth and granite—jutting skyward, then leveling off into verdant meadows of the southwest, near Sarajevo.

Both boys were drenched with sweat; their legs felt like lead and their lungs burned from their climb. They sat, looking out over the Drina River and the swelling countryside. Inhaling, he smelled the fresh scent of pine resin. He shivered in the cool shade. The place reminded him of King Arthur's castle in the story of *Camelot* which his father used to read to him at night before bed. He dreamed of being among the greatest and most chivalrous warriors in Europe, the Knights of the Round Table. After his father had been taken from him, he came to view Camelot not only as a place, but as a beacon—guiding him back to a better, happier time.

"Here's where we'll find the boars," Celo announced confidently. He sat on one of the ancient, stacked, white granite blocks that were once an outpost or a landowner's perimeter.

"Boars?"

"Mmm," Celo nodded, pointing below them to the right. "Look, their tracks."

He focused his gaze through the thick vegetation in the direction Celo indicated, and could make out a clearing some thirty meters away.

"And there is where they were today and yesterday." Celo pulled the Makarov from his belt and handed it to him. "You can see where they've dug up the ground. Their shit is everywhere."

Suddenly, as the weight of the pistol—the cold metal—was placed in his hand, the scenic view no longer mattered. He'd never handled a pistol before, and he felt a rush of adrenaline. He concentrated on not letting go of the handle, for fear he'd lose it or shoot himself by accident.

His anxiety was doubled with Celo's simple admonition: "Be careful, it's loaded."

Celo rested the shotgun on his lap. He looked comfortable with it, natural even. "It's better to wait quietly than to search for them. If we're moving, they'll hear us."

They waited in silence. The sun had begun to set and the sky darkened. His heartbeat slowed as his grip on the Makarov became looser and finally felt more natural to him. His hands no longer shook. He looked at Celo, who stared intently in the direction of the clearing.

He admired Celo. With all of his hot air and showing off, Marko saw him as a natural leader. He looked the part too. His adult face had still not settled on him, but he bore a strong resemblance to his father with his jet-black hair and piercing blue eyes. And he spoke with the authority of someone twice his age. Once, Marko had seen a classmate a year older challenge him at school. Celo had ended the brewing fight before the other boy had an opportunity to start it. Girls were attracted to him—a source of fascination and envy for Marko, especially when Celo introduced him to them as his brother.

Their daily routine helped to take his mind off his own father, who was sitting in a jail somewhere in Zagreb or Belgrade; he didn't know which. Although Marko knew his father was in trouble with the government, he didn't know why he'd been arrested. No one had ever explained it to him.

Nor did they explain why they'd forced him into the orphanage in Zagreb. While he was there, he missed his father. He never knew his mother because she'd died when he was only two; but he'd seen many photos, and in the orphanage, he found that he missed her too. Each night, his hearing grew acute to every sound, and he would lie awake listening to every footstep or whispered conversation in the hallways.

His aunt and uncle had brought him to their home about six months ago. They told him only that his papa had a disagreement with Tito, as if he were one of their neighbors, instead of the country's communist leader. He listened silently, but still didn't fully understand. All he knew was that he missed his papa. Still, there were the bad dreams of being led away from his father. In the orphanage, they came to him as anxious shadows, and every night they returned and woke him from his sleep—the same, familiar sense of loss that flooded back to him like the rising of a tide, plunging him into darkness.

Every night, as the darkness and the shadows returned, he was thrust into a living nightmare. The sound of loud knocking, doors being kicked in, shouting, his father's protests, screaming sirens, and crying—always his own—startled him out of sleep and kept him awake. Only when he imagined the sound of his father's violin would sleep finally come to him.

Celo nudged him and pointed behind them and to their left. He heard the rustling before he actually saw the black shapes in the streambed. Celo motioned to him as he dismounted the granite slab slowly and attempted to approach the boar from their right side in a kind of fishhook maneuver that would allow them to remain on the high ground, allowing Celo a clear shot.

He tried to emulate Celo's stalking movements, but as much as he tried and as slowly as he moved, he was painfully aware of the noise he made with every step. Celo looked back and motioned him forward, but at that instant, they heard the sharp, rhythmic crack of rifle fire echo around them. It startled the boars; they grunted and squealed and ran into the underbrush before Celo had the chance to fire at them.

The automatic rifle fire came from the west, in the direction of the lake and dam. Celo cursed loudly then threw his father's shotgun on the ground in front of him, kicking the leaves and dirt in frustration.

"It's the army, isn't it?" Marko asked with a nervous smile. They'd seen the trucks rolling through the village that morning on the way to school.

"The bastards! What are you smiling about? The fucking bastards ruined my shot!"

He nodded and tried to keep from laughing, but he couldn't conceal his grin.

Celo shook his head. "I'm going to teach you how to move in the forest, Marko. You're like a freight train at night!"

"I know. I tried to copy you, but I'm still too loud," he admitted, then attempted to change the subject. "We should go home before your father returns and sees his guns missing."

Celo nodded, and Marko could see a renewed sense of purpose in his eyes. "We'll take a different way, along the lake."

"And the maneuvers?"

"Don't make so much noise. Walk toe to heel and they won't hear us." Celo gripped the middle of the shotgun. "Just follow me."

"Toe to heel," he repeated, close behind Celo, still tiptoeing like a ballerina.

As they approached the lake, they could hear trucks moving around at the base of the dam, coming and going. The lake was a dull orange and smelled of sulfur. Large deposits of a flaky white substance ringed its banks. Celo pointed at the steel pipes that emerged from the ground and emptied directly above the water. Although his mouth was very dry, Marko looked at the lake and had no desire to drink from it or from the streams around it.

"They dump the chemicals and shavings from the aluminum plant," Celo said, "so the lake is dead. No fish, and the water looks like orange soda."

"Fanta Lake." Marko replied, referring to the western beverage that had recently arrived in Yugoslavia.

"A good name for it," Celo agreed, and pointed toward the opposite bank. "We'll go around the lake and come out in the woods in front of the dam, so we can see the army's maneuvers without being seen, but we have to move quickly."

The sun was sinking below the line of pine and oak trees atop the dam. He walked by his cousin's side, anxious. "It's getting late, Celo. What will your mama and papa say?"

"We're on our way now. There's no shorter path." Celo replied. "If we'd killed one of the pigs, it'd be easier to explain."

"You can tell them I got lost, and you came to search for me."

Celo turned to him, smiling. "With guns?"

"Well, you can say that you were afraid the army would arrest me, too."

There was the very subtle, if accidental, reference to his father. During the past month, Celo had done his best to keep Marko's mind off all of that. He walked a few more steps before responding.

"I said, don't worry," Celo replied impatiently. "We'll hide the guns in the shed tonight and sneak them into their bedroom tomorrow after school. They go under the bed, so they'll never know they were missing."

Marko grunted and nodded his head.

As they approached the dam, they could hear voices and laughter. Just ahead, they could see a wooden guardhouse at the top of the dam. To avoid being seen or heard, Celo turned deeper into the woods and slowed their pace. *Toes to heel,* Marko reminded himself. Soon they were walking downhill, parallel to the dam, and away from the lake, holding branches and trees whenever possible to control their descent. The voices were louder now. Celo stopped and silently knelt down next to Marko, motioning toward the hilltop opposite the dam, not far from the main road that led to their house. Marko nodded.

As the boys began climbing the hill, the soldiers' voices were muffled by the loud arrival of more trucks struggling up the dirt road to the dam. Marko noticed that Celo used the trucks' noise to mask their own as they climbed up the hill at a more rapid pace.

Another good lesson, Marko told himself.

At the top of the large hill, they slid on their bellies and crouched behind a boulder where they could see across to the police guardhouse over the darkening horizon. It was lighted, but appeared unoccupied. Long black pipes stretched along the width of the dam, their release valves rusting, pointing in the direction of "Fanta Lake."

Below, at the base of the dam, Marko counted three jeeps parked on the far right side near the entrance. Two bulldozers were parked on opposite sides of a large rectangular hole that had been cut deep into the ground. Piles of earth surrounded the hole, except on its western-most end, where one of the 'dozers had created a dirt ramp entranceway to the bottom. Soldiers with machine guns and rifles congregated by the parked vehicles talking, smoking cigarettes and laughing.

From Marko's vantage point in the gathering darkness, he could see both trucks parked on the dirt road at the entrance to the dam, their engines still running where the two guards stood. A jeep drove around the trucks, and the guards saluted as it passed. It stopped in front of the group of soldiers, and a tall, thin man in an officer's uniform stepped out. He carried a pistol holstered in black leather on his hip. He returned their salutes crisply, and the group immediately ran to positions atop the piles, standing in a semi-circle, their guns facing the dam.

Four soldiers were posted at the entrance of the hole on each side. One of the trucks moved forward, and then backed into the entrance. Two soldiers gave the driver directions from the front and rear. They stopped the truck just as the rear wheels began to descend down the earthen ramp. The rear tarp was lifted by two other soldiers with guns, who quickly jumped off the back and took their positions on each side of the truck, weapons raised. At the other end, another soldier lay down with his machine gun on a bipod, its linked ammunition pouring out, aimed at the rear of the truck.

Marko shook Celo's arm. "What are they doing?" he whispered.

"Sshh! They'll hear you!" Celo placed his hand on Marko's shoulder and forced him down to the ground. "Don't say a word."

They heard a series of orders barked out by one of the soldiers near the truck. Marko watched in horror as men, young and old, jumped off the back of the truck, fell to the ground, and struggled to stand.

From the distance, he could finally see why: each man's hands were tied behind his back. Some of them had their mouths bound with cloth. As one truck emptied and then departed the ramp, the other was moving into position, preparing to go through the same drill. Marko estimated that there were thirty prisoners falling off the truck and shuffling together into the hole.

"Look!" Marko said, pointing. One of the prisoners, dressed in filthy street clothes, had broken away from the group, alternately shuffling and hopping toward the dam steppe in an attempt to escape. They watched as one of the guards calmly raised his rifle and took aim. There was no warning given to the prisoner or any order to stop. Only a single shot. The man collapsed in a heap to the gravel. Another guard walked over to the prisoner's body and kicked him down into the hole.

The terrible significance of the scene tore through Marko, and his heart began to flail ominously. Tears streamed down his face. So Celo would not see, he buried his face on top of his hands—one of them still holding the Makarov loosely in the dirt.

They dared not move.

A moment later, the staccato rattle of gunfire tore through the forest, echoing at once against the side of the dam, projecting the noise back upon them in a seemingly endless wave. The groans of those wounded were cut off with short bursts, and then single shots rang out. Celo reached across and gripped Marko's arm, drawing him closer. When the noise finally subsided, Marko realized he was sobbing silently against him.

Celo whispered close to his ear. "Come on, Marko! We've got to get out of here." As he began to help Marko up, the last truck pulled away from the ramp with its headlights on. The truck slowly drove off, its headlights silhouetting the officer Marko had seen earlier, casting a long, thin shadow that intersected the group of soldiers. The soldiers had all descended from the piles of earth around the grave, and now stood at attention before him. His voice was deep, authoritative, and seemed accustomed to giving orders. But Marko was struck by how calm he appeared in the wake of the slaughter he'd just supervised.

"It's too dark to bury them now. Post guards here tonight and we'll finish tomorrow morning, when it's light."

There was no discussion in front of the officer, but as soon as he departed the area in his jeep, the arguments began in earnest.

"Fuck him . . . and fuck them too! They're all dead. They don't need guards!" The dim glow of cigarettes being lit illuminated the soldiers' young faces. A small mob of troops began to walk toward the trucks, joking and laughing. After they loaded on the trucks, Marko heard another soldier shouting over the noise of the engines. He barked out names, then there was more laughter as two soldiers jumped off the back of the truck closest to him and Celo.

Celo pointed at them. "Those must be the 'volunteers,'" he muttered sarcastically.

As the trucks drove away from the dam, gravel crunching under the tires, both soldiers that had been left behind continued to be teased loudly by their comrades who had escaped guard duty for the night. As they drove by, one of them taunted: "Why don't you go over there and have a *rest* with your friends!"

The guards stood by at the base of the dam, smoking their cigarettes, weapons slung over their shoulders. One of them stamped his cigarette into the gravel. The other was urinating in the hole, and as he did so, dismissed the taunts with a final obscene gesture that he directed toward the last truck: "Fuck your mothers!" The guard's insult was returned with howls of laughter from the back of the truck.

Marko followed the cluster of truck headlights down the road until they were out of sight. He looked back toward the dam and saw both the guards light fresh cigarettes as they walked away from the hole along the same dirt road.

"We're going home," Celo whispered. "Do you hear me?"

The truth suddenly dawned on Marko. "They killed them all, didn't they?"

Celo rose from his prone position with the shotgun in his hand. Squeezing Marko's arm and pulling him up, he replied firmly. "We need to go *now. Come on!*"

Marko sniffed and nodded slowly, rubbing his hand against his nose and mouth, now caked with dirt. "Are they all dead?"

Celo knelt to face him and looked into his eyes. "Yes! They're dead. *All of them.* And we shouldn't have been here to see it happen." Celo grabbed Marko's arm insistently. "Listen to me! If they catch us, they'll kill us, too—"

Celo was interrupted by a low, wavering moan below them. He forced him back down onto the ground and held his index finger to his mouth, signaling Marko to be silent, then pushed his chest off the ground to see over the boulder. Bringing his knee to rest beneath him, Celo searched for any sign of the guards. The noise came again, from the direction of the grave, a low constant groaning that sounded more like a wounded animal than a human.

Marko, now kneeling beside him, tugged at his shirt. "Someone's alive down there!"

"No! I told you, they're all dead!" Celo insisted, staring at him fiercely. "And we're leaving."

Marko placed his hand on Celo's back, pleading. "Celo, you heard it too—there's someone alive down there! We gotta help him!"

Celo shook his head defiantly. "I said no. We don't know them, and we aren't in a position to help *anyone*. They're prisoners! Look, we're going home now!"

Celo rose and started to walk down the opposite side of the hill. Marko ran up to him, nearly stumbling into him, and grabbed hold of his arm with a surprising strength.

"Celo, listen to me! Someone *is* alive down there, and he's been shot just like all the rest. He'll die if we don't help him." His tears were rolling down his face, causing the dirt to streak heavily. "Don't you see? It could be Papa.

He's a prisoner too. We gotta do something!"

Celo looked at him. This was the first time Marko had directly referred to his father.

"Where are the guards?" Celo asked quietly, looking around.

"I don't see them. They must've left."

"They're behind us . . . over there," Celo said in a whisper, pointing behind them. "On the road."

Marko looked back, but could see nothing through the forest. "Don't stop me. I'm going down there."

Celo looked at Marko for a moment, as if sizing him up. Finally he said, "I'll watch for the guards up here and cover you. If I start shooting, you run. Understand?"

Marko nodded silently and began descending—sometimes sliding— down the steep hill toward the base of the dam. He stopped when he heard the moaning again, this time louder and more distinct, more human. *It was not an animal.*

As he inched closer, he realized that in order to get to the mass grave, he would have to go below the gravel base another fifty feet to the bottom of the hill, and then climb up to the dam steppe. Directly across from the hole, he was overcome by the putrid smell of decay, human excrement and loam. He choked back the heavy bile that rose in his throat. He tried to hold his breath but it only made the smell worse when the lack of oxygen forced him to inhale the thick rancid air. He dropped to his knees and elbows, pressing his mouth to his free hand to muffle the sound of his gagging.

He clung to underbrush and pulled on tree saplings to assist in negotiating the steep parts of the climb. Drawing closer, zigzagging between trees and boulders, he saw the guardhouse with the corrugated metal roof on top of the dam. A moment later, he heard the voices—faint, indecipherable. He froze, then slowly moved to flatten his body against the steep incline. His arms were outstretched in front of him, holding onto a sapling to prevent from sliding down.

Who were they? Guards or survivors?

The sound of crunching above startled him. Seconds later, he felt an avalanche of gravel, branches and leaves falling around and on top of him. He reached for his pistol, but before he could remove it from his belt, a giant hand suddenly took hold of his wrist. His pulse raced. Reflexively, he pulled back, but the man's grip was too strong.

"*Comchye*...Neighbor...." It was a rasping, barely audible male voice,

10

heavy with desperation. "Please . . . help us!"

Marko found the pistol grip with his other hand and pulled it out in one swift motion, pointing it at the bridge of the man's nose directly above him. He felt a sudden shock at the face he saw—covered with mud and blood. His eyes were a liquid black, and were glazed over in a vacant, mad stare.

"Ll. .let. .tt go of me, now . . . or . . . or I'll sh . . . shoot," Marko stammered, every nerve of his body on edge.

He saw the man close his eyes, and noticed that he was struggling to breathe. His eyes opened and stared back at him. *"Neighbor . . . I am already dead . . . others are alive . . . help them before the soldiers return."*

He felt the man's grip release completely, leaving his own arm wet with blood and slime and dirt. He lowered the pistol and pulled himself up parallel to the man's head. He could see the grave directly in front of him. The dam was its backdrop. "How many are alive?" he whispered.

"Two, three . . . I don't know"

Marko dragged the man down by his belt like a sack of flour, his limbs boney and wasted, and rested him against a tree. Only then did he realize that the man had been shot in his chest. He knew the man was dying in front of him, but he could do nothing except try to make him more comfortable.

"Help them . . . please. . . ."

"Rest here—I'll be back for you."

The man nodded weakly, and Marko saw him close his eyes. Fear gripped him, as if he were clutching the side of a cliff. *How could this possibly be happening? From a simple hunting trip to this?*

Attempting to stay in the shadows, he ran up to the dirt mound closest to him and found the bulldozed entrance to the mass grave. Turning the corner onto the ramp, he was hit by another wave of stench—the coppery stench of blood and death. His mouth filled with bile. The dry heaves that followed caused his eyes to flood with tears, momentarily blinding him. He put his hand to his mouth and lay still. He blinked his eyes hard and his vision cleared.

He looked below and saw faint silhouettes that seemed to float noiselessly. He leaned forward to get a better view. Bodies illumined by the moonlight. Scattered grotesquely. Many were intertwined with others, as if they had all been dancing in celebration together, and had suddenly collapsed from exhaustion—their mouths agape, grinning at him in an odd, disconcerting levity. But they were dead, mangled and still bleeding in front of him. No one else had survived the slaughter. Other bodies had been buried before, in previous executions, but hastily, and occasionally he could see a face staring at him in lifeless disbelief. Shoes and hands seemed to be reaching to him out of the ground. Shiny, metallic-colored flies buzzed around, reflecting the moonlight, swarming onto the corpses and on the pools of blood on the ground around him. The grave was cluttered with shell casings that had fallen from the dirt mounds above. Papers, photographs and identification cards were scattered about.

He remembered promising Celo he'd return quickly. Now that seemed an impossible task. Not in this darkness, and not in this hell. But now he wanted nothing more. He searched for Celo on top of the hill, but his sweat and tears stung his eyes and made everything foggy around him.

He turned to step off the ramp, and the man he'd left in the woods appeared suddenly in front of him, like a ghost. Marko gasped. The man was standing now—hunched over, and fell heavily into Marko's arms.

"Not here . . . I'll show you where they are."

Marko quickly took hold of the man and placed his arm over his shoulder. The man guided him around the grave to the end opposite the entrance. In front of them, two men were lying down on the gravel along the large dirt piles. He helped the man down to a sitting position on the dirt mound, then moved to the other men. Their eyes were open, but only one was still alive. He knelt down and closed the dead man's eyes. He looked up and noticed the other man was weeping.

"They're brothers."

"We can't take him with us."

"No! We must!"

This was taking too much time, Marko realized—time they couldn't afford—with men who had barely survived their own executions, now giving *him* orders! *"I'm arguing with the dead."* He looked over and saw that the brother who was alive was holding the other's hand, breathing querulously. "I'll take him into the woods and hide his body. Then I'll come back for both of you."

Both men nodded at one another.

He reached over, separating the brothers' hands, looking at the one who had survived. The man nodded and covered his face with his hands.

Marko managed to drag the man's body, little by little, to the edge of the woods, and dropped him there. Reaching for branches with his free hand to control his descent, he slid the body to the bottom of the hill between two trees and covered it with branches and leaves. Gasping for air, he hurried back up the hill, and found both men slowly making their way to the woods, unassisted. Marko ran up to them and helped the other brother, draping the man's arm over his shoulders.

"Walk with me . . . lift your bad leg off the ground, and rest your weight on me." He looked up and saw the other man standing a few steps ahead, watching them. How could he have survived a bullet in the chest? He should be dead!

"Get into the woods! I have him." His voice was no longer a whisper.

In the distance, he saw the reflection of headlights against the trees bordering the dirt road, followed by the sound of a small engine approaching. The ground erupted around them, and an instant later he heard the deafening sound of automatic gunfire from above accompanied by voices, sharp and hectoring. He lunged forward to a nearby tree and pulled his pistol out of his belt. He looked up at the guard shack, where he saw the guards standing up in full view, firing directly at them from atop the dam. Without aiming, he fired the pistol twice in their direction and he saw them disappear, taking cover.

A loud boom filled the night air, and he realized it was Celo, firing the shotgun. The guards returned their fire, above and below. He heard a pronounced grunt, then felt the man's arm around him go limp. Unprepared to bear his full weight, Marko's knees buckled. He looked at the body of the man next to him, face down; his shirt stained a dark crimson. He searched for a pulse, but found none.

He felt all of the muscles in his body propel himself forward, toward the woods only a few yards to his front. In only a few moments, he was tumbling down the hill in a headlong plunge through all the saplings in his path. The full weight of his momentum carried him to the bottom of the ravine, where he careened into a fallen log and twisted his back painfully.

He tried to breathe as he quickly assessed his surroundings. Looking up at the dam, he could see the headlights above him. Suddenly, there was a tumult of shouting and cursing—first questions, then accusations, and finally orders. The tall officer he'd seen during the executions was standing above him. Glancing back down at his hands, he knew they were badly cut, but he could feel a dull, throbbing pain in his right hand. A shiver ran through him. The guards were now using the headlights of the jeep as an improvised searchlight, illuminating the hill opposite them, where he was hiding. They were randomly firing their rifles in the direction of the beams, and one burst impacted only an arm's length beside him.

13

There was more gunfire. Some of the rounds erupted in the dirt and leaves in front of him. He crawled as quickly as he could through the creek bed, toward the road and around the hill. He was panting. Sweat soaked through his clothes. The scent of human decay was still sharp in his nose.

Celo fired twice again above him. More shouting, and this time screaming, came from the dam. Celo had hit one of the guards.

Marko stood up and sprinted forward to a log twenty or thirty yards away. Crashing into the log, he heard a loud grunt, revealing the unearthly body of the prisoner who had been shot in the chest. The man's hand enveloped the back of his head and pushed it forcefully down into the dirt.

"Quiet!"

After a few moments, the guards were firing away from them. With the initial surprise now passed, one of them was taunting Celo.

"Come down, *Chetniki*, or we'll hunt you and your families down and kill you! If you surrender now, we'll let you live."

"If they're calling us 'Chetniks,'" Marko asked, "who are *they?*"

"Tito's secret army," the man next to him whispered, looking over the log. He did the same. Men seemed to be surging toward them from all directions. Just ahead of him on the side of the dirt road, he saw the tall officer. He was alone, skirting the hill, moving deliberately and quietly, ghostlike.

Marko turned to the man next to him, whose ashen white complexion, mixed with blood and dirt and eyes black as death, almost glowed in the moonlight. "Who are you?"

The man appeared delirious, hardly human. His voice was choked and cracked. "Thanks to you, you can call me Lazarus, like in the Bible."

The name had no significance to him, except that it had a unique sound to it. *Lazarus.* "Well, I can't help you anymore, Lazarus. My cousin is on top of the hill," he whispered, then pointed at the officer. "And *he's* going to kill him. If you can, get to the church just down the road. It's not far, and there is a wood shack behind it. I'll look for you there tomorrow."

The man nodded in a way that made him appear drunken. Before Marko could leave, he felt the man's hand firmly take hold of his shirt, causing him to turn around, startled. Lazarus' eyes suddenly appeared lucid, alive, but his voice was weak he seemed to be scarcely breathing.

"*Hvala, Comchye*—thank-you, neighbor. I am indebted to you."

Marko looked at him, but said nothing. He doubted the man would live much longer in his condition, even if he escaped the guards. More guards would certainly be on the way.

Marko saw the officer, pistol in hand, quietly, deftly, ascend the hill. He was even taller than he looked at first. Powerful, but not fast. Fifty yards up, Marko left the man who called himself Lazarus at the log and began walking up the hill also, matching the officer's steps one-for-one, toe to heel. Copying his movements, Marko realized he would have to stop this officer to save Celo's life.

He struggled to keep up with the officer, whose movements up the hill seemed quick and effortless. In the moonlight, he could see that the officer was holding a small pistol in his hand. Only fifty yards remained to the top. Exhausted and gasping for air, his lungs burned and his legs screamed in agony. Clawing frantically at the ground, he felt his hand pounding. It was swollen and he could barely move his fingers. He was confused when he felt his knees and shins crashing forward into a rock outcropping.

Something was grinding into his back, between his shoulder blades, driving the air from his lungs.

"If you move, I will kill you." The voice was caustic, yet matter-of-fact. He felt a rough hand grasp the Makarov, then forcefully remove it from his hand. He turned his head out of the dirt and leaves to breathe, only to find himself staring into the barrel of the officer's gun. He tried to look away, but the officer buried his knee further into his back. A hand took hold of his hair and jammed his head into the ground. His neck crackled in protest. He struggled to spit out the dirt in his mouth and felt his lungs beginning to collapse.

"Please . . . let me go."

"Shut-up. Is that your friend up there?" The officer pulled his head up with such force that he could feel the muscles in his neck tear, and the center of his back felt like it was being cut in two. Spasms wracked through him, and he began to choke.

"Yeah. . . ." He felt himself begin to black out.

The officer pulled him by his hair, to his knees, then drove his knee between his shoulder blades. He gasped for air. Streaks of yellows and reds shot through his clenched eyes.

"Call him down here . . . now," the officer growled, smiling derisively. "Or you will both die like the rest."

Marko inhaled, smelling the sourness of his breath and coughed violently. He spat out a spray of bloody saliva and nodded. "Okay," he gasped. He felt the officer's grip loosen, and he gasped for air.

15

"Tell him!"

Again his hold slackened, and Marko shouted as loudly as he could manage. "Celo! *Run!*"

The officer's boot heel crashed into the back of his head, a heavy weight struck him in the back and pitched him forward into an abyss . . . and then, everything went black. The searing flash of pain in the back of his neck was what caused him to regain consciousness. He opened his eyes and the world was spinning around. He wanted to scream, but his vocal chords had shut down. He tasted the dark, coppery tang of his own blood in his throat. He coughed and gasped violently, fighting off waves of nausea.

His eyes gradually focused on the officer directly above him. The face was long and narrow, with eyes that were cold and hollow, displaying no emotion—only calculation. He was lying on his back, with the officer's heavy boot on his chest. A wave of nausea passed over him.

"That was foolish," the officer snarled. "Because now both of you will die, and you will be first."

"Why are you doing this?" he half-cried, half-screamed. He swallowed convulsively. His stomach cramped and his body instantly seemed to draw in upon itself in anticipation of what was to come. He peed himself just as he saw the pistol aimed at his head. He closed his eyes to say a prayer . . . any prayer. . . . And then there was a loud noise, shattering the darkness like a clap of thunder. Not one, but two shots, one distinctly louder than the other. Dirt flew onto his face and he crashed to the ground.

I'm dead, he thought. But he could open his eyes and his ears were ringing. He was breathing in shallow, panting gulps. The dirt on his face obscured his vision, and he realized the officer had released him.

"StopStopStopPleaseStop!"

It was Celo's voice, loud and high-pitched. Desperate. Interrupted by the sounds of fists striking bone and flesh. Everything was in motion. The officer was on top of Celo punching him viciously, relentlessly. A shot rang out, followed by another one soon after, but the second shot sounded different, louder than the first. He scrambled awkwardly to his feet and ran to where he heard Celo's voice. He found his cousin laying face-up on the ground, wide-eyed and panicked. He was holding his side, blood oozing between his fingers.

The officer was lying beside him.

Marko looked back and could see a group of soldiers assembling at the base of the hill, now surging toward them.

"Celo! Get up! We have to go!" Marko screamed. "They're coming!"

He was hyperventilating. His bones popped and cracked. Rivulets of pain shot through his neck and back. His face was raw and numb.

Celo was struggling to speak. Blood welled from his badly battered mouth. "Marko . . . go without me . . . I'll be okay."

Marko tugged on his arm. "No! *Get up!* I won't leave you!"

The officer groaned beside them. *He was still alive.*

Where was his pistol?

The panic receded as he flexed and rubbed the circulation back into his hands. He found the shotgun beside Celo and took it in both hands. His head pounded and his mouth was dry from swallowing blood. He swayed heavily, dizzy from the pain shooting through his body.

He looked down at the officer, and could see that he was breathing and his eyes were blinking. His shoulder reflected a mass of dark red in the moonlight.

He heard Celo's faint voice. "I have his pistol!"

Ignoring his cousin, Marko raised the stock of the shotgun to his left shoulder and aimed the barrel at the officer's head.

"Marko! *No!*" Celo gasped.

He pulled the trigger, but it only clicked. He lowered the shotgun to the ground with his good hand, and pumped it to inject another shell. Raising it in a single motion, he pulled the trigger again. The click echoed against the trees.

The officer stared at him, then at Celo with a wide grin. "Thou shalt not kill," he recited.

Celo managed to lift himself to a knee. "The guards, Marko! We don't have time!"

With a stiff, jerky gait, Marko stepped forward, away from his cousin, and reversed his grip on the shotgun as if it were a hammer. He glared at the officer with a hatred he'd never before experienced. *These are the people who took my Pa from me.*

Marko raised the stock of the shotgun above his head with his left hand and brought it crashing down with all his power. There was an audible *CRACK!* as the wooden stock shattered the officer's jaw. He felt the reverberation throughout his entire body. Blood sprayed across his face. Pulling the shotgun away, he looked down and saw the man's body lying on the ground, motionless. He took Celo's arm in his and pulled him to his feet.

"Let's go."

The darkness of the forest seemed to close in upon them. Using the shotgun as crutch in one hand, grasping Celo's waist with the other, Marko stumbled through the woods along a faint depression, away from the dam. They waited in the woods until the trucks roared past them. Outside the forest and over the ridge, the moon was low and full.

"Do you have the pistol?" Marko asked suddenly.

Celo looked up at him and handed him the officer's pistol.

"No! I mean your Papa's pistol!"

"I thought you had it!" Celo grimaced.

Marko stared back at his cousin blankly, blood and sweat oozing from his hair. He shook his head. "I had the shotgun."

Celo tensed and looked back at the trucks approaching the dam. "If they find it. . . ."

Marko shook his head, anticipating his reaction. "No, we can't go back there. They'll kill us!"

Celo, still holding his wound, looked back at him and reached with his free arm. "Help me up then. We can't rest."

Casting a glance at the horizon as he helped his cousin to his feet, he was suddenly conscious of a terrible fear—raw, intense, and sickening, submerging him like an anchor, made heavier still by overwhelming dread of what was yet to come....

PART II

APPARITIONS

CHAPTER 2

MARK LYONS HAD DEPARTED Belfast, Northern Ireland, in a shroud of fog at five in the morning. Nine hours and two layovers later, the plane began its rough descent into the valleys of southern Bosnia. As a distraction from the turbulence, he picked up the copy of the *New York Times* folded in the seat pocket in front of him. Scanning it, he noticed the headline on the front page, above the fold.

> **Renewed Fighting in Bosnia Threatens Balkan Peace**
> By Kate Kamrath
> ***New York Times* News Service**

His eyes widened when he saw the author's name . . . Kate Kamrath. *It shouldn't come as any surprise*, he thought. He inhaled deeply. But it was, nonetheless, and it was unsettling. As one of the premier war reporters, he knew Kate Kamrath reported on only the most serious world crises—the most dangerous ones—and often the ones that hadn't fully revealed themselves. That was her role.

Why couldn't you find another war, Kate? Somewhere else this time. Somewhere I'm not.

He continued reading as the turbulence worsened.

> Mostar, Bosnia-Herzegovina, January 22—More than a decade after the Dayton Peace Accords, bloody clashes between Serb and Croat forces in southern Bosnia are threatening a fragile Balkan peace.
>
> Western envoys arrived in Sarajevo today for talks aimed at pressuring the warring sides to reaffirm the Dayton Accords as renewed shelling in Herzegovina Province destroyed dozens of homes and left an estimated eight people dead.
>
> Chief American envoy Ambassador Jack Fulbright characterized the planned talks as "crucial to the future

stability of the Balkans," and a vital precursor to a renewed agreement to be formalized in Lyon, France next week.

Recent hostilities have centered on the small Bosnian Croat village of Ravno, where Serb paramilitaries killed eighteen Bosnian Croat police officers. Last week, Croatian President Milo Stanic responded by dispatching tanks into Bosnia, to an isolated stretch of forest ridgeline where they continue to shell the hills at regular intervals.

Tens of thousands of refugees have poured into neighboring Croatia and Montenegro. Mobs and riots quickly turned into armed conflict between paramilitaries. As the violence intensified, Serb and Croatian armies rushed to the Ravno area, razing the village and emptying it of their Serb and Muslim residents.

Seventeen years ago, Ravno was the site of one of the worst massacres of the Bosnian War. In August 1995, following the lightning Croatian military offensive known as Operation Storm, hundreds of thousands of Krajina Serbs were forced out of their homes and into neighboring Montenegro, Serbia and the Serb half of Bosnia known as the Republika Srpska, or RS. Thrown out of Croatia, fleeing Herzegovina, and impoverished in the RS, the Krajina Serbs are loosely represented by Celo Mescic.

"This is our land!" Celo Mescic shouted yesterday to the busloads of Serbs that surrounded him in the RS capital of Banja Luka, wearing his trademark red Gore-Tex warm-up suit and thick gold chains around his neck. A self-styled politician and advocate for ethnic Serbs throughout Bosnia, he has threatened to use violence to compel the UN to deal with the Krajina Serbs' repatriation. "The world has not left us with many choices, so we will continue to bleed, and we will make others bleed until we are allowed to return to our homes," he said.

Mr. Fulbright refused to rule out force as an option in returning stability to the region if his talks fail. The European Force Commander, British General Ian Rose, reinforced Fulbright with his own admonition: "When we are directed, we will not hesitate to act decisively against either side if the situation warrants it. One thing both factions must not do is to confuse our impartiality with a reticence to act decisively."

Mark set the newspaper down and closed his eyes. There was the mention of Celo, and the inevitability of their encounter weighed heavily on him. After three and a a half decades, he struggled with his desire to avoid his cousin altogether, and his aunt's repeated pleadings to actively seek him out. But it was the mention of British General Ian Rose in the last paragraph that made him begin to second-guess his decision to return. His heart began to pound. with the sudden recognition of both men in the same article. Like a perfect storm, they seemed to converge upon him again. Setting the paper down on his lap, he was left with a debris field of memories to contemplate.

Well, best to just wait and see.

CHAPTER 3

IT WAS TWO O'CLOCK in the morning; the shelling had stopped the previous afternoon. Doctor Jean Renee Lauvergeon had been in Bosnia for three months now—one of the first doctors from Médecins Sans Frontières, Doctors Without Borders, to arrive after the outbreak of hostilities in Ravno. He'd driven four hours along muddy, rutted, back roads crowded with refugees—men, women and terrified children on foot and in packed, horse-drawn carts and tractors with livestock in tow. Their vacuous expressions reminded him he was heading in the wrong direction—toward the violence they were fleeing.

The acrid stink of fear and death confirmed his arrival at the outskirts of Ravno. He passed the smoldering, shattered ruins of homes and businesses, dodged blasted remnants of brick and cinderblock and the burning hulks of cars . . . some still with the charred remains of their human occupants.

The call for a doctor had come over the radio from a United Nations High Commissioner for Refugees (UNHCR) representative, who was now nowhere to be found. He found his own way to the barn, which was his destination. It was lit dimly with four kerosene lanterns, one hanging from a post in each corner. Struck by the utter lack of modernity, he entered and saw the Bosnian Serb family huddled around the eleven-year-old girl. She was lying unconscious in a makeshift bed of straw, covered with several wool blankets and torn sweaters. Drawing closer, he was accosted by the combined stench of vomit, urine and feces. The smell of sickness and death.

He felt her forehead. She had a high fever and her skin was cold, loose and clammy and her hair was falling out in clumps. He opened her eyelids and found her eyes had rolled up into her head. He opened her mouth and found a mottled, blue tinge to her gum line. Her palms and fingers were red and blistered, as if they'd been placed on a hot stovetop.

"How long has she been like this?" He said with a thick French accent. He repeated the question in French, louder this time, and realized that no one spoke either of his languages. Finally, the mother held up two fingers. *Two days.*

He went on with the examination. He lowered the blanket to the girl's waist, and ran his hands along her lymph nodes on her neck and then her pelvic region revealing hip bones that were shockingly protuberant. He pointed at a lantern in the corner and requested that it be brought over to him and held aloft so he could better see. He felt himself recoil with his first glimpse of the girl's condition. Blue and orange skin rashes covered her body like a spreading fungus. He quickly regained his composure, recognizing what was in front of him only from the classes he'd taught at Pierre et Marie Curie University Medical School. Her condition was symptomatic of only one cause. Without explanation, he rose to his feet and took a step back toward the door. His knees weakened as he looked silently at her parents, who were standing across from him. He looked out of the barn into the night void and held the bridge of his nose between his thumb and index finger. He took a moment to inhale deeply, trying to expel the terrible reality before him.

Dear God, not here, not now. . . .

SARAJEVO, BOSNIA AND HERZEGOVINA

"WEATHER BE DAMNED," said Ambassador Jack Fulbright, throwing the message he'd just been handed across the conference table. "Screw the choppers. Get me the keys to that Suburban out there. I'll drive us to Banja Luka—driven there hundreds of times myself." He nodded in the direction of a dark blue Suburban and a black Chevrolet visible outside in the embassy driveway.

Joseph Steinberg, the U.S. Ambassador to Bosnia, and one-time protégé of Fulbright, looked at him. "Well, you can count me out, then. I know how you drive. And I clearly recall that five hour tour of the farmyards of Herzegovina you took me on about fifteen years ago. You swore it was a short cut."

Fulbright chuckled. "Not true. It was only about three hours, and I didn't really hurt that goat we had to pay for—I only grazed it."

"Be that as it may," Steinberg said, "we already have alternate transportation set up, a convoy, in case the helicopters can't fly. Snowstorms, as you know, aren't uncommon here. That's why the limo is out there. Complete with driver. As diplomatic protocol would have it."

"To hell with protocol," Fulbright grumbled.

Steinberg smiled faintly. "It's not the protocol, Jack. It's the insurance."

Fulbright's arrival at the U.S. Embassy in Sarajevo, known as "The Residence," was in itself an unmistakable sign that the country was again in the midst of a serious crisis. Steinberg looked at his friend and patron and marveled. Fulbright's career had spanned thirty-four years, from Kennan to Kissinger to Powell and Stone. From Vietnam to Lebanon to Yugoslavia and Korea. His methods were unconventional and geared toward systemic fixes, rather than expedient ones. Over the years, when confronted by diplomats who objected to his trademark political incorrectness, he would respond with an engaging smile and a slow, thick Boston accent, explaining, "Well, you see my friend, I don't work for the status quo."

The prevailing view among the presidents he worked for, however, was that Jack Fulbright was the indispensable man abroad who solved the seemingly unsolvable problems. When President Gerald Ford called him "The Fireman," following his intervention in the infamous Mayaguez incident, the capture of U.S. ship by Cambodian Khmer Rouge communists, the name stuck.

The Fireman came with his own stable of diplomatic fire chiefs and a coterie of supporting Department of Defense and State Department advisors. They all had rushed to occupy the awaiting SUV's as they saw Fulbright get in the first armored Suburban.

Now, driving through the heart of Sarajevo under police escort along the Miljaska River, Lieutenant General Leslie "Butch" Sterns, an Army three-star military aide, passed the yellow folder marked **"TOP SECRET/UMBRA NOFORN WNINTEL"** to Joe Steinberg, and handed a duplicate copy to Jack Fulbright. Each man knew that folders so marked contained top secret information restricted only to those with a need to know, and contained the source of that information.

"Two items, sir. This, and then the last item you'll see there is a medical report from Doctors Without Borders that came in this morning."

Fulbright nodded and opened his folder.

General Sterns continued. "Here are the personality profiles of the players you'll be meeting in Banja Luka. Familiar faces, in most cases, but several are new. There's been a lot of eleventh-hour jockeying for position. We noticed that after the Serbs promoted their military representative to his third star, the Bosniaks and Croats promoted theirs the same day, to the same rank."

Fulbright smiled as he flipped through his folder and looked up at the impeccably uniformed officer. "Of course, they're matching you, Butch—star for star. So everyone's equal. It's all bullshit."

"Endgame politics." Steinberg nodded in agreement, reading through the individual portfolios. "They've brought in the good, the bad and the ugly. Some of these folks should be under sealed indictments for war crimes . . . Celo Mescic, Milo Stanic . . .." Steinberg whistled softly, shaking his head. "A virtual rogues' gallery."

"A few of them are still under investigation, but no indictments yet," Sterns responded.

Fulbright shifted in his seat. "Yeah, and because of that, they've become either elected or unofficial leaders, and so as long as their indictments are sealed we have no choice but to deal with them." He removed his glasses and handed his packet back to the general. "Most of those investigations are for crimes committed nearly two decades ago. That's the largest hurdle we're facing now—until the war criminals are put away, peace will continue to be elusive."

"I know General Rose has a plan," Steinberg commented. "About the only positive thing to come from the Ravno Crisis is that it will allow him to pick up the pace in making those arrests."

"Well, Joe," Fulbright insisted, "General Rose needs to understand that time is short. He needs to be more aggressive. In Ravno, all he's done is provided a ring around the area so all three factions can continue to duke it out."

"There's more that can be done," Sterns agreed. "Tomorrow in Brussels, they'll be coming to a decision on air strikes."

"Air strikes!" Fulbright scoffed, placing a hard candy in his mouth and sucking on it. "We've been swatting flies, when all along we should've been draining the swamp!"

He pointed outside the Suburban window at the many buildings, windows blown out, still pockmarked from shelling and in ruins since the last war. "Look, if the last war taught us anything, it's that peace doesn't just happen here. Too many folks've died during the last war, and those who lived generally hate each other too much to forget." He looked out the window and shook his head, then looked back at Steinberg. "If we don't change our approach, quick, Ravno may just be the beginning."

Steinberg solemnly nodded his agreement.

CHAPTER 4

MARK LYONS WAS GREETED on the tarmac of the Sarajevo Airport by a gust of icy wind that whipped at him relentlessly. The cold air was palpable and heavy, and the sky was an overcast, gloomy gray. He shuddered and drew his overcoat close to him to warm himself.

As he waited inside the customs area for his remaining baggage, he saw the UN policeman entering through a side door. He wore a British police uniform—probably from the Manchester Department—black military-style boots, and carried a dark blue overcoat in his arm. He was tall, with cropped, light brown hair, a beard that was neatly groomed and a face that was weathered and creased.

As he looked around the room, his repeated glances clearly conveyed his belief that Lyons couldn't possibly be the EUPM's new assistant commissioner for the Balkans. His fleeting glances at several of the other passengers betrayed his search for another man, an older one, with shorter hair and without a musical instrument.

Mark smiled; he was used to being underestimated, especially in times like this, when his windswept hair, unshaven face and the violin case in his hand added to his disheveled, travel-weary appearance. He extended his hand to the policeman and introduced himself.

The policeman's posture stiffened momentarily, but he met his grasp with a smile. "Sergeant Mike McCallister, sir, with the European Union Police Mission Headquarters. Welcome to Sarajevo."

"Thanks, it's a pleasure." He looked around the airport toward the coffee and snack bar, then at the people standing idly around. Cigarette smoke hung heavily in the small ramshackle terminal. "It's good to be back, I reckon."

McCallister turned to him. "You've been here before then?"

He nodded and then abruptly reached for his suit bag that was passing by on the carousel. He looked up thoughtfully. "I have . . . in a different time."

McCallister took his bag. "Well, Commissioner, you've picked a bloody helluva time to be arrivin' now then!"

Mark picked up his other suitcase and grinned at McCallister. "I've been known for my impeccable timing."

Outside, they walked past two French soldiers who stood by one of several barricades and guard shacks that blocked vehicles from approaching the terminal. Surveying the hills surrounding Sarajevo, then fixing his gaze to the west, he could make out the outline of Mount Igman in the distance, shrouded by a dark curtain of clouds. He lifted the collar of his overcoat in response to the strong wind. Along their way to the United Nations parking lot, a Bosnian policeman asked him for identification.

McCallister had already pulled out his Police Mission identification card and began to explain Lyons' status, but the Bosnian policeman only glanced at McCallister and maintained his gaze on him. He waved a hand at McCallister "No, it's quite all right, Mike."

He pulled out his wallet to display his police identification from Belfast. *"Dobar don, gospodine. Ja sam Mark Lyons, ovo je moj kolega. Mi radimo u EUPM-u. Ja sam upravo dosao iz Irske."*

"Irska . . . Gdje idete?" the policeman asked. Mark turned to McCallister, who was visibly surprised at his display of fluent Serbo-Croatian. "Tell me, where we are going now?"

"To the UN Headquarters. You have an appointment there in fifteen minutes."

He nodded and calmly answered the Bosnian policeman. *"Idemo u svoj ured."*

The policeman nodded after a brief pause, then stepped aside. *"Hvala."* Thank-you.

McCallister looked at him, surprised. "Obviously, you won't be needin' a translator?"

Mark shook his head and smiled. He looked at his watch. "And who's my three o'clock appointment?"

"Your new boss, Commissioner, the High Representative."

CHAPTER 5

SANDY EVENSON, LEAD INVESTIGATOR for the International Criminal Tribunal for the Former Yugoslavia, or ICTY, rushed out of her Sarajevo office for the last time, ever, carrying a black leather back pack. This trip to Banja Luka would be her last in Bosnia. After this last interview, she'd drive to the airport in Zagreb, and that would be it. On to The Hague and then home to Connecticut to decompress.

She checked her official car, a white Toyota 4Runner, complete with a two-way radio and the UN's blue wreath logo on the doors. It was all there — her luggage in the back, and the CD player she'd persuaded the UN mechanics to install, in exchange for two fifths of Jack Daniels.

Pulling herself away from Sarajevo was never an easy task. And today was no exception. The ICTY's most visible war crimes trial to date was only a month away. After the sudden capture of Serb "general" Vojislav Razic during the World Cup Soccer Tournament in Paris the year before, eight years of her own exhaustive efforts were finally coming to fruition. Razic had been commander of an infamous Serbian "Black Tiger" militia, and responsible for the worst war crimes in Croatia and Bosnia. She was due to fly back to Amsterdam in the morning to attend his deposition, and ultimately to testify in his trial. She'd extended her stay in the Balkans by years, and long after all of her "wartime" friends had departed, she realized, belatedly perhaps, that it was time to leave.

She weaved the 4Runner through the Sarajevo traffic along Tito Street, occasionally jumping curbs to pass other cars that blocked her way along the road that had become known during the last Bosnian war as "Sniper's Alley." Gradually, between sips of coffee, and thoughts of the last-minute tearful goodbye's, she forced her way out of the city and along the road leading through Rajlovac, toward the Bosnian Serb capital of Banja Luka.

Along the way, the terrain began to ascend dramatically. Snow-covered hillsides, white limestone outcroppings and rounded peaks gradually became mountain-like hybrids with terraces cut into their sides by generations of villagers long past. Lush forests of oak, beech and pine enclosed the winding road and made it difficult for her to pass the logging trucks that lumbered slowly uphill. The BBC station she was listening to faded to static, and was replaced by a local Bosnian newscast, reporting on the crisis in Ravno, more house burnings in Stolac, Razic's upcoming trial at the Hague, and the Serb protests against the Pope's visit to Medjugorje the next month.

It was 1992 all over again—the feeling was palpable and it was real, and that was why she was leaving. Now it would be someone else's war.

Not mine.

As she followed slowly behind a tractor, she opened a Van Morrison CD and loaded it. Shifting down, she passed the tractor and prepared for the next hairpin curve in the road ahead. The snow flurries had become heavier. The windshield wipers were batting away in a synchronous rhythm. The weather in the pass would be even worse, and as she felt the rear wheels of her 4Runner struggle, slide and finally grip the icy road. She passed a Yugo that had overheated and a Lada, with its tire in shreds. Through the heavy snowfall, she saw a sign: Oborci, five kilometers ahead.

She followed four logging trucks, moving slowly, steadily uphill. She reached over to change CD's and glanced up to see the back of the truck rushing up on her. Slamming on her brakes, her vehicle slid sideways on the ice. Gripping the steering wheel tightly and down-shifting, she regained control and stopped only a car's length from a bundle of logs jutting out from the rear of the truck.

"Jesus! What the—?"

The truck began to slide back in short, jerking movements, unable to maintain its own traction. The logs in the bed of the truck bounced around like a box of toothpicks. Instinctively, she threw the 4Runner into reverse and then into first gear, passing the convoy until she could see why the trucks had stopped so abruptly.

CHAPTER 6

MIKE MCCALLISTER LED Mark Lyons through the security station of the Office of the High Representative complex. As they entered, Mike mentioned that in Sarajevo, it had early-on been nicknamed "The White House," because it, rather than the shared Bosnian Serb, Muslim and Croat presidencies, was where the real decisions of government were made. They progressed upstairs to the outer office of the United Nations High Representative. After waiting several minutes, a tall man dressed in an exquisitely tailored three-button, dark blue pinstripe suit emerged from the office, extending his hand to Mark. His hair was a closely cropped light brown, like a soldier's. His nails were manicured and his watch was a Rolex, studded with diamonds along the bezel.

"Mark Lyons? I am Roman Polko. Welcome to Sarajevo."
Mark met his handshake and nodded politely. ""I wish we could've met under better circumstances, sir."

Polko smiled. It was the easy, immaculate smile of a diplomat. Well-practiced and confident. "And I must apologize to you for the conditions—both the atmospheric and the political." He shrugged. "Unfortunately, it seems we can do little about either at the moment."

Mark followed him into the spacious office. During the drive from the airport, Mike McCallister had already informed him that Roman Polko enjoyed a power base that extended well beyond Europe. As Poland's former Minister of Finance and a former Deputy to the UN Secretary General, the rumors were his tenure in Sarajevo was to be short-lived. Polko was widely viewed as the next UN Secretary General.

Polko gestured to the white embroidered sofa and sat opposite him in a leather armchair, crossing his legs.

"Lyons, people disagree with me, but I believe the violence in Ravno is a resumption of the last Balkan War. Today I met with Ambassador Fulbright, and although he is a remarkable man, I confess that I am somewhat doubtful that he will succeed. All three factions would rather fight one another than negotiate." Polko sighed. "Two hundred fifty thousand dead from the last war are not easily forgotten."

Polko's English was perfect, with hardly a trace of an accent.

Mark nodded at the diplomat. "I'm aware of what's transpired, sir, but I've much to learn. I'm here to assist in whatever way I can." *Keep it short, positive...in and out.*

"We are fortunate to have you here," Polko said, handing him a cup of tea. "Your experience in Northern Ireland with Britain's Special Air Service, the Northern Ireland Police, and your earlier years here as a youngster...all make you unusually suited to assume your position, especially now, at this crucial time. My only concern was if you would be impartial toward each of the factions. I was assured by your prime minister that impartiality was a trait that defines you."

Mark sipped his tea, shifting slightly in his seat. "There's no doubt I've managed to upset people on all sides of the Troubles in Ireland. Now that things are on the mend there, I suspect that's why they sent me here."

Polko shook his head insistently. "No. Now you must understand: *That is why I requested you... over many others.* Polko chuckled and it caught Mark off-guard. "You can blame me. I know your experience in Belfast was particularly difficult at times, but I needed someone here with your perspective. Bosnia is a place where one man can make an enormous difference." Polko held his finger up. "*If* he cares!"

He inhaled and paused to collect his thoughts. Polko seemed to know much more about him than he'd expected—with his mention of the SAS and incidents no longer part of the public record in Northern Ireland—all things he'd done his best to put behind him. Even more unnerving was that based on that knowledge, Polko was making it clear that he would be relying upon him heavily to change the course of this re-emerging war. *Was this a technique he used with all of his people?*

"Wait, I don't want you to think—"

Polko waved him off reproachfully, anticipating his response, but with a smile. "You understand the dynamics of this country, where others do not, Lyons." Polko paused as if in deep thought. "While you are here in this post, there is something I would ask you to consider...a way *you* can make an enduring difference."

33

Mark looked up at Polko with contrived interest meant to conceal his growing skepticism.

"Many of those who are fighting in Bosnia now were no more than children during the last war. A decade ago, they were the same children who were taught to hate by their teachers and parents, by filing them past mass graves, telling them stories about their relatives who were tortured and killed by their neighbors." Polko shook his head. "So, you see, the effect of all this is devastating and...," he shrugged. "It is indelible. The trauma . . . the hatred... it is passed on to the next generation." He paused again. "I am Polish, Mark Lyons. As children, the Communists programmed us in our schools, too. When the Communists left, we had to deprogram our children so they could think like normal children. It took time, but everyone agreed that we had to begin the process."

Mark leaned forward and nodded. "I can tell you, in an environment like this, it's easier for a young boy to be drawn to the violence than repelled by it. Violence and a warrior ethic are part of the fabric of the culture here, much more so than religion."

He wanted to say more, to convey the experience of his own youth. He began to speak and reconsidered, looking back at the elder statesman.

Polko nodded and set his tea on the table, then leaned back into his chair. "For two years, I was subjected to their propaganda as a political prisoner not far from here. That experience taught me that politics is only an excuse." Polko paused and leaned forward. "You understand this dynamic, where others do not. Let me tell you why I fought to have you in this posting. I know what the police mission does. I know what the commissioner's job has been in the past. You monitor the other police forces, you communicate with the other police chiefs. That is all very important, but I want to add a dimension to your job description—"

He tensed and sat back in his chair as Polko continued.

"You can communicate with the children in their language. No one else in your position could do so. I want you and your people to visit the schools, to talk to the children. They have to begin to see the futility of hatred."

He felt his heart pounding. He hadn't signed up for this, he was *not* qualified to fill that role, nor did he want to set the expectation that he could accomplish such a dramatic change. He was a policeman, not a goddamned child psychologist! But Polko had reeled him in as expertly as a champion fly fisherman.

34

"Ambassador, please understand . . . I've been away from here for thirty-five years. I've been a soldier and policeman for twenty-five of those. I'm afraid I'm probably more Irish in my thinking than Yugoslav. I'm not good with the kids. There must be someone—"

The diplomat inclined his head respectfully toward him. "Ahh," Polko interjected, smiling broadly. "I knew you would be the reluctant warrior. I will not rush you or force you into a role that you are not comfortable in. All I ask is that you consider the enduring contribution you can make here, if you choose to do so. Certainly, it is not Camelot for the children here, but if people in positions like ours cared to make it so, it could be, could it not?"

Camelot.... Vivid memories of the stories his father told him of Camelot returned to him in a torrent. After a moment, he looked up at Polko. "Yes, sir. Of course."

Polko stood up and shook his hand as they walked to the office door. "Good. I know you are anxious to meet your men. Your office is right down the hall from mine. This door is always open to you. "

"Thank you very much for your time, Ambassador."

"Thank you for yours," Polko smiled. "And welcome back, Marko."

"How...?" At the mention of his original given name, he felt as if he was falling down a deep well. He paused in the doorway to regain his composure. He was barely aware of Mike McCallister, who had been waiting for him in the outer office.

"I'll take you down to your office, Commissioner."

He nodded absently, still in a state of half-shock.

"Judging from his smile," McCallister said, gesturing back at Polko's office. "It looks like you've already found favor with the old man."

35

CHAPTER 7

AFTER RETURNING to the Suburban following their rest stop at the Dutch EUFOR Base, General Sterns pulled a three-ring binder from his aluminum briefcase and handed it to Steinberg, who held it in both hands. "Jack, we've developed a strategy to deal with the Ravno Crisis, and although neither side will be very happy with it, I think it's a good one."

"Well, I'm not here to make anyone happy. What do we have to back it up?" Fulbright asked.

General Sterns handed him a single sheet of paper. "Sir, we're bringing another Carrier Strike Group into the Mediterranean—the *ENTERPRISE*— and the remainder of the 1st Infantry Division from Germany will be augmenting the French Division in Ravno. They're due in to Dubrovnik within the week."

"So we have two carriers, a U.S. Division and tomorrow we'll find out if we can launch air strikes. What about sanctions?"

"They're being approved by the president to coincide with the authorization for air strikes."

Fulbright scanned the paper and looked at Steinberg. "Okay, what's your plan, Joe?"

Steinberg handed Fulbright the binder and reviewed the strategy he and his staff had developed with the Office of the High Representative. "It's aggressive and not without risk. It places several contested municipalities, Ravno, Stolac, Mostar and Trebinje, under UN arbitration and a UN administration indefinitely."

Fulbright closed the binder and handed it back to Steinberg. "It may work if Roman Polko is willing to commit, but he'll be bearing the lion's share of the burden. The key is to back the factions into a Hobson's choice— where they have no real choice but to accept our terms."

"The problem lies with the hard-liners on all three sides," Steinberg said. In Ravno, the Serbs, the Croats and Muslims, they've all used the situation as a land grab, with the rather transparent subterfuge of 'protecting their countrymen'."

"It's all bullshit," Fulbright sighed. "The whole goddamned place is still awash in weaponry. The fighting has escalated beyond the European Force's ability to confront it, let alone control it. So whatever plan we arrive at, we just need to be damn sure we're able to enforce it when we say we can."

Steinberg nodded his agreement.

Fulbright pointed at the binder on Steinberg's lap. "Well, my compliments on that. It'll at least give us some room to improvise."

Fulbright looked out the window at the heavy snowfall across the Travnik Valley. In the distance, the city of Travnik was nestled at the base of the mountains. Narrow white minarets rose over the rounded domes of mosques, old and new. Terraced ledges held the snow tightly against a central hillside that led to an ancient Turkish fortress standing guard above.

"Travnik," Steinberg commented, pointing out the window. "It was the capital of Bosnia under the Turks for two centuries. In Turkish, it translates to 'grassy town.'"

Fulbright nodded and smiled. "They obviously never lived here during the winter."

"Maybe not," Steinberg agreed. "Fair-weather occupiers, the Turks. The Austrians were a hardier lot."

"Well," Fulbright said, "World War I ended that empire too, so it's all relative. After the Second World War, came Tito, who in many ways set us up for this trip."

"The old geezer's doing cheetah flips in his grave, telling us *'I told you so!'*" Steinberg answered dryly. "He ruled Yugoslavia with an iron fist for thirty-five years."

The bodyguard in the passenger seat turned around to address Steinberg. "Sir, the roads are getting worse and the trucks are having difficulty making it ahead, so the pace'll be slower through the mountains. We're going to pass the slower moving traffic where we can, without losing contact with the rest of the convoy. If we have to, we'll turn the flashers on."

The windshield wipers were shifting back and forth at full speed, deflecting the heavy flakes of snow whipping at the windshield. Steinberg leaned forward and tapped their driver on the shoulder. "Al, we're not in a hurry. We've got plenty of time—just get us there safely."

Fulbright nodded and held out his hand. "And look, no goddamned sirens! Hell, I'm just enjoying the scenery . . . what I can see of it. Take your time!"

He turned to General Sterns. "Okay, Butch, you said you had something else that you wanted to brief me on? A CIA analysis, was it?"

"Yes, sir. And a medical report from Ravno," Sterns said, reaching across to his briefcase for the folder. The Suburban began to slow down.

AS SHE PASSED the stalled truck convoy, Sandy Evenson saw the overturned cart and horse lying in the road. She stopped her 4Runner in the oncoming lane, next to the first logging truck in the convoy. An old, red BMW was tipped on its side along the shoulder of the road, its windshield shattered and side fender crushed. At a glance, it appeared that the car had hit the horse over the centerline as it tried to pass the truck around the corner, causing the cart to flip onto its side. Hay and farm implements were scattered on the roadside. Three farmers in worn clothes were standing around the accident site, and appeared unhurt. One of them was arguing with the truck driver, gesturing wildly.

The cart's wreckage blocked the oncoming lane and the horse carcass and BMW blocked the other lane, preventing any traffic from passing in either direction. Sitting in her vehicle until the situation resolved itself would mean an interminable wait. She left the engine running and stepped out of the 4Runner, slipping on the icy road before finally regaining her balance. The air was freezing, but it had stopped snowing. Buttoning her overcoat and crossing her arms to stay warm, she walked to the men who were still arguing near the logging truck.

"Excuse me! . . . *Izvolite!*"

Both men turned and glared at her. One stepped forward and spoke calmly, his English accented, but fluent. "No one is hurt, only the horse. Please, return to your automobile until the police arrive."

"You are required to make room for us to pass through. Do you understand?"

The truck driver spoke excitedly, first pointing to the cart, to the horse, and then to the farmer in front of him. The farmer was insisting that the police intervene first and write out an accident report before any traffic could proceed.

Sandy shook her head and pointed at the wreckage. "No, move the cart *now* and make a lane for other cars to pass."

The farmer pointed to the horse lying on its side, and threw up his arms. "Dead. She was hit by the car."

Sandy walked over to the horse. It was a young mare with compound fractures to both front legs sustained from the car's impact. Her harness was still connected to the cart and her eyes, although open, were lifeless. Evenson put her hand on the mare's neck to confirm that she was dead. She checked in vain for any signs of a pulse, and saw a mass of blood behind the mare's left ear. She traced her fingers over the bloody mass and her middle finger sunk—a gunshot wound. She stood to face the other two farmers. One of them held out a large, nickel-plated revolver.

"She was dying. We had no choice."

Sandy nodded. This was not the first accident of this type she'd seen in Bosnia. In many ways, it represented a clash of eras and of civilizations. Past methods, no matter how antiquated, continued to challenge modern technology on roads like these, often leading to fatal results. Given her condition, shooting the mare was surely the only compassionate thing to do. She knelt down and scooped up some snow to wash off the blood from her hands.

Looking up, she saw the farmers' shoes before he abruptly covered them with snow. Brown leather dress shoes, wingtips—she was certain of it. Glancing over at the other farmer, she realized he didn't *look* like a farmer after all. He was muscular, conspicuously well-groomed and clean-shaven, and he was carrying a small two-way radio. Another glance confirmed that his tan work trousers were too short, cut on the sides to fit over his black pants that were bloused into black military-style boots.

"Okay, Sandra Lee, what's wrong with this picture?" she whispered as she rose to her feet. Suddenly, this accident seemed entirely different than she had first observed. *Where was the driver of the BMW? Why did they have radios? Why weren't any passengers injured? There was no oncoming traffic . . . no congestion in the opposite direction!* She looked back at the mare's carcass. An uneasy feeling overcame her—that the mare had been sacrificed . . . nothing more than a macabre prop of sorts. Her heart pounded furiously. She was now certain these were not farmers. And this was no accident.

The men seemed to swirl and hover around her. She had the distinct feeling that she'd sailed into the eye of a developing hurricane. They stared at her as she walked back to the 4Runner. Her mind raced when she considered the purpose of this gruesome roadblock. It wasn't the standard "rent-a-mob" that she'd seen so often in Bosnia to protest rival ethnic disparities and refugee returns. She knew that mob and riot organizers in those cases were often Ministry of Interior people and Special Police in civilian clothes. There was a good possibility that's who these men were, but their tactics were different, and too extreme. Mob planners typically cut down trees and parked trucks across roads. They didn't attempt to hide their identities or stage an accident, and they *never* killed livestock. And Bosnians, she knew, by their very nature, only rioted when the weather was good, mostly when *schlivovitz* — the local plumb brandy — was in season.

She let her breath out very slowly and walked calmly back to the 4Runner. She sat inside for a moment before starting the engine. The road was filled with debris. One of the cart-wheels blocked the shoulder of the road, but it afforded the only real way out. When she started the engine and switched into four wheel drive, she noticed each of the men look in her direction. One of them spoke into his radio as she pressed her foot on the gas, turned hard into the shoulder of the road, and ran over the cart wheel, barely avoiding the major pieces of wreckage.

She looked back in her rearview mirror and felt a wave of panic pass through her. Several other men, dressed in black, emerged at the other side of the underpass, with handheld radios. She saw them briefly confer with one another and point in her direction. A moment later, they disappeared through the underpass and around the hairpin curve in the road. One of them, she was certain, was carrying an assault rifle. She pulled her cell phone out of her backpack, and dialed the phone number for the UN headquarters, but realized that the attempt was futile. The mountains on either side of her masked any potential cellular signal. She shoved the phone into her backpack and drove past the bombed-out ruins of Komar into Oborci village. She turned onto a service road that led to the parking lot of the *"Restauran Slap,"* a restaurant she'd eaten at several months prior. Clean. Good food. Modern bathroom. She remembered that they also had a telephone.

She parked in the lot beside a covered waterwheel-generated rotisserie grill that was roasting a lamb. On a footbridge beside the driveway, a family was walking their small herd of cattle toward a white stucco farmhouse across the street. She shivered.

Entering the restaurant, she walked purposefully toward the owner behind the bar.

THE HEAD OF JOE STEINBERG'S security detail saw the backup of cars and trucks as their Suburban slowed, and turned to the driver. "Can we get by?"

The driver nodded. "But the boss won't like it."

The detail leader turned around to brief Fulbright. "Ambassador, if we're going to make any progress here, we'll need to turn on the flashers."

Fulbright leaned forward to get his own view of the scene ahead. "What happened?"

"An accident, sir," the detail leader answered. "Looks like someone hit a horse-drawn cart—quite a mess."

Fulbright nodded. "All right, but turn 'em off when you can."

The driver flipped the switch under the dash, and the detail leader spoke into the Motorola radio, giving instructions to the lead and trail vehicles. They too, turned on their flashing lights and sirens.

Fulbright laughed. "Well, if they didn't know we were coming, they do now!"

SANDY ASKED the restaurant owner, who was washing glasses at the bar, to use his telephone. At the same time she dug into her backpack and handed him a ten euro bill. "To Sarajevo please, one or two minutes only."

He nodded and pointed at the telephone behind the bar, near the espresso machine. As she dialed the number and waited for the operator to connect her to the U.S. Embassy in Zagreb, she realized no one else was in the restaurant but her, a waiter and the owner. Looking at her watch, she saw that it was five-fifteen. Not dinner time yet, but the place still shouldn't be deserted.

She heard the connection go through and when the UN operator answered, she asked to be connected to Robert Childs. As a long-time friend and the CIA Station Chief for Southern Europe, he was the only one she absolutely knew would still be at work. Three monotonal rings, and Bob Childs steady voice was on the other end.

"Bob, something's terribly wrong," she said without preamble. "They're blocking the roads here and they've got guns, radios—"

"Sandy? Is that you? Wait, slow down, tell me what's happening! *Where are you?*" Childs asked.

"I'm just outside Oborci, at that restaurant we went to a couple months ago on the way to Banja Luka," she said, out-of-breath. "Bob, they killed a goddamned horse and made it look like an accident. *Why would they do that?*"

"Okay, I'm trying to understand. Calm down. Where's the roadblock?"

"Just down the road! *Why would they kill a perfectly good horse?*" She realized she was yelling and tried to calm herself. "Listen, something *way* odd is happening, and I'm worried! *Do you hear me?*" She stared outside the windows. There was still no traffic on the road in either direction, except the family leading its cows. *The same cows and the same family. They haven't moved!* "You can't graze cows in the fucking snow!" she exclaimed.

Bob Child's voice was calm. "Wait—hold the line."

There was an extended pause and she heard Bob's voice again, this time it was urgent and directive. "Listen to me, Sandy. I just checked with Embassy Sarajevo—that's the route Fulbright's delegation is taking to Banja Luka. This may be the prelude to another one of their demonstrations. I'll call the EUPM and EUFOR to let them know, but you should get away from there before you get caught up in it!"

"Jesus!" she exclaimed. "Okay, I'm leaving now." She gave an abstracted "goodbye" to Childs and hung up the phone, even more distraught and confused. She'd heard that Jack Fulbright was in town, but he was only background noise to the perpetual undercurrent of chaos in Bosnia.

She put her coat on, grabbed her backpack and rushed out the door toward her vehicle. Looking over, she saw a black BMW 740i parked in the opposite corner of the parking lot with dark tinted windows partly rolled down. She turned away abruptly and quickened her pace.

When she reached the passenger side of the 4Runner, a new, grey Mercedes-Benz drove up next to her car. The passenger window rolled down and she saw a middle-aged man staring in her direction. His face was long and narrow, and his features chiseled and hard. His hair was a mane of curly black. But it was his eyes that were so striking—cold and expressionless, with an intense light blue caste. When he opened his door, she reached into the passenger-side window to grab her camera, as if she'd forgotten it.

Returning to the restaurant, she sensed his eyes following her and quickened her steps. Approaching the entrance, she looked over at the road. The cows were still blocking traffic and the group of people she initially assumed to be a family of farmers no longer appeared so innocuous. A closer look revealed that they were six men, each in their twenties or thirties, dressed and equipped much like the previous crowd she'd encountered.

Not farmers.

She sat at a corner window table with her camera in hand and looked out at the road. She aimed the zoom lens of her Nikon F5 at the group and clicked the shutter two times in quick succession. All of the men were tall and athletic, with crew cuts and strong, narrow faces . . . like Aryan clones. All of their white coveralls were several sizes too large. In their back pockets, they were carrying walkie-talkies. Two men were driving the cattle into the road, while the others were arranging ropes that extended flat across the road at uneven intervals. Following the ropes, she could see that they had been tied to telephone poles that extended across the road to service the white farmhouse.

This, too, was a familiar scene, and she struggled to remember where and when she'd seen it before. She heard the distinct sound of sirens approaching in the distance. The woman in coveralls and combat boots moved to the opposite side of the road, pulled the radio from her pocket and held it to her mouth. Another man ran across the road where the ropes were tied off and removed snow-covered burlap bags to reveal round, metal, rim-like objects that had been stacked on top of one another—six or seven to a stack, linked together with chain. She heard the rasp of metal dragging on gravel. Men in the opposite culvert were pulling the ropes and rims to the edge of the road.

Why?

"Oh, my God...what...?"

THERE WERE CATTLE in the road as the Suburbans turned along the hairpin curve. The lead one slowed down and then stopped behind the livestock.

"Here we go again . . . ," the driver sighed.

Ahead were several vehicles in a restaurant parking lot, one of them a white sport utility vehicle with black and blue UN markings. "Let's see if this works. If not, we can turn into that parking lot and go around them. Be careful we don't hit any of their livestock."

The Suburban slowed, following closely behind the lead one, flashing lights and siren switched on in an attempt to scatter the herd of cows from their lane. Suddenly, in front of them, the Suburban came to a complete stop. The detail leader spoke into his radio and held the earphone tightly to his ear. After a few moments, he turned around to Steinberg.

"Sir, our lead vehicle tells me one of the calves fell down the ravine in front of them. I understand there are some pretty angry farmers up there."

"Okay, let's see if we can go around."

Steinberg's expression turned incredulous as he pointed at the men on the side of the road now standing in front of and behind the Suburban, pulling on what appeared to be ropes, and then disappearing behind the ravine to their right.

The detail leader looked over and immediately recognized the objects attached to the ropes as anti-tank mines. "Jesus Christ! Get down on the floor! *Now!*" He pulled out a submachine gun from one of the vehicle's custom-made side panels. The driver shifted into reverse to begin a well-practiced evasive maneuver. The detail leader turned back and grabbed the driver's arm. "Wait! *Don't move!*"

CHAPTER 8

THE SUBURBAN'S RIGHT REAR TIRE ran over the mine first, detonating it and all the others in a massive, deafening chain of explosions that cut the vehicle in half. Three antitank rocket volleys screamed out from the top of the cut away hillside above and slammed into the side quarter panels of both vehicles. The force of the rockets tossed the Suburban to the front, onto its own chain of mines causing it to burst into a ball of brilliant flames and launching it like a burning matchbox in front of the restaurant parking lot.

With the first explosion, the glass exploded. Chunks of asphalt, car parts and shrapnel flew everywhere. Sandy Evenson threw herself to the floor of the restaurant, reaching up to the windowsill to press the shutter release of the camera, pointing out toward the ambush.

The explosions were followed by continuous bursts of machine gun fire from the white house, strafing the vehicles and the front of the restaurant relentlessly, shattering the remaining windows and glass in a deafening cacophony. Ears ringing, she pulled the camera down and sank to the floor in a fetal position, her arms alternately covering her head to protect against flying glass, all-the-while attempting to keep the camera above her head.

"ShitShitShit!" She alternately lowered and raised the camera, pointing it outside randomly in the direction of the gunfire.

The machine gun fire tapered off after a few moments, then stopped altogether. She raised herself to the windowsill behind a curtain and looked through the broken glass at the wreckage to her front. The attackers fled on foot, disappearing through the thick forest behind the restaurant, their retreat obscured by the heavy black and white smoke pouring out from the burning wreckage. The bloody carcasses of dismembered cattle were lying in the road, in the ravine, and the parking lot; grotesque, scattered vestiges of a murderous and senseless slaughter.

She took a photo of the diplomatic plates on the overturned, windowless

Suburban. In the corner of her eye, she could see movement from the road. A series of single shots erupted from the other end of the parking lot. She looked out and aimed her camera at the sound of the gunfire. Through the dense smoke, she could see the man in the Mercedes firing an AK-47 rifle as it backed up and stopped directly across from her position in the window. At the sight she froze, unable to move or speak. He was a giant of a man with piercing blue eyes—an imposing figure with black hair that fell in curls around his shoulders. She looked directly at him, aiming the camera in his direction and pressing the shutter release. Her stomach turned over when she saw him raise the barrel of the rifle and point it at her head.

She went rigid with shock.

He eyed her speculatively with his finger on the trigger, cast an indifferent smile toward her, and lowered the rifle. The window rose abruptly and the Mercedes retreated to the south, unscathed.

She drew several deep breaths as she looked out and saw the rest of the ambush party retreating into the woods, quickly but deliberately, over burning phosphorous and oil-soaked snow. The air reeked of scorched rubber and burning oil. She looked through the remnants of the restaurant's windowpane at her 4Runner. It was riddled with bullets and gaping holes gouged into the fenders from flying shrapnel. The windshield was blown out entirely. Shards of glass silhouetted the vehicle and reflected grey light. The pungent smell of sulfur, burning diesel, cordite and gunpowder hung in the air, mixing together to form a dark blue haze. The asphalt road had been transformed into a mass of stone and mud.

The thought occurred to her that there could be survivors in the wreckage—survivors she possibly knew. She ran outside with her camera still in hand. Approaching the broken Suburban, she realized that she was not at all prepared for this. It was the smell that overpowered her first—the acrid, putrid smell of burnt human flesh made the air caustic. She recoiled, placing her hand over her nose and mouth to fight the nausea, sucking in air to breathe. Pushing herself forward, she glanced inside the passenger section of the Suburban through the thickening acid smoke.

She gasped and jerked backward at the sight. She went cold at the realization that the occupants were not only dead, but completely burnt...still, oddly like scorched mannequins after a department store blaze.

No one could have survived this.

She stepped back from the pile of destroyed vehicles and surveyed the scene before her. Her breath hung in front of her face. There was a stillness, interrupted seconds later by the echo of sirens in the distance.

She ran back to her 4Runner and threw her overcoat on the fragments of glass covering the driver's seat. Inserting the key, she prayed the engine would start. Haltingly, blessedly, it did. She backed the vehicle up and tore out of the parking lot, windshield fragments falling in piles from the dashboard to her chest and lap. She drove north toward Jajce, coaching herself to breathe, to take deep breaths, to focus on the road through her shattered windshield. Police cars flew past her, sirens blaring, oblivious to her broken vehicle.

CHAPTER 9

MARK LYONS WANDERED around the EUPM office, shaking hands with secretaries and policemen from around the world—Americans, South Africans, Pakistanis, Australians, Turks and Canadians. Mike McCallister made the introductions effortlessly and Mark struggled to remember names.

As Mike led him to his new office, Mark asked how many people worked for the European Police Mission. McCallister looked around the room for a moment with a wry smile. "About half," he whispered conspiratorially. "Not everyone has the work ethic we're accustomed to, I'm afraid, but you get used to it."

Mark laughed. Just as they were approaching the outer doorway, the elevator door opened, followed by a brief commotion.

McCallister grasped Mark's elbow and nodded toward the elevators. Roman Polko was walking toward them, accompanied by a bevy of staff members by his side. "Commissioner, it's the boss—again. I reckon he's not finished with you yet."

Roman Polko apologized briefly. Behind him was a man wearing civilian khaki pants and a gray nylon aviator's jacket. Polko's expression was worried, the tone of his voice, urgent.

"Lyons—there is a report that Ambassador Fulbright's delegation hit a mine as they were driving north along Route 5, north of Travnik in the mountains. I'm told local police are at the scene. I must ask you to go there immediately to investigate what has occurred...to see if there are survivors."

"Yes, sir. How—"

"You can use our helicopter, it is fastest." Polko turned to the man in tow. "This is my pilot, Vladimir. He assures me he can get you there safely through the weather. Please call me when you get there. Tell me what the hell has happened."

Chapter 10

BOSNIA'S VLASIC RANGE was serene under the blanket of fresh snow. Dim sunlight radiated through clouds against jutting hilltops, casting pale grey shadows on the valleys below. The Lasva River circulated through quiet towns, waiting for the spring thaw that would transform the Lasva's gentle flow to a torrent. Narrow, dirt country roads ascended steep slopes through tightly wound switchbacks, lined at irregular intervals with piles of firewood. Giant coned haystacks dotted the fields and farmyards, like giant toy soldiers standing guard over homes modestly constructed of cement cinderblock, red brick and clay tile.

Maneuvering between a maze of dispersing clouds and mountainsides in the turbulent air, the old Soviet-made MI-17 HIP helicopter descended upon the village of Oborci. Sitting in the co-pilot's seat, Mark glanced back at McCallister, who was sitting on a webbed nylon seat, watching—with some concern—the hydraulic fluid dripping from the ceiling to the floor of the aircraft.

Circling several times before coming to a hover high above the wreckage, Mark could see the aftermath of the ambush through the fogged windshield. Three destroyed vehicle hulks were scattered like coals from a campfire intersecting the parking lot and road. Clouds of white smoke billowed out of the clumps of twisted metal and steel. One of the vehicles lay overturned, submerged into the roof of a second car in the restaurant parking lot. The third vehicle, another burnt Suburban, lay diagonally across the road. Three deep trenches cratered the road in symmetrical lines. The windows in front of the restaurant were blown out. Carcasses of cows were strewn onto the road, in the parking lot, and in the ditches alongside the road. Several sets of tire tracks led to the restaurant and then out again, heading north into a web of other tire tracks. Bosnian police cars had surrounded the scene, their flashing lights reflecting blue on packed, crystallized snow.

Vladimir pointed at a road intersection several hundred meters from the scene. "We'll land there—if we move any closer we'll blow away any evidence."

Mark nodded and gave Vladimir a thumbs-up sign and the helicopter banked aggressively to the right, its body vibrating under the exertion of a controlled descent. Over the engine noise, he heard McCallister curse behind him. He looked back to see that the hydraulic fluid's drip was now a steady stream, pouring down, splattering McCallister's shoes and pants. Descending farther, the spinning rotors caused the snow on the ground to lift, surrounding the giant helicopter in a blizzard of white powder. Vladimir calmly steadied the aircraft into another brief hover until the whiteout subsided. A moment later, he rested the massive aircraft on the ground. Mark released his seatbelt and exited the side door behind McCallister.

"I'll be walking back to Sarajevo tonight," McCallister shouted.

Mark stopped mid-stride, surveying the scene in front of him. "Mother of God. . . ."

Two uniformed policemen were walking up to them from the ambush site.

"Our welcoming committee," McCallister said.

Mark turned to him. "Alright, after the introductions and formalities, see if you can keep these folk occupied while I take a look around."

McCallister nodded.

It was cold; even colder than it had been in Sarajevo with the higher elevation, and with dusk less than an hour away. Viewing the scene while there was still light was crucial. Dealing with the local police was not. One of the policeman extended his hand to Lyons and then to McCallister, introducing himself as Sergeant Maric.

Mark shook his hand and introduced himself and McCallister. "Can you tell us what happened?"

"Mines." The policeman pointed to the wreckage directly in front of them. "The road is cratered there...and there."

"A deliberate attack?"

Maric shook his head. "It was random. An accident. The mines were dumped on the roadside and left."

He looked down at the snow-packed asphalt, then up at the dead cattle, the pieces of metal littering the road, focusing on the destroyed vehicles ahead. He signaled McCallister with a tap on the shoulder. "I'm gonna walk around a bit." Turning to Maric, he nodded. "Thank you."

His feet crunched in the inch or so of accumulated snow. Before he reached the Suburban, he could smell the distinct, pungent odor of burnt rubber, cordite and plastique explosive residue in the frozen stillness. The devastation was already apparent—there would be no survivors. The Suburban's rear wheels had been torn from the axle and its tires were partially burnt off their rims. The rest of the vehicle was charred and oxidized blue-grey. The metal on the remnants of the hood had turned white from the searing heat. Splotches of black paint were only visible around the grill. The roof had ballooned, compressed, and separated from the chassis. The bullet-resistant windshield melted, leaving it and each of the windows liquescent and opaque.

Walking around the rear of the Suburban, he slipped in the mud and filthy, half-melted slush. Debris—broken metal fragments from vehicles, wood from trees and clumps of asphalt—was everywhere. Regaining his balance, he could see the Chevrolet symbol on the trunk still intact, but the trunk itself was a tangled mass of steel. Sticking out of the bumper was part of the diplomatic license plate. The burned and shredded rubber from the tires turned the asphalt a light blue, and left a black residue that stuck to the ground.

Circling the vehicle, he drew a deep breath. The dense air caused him to cough violently. Large circular holes had been punctured into what remained of the driver's door and the rear window. The roof had been blown open. To his left, on the foot bridge, boot tracks extended more than a hundred meters from the trees and terminated in the road, roughly at his position.

"Random," he muttered almost inaudibly, looking over at the two policemen still talking to McCallister, each taking turns pointing in different directions. He felt an eerie sensation in the pit of his stomach that was all-too-familiar. He'd seen enough of these scenes to know a deliberate ambush when he saw one. He hesitated, took a deep breath, then peered inside the window.

He closed his eyes at the sight of the carnage inside. The vehicle's armor plating had been no match for antitank rockets. The blackened, charred bodies were slumped over and grotesquely contorted in their seats, mouths agape and arms extended, frozen in a surreal display of bewildered desperation. He recoiled at the sudden acrid stench of burnt fat and flesh.

The smell made his head begin to ache.

Stepping back, he felt something under his shoe—a severed piece of rope, less than a meter in length. He knelt down and looked around. Other smaller rope fragments, many charred, were strewn about the road amidst the countless pieces of shrapnel, large clumps of mud, asphalt and debris. He remembered the three dark thick lines he had seen from the helicopter. Those lines, he saw now, were solid one-foot craters in the asphalt, extending the width of the road in evenly spaced intervals of approximately twenty-five feet each. Three telephone poles bordering the road leading to the parking lot had ropes tied at their base. Whoever the attackers were, they were both savage and methodical.

"Lordy. . . the poor sods never had a chance." McCallister was behind him now, and he saw Sergeant Maric approaching.

He looked at the tall Englishman and pursed his lips. "Were there any witnesses?"

"Over there, McCallister pointed to the outdoor rotisserie beside the restaurant. "—the owner and his son. They didn't see much."

"Well, I think they did. They've probably had the living daylights scared out of 'em, but if they were here, they saw something. Look at those tire tracks in the snow, in the corner of the parking lot. There are at least two sets. That means they had guests . . . and you can see they both left here in rather a hurry."

"In different directions. . . ."

He nodded. "I'll go talk to them. While I'm doing that, see if you can get EUFOR over here to secure the site."

"Ye know, Commissioner, only the American delegations drive Chevy's," McCallister said abruptly, as if an afterthought. "...The police said there's a phone in the restaurant. I'll call back to Sarajevo from there."

Mark nodded and moved with the policeman toward two men who were looking anxious and dazed. He shook their hands.

The Bosnian policeman, Sergeant Maric, stepped forward and faced the men. Speaking quickly and officially in Serbo-Croatian, Maric apologized to them for the additional intrusion, and stated that for their own welfare and in the long-term interest of their business, it would be best if the only information they gave be limited to what he had discussed in their earlier conversation. As Mark listened to Maric's instructions, his eyebrows rose, but he otherwise stood by impassively, waiting for him to finish.

Sergeant Maric turned to Mark and made the introductions. "This is Riso Siric and his son, Refik. They are the owners of this restaurant."

He smiled and turned to Maric. "Could you ask them what they saw?"

Maric translated the question, and he could see that both men were growing increasingly nervous. Riso Siric spoke haltingly, pointed down the road and then at the scene in front of them as he explained their surprised reaction, and the fact that they'd taken cover behind the bar.

"We only heard the explosions . . . they blew out our windows," Siric said, his voice hollow and stiff.

Mark nodded as he looked at the stucco finish on the outside of the restaurant, severely pock-marked from gunfire and flying shrapnel. When Riso finished, Maric delivered a rough, but obviously modified translation. Mark listened, and realized that the translation was dramatically altered, designed to support his original theory that what had occurred was a random mine accident.

"It happens from time to time," Maric commented. "The farmers . . . they find the mines and stack them on the side of the road for the military or the police to pick up."

"You're very lucky to be alive," Mark commented politely, and he heard Maric echo the statement in their language. Both men nodded slowly.

Riso nervously turned to Sergeant Maric, who answered for him. But now Maric's tone was impatient. "Is there anything else you would like to know from these men?"

Mark placed his hands in his pockets and looked at the covered patio and grill. The roof was pierced with shrapnel and bullet holes, but the rotisserie was still turning the charred, torn remnants of a spitted lamb, its meat cooking, hanging in shreds over lit wood embers. In the distance, he heard the sound of helicopter blades beating through the valley.

"I'm afraid your lamb is ruined, Mr. Siric. You'll have to get a new one to replace it." He kicked the base of the grill absently. "But, fortunately, your rotisserie is still functional."

"Do you want me to translate that?" Maric asked incredulously.

He looked over to the father and son, then back again at the policeman, eyebrows raised. "Oh, I beg yer pardon," he said with an exaggerated Irish brogue. Then he pointed into the air and transitioned to a rapid-fire, directive stream of fluent Serbo-Croatian: "I'm assuming those helicopters are EUFOR. As a matter of professional courtesy, you may want to greet them when they arrive. I can stay here and talk to these gentlemen myself."

Maric glared at him, aghast. He was flustered, speaking first in English, and finishing in Serbo-Croat. "I . . . I am sorry. One of us must be present when you question our witnesses."

Mark smiled, feigning amusement, and continued in their language. "Sergeant Maric, walk away from here *now,* before I have EUFOR arrest you for obstruction of justice, witness tampering and as a possible suspect in this attack. Do I make myself clear?"

The Bosnian policeman's face was red with anger. He turned and strode through the parking lot and toward the EUFOR helicopters now preparing to land on the road in front of them.

Mark turned and exchanged glances with Mike McCallister at his side. "Was it something I said?"

"I reckon it was how ye said it," McCallister answered off-handedly. "I managed to get hold of the office. I told them we were on site and they're in contact with the U.S. Embassy and Washington D.C." He lowered his voice. "There were two vehicles in the convoy, both armored Suburbans. The BMW over there was an unfortunate bystander."

"Okay, I'm going to finish up with our restaurateurs before they dust all the evidence from the scene."

McCallister looked up at the approaching black UH-60 Blackhawks and AH-60 Apache escorts and nodded. There were four helicopters in all. "Ahh, that's gotta be General Rose—no one else travels like that around here."

He nodded. "It appears we've been upstaged then, haven't we? I'll be right there." He turned to the father and son, switching again to their language. "Mr. Siric, you have a choice. You can tell me what happened here and who else was in your restaurant when it happened, or I'll recommend that EUFOR detain you in Sarajevo for further questioning."

"I . . . I can't. . . ." the elder Siric stammered. His shoulders slumped and his hands twitched.

"Look, those tire tracks in your parking lot tell me there were at least two cars here. Twelve people from the American Embassy were just murdered, and you both saw it happen. So, I don't have much time for semantics. Either answer my questions truthfully *now* or I'll have you arrested by EUFOR. It's as simple as that." The Blackhawks hovered over them, and he looked down to see the tracks being swept away in their rotor wash with the rest of the snow. He shouted above the noise. "Who were they, Mr. Siric?"

The elder Siric coughed uneasily, his hands twisting together tightly. At once, his son moved forward, grasped Mark by the arm, and led him inside the restaurant to the damaged wooden bar. His father had followed them inside. Reaching underneath the counter, the son handed Lyons a ladies' brown leather wallet. Mark unsnapped it and saw the UN I.D. card inside. On it, there was a photo of a woman with brown hair, brown eyes, high cheekbones and a very attractive, bright smile. He pulled one of the business cards out of the front pocket. A symbol of a blue globe and a wreath surrounding it was in the top left margin of the card; below it, there was a blue diamond with a globe between two ends of a scale. The printing was in both English and French:

Sandra Lee Evenson

Expert-on-Mission
International Criminal Tribunal for the Former Yugoslavia (ICTY)
Tribunal Penal International pour l'ex-Yougosalvie
Churchillplein 1, 2517 JW The Hague Netherlands

He looked at both men. "Who does this belong to?"

Riso Siric looked down at the floor, and again it was his son who spoke excitedly. "To the woman who drove the UN car. She saw everything." He pointed at the broken plate glass window and then at the overturned furniture. "And she took photos! When it was over, she drove off. We saw nothing! You must believe us!"

"Who else was here, Mr. Siric?" Mark demanded. "Tell me, now."

The younger Siric was visibly shaken. "I . . . we didn't know who he was. He drove a grey Mercedes . . . a very large, new Mercedes. He was tall, had long hair and was calm, but he didn't come in. He had a Kalashnikov and he fired at the cars."

"Did they leave together?"

"No! He left first, going that way." Riso Siric pointed south. "And the UN woman drove north toward Jajce!"

"How long ago?"

"Right before the police arrived, less than an hour," Riso said.

He looked outside through the broken glass windows. The EUFOR helicopters landed in succession beside one another on the road, their engines whining. The rotor wash blew debris from the road and parking lot into the restaurant. The Apache attack helicopters flew overhead, bristling with armament, ready to strike at any threat or provocation. The door to the lead Blackhawk opened. Three men in civilian clothes and with thick moustaches jumped out, carrying short automatic rifles. Moments later, a tall man wearing a Gore-Tex camouflage jacket stepped out. From a distance, he could see the familiar face of General Ian Rose approaching. His entourage followed close behind.

CHAPTER 11

LIEUTENANT GENERAL JOHN THORPE, Commanding General for the United States Joint Special Operations Command, entered the ground floor entrance to the West Wing, escorted by the director of the White House Military Office or "WHMO." After showing the Secret Service agent seated at the desk their I.D. cards, they proceeded past him and turned down a hallway leading to two doors: the White House Mess on the left and the White House Situation Room on the right. Directly in front of them was a bar for fast food pick-up orders from the mess. The WHMO director picked up the telephone at the door to announce their arrival, and the door lock clicked open. Standing at the door, the director of the White House Situation Room greeted Thorpe.

"They just started, sir," he whispered. "I'd advise you go around to the side entrance. There's a seat open to the right of the door."

Thorpe thanked him and stepped past the desks, through the dimly lit operations center and entered through the side door to the large conference room. Technically, he knew, this was what was commonly known as the "Situation Room." Actually, however, the SITROOM consisted of larger complex of offices and broader video teleconferencing sites that extended well beyond the 18 acres of the White House. Because he was already at the Pentagon for another series of meetings, the Secretary of Defense had called from the White House and sent a "white top" helicopter to fly him across the Potomac to a field near the Washington Monument. He was then driven to the White House—only the President was authorized to land on the South Lawn. All he'd been told was that a serious incident had occurred in Bosnia and his presence was required immediately.

He slipped quietly into a chair behind the oak table at the near wall of the conference room. He appraised the room in a single sweeping glance. It was only the third time he'd been invited to the SITROOM, and each time he was struck by its size. What was typically billed in Hollywood as the ultimate command center, was in fact far smaller than he'd imagined it would—or should—be, occupying only a corner of the West Wing's ground floor. But from his previous visits, he knew that it was equipped with the most extensive state-of-the-art array of communications and audiovisual equipment available, to include a simultaneous satellite downlink capability that streamed information in real time, which had only recently been installed. It was all tastefully hidden from view, behind oak paneled walls. Everything was monitored around the clock by the military's best communications experts.

Grouped around the oval table, Thorpe recognized the members of the president's cabinet who also comprised the National Security Council. Many of them he had only previously seen on television. President Thomas Sells leaned back in his seat. At the opposite end of the table, oak panels opened to reveal a large, flat plasma screen. There was a pained look in the president's eyes as he briefly surveyed the room. His eyes came to rest momentarily on General Thorpe before looking over to his national security advisor beside him. The president greeted Thorpe's appearance with a nod.

It was Rachel Cook, the national security advisor, who spoke. "Good morning. A little over an hour ago, we were notified by the United Nations High Representative in Sarajevo that two vehicles carrying Ambassador Fulbright and his delegation were hit by mines scattered along a mountain road between Sarajevo and Banja Luka. There were twelve occupants, according to the last count we received from the embassy. They included Ambassadors Fulbright and Steinberg, Ambassador Fulbright's military aide, four political advisors, and five members of a protection detail from the Joint Special Operations Command, who regularly accompany delegations like these." She handed out copies of a one-page paper. "Here are the names of those assigned to the delegation. Twenty minutes ago, the U.S. embassy informed us that European Union Police Mission representatives were on the scene with the Bosnian Police. The EUPM Commissioner reports no survivors."

John Thorpe felt like someone had just kicked him in stomach. He knew Butch Sterns well—knew his wife and kids. The five members of the Special Operations Command protection detail were his men. Looking at the paper from the director of Central Intelligence, he only recognized a few of the names; the driver had been one of his Squadron Sergeant Majors. But they were all members of the Combat Applications Group or "CAG"—referred to more commonly as Delta Force—which he'd commanded seven years before.

"Was it confirmed as a deliberate attack?" The Chairman of the Joint Chiefs asked.

"That is the EUPM's conclusion, at least," Rachel Cook answered. "But I'd like to let Jim Goodwin show you the satellite imagery and let you decide for yourself. Jim?"

Thorpe knew Goodwin well. They were both White House Fellows together nearly two decades ago when the first war in Bosnia started. Jim was now the Deputy Director of the CIA.

The screen lit up with a black and white satellite image of the Bosnian countryside, covered with snow. The image shifted and centered on the ambush site.

"Thank you," Goodwin began, looking at the screen. "Before you is a live NSA downlink of the scene from one of our Condor satellites. Those helicopters that are landing are General Rose, the EUFOR Commander, and his party." Goodwin pointed with a red laser pointer to the two Blackhawks on the road and the Apaches circling overhead. While the image was reasonably clear, it was delayed several seconds, producing a slow-motion strobe-like effect. "You also see the Bosnian police cars surrounding the site."

"The white helicopter, to the far right on the road? Looks like a HIND or HIP, on the road?" the chairman asked.

"Yes. It's a MI-17 HIP. Belongs to the UN—it brought the EUPM commissioner into the site about an hour ago."

"And who is he?" the secretary of state asked.

"He's newly appointed. From Ireland we're told—name is Lyons. He and another EUPM man have been our only reliable sources of information on the ground since this happened. General Rose will now be able to assume control from them."

"Mark Lyons?" Thorpe asked quietly. Heads turned to face him.

"Yes. Thanks for being here, John," Goodwin answered.

Thorpe nodded.

The secretary of defense leaned back in his chair and pointed at Thorpe. "Some of you may already know General Thorpe. I asked him to come here. As the commanding general for the Joint Special Operations Command, JSOC, he brings a valuable perspective to the table. He was in Panama in 1989 and played a key role in capturing Noriega. He was in Somalia in '92 during the hunt for Aideed, and he's helped us find Pablo Escobar, Saddam

Hussein, Omar Sheikh and others."

The president nodded at Thorpe approvingly. "Good to see you, General."

Goodwin resumed his review of the scene in detail, identifying the destroyed vehicles and establishing the facts and assumptions he had drawn from the collective imagery analysis from the National Reconnaissance Office. "The wreckage is scattered along this debris field, representing what we also estimate to be the kill zone from the ambush, between the parallel lines you see on the road here. These lines are, in fact, trenches and craters blown into the road by explosives, in this case antitank mines."

"Daisy-chained?" Thorpe asked, noticing that several cabinet members had turned to face him.

"We believe that's the case, John."

The vice president spoke up abruptly. "Can I ask you what 'daisy-chained' means?"

"A series of explosive devices tied together, sir." Goodwin answered.

"Okay, I'll be the devil's advocate," the vice president continued skeptically. "How do we know that this wasn't a random pile of mines someone put there to have the military pick up? Aren't these detonated electronically?"

Goodwin nodded, anticipating the question. The screen turned a sky blue momentarily, and another black, white and grey satellite image replaced it. It was the same location, the same scene—but the road was clean of wreckage. There were vehicles in the parking lot and a herd of cows scattered along the road in front of the restaurant. Goodwin froze the image and took a sip of water.

"Our satellites were turned on to this location after radio communications were intercepted by our listening station in Bad Aibling, Germany. The team of analysts there were sufficiently concerned to call the National Surveillance Office at Fort Meade and within five minutes, we were able to switch over from Kosovo to Bosnia. This footage was taken at 10:05 A.M., 4:05 P.M. in Bosnia. We tried to reach the cell phones with the delegation to warn them that they were heading into an ambush, but getting a signal through the mountains is damn near impossible. I'll begin the sequence of what occurred there now—watch carefully."

Thorpe listened to Goodwin's commentary. His heart pounded as the footage progressed, showing the convoy approaching in the distance, slowed initially by the first road block and then slowed again by the herd of cows. Goodwin stopped the tape and pointed to the blown up images of all three vehicles. "The UN vehicle you see here has been traced to the International Criminal Tribunal. The others have no license plates or markings to speak of, so we're assuming them to be stolen."

The image panned out as the two-vehicle convoy stopped in the middle of the roadway. Those who initially appeared as villagers herding cattle could now be seen jumping down the ravine with radios and weapons in hand. Three men pulled ropes across the road with antitank mines in tow.

Thorpe was struck by the silence of the images on the screen as he watched the initial blasts, appearing as small white puffs, followed by larger explosions of rockets impacting both vehicles from all directions. Thick streams of black and white smoke and scattering debris prevented a clear picture of the scene for nearly thirty seconds. People could be seen running on the periphery of the wreckage, firing weapons point blank into the vehicles and then retreating again.

Goodwin zoomed in on the man firing an AKM sub-machine gun from behind a grey Mercedes, in the direction of the convoy. As the man's image became larger, it was less clear; but it did provide an oblique-profile view of a tall, muscular man with sharp features and a strong, pronounced chin that was bonded to the stock of the AKM. The satellite still-photo had its effect. Thorpe heard Goodwin talk, but he was no longer listening. His shock at the loss of his men was suddenly replaced by anger, and a determination to see that those responsible be held accountable.

"We believe this to be the man behind the attack. We've identified him as Goran Mescic, widely known in Bosnia by his alias or nickname, "Celo." Celo is a radical Bosnian Serb living in Prijedor. He owns a café there, deals in the black market and owns a construction firm. He's the Bosnian Serbs' unofficial representative. Wildly popular. During the Bosnian War from '92 to '95, he was the commander of a Bosnian Serb Brigade. At the time, the youngest brigade level commander in the Serb Army—"

"Wait." The secretary of state was reading a note from one of her staffers. She looked up. "Are you *sure* this is him?"

Goodwin nodded. "It's as positive an identification as we can get on short notice."

The secretary of state's eyebrows rose incredulously. "Celo Mescic is also a sealed-list indictee with the ICTY."

"Yes, ma'am. We know who Celo Mescic is," Thorpe interjected. "We've been tracking him for several months now and assess him as low-threat. When the time comes, we'll pick him up."

The lines around the secretary of state's eyes and forehead betrayed her indignation. Her cross tone followed. "General, I don't understand. If you know where this man is, why don't we arrest him now? He's a war criminal, and from all we've seen here, it seems certain he's responsible for the murders of two of our ambassadors and five Foreign Service officers."

Thorpe's voice was resonant and even. "Madam Secretary, four of those killed came from my command also. I'm as pained as you are by this incident, but emotionalism has never been a rationale for us to jump into an operation. When the facts are assembled, when I am given the order, we'll launch." He paused without diverting his eye contact from the secretary of state. "Between now and then, I'd suggest we sort out some loose ends before we jump to any conclusions." Thorpe glanced over at the FBI director and back at the secretary of state. "You have one of the finest soldiers and investigators now on the ground in Mark Lyons. You can trust him. Right now, my advice would be to listen to him."

There was a stunned silence. The secretary of state bristled, shifting irritably in her seat. The FBI director nodded, but kept silent, unwilling to enter the fray.

The secretary of defense, waiting to intervene, leaned forward. "None of us has all the answers at the moment, and none of us are advocating that we do anything rash." Turning to Goodwin, he made an attempt to divert the increasingly heated discussion developing between Thorpe and the secretary of state . . . all in the presence of the president. "Jim, any other thoughts on this?"

"At this point," Goodwin said, "determining who's responsible for this attack is purely speculation. We've got some significant work yet to do."

Thorpe nodded. He knew he was treading on thin ice. As a three-star, he was a small fish compared to the others in attendance. He also knew that both cabinet members were friends and past associates in one of the largest New York City law firms. His comments were a subtle directive—"end of discussion." Thorpe had already approached that invisible line, and he knew it was time to back off. "We'll assist in every way we can. My concern is that we don't jump to conclusions before we have a clear view of what's transpired."

The president nodded, having listened intently to the preceding debate. He leaned back in his chair. The room was silent, except for the air being pumped through the overhead vents. He looked at Thorpe. "We're all sorry about your men, general. They're irreplaceable and this is a tragedy any way you cut it." The president shifted his gaze to the FBI director. "I'm not prepared to characterize this incident until the investigation is complete. So until then, we'll refer to this as a land mine accident."

"Mr. President, I'm not advocating that you call this anything but what it is," Thorpe said quietly, but forcefully.

The president paused momentarily, obviously annoyed by Thorpe's interruption, and held out his hand to placate. "General, right now we need to err on the side of caution right now. If, as you say, we act impetuously, we run the risk of escalating our involvement in a war none of us wants to relive, and I'm not going to trip our way into a civil war where I'm forced to fight all three sides. Lord knows, we have our hands full as it is." The president looked at the secretary of state and at the chairman of the joint chiefs, and tapped his pencil on the pad of paper in front of him. His tone was suddenly firm, with a distinct edge. "So everyone's clear on this, you can be goddamned sure we'll find out who's responsible for this attack, but we'll do that behind the scenes, rather than under a media spotlight. Has everyone got that?"

The room went quiet for a moment. Thorpe shifted uncomfortably in his seat.

The White House chief of staff looked to the secretary of state. "Okay, State has the lead. Do you have enough right now to deal with the press?"

The secretary of state looked up from her papers and nodded quietly. "Yes, I believe we do. We'll treat this publicly as an accident, pending completion of General Rose's investigation."

Thorpe sat back in his chair, aghast. His cautionary—perhaps overzealous—push for a pragmatic approach had clearly been misinterpreted, or worse, used to validate a policy decision that he judged to be, at the very least, ill-advised. Whatever this incident was, it was not an accident. To say otherwise was a deliberate misrepresentation. His men had *not* died in an accident—*they'd been attacked!*

"Sir?" Thorpe interjected evenly, addressing the chief of staff. "I request that I be allowed to notify the families of these soldiers who died before we announce it to the media. I don't want them to find out about this on CNN."

The president nodded and answered. "No, none of us want that. How much time do you need?"

"Can you give me two hours?"

"You have them," the president said, looking over at his chief of staff. "All right, make sure we're following the same procedures for the families of the others in the delegation." Looking around the room, the president found the director of the FBI at the far wall. "I'd like you involved in this also— whatever help they need."

The FBI director gathered his papers and nodded to the president. "I'll have a team from Quantico on the way to Sarajevo to augment this afternoon."

The president turned to his chief of staff, and exhaled. "Okay, can we can get a hold of Ten Downing?"

The chief of staff walked to the side door and a White House communications technician was ushered into the room; a twenty-something female technician in a grey suit. Her green access badge was marked with the acronym "MIL," associating her with one of the military services. She dialed the secure telephone beside the president and laid the handset on the table. She pressed the intercom button so that the NSC members could hear it ring. "Sir, the Prime Minister is connected to a satellite telephone. He may fade out periodically, but you'll be talking securely."

Watching the scene before him…and the president's responses, Thorpe suddenly had the haunting feeling that much of the plan had been scripted behind closed doors, before this meeting in the SITROOM had been convened.

Chapter 12

SANDY EVENSON FELT NUMB, operating more on instinct than reason to distance herself from the scene at Oborci. She had been on the road less than an hour. She held her hand up to her face to shield herself from the freezing air that came through the shattered, bullet-riddled windshield. Her eyes teared and her vision blurred. She negotiated the tight curves in the road, struggling to maintain control of the damaged 4Runner, but also pushing it to go even faster, passing other, slower vehicles along the way.

The whole situation seemed so unreal, and the questions were as elusive as the answers. Who would attack a diplomatic convoy from the U.S. Embassy? Who was the man who had pointed the rifle at her? And why hadn't he shot her?

She reflected on the years she'd spent in Bosnia during—and since—the war. Two failed engagements to men she loved . . . the graves . . . and her friends killed, senselessly and suddenly.

Why was this happening now? When does it all stop?

It was the high-pitched ring from within her backpack that caused her to refocus. She wiped the tears from her eyes, reached inside and pulled the cell phone out. Through the static, she recognized the voice on the other end as her friend in Zagreb, Jon Schauer.

"Sandy? Is that you?"

She held it to her ear for a moment, and swallowed before answering. "Christ . . . the bastards killed them! They're all dead!"

"*Whoa!* Wait! *What* are you talking about? I've been trying to call you for the past forty-five minutes. Everyone's calling, looking for you. Where are you? Are you all right?"

"I'm fine. *An American diplomatic convoy was blown up . . . right in front of me!*"

"Listen to me Sandy . . . where are you? Tell me where you are."

She replied in a restrained tone that belied her state of panic. "I'm just south of Banja Luka and I'm going to try to get into Croatia. I can't stay here. I'll call when I cross the border."

Schauer reacted quickly. "Okay, look, there's a EUFOR Base in Slavonski Brod, just east of where you cross the border. I'll call them and have them meet you on the Bosnian side."

"Jon, please, I don't want an escort. Being detained by EUFOR is the last thing I need right now. Call Bob Childs at the embassy. I spoke to him just before all of this happened. Tell him you talked to me, and that I'm going to try to make it to Zagreb and catch my flight to The Hague tonight."

"Who will take you? Can I meet you?" Schauer asked with a clear tone of desperation.

She remembered that her flight to Amsterdam didn't leave until the morning. She looked down at her backpack. There, underneath it, was the camera that she had thrown into the passenger seat. Downloading the photos had to be one of her priorities, and Jon Schauer was the one person she could trust to do that quickly and privately.

"Okay. . . ." She hesitated, knowing she was talking over an open line that could easily be monitored. "Meet me at the airport then."

"I'll be waiting for you at the departure terminal," Schauer answered. "Sandy—be careful."

"I'll be careful . . . listen--can you find out from Bob who was in that diplomatic convoy? I need to know."

The phone went dead.

She was at least 250 kilometers from Zagreb . . . another three hour drive. She looked down at her gas gauge. With slightly more than a quarter of a tank left, there was only a slight possibility she would have enough gas to make it, but there would be gas stations on the Autobahn to Zagreb. Reaching into her pack again while also turning along a hard right curve in the road, she searched for her wallet.

The wallet with her money, credit cards and I.D. was gone.

OBORCI, BOSNIA AND HERZEGOVINA

MARK LYONS APPROACHED the familiar, tall, uniformed man striding in front of the other dismounted passengers. He knew that General

Ian Rose was no stranger to violence, and he knew to tread carefully with his old nemesis. The irony of their meeting in these circumstances was not lost on him or, he was certain, on Rose. Rose did not look directly at him as he surveyed the grim scene.

After a brief moment, he extended his hand to Rose. Rose shook his hand absently.

"I heard you were taking over the Police Mission, Lyons." It was difficult to hear over the loud helicopter rotors, but nothing followed. No congratulations offered.

Mark looked at Rose's long, weathered face. He projected a commanding presence. His eyes were squinted and his jaw was tight; clearly, he was disturbed by the sight of the wreckage and by the gravity of the situation before him.

"It was a deliberate ambush, set up over here, on this side of the road," he said, pointing to the culvert. He walked with Rose to the limousine hulk and the other vehicles in the restaurant parking lot, briefing him on the likely sequence of events. At one point, short of the limousine, he stopped and showed him the evidence from the mines and rocket-propelled grenades. Rose nodded his understanding, following his gestures silently. All the while, the Apache helicopters hovered like massive wasps above the damaged roadway. Mark faced Rose. "I'd say whoever did this knew that the delegation was coming and came prepared to engage a moving target."

"How would they know they were coming, Lyons? If you make that assumption, you've also got to assume they would've known their route and time of arrival," Rose challenged. "And why did they not use an IED...electronically detonated...rather than this rather primitive use of mines?"

Mark shrugged slightly, placed his hands in his pockets and looked out at the grizzly scene. "Any number of possibilities. Fulbright's arrival here yesterday was well-publicized. They may have been observed and followed from Sarajevo. And there's the whole question of capability—"

"And intent," Rose added gruffly.

Mark nodded. "The effect was every bit as devastating. As to motive, we don't know who else was in the convoy, except Ambassador Fulbright."

Rose handed him a folded sheet of paper with a list of names scribbled in pencil. It took him a moment to realize it was a complete list of the delegation, probably obtained in-flight. Fulbright, Steinberg, Sterns,

Dempsey, Gillem, Ugresic, Grimes. Names he didn't know.

An officer, who he guessed to be Rose's aide, approached quickly.

"Sir, you have a call on the INMARSAT. It's the Defense Minister."

The INMARSAT, he knew, was a secure satellite line. Expensive to use, but very effective. Rose nodded and turned back to him, excusing himself.

McCallister walked over to him as General Rose departed. "Who was this lady witness?"

Mark handed him Sandy Evenson's business card. "She's driving north on this road according to those two in the restaurant."

McCallister studied Sandy Evenson's business card. "ICTY? How in the bloody hell—"

Mark took the card back. "We need to find out. Maybe we can catch up with her," he answered. "Tell Vladimir to be ready. Can you handle another flight?"

"I wouldn't miss it, Commissioner," McCallister replied, eyes wide, trying his best to smile.

Lyons looked at Ian Rose approaching him again.

"Ah," McCallister murmured, "This is where he politely says 'Thank-you very much for all your help, lads, but I'm in charge now—ye can go.'"

"Go ahead and give Vlad a heads up, and I'll be right there." He saw Rose's serious expression and long, purposeful gait as he drew closer.

Rose had taken out his leather gloves from his coat pocket and was putting them on as he drew near. "That call was from Ten Downing Street. The Defense Minister conveyed to me that Washington has received your notification. I'm sealing this area off completely until families can be notified and our investigators arrive. Anyone who is not EUFOR must vacate the area."

Mark glanced at McCallister in the distance and smiled slightly, understanding that they were effectively being evicted—without grounds, but locking horns with the EUFOR Commander wasn't something he was inclined to do at this moment. He shook his head and smiled sardonically. "Of course, Ian. Wouldn't want to upset Ten Downing, would we?"

Rose nodded, still apparently distracted, but also visibly relieved at his willingness to disengage. "I'll be in touch, Lyons."

CHAPTER 13

SANDY EVENSON HEARD the police sirens behind her long before she heard the helicopter's rotor blades pounding above. Her heart raced as she considered the options available to her. She could continue toward the border crossing, stop and try to deal with Customs, or as a final option, try to make her way to the Joint Commission Observer house—a British Special Air Service team that had lent their assistance to the ICTY during several mass grave exhumations. The disadvantage in going there was that they lived on the western edge of town, along a route that led away from the border.

Continuing to evade the police in an attempt to cross into Croatia, however, would be impossible without her identification. By now, the police would have certainly radioed ahead to the border police.

Eventually the police would catch up with her. Two other police cars were now approaching from the opposite direction, and stopped abruptly, adjacent to a large Shell station, blocking the entrance into the town of Bos Gradiska, but they had not blocked off the cross road leading east and west. She started to slow the 4Runner as she approached the police road block, and abruptly swung the vehicle left along the back road leading to the JCO house less than a mile away.

MARK LYONS HAD BEGUN to give up hope of locating the UN vehicle belonging to Sandra Lee Evenson from above. They'd flown from Oborci along Route 5 toward the border to Croatia, and he knew the helicopter was running at half a tank of fuel. Vladimir had established the Sava River, the border between Bosnia and Croatia, as their turn-around point, where they would have no choice but to return to Sarajevo.

"There!" Vlad exclaimed, pointing at the severely battered white SUV passing cars on the right-hand shoulder of the road, around blind turns, and creating a middle "third lane" in order to avoid head-on collisions. The car had to be hers.

Just a short distance away, he could see a house with a British flag flying overhead.

"She's gonna kill herself any minute," McCallister commented dryly from the back.

Bosnian Serb police cars were trailing close behind her. "That's what she's trying to get away from . . . she's probably heading to that house with the Brit flag."

"The house belongs to the British JCO's," McCallister shouted.

He saw armed soldiers pouring from the house, occupying positions behind sport utility vehicles in the driveway. "JCO's?"

"Joint Commission Observers," Vladimir replied. They're Special Forces teams that work directly for the EUFOR Commander. The ones down there are British SAS."

"Can you land there?" he asked.

Vladimir nodded, and Mark turned around to McCallister. "Prepared to make a hasty exit?"

"Ready!" McCallister shouted. "I'll handle the police!"

Vladimir maneuvered the HIP aggressively forward and in front of the two police cars blocking the road, then descended sharply. Simultaneously, he turned the aircraft 180 degrees and lowered the tail rotor, buffeting the cars with debris and dirt until they retreated from their positions in the road. He leveled the nose of the helicopter and landed on the road. McCallister had already opened the side door and was poised to jump out.

The police were pulling up behind the white 4Runner. Seeing the vehicle's battered condition, he was amazed that it was still running. Two policemen approached her car from behind, ignoring the HIP and ignoring its UN markings in their rush to detain her. Jumping off onto the road, he felt the intense buzz-saw-like rotor wash overhead. He walked under the rotors fully erect, disregarding the natural inclination to crouch or to run, knowing there was at least three feet of clearance above him. Both policemen stopped in their tracks, facing him.

McCallister came up behind them and guided them away from the 4Runner. The driver's door to the 4Runner flew open and an attractive woman stepped out. She perfectly matched the photograph on the UN identification card.

"Would you happen to be Sandra Lee Evenson?"

"Yes! But how—"

"Mark Lyons," he preempted. "Assistant Commissioner of the European Union Police Mission." He pulled her wallet from his overcoat pocket and handed it to her. "I believe this is yours. May we offer you a ride?"

He regarded her in her blue wool overcoat, arms crossed. Small shards of glass were stuck to her coat. Her thick, dark brown hair slid over her shoulders in disarray. She pushed it back, exposing bright hazel almond-shaped eyes and dark lashes that boldly held his gaze. She was only slightly shorter than he. Despite her composure, her cheeks were tear-stained.

"I need to get to Zagreb—"

"We'll get you to Zagreb, Miss Evenson, but it would be better if we didn't stay here long. I'm not sure how long we can keep the neighborhood police at bay."

"The JCO Team can handle them; they're friends of mine," she answered, pointing in the direction of the soldiers assembled on the driveway of the large two-story house.

One of the soldiers was approaching—brown hair, sharp features, medium height, with a lean athlete's build, wearing blue jeans with one hand casually gripping an automatic rifle. He recognized him and turned to Sandy Evenson. "Chris Ryan?"

"Yes, he's the team leader. You know him?"

He nodded, and smiled faintly. "Aye, indeed I do."

Ryan walked up and extended his hand. "Well, Colonel Lyons, I'd say you're a long way from Belfast."

He met Ryan's grasp and nodded. "Just arrived, Chris. Small world" He nodded toward the local police. "As you can see, we're in a bit of a situation. Could ye lend us a hand?"

"Certainly," Ryan responded, then turned to Evenson. "Sandy—you okay?" He glanced at the 4Runner. "What the bloody hell happened?"

Sandy nodded. "Wrong place at the wrong time—what I really need at this moment is to get away from here."

Ryan nodded his understanding and relayed a series of orders into his handheld radio. "All right then, we'll handle things here. You're in good hands with this bloke," Ryan replied, reaching over to grasp his arm. "Finest police chief in all of Ireland!"

Mark slapped Ryan on the shoulder, thanking him. He saw Sandy Evenson silently take in the scene.

McCallister joined Lyons in transferring Sandy's suitcases from the back of the 4Runner to the helicopter as two policemen looked on— one conspicuously taking notes and the other talking on their car's two-way radio.

After she retrieved her backpack, her car's compact disk player, her CD's and her camera, Sandy ran to the side door of the helicopter. Its engines were whining. Three SAS soldiers in blue jeans and camouflage Gortex jackets stood between the police and the helicopter.

Mark walked over and shook Ryan's hand. Both men regarded each other with an unspoken familiarity. As he started toward the helicopter, Ryan called out to him.

"Sir, you know General Rose is here, in Banja Luka?"

Mark paused and nodded his head. "Yeah, we've already run into each other."

He boarded, and with a deafening roar, the massive aircraft lifted off in the direction of Zagreb, Croatia. He and Sandy looked below, in time to see the wind hit the policeman's papers, causing them to take to flight.

CHAPTER 14

FIVE HUNDRED FEET above the Sava River, crossing into Croatia, Mark knew well where he was. The smell of the winter air combined with the manure fertilizing the farmers' fields—the same smell he'd remembered as an eleven-year-old boy, the night his father had been arrested.

He'd gone to bed that evening, and his father had been at his desk, grading his students' papers, reviewing lessons for the next day. The car engines and lights flashing outside their first floor apartment startled him from his sleep and shot him bolt upright. Within moments, he'd heard the door forced open, and when he opened his bedroom door, his father was gone.

A single moment, seared in his memory.

The police ordered him to pack a set of clothes. He'd already soaked his pajama bottoms. He'd been too terrified to speak that night—and for days afterward; and yet, deep within, he was screaming.

The "boarding school" was one of Zagreb's numerous orphan asylums. The gates and walls could not contain the damp, airless stench of backed-up toilets in the dormitory, the creak of the old iron beds and the footsteps echoing relentlessly on the cold cement floors. He remembered how daylight would take forever to come through the narrow windows, caked with dirt. After he'd regained the courage to talk, the prefect finally looked at him with cold, black eyes and announced with finality, "This is your home now."

The spring seemed to evaporate, and as the seasons changed his loneliness grew. Weeks later, in the middle of the night, he'd heard pounding at the prefect's door, and a booming voice demanding that his nephew immediately be released to his custody. After the shock, he'd quickly realized that his uncle had come for him. When the doors to the dormitory opened, he was already dressed and waiting by the side of the bed, clothes stacked in his arms. A large, imposing shadow approached, blocking the bright light from the doorway.

"Marko. Come with me." It was his uncle—his father's brother, Milan. He stared up at him—a giant of a man with long, black hair and a beard that made him look like Moses. He had come to rescue him from a living nightmare, and bring him back to his home.

Driving in the old, rusted Lada toward eastern Bosnia, he had been too frightened and emotionally exhausted to speak. The same soothing, wonderful voice resonated as they crossed the Sava River into Bosnia.

"You will see your father again. . . . You are part of our family. You and Celo . . . now you are brothers. . . ."

As an only child, he did not know what to expect. All he knew was that he was grateful to be liberated from that hell. The fog of despair and anxiety slowly began to lift.

They arrived in Zvornik early in the morning, and entered the small house, exhausted. Effortlessly, Celo assumed the role of older brother. Celo showed him their home, his new bed, and introduced him to his friends. They explored the shallow limestone caves and ancient ruins above Zvornik. He was treated as if he had always been Celo's brother; like his twin, even if he was nearly a year younger. Over the months that followed, Celo became the role model and brother he'd never had.

Years later, one bitterly cold winter day in Belfast, he'd discovered the official government paper declaring that his father had been imprisoned as an "enemy of the state, without the right of correspondence."

It was Tito's Death Sentence.

The searing memory of that realization forced his eyes open as the helicopter came to rest on the tarmac of Zagreb's Pleso International Airport.

WASHINGTON, D.C., THE WHITE HOUSE

"John?"

Lieutenant General John Thorpe stopped and turned around as he was walking out of the Situation Room. It was Jim Goodwin.

"Jim! It's been a long time. When was the last time I saw you ...at Walter Reed, was it?"

Goodwin nodded. "After that warm reception in Kabul. . . ." He smiled thoughtfully. "Not one of my more stellar moments."

"You're damn lucky to be alive." Thorpe smiled and slapped his shoulder. It had been several years ago, and Goodwin had been a UN observer aboard a Russian military transport plane that was attempting to land at the Kabul Airport when it had come under fire. One of the antiaircraft bullets hit the femoral artery in his leg, and with no first aid kit on board and no one who knew how to effectively stop the bleeding, he did it himself, using his belt as a tourniquet, saving his own life. He fell unconscious from blood loss and slipped into shock, nearly dying. "You even managed to take the scenic route to Walter Reed; from Kabul to Landstuhl, and all points in between."

"That's what I hear. I'd like to say I enjoyed the trip but honestly, I don't remember any of it."

"Best way to fly," Thorpe quipped. "How are you? *Honestly?*"

Goodwin looked up at him. "Good days, bad days. My doctors tell me I won't be running any more marathons, but I'm much better, thanks to you."

"Thank Mary Pat. She was by your side all the time, and she made the phone call."

Goodwin shook his head and laughed. "She's a doctor's worst nightmare, but I have you both to thank. How you convinced them not to amputate my leg, I still haven't figured out."

He shrugged. "I told them to save the leg, because without it, it would be hard for you to get around the West Wing!"

Goodwin's smile faded and he nodded. "I'd rather be in the fight than here, quite honestly."

"Well, I have to tell you, it's good to see a friendly face in these hallways, especially today."

Goodwin grasped his elbow and walked close by his side. "I'm sorry about your men, John—it's a terrible loss."

He nodded solemnly as he looked down the hallway. He pursed his lips and lowered his voice. "Not telling the truth about what happened to that convoy is a mistake." He paused, his voice now a whisper. "Jim, you know I'd die for this country, but I won't lie to those families."

Goodwin nodded and looked around. "I know you're in a rush. Let me walk outside with you."

Thorpe immediately understood. *"We can't talk here."*

Both men continued up the narrow stairway silently, passed a uniformed Secret Service agent at a desk, and a hallway adorned with a series of four original Norman Rockwell paintings, entitled *So You Want to See the President?* outlining Rockwell's depiction of what a visitor could see while waiting to enter FDR's Oval Office. They stepped out the rear doorway of the West Wing directly into the Rose Garden. The cherry and magnolia trees had not yet blossomed and the soil under the flowerbeds was freshly tilled. He was struck by the impression that the surrounding South Lawn could easily be the grounds of a small country club.

"Is there something I'm missing here, Jim? Because if there's a rest-of-the-story to this and I don't know what that storyline is, things will quickly get out of hand."

Goodwin nodded. "I believe there is. Whether or not it'll provide a rationale for what went on in there, I can't say, but you should be aware."

"What is it?"

Goodwin stopped on the brick pathway and faced him with a solemn expression, like a doctor about to deliver a fatal diagnosis. "This morning I got a call from a friend who works for Doctors Without Borders. He's in Ravno right now running a field hospital for refugees. Two days ago, he was led to a twelve-year-old girl in a coma who later died. She had lesions all over her body."

"Yeah, but given the circumstances—"

"I know, not so significant. But what *is* significant was the cause of death." Goodwin looked over in the direction of the Oval Office and back at Thorpe. "They determined she died of severe radiation poisoning."

"How—"

Goodwin held up his hand and spoke in a low voice. "We're still trying to figure it all out, but her *entire* body was radioactive. She ingested a concentrated weapons-grade material. We have forensics on the scene and they're checking out the area where she was found. We believe that she was playing with or handling a piece of plutonium."

"*Plutonium?*" Thorpe said in disbelief. "Christ . . . but how?"

"We're still trying to determine that," Goodwin answered. "But it's the kind of report that makes your blood run cold."

Thorpe nodded solemnly. "Can your friend meet me at EUFOR Headquarters tomorrow night?"

"Of course," Goodwin replied, surprised. He pulled a card and a pen out of his inside jacket pocket and scribbled on it. "His name is Jean Renee Lauvergeon. He goes by 'J.R.' I'll tell him you're coming." He hesitated a moment. "Will you see Mark?"

"I had no idea he was over there until you mentioned it in your briefing."

"Well, I suspect he's there for good reason. Do you stay in contact?"

Thorpe shook his head. "Not since Annalisa died." He knew Goodwin would understand his reference to his daughter.

Goodwin nodded silently, gazing over the South Lawn of the White House toward the Washington Monument and the Jefferson Memorial.

"John, the last thing I want to do is start a mass panic or a media feeding frenzy, but if there's loose fissile material out there or anywhere else, we've got a helluva mess on our hands."

He slowly nodded his understanding and extended his hand to Goodwin. "I'll look into it. Be safe, my friend."

"No, you be safe, John," Goodwin said. "Godspeed."

CHAPTER 15

SANDY EVENSON RETRIEVED her backpack and Mark offered his hand to help her off the helicopter. He walked beside her on the tarmac.

"Can we talk, Ms. Evenson?"

She nodded and stopped abruptly, looking up at him. "I don't want to understate my appreciation for flying me here, because I'm grateful for the ride. But you have to understand that I *must* make this plane to Amsterdam—it's not an option. I'm testifying at The Hague tomorrow morning. You're welcome to walk with me to my plane."

He nodded silently, matching her faster pace toward the white shuttle bus marked with the black letters "UN" on each side. "So, what time do we depart?"

"We?" She stopped in midstride and turned toward him.

He nodded. "Of course, you're a material witness in two cases now."

She eyed him narrowly. "What do you mean '*two*'?"

He shrugged nonchalantly. "Well, yes, two. Your case at The Hague tomorrow, and the incident you're running away from—the one I'm now investigating. So I'm glad to join ye, if that's what it takes."

She sighed heavily and boarded the bus. Sitting down opposite him, she leaned her head back and shut her eyes. After a few moments she opened them.

"Mr. Lyons, *who exactly are you?*"

He was momentarily caught off-guard by the question. He smiled. "I'm the new Assistant Commissioner –"

"Yeah, I got that," she interrupted, casting an appraising eye. "Then why haven't I heard of you?"

"I just arrived actually. Can't say I expected any of this."

"You were there? Then you saw what happened."

"Indeed, I did see it." He nodded and paused, changing the subject. "Can ye delay your departure?"

She exhaled, shaking her head slowly, resolutely. "You don't know what you're asking me to do."

"Aye, I think I do," he replied casually. "You've been here a long time and you obviously want out of here. I can understand that. Any sane person would want to get on that plane. But these are extraordinary circumstances. And you—well, you're our only witness at the moment."

"Who were they, the people in the cars? Was it Ambassador Fulbright?"

He nodded. "It was." He handed her the slip of paper that General Rose had given him. "Here are the names." The bus stopped at the passenger terminal. A blast of cold air greeted them as the driver opened the door and they stepped off the bus.

She surveyed the list on the tarmac and seemed to take a deep swallow. "They're all dead then, aren't they?"

He nodded again and looked directly into her eyes. "Yes."

She began walking at a quick pace.

He walked beside her, matching her steps. "Can you tell me what happened?"

At first, she did not answer, but then turned to him with an appraising eye. "How do I know I can trust you?"

He shook his head and smiled. "Aye, well," he said. "At the moment, it looks like I'm the only one here who's in a *position* to help you."

She eyed him dubiously. "I'm afraid that's not good enough. Not here, it's not."

"I'm hopin' it's a start then," he said with a slightly desperate tone. "Look, Miss Evenson, we . . . I . . . need you, if we're to get to the truth of what happened back there. . . ."

Annoyed, she turned to face him. "What do you mean, *the truth?* They were killed in cold blood! Isn't that obvious? What else do you want from me?"

She walked, faster now and he continued by her side. "Without you, I'm afraid the picture won't be so clear."

"*What?* What are you saying?" She stopped and turned to him. "That they'd cover this up?"

Before he could respond, the high pitched ring of a cell phone interrupted. Sandy reached into her coat pocket to retrieve it and stepped away from the bus, talking over the noise of the airport, with a finger in her other ear.

She walked back toward him. He overheard only part of her conversation before she disconnected. "Tell them to postpone it."

She stopped in front of him. "Mr. Lyons, all I've wanted . . . all I *want*," she said wearily, "is to finish here; to finish digging bodies out of mass graves, talking to people who've committed atrocities against their neighbors, to survivors and the families of those who were murdered, to leave this and go back to a normal life—to live like a *normal* person. Is that too much to ask? What you're asking me to do is stay here in this shit-hole and I absolutely can't endure that any longer."

"Just for a few days—"

"You're asking me to trust you," she interrupted pointedly. "And I don't even know you."

He smiled and nodded sympathetically. "Ah well, I suspect there are worse folk ye could trust in these parts."

"You're killing me...." A faint, fleeting smile crossed her face. She was momentarily taken by his low voice and his understated humor. "All right, Mister Commissioner. I'll give you two days, but that's it. A friend of mine who lives here in Zagreb is picking us up. That was him on the phone. We can talk at his place."

She stopped and extended her hand toward him.

"Mark...you can call me Mark."

She shook his hand, but her hand remained extended.

"Yes?" he asked, confused.

"Can I have my camera and passport back now, Mark?"

CHAPTER 16

KATE KAMRATH FINISHED typing and read the article before sending it to her editor in New York. It was a story that had not yet taken hold in the mainstream media outside Europe, but with the Ravno crisis worsening, the story of Archbishop Alojzije Stepinac's canonization to Catholic sainthood had all the signs of a gathering international political storm. She was certain other print and broadcast media would quickly snap it up as well.

Croatia's Stepinac to be Canonized Amidst Controversy
By Kate Kamrath

ZAGREB, January 24 (*New York Times* News Service)—Pope Vincent will visit the Balkan States next month to canonize one of the most controversial figures in Roman Catholic history, World War II Croatian Archbishop Alojzije Stepinac—a hero to Roman Catholics, but long a symbol of division in the Balkans. In 1953, Pope Pius XII recognized Stepinac's service in a difficult era by making him a cardinal.

Addressing a congregation in Stepinac's birthplace, Krasic, Croatia, Croatian Archbishop Vojislav Pijadje said the Pope would visit Bosnia and Croatia to canonize Stepinac in a Mass at the site of a pilgrimage shrine in Medjugorje, Bosnia next month, where the last of three miracles attributed to Stepinac was recently confirmed by a Vatican Commission. Canonization awards the full title of "saint." The Pontiff's Mass is expected to draw up to seven hundred thousand Catholic visitors to Medjugorje.

But the ceremony, for which Croats have waited years, comes despite serious differences among historians on the role Stepinac played under the fascist regime which ruled Croatia during World War II.

CLASHES WITH HISTORY

While serving as Zagreb's archbishop in 1941, national

fervor drove Stepinac to rush into welcoming an independent Croatian state, which was established after Germany invaded Yugoslavia in April 1941.

The head of the new Croatian State, Ante Pavelic soon gained notoriety for his new government for fiercely persecuting its Serbs, Jews, Gypsies and Croats who did not support the Ustashe, which was allied with the Nazi regime. Although Stepinac denounced the Pavelic regime, many Serbs still consider him a war criminal.

The Simon Wiesenthal Center, a U.S.-based Nazi-hunting group, also had asked the Vatican to postpone the canonization pending further study of the cardinal's actions. Some local Jews have defended Stepinac, insisting that he protected the Jews during the Nazi puppet regime's reign.

Stepinac continues to be hailed as a hero by Croatians for his resistance to communism and refusal to separate the Catholic Church from the Vatican. For this reason he remains a symbol of endurance and survival for all Croats, the overwhelming majority of whom are Catholic.

During his visit to Zagreb in 1994, Pope John Paul II called Stepinac the "bulwark of the Croatian Catholic Church." Of Croatia's 4.7 million people, an estimated 80 percent are Roman Catholic. The Vatican views the country as its representative state in the Balkans, otherwise surrounded by orthodox Christians and Muslims.

A CLEAR CONSCIENCE

Stepinac was arrested and tried by Yugoslav authorities for allegedly supporting the Nazi-backed Ustashe fascists. Stepinac defended himself by saying: "My conscience is clear." Modern historians generally recognize that he asked his priests to actively work to assist people of other religions who were threatened, and to help save lives wherever possible.

Former President of Yugoslavia, Milovan Djilas, later admitted that Archbishop Stepinac would never have been tried for his conduct during the war "had he not continued to oppose the new Communist regime."

After serving five years in prison, Tito placed Stepinac under house arrest in his birthplace of Krasic. He died there nine years later from a rare blood disease, exacerbated by the exhaustion of his captivity.

Bosnian Serb officials warned yesterday that allowing the Stepinac canonization to be held in Medjugorje would further destabilize the region at precisely the time when diplomatic efforts there are at their peak. A Vatican spokesman responded yesterday by stating that the Stepinac canonization was long overdue, and that they saw no substantive reason to reschedule the event or move it to another venue.

After reading it through a final time, Kate Kamrath pressed "Send."

CHAPTER 17

CELO MESCIC SAT in silence in the Café Prijedor opposite his deputy, Dragan "Ivo" Bostic. As the owner, Celo felt most comfortable there, and he had spared no expense in constructing it, with a simple, yet elegant contemporary Scandinavian teak and aluminum design. The table-tops were stained glass, with ground stainless steel frames. The bar and restaurant were Celo's showcase in wooing potential clients for his construction company.

Bostic knew that Celo's patience had worn thin. Celo had called from his car, ordering him to drive to the café and to wait for him there. He was offered no explanation, and knew better than to question the directive. Celo wore black jeans, a tight military green tee shirt, several heavy gold chains around his neck, and a leather bomber's jacket. He was carrying his Smith and Wesson .357 Magnum tucked inside his belt in full view, rather than in a holster behind his muscular back, where he typically kept it.

He was accustomed to Celo's silence in tense situations. He had seen it countless times during the Bosnian War and on several occasions since, but he knew never to confuse Celo Mescic's silence for restraint. In moments like these, when he faced an unknown threat, he knew that Celo was far less calculating and far more dangerous as his instinct for survival became more acute.

"Those Ustashe bastards tried to kill me," Celo stated finally, looking up at him. "If they wanted a reaction from me, *now* they'll have it."

He sat back in his chair and smiled faintly in an attempt to calm Celo, but also himself. "Who? How can you be sure it was the Croats? There are a lot of people who would love to have a pound of your flesh—the Turks, the Ustashe and even many Serbs. The last couple months you've managed to piss them all off."

"Savo Heleta was there."

"Heleta?" He was incredulous. Savo Heleta was one of Croatia's war heroes from the last Balkan war. During an internecine blood feud between Croatian clans in Medjugorje during the last war, Heleta led a Croatian Army counterattack against one of the clans who had rounded up a hundred villagers and executed them all in a ravine. Celo's men had fought Heleta during the Croatian offensive on the Serbs in Knin, called "Operation Storm." He had been reported killed in a car accident over a year ago, after his surprise announcement that he was entering the seminary.

"It couldn't have been him. He's dead."

Celo glared back at him. "He was there, goddamn it. I saw him . . . it couldn't have been anyone else."

As Celo began to tell the story of the attack he'd witnessed at Oborci, his tone became more urgent, angrier, his diatribe peppered with more questions than answers. Celo was convinced that the attack had been launched to prevent a Serb company from being awarded the contract to rebuild the Catholic church in Derventa, formerly an ethnically Croat-dominated town in North Central Bosnia. During the last war, the Croats had been thrown out of Derventa and displaced almost entirely to neighboring Croatia. The church was a world cultural site that had been destroyed by the invading Serb militias and had been in ruins ever since. Several attempts by the Croats to conduct Catholic services at the site of the ruins resulted in violent riots. And then only a week ago, Bostic had been called by someone claiming to represent the Archbishop of Sarajevo, asking if they, as a Serb company, would consider building them a new church in the town center as a symbol of reconciliation.

Celo could have cared less about the symbolism. With matching UN funds, the contract would be worth two million dollars, and that was all that mattered to him. Nonetheless, it was a brilliant political maneuver on the part of the Catholic Archbishop. The Croats could not rebuild it themselves; riots would break out, as they had so many times before, and they wouldn't be able to even start construction. Awarding the contract to a Serb company—especially one employing Serb workers from the impoverished town to build it, on the other hand, could defuse the emotionalism and violence that would otherwise erupt. Celo's construction would bring jobs to a town ravaged by unemployment and poverty, the town could then accept the existence of the Church, and at the end of the day he'd be two million dollars richer. Brilliant indeed.

"I agreed to meet the Archbishop's secretary at the restaurant there to talk about contracts, and instead!" He shook his head in disbelief, jabbing his finger into the table. "There is Savo Heleta launching a fucking ambush!"

"Are you sure you were the target?" Bostic asked carefully.

Celo looked away momentarily toward the bar, and then back at him. He was calmer now, preoccupied. "What do you mean?"

"Was anyone killed?"

Celo nodded. "Cars were hit . . . all of them . . . mines, rockets, AK-47's. I don't know who was inside. . . ."

Bostic nodded and leaned back. "But yours wasn't," he said with finality. "It's possible that you were called there for another reason then."

"As a witness?"

"Or to take the blame. We need to find out who brought you there, and why. Who saw you?"

"A woman. Thirty years old maybe. Dark hair. She looked too afraid to have anything to do with it, and she was good looking so I let her live. She had a camera and she was taking photos."

"Who is she? A reporter?"

"I don't think so. She was driving a car with UN markings."

He nodded. "We need to find out who she is. Those photos could either exonerate you or condemn you." He leaned back in his chair, and stared over at the bar. After a moment, he pulled out his cell phone from his coat and pressed the speed dial for the French intelligence battalion commander in Sarajevo. He looked up at Celo over his glasses. "We will find her, and if Heleta is alive, we'll find him too."

ZAGREB, CROATIA

STANDING OUTSIDE the Zagreb "Arrivals" section, Mark Lyons nodded at Jon Schauer. Schauer had classic Germanic looks—a lined, weathered face, blonde hair, and a medium athletic build. He was dressed casually in blue jeans, a flannel shirt partially covered by a green Gore-Tex ski jacket, and tan work boots.

Sandy Evenson introduced both men but it was too quick of an encounter to even shake hands. She climbed into the back seat of Schauer's Saab.

Schauer smiled and shook his head as he made his way to the driver's side door. His voice betrayed a slight German accent. "You've both had a difficult time today, I know. We'll go to my flat directly."

Before Mark could seat himself in the Saab, Mike McCallister ran out, shouting for him. He breathlessly unfolded a piece of paper to show him. "I just got a call. General Thorpe, an American, is coming in to Sarajevo to see you tomorrow afternoon. Do you know him?"

He looked up from the paper, surprised. "John Thorpe?"

McCallister nodded. "That's him, I reckon."

He looked down at the pavement for a moment. "Can you arrange a time and place I can meet him privately?"

"Of course," McCallister replied. "He may already be on his way. Who should I talk to?"

He took out his wallet and pulled out a piece of metal and handed it to Mike. It was heavy brass, cut in the shape of a military dog tag. An enamel red flag with three white stars and the logos of each of the four military services decorated one side. Centered below the flag was the inscription: *"Presented by Lieutenant General John Thorpe, Commanding General, Joint Special Operations Command."* On the flip side of the tag there were two blue enamel swords crossed over two other swords surrounding the grids of a globe, with the simple title, *"Quiet Professionals."*

"His office is at Pope Air Force Base near Fort Bragg, North Carolina. You can call them. See if we can meet at a restaurant in Sarajevo when I get back there—the sooner the better."

WASHINGTON, D.C., THE WHITE HOUSE

JIM GOODWIN STOOD inside the Roosevelt Room of the West Wing as he waited for the door to the Oval Office to open. It was one of his favorite rooms; a conference room that was quietly elegant and immersed in history. He stood next to the fireplace on the east end of the room. A portrait of Teddy Roosevelt atop a horse in his Rough Rider uniform hung above the mantle. He recalled that it was painted by Tade Styka in Paris, sometime after Roosevelt's presidency. Below it, encased in an alarmed plastic box, was the Nobel Peace Prize that had been awarded to Roosevelt in 1906 for his intervention in the Russo-Japanese War of 1905—the first Nobel Peace Prize awarded to an American. All of it had special meaning to Goodwin because he was a great, great grandson to Teddy Roosevelt. And it was the former Rough Rider's example that he tried to follow after joining the CIA twenty-five years ago.

Goodwin entered with the others when the door to the Oval Office opened. He took his usual seat on the sofa, as he did every morning at 7:00 A.M. Next to him was the national security advisor, and in the other armchair beside the president, the vice president. On the opposite sofa: the national intelligence director or "DNI," the secretary of homeland security, the secretary of defense or "SECDEF," and the White House chief of staff. Goodwin passed the single-paged intelligence summary to the president and vice president.

"Mister President, we've been tracking a number of events that have coincided to paint a rather disturbing picture." Goodwin paused and looked around the room for a brief moment before handing the photos over to the president and the others assembled. "This eleven-year-old girl died yesterday in a farm house in southern Bosnia, near Ravno, close to the fighting. The cause of death was confirmed as acute radiation exposure. When we searched the barn later, we found seven pellets of raw, unshielded plutonium-238. They were small . . . about the size of a pea. She'd somehow ingested one of them. Two others were found near where she was playing—larger, softball size. The configuration of the pellets was the same one used at the pebble-bed style South African reactors." Goodwin produced a chart with a photograph of a nuclear reactor and a map. "We've been able to trace these to the nuclear reactor in Koeberg, South Africa. There were likely more pellets, but they're gone."

The president removed his glasses and looked at him. "Well, Jim, this begs all of the questions, doesn't it?"

He nodded and opened two folders marked **"Top Secret, Special Compartmented Information."** He leaned over and handed them to the president and the vice president. "This is what we know, gentlemen."

After several moments, the vice president asked, "Has anyone spoken to the South Africans about this?"

"No, sir. We haven't yet," he replied. "We learned of this only recently and of course it's very sensitive. If the media got wind of it, it would cause even more chaos in Bosnia than already exists."

"And it would have the same effect here in the United States. It would make an already bad situation worse," the homeland security advisor added. "If there's more of this material out there, there's no question that we should put a full-court press on finding it."

Goodwin nodded, and deferred to Rachel Cook, the national security advisor who was now leaning forward in her chair. "We've formed a task force consisting of our Special Mission Units, the FBI, CIA and the CDC to investigate the origin. It's possible that whoever's behind this has the construction of a nuclear device as their goal."

"Or *devices,*" the national intelligence director interrupted, emphasizing the plural. It's always been a declared priority for al-Qaida," the national intelligence director said.

The president tapped his pen on the notepad in front of him. "I don't think I have to tell you. We don't have any other options but to find and interdict it, before they can use it against us or someone else."

"Is there a chance we may be overreacting here?" the vice president asked.

There was a momentary silence in the room, which the president broke, shaking his head. "I don't believe too much in coincidences. So, let's assume that all of this is connected. Who do we have over there to deal with this?"

The defense secretary leaned forward and crossed his forearms on the table. "General John Thorpe. You'll recall he was at the meeting in the SITROOM yesterday. He and his emergency response experts are en route as we speak. The problem is that the material could be anywhere. We need a good intelligence picture to guide us."

The DNI nodded. "Well, it's quite a challenge. The NSA has focused their communications intercept assets on the area in and around Bosnia, and we've got our human intelligence networks working overtime." He paused and looked up at the president. "If that material ends up shielded in some kind of lead container, we may never find it."

The president caught the SECDEF's eye. "Let me know when General Thorpe arrives on the ground. I'd like to talk to him . . . it doesn't matter what time. Wake me up if you have to."

"We'll do that, Mr. President," he answered.

The president stood and closed his leather binder. He looked up over his glasses at the small group, with a grim expression. "Okay, let's get in front of this."

ZAGREB, CROATIA

MARK LISTENED to Sandy's account of the ambush as Jon Schauer maneuvered his Saab through Zagreb's city center. She knew Schauer and trusted him so she spoke freely. Schauer was both responsive and perceptive. He was compassionate, but seemed to have an instinctive talent for asking the follow-up questions that Mark was most interested in: "Who else witnessed the attack?" "How many attackers were there?" "Did they see you?"

One of her responses intrigued Mark. "One of them pointed his rifle at me, but didn't shoot . . . he let me go."

"He let you go?" Schauer asked.

She nodded. "I don't know why."

"No doubt you charmed him," Schauer replied.

"No doubt," she answered.

Mark turned around to face her. "What did he look like?"

"Tall, muscular ... like an athlete, long curly black hair, a narrow, face ... pockmarked, black leather jacket. I think I've seen him before, somewhere. He should be in the photos I took."

Schauer glanced into the rearview mirror. "We can print them out at my flat. It won't take long." He smiled. "And we can see if you listened to any of the photography lessons I gave you."

She reclined against the door and closed her eyes. "Please, spare me."

Schauer looked over at him. "She's never liked tests."

From the backseat, she exhaled her exasperation loudly.

CHAPTER 18

MARK LYONS FOLLOWED as Sandy entered Schauer's fifth story apartment, which looked down over Zagreb's town center, and dropped her coat on the sofa. The apartment was small but elegantly decorated with high-end contemporary furnishings. On her way to the kitchen, she picked up the TV remote and turned on the plasma screen television. She opened the refrigerator and pulled the cork from an opened bottle of Merlot. Holding the bottle up to him and Schauer, her tone was nonchalant and clipped.

"Like some?"

Mark shook his head and held up his hand. "No, thanks." He watched as she moved deftly around Schauer's apartment.

She poured the single glass of wine, then walked quickly down the corridor to what he assumed to be the bathroom.

Schauer looked at him. "I must say, how you managed to stop her from getting on that plane is quite impressive."

He shook his head. "I only told her she's the only witness we have. What was impressive, really, was how she managed to survive and evade the local police."

Schauer smiled. "That's something you have to know about Sandra Lee Evenson, Mark . . . she's a survivor and, you'll find, a rather outspoken one at that."

He raised his brows and nodded. "So I've gathered." He paused, feeling suddenly out of place. "Look, I'm sorry to impose."

Schauer shook his head as he pulled his cameras from a black nylon backpack, setting them on the shelf. "You're not imposing at all. She's safe, and you are responsible."

"No, I'm not—"

"Please, sit," Schauer interrupted, gesturing to the sofa.

Schauer sat down opposite him and pulled a bottle of mineral water from beneath the mahogany-and-glass table and poured two large glasses.

"You are from Ireland?"

He nodded.

"So you understand. There is an expatriate community of several hundred here—people like you and me and Sandra. That's what we do . . . we help each other because there's no one else who will, especially during times like this." He sipped the mineral water. "And some of us never leave. We're Balkans junkies, you might say . . . there's always the underlying excitement, and subconsciously I think many of us are just waiting for the next war. Now, it seems, we won't be disappointed."

"It seems so," he said. "I just didn't expect—"

Schauer held up his hand. "That's the first lesson I learned about this place—expect the unexpected! You've been here before?"

He nodded. "Aye, but it's been a long time, and things've changed, I think."

"Possibly," Schauer replied. "But perhaps not as much as you may've thought."

He looked around the living room, at the enlarged, glossy framed photographs of world events. He stood up to look more closely: the fall of the Berlin Wall, the Sarajevo library in flames, Nelson Mandela's release from prison, the bridge in Mostar under bombardment, President Bush with New York City firemen and police after the September 11th terrorist attacks, the capture of Saddam Hussein. He came to another photograph of Schauer and Sandy together, hugging one another and smiling in Moscow's Red Square. "You're a photographer?"

Schauer nodded. "For *Der Spiegel* and then *Time* Magazine . . . out of Berlin, but they let me live here."

"*And* he nearly got us killed because of his goddamned photographs," Sandy announced from the hallway, walking over to her wine glass. "The lesson is, never trust a photographer to lead you to safety, when he's trying to take the perfect photograph and you're in the middle of a mortar attack in downtown Sarajevo."

"Yes, but look where you are now! Always back to the same safe place!" Schauer rejoined, pointing his finger upward in mock triumph.

"Yeah," she answered, feigning exasperation. She leaned over and reached into her coat pocket, pulling out a memory stick. "Can you download these photos, Schauer, or should we just go to the neighborhood Moto Photo?"

He took the memory stick and pointed at the news report that was on the television screen. There were fleeting scenes of the charred wreckage at Oborci from above. EUFOR troops were guarding the scene. He stood and held out the stick. "Does *this* have something to do with *that?*"

CHAPTER 19

JON SCHAUER WALKED out of his office with a stack of photographs in hand. Mark could see that he was shaken by what he'd just seen, and leaned forward to take the photographs from him.

"It's a rather terrible sight," he said calmly.

"They said on television it was an accident," Schauer replied. "But from these photos, it's obvious that's not the case. Do they know about these?"

Sandy interrupted. "No they don't know. No one knows except us."

Schauer shook his head and pointed at the photographs in Lyons' hands. "Unless this gentleman you photographed at point-blank range is dead, he also knows—who is he?"

"The guy who let me go," Sandy answered, glancing at the photograph.

Mark pointed at photograph. "This fellow here?"

Sandy finally studied the photo. "Yep, him."

He handed the photo back to Schauer. "Could you get any better resolution on some of these? Hard to see the faces."

"It'll take a few minutes to refine the images on my Mac," Schauer said. "Let me see what I can do."

CHAPTER 20

MARK LYONS STARED at the freshly printed stack of 8x10 photos laid out on Jon Schauer's dining room table. Sandy leaned forward on the sofa, arms crossed. Many were still blurred, unfocused and not aimed. And yet, they showed beyond any doubt that what had occurred.

Schauer was silent as he looked on, but clearly troubled. "Why would they be saying this was an accident?" Sandy and Mark were both silent. He looked at Sandy. "How did you get yourself in the middle of *this?*"

She sat down on the leather sofa and leaned her head back.

Mark continued to pick up the photos individually and examine them. They were obviously taken from inside the restaurant. Through the window, the photos showed both vehicles stopped in the middle of the road. With each successive photo, smoke and fire emerged from their chassis, obscuring the view of the opposite side. In one photo, three masked figures dressed in white, with AKM assault rifles, were firing on what was left of the black Suburban at point blank range from the white house across the street. Schauer passed another photo to him. It showed another person in the restaurant parking lot, facing toward the camera. He wore a black leather coat, and was standing up calmly--carrying an AK-47 Rifle.

"I think I know him."

He looked at Schauer, surprised.

"His name is Celo," Schauer continued. "A radical Bosnian Serb and syndicate leader in Bosnia—from all reports, a very dangerous fellow."

Sandy stood up and strode over to see the photo. "*That's* Celo?"

Mark stared at the photo in disbelief. "Celo?" It came as a whispered utterance, but loud enough for both Sandy and Schauer to hear.

CHAPTER 21

KATE KAMRATH COUNTED four bodyguards strategically placed outside and inside the Banja Luka Café. They were oddly out of place, sitting at tables that offered unobstructed views of those coming and going. They all seemed to hover around, wearing black leather jackets with pistols bulging from shoulder and ankle holsters.

He asked to see me, she repeated in her mind. *But why?*

Ivo Bostic, a self-proclaimed associate of Celo Mescic, led her upstairs. She made a mental note, assuming "associate" to mean "under boss," or something above the status of mere bodyguard. Walking up the aluminum spiral staircase, she noted empty wicker chairs above her. At the top of the staircase, Bostic gestured to the corner of the room, where a very large, imposing figure of a man sat at a table overlooking the entrance to the café. The window behind him caused the sunlight to shine around him, giving him a divine presence that she gathered wasn't at all unintentional.

As she approached, Celo Mescic stood and extended his hand to her. His arms were thickly muscled and his hair was long and curly black with threads of grey. His face was slightly pockmarked. He wore black leather pants and a matching leather jacket, and around his neck, a heavy gold chain with a Serb Orthodox cross. Sitting down on the padded wicker chair, the theme song from *Shaft* began playing in the background. She shook her head dubiously. She had the distinct feeling she'd just walked into a cheap "B" movie.

Celo greeted her in Serbo-Croatian, and she responded in kind. Her own fluency in the language originated from her mother, who was half Croatian. Kate had met Celo during the last war at a raucous, smoke-filled press briefing when the Croats were burning houses at five per day in Stolac, south of Sarajevo. She also saw him use his impressive intellect and rhetoric to sway people's opinions when the stakes were high and when the odds were stacked against him. She had previously observed that he had a deep understanding of Yugoslav history that allowed him to manipulate it to his advantage, and to silence those who sought to oppose him. Combined with his imposing physical presence, it made him rather intimidating, even for a seasoned *New York Times* reporter who was well-accustomed to dealing with generals, criminals and politicians.

Celo was a different breed altogether.

"Would you like some coffee?" Celo asked.

"Cappuccino, please."

He motioned to the waiter and ordered a cappuccino for her and a glass of mineral water for himself.

"You survived our last meeting in Ravno, I see."

She remembered that scene well. He'd spoken calmly to her as cars were overturned and set afire, with clouds of black, putrid smoke surrounding them. She nodded and smiled. "Despite the riot that you started there, yes . . . just barely."

"Riot?" Celo exclaimed, feigning shock. "No! It was a simple demonstration; we were exercising our democratic rights! You . . . ," he pointed at her reprovingly. "You should be more balanced in your reporting!"

She gave him a canny look. "Something tells me that you don't really favor balanced journalism unless it favors your cause."

Celo leaned back in his chair and shrugged. "That depends."

"On what?"

"On whether or not you believe the ends justify the means," he said laconically.

"Sorry, I don't think I'm following you," she replied.

He paused and shrugged, "You need me to show the struggle of the Serbian people while your politicians and their generals are killing us. The front page story...that is your endgame. I am your means to that end."

"I'm afraid there's not much sympathy for your cause right now, however you want to portray it."

Celo extended both of his hands across the table, palms down. It appeared he was about to spring up from the table in a rage. "We don't need your sympathy. We are Serbs!"

The waiter arrived with their order. U2's "Beautiful Day" was playing.

Just in time, she thought.

"Why did you ask for me, Celo?" She sipped her cappuccino placidly.

"Why now?"

"Why?" Celo smiled. He paused only briefly and looked up at her. "For your good, balanced reporting, of course."

She shifted in her seat. She knew instinctively when she was about to be used, and she knew Celo was a master at the game. She looked at him for a moment, deciding to take a more assertive approach. Her voice was conversational, but her question was direct. "Okay, good, balanced reporting it is, then. Maybe we should start with the 'mine accident' down the road a piece?"

Celo's eyebrows raised, and she detected a faint surprise. "That is precisely what I wished to discuss with you. You have read my mind!"

"No, I read *people*, Celo, and I know you brought me here for a reason, whether it's lies or truth, so I'm here to listen. Nothing more."

"Do you believe that it was an accident?" Celo asked.

"It doesn't matter what I believe."

"Of course, but perceptions . . . they can make facts irrelevant."

Her brown eyes narrowed and she sat back in her seat, her exasperation apparent. "Okay, I surrender!" she exclaimed with her arms crossed. "Just tell me what's on your mind. Or should I be on my way?"

Celo smiled, but it was a humorless, silent, even threatening smile. His green eyes were cold, and seemed to pierce through her. "No, you will stay here until we have completed our business, and then you can be on your way."

She stared back at him, hoping he would not notice that her heart raced, her legs shook, and her breathing grew shallow. She knew that if she tried to speak at that moment, she would fail.

"You have seen what happened at Oborci?" Celo asked.

"Yes, I have. I arrived there an hour or so after it happened."

Celo nodded, and paused. "They will say I did it—"

"How—?" she interrupted, but was stopped by Celo's raised hand.

"Listen to me, Miss Kamrath. You know this place. Things are not always as they appear. It was not an accident that happened at Oborci. It was an ambush. And a very good one."

"How do you know?" She pulled out a notebook and pen from her backpack.

"Because I was there," he said flatly. "I saw them do it. The same as the ambushes we would do against the Turks during the war."

"Why were you there?"

"To meet some people about a construction project we have been trying to get for many months. I had two of my men with me. One of them was killed."

"Can you prove this?"

Celo shoved an envelope across the table to her. "Here is his passport, and his employment records. Everyone knows he works for my construction company. You can check. I am now responsible for his family."

She took the envelope and placed it in her backpack. "This could work against you, Celo. You must realize this, don't you?"

He nodded tentatively and looked away. "There was someone else there. I do not know her, but she is with the United Nations. She drove a white UN Toyota. Pretty...dark brown hair. She must be American or British, I think. You should have no trouble finding the car because it was torn apart by shrapnel and bullets when she drove away in it. The windows were blown out and it was leaking petrol."

"Why was she there?"

Celo shrugged his shoulders and smiled, his eyebrows raised. "You are the reporter, you ask her. And ask her to see the photos she took."

She stopped writing to stare up at him, unable to conceal her surprise. "Photos?"

He nodded. "Yes, she took many from the restaurant, you will be happy to hear. I could have shot her, but I let her go."

"You had a gun?"

"Of course! A Kalashnikov. I always have a gun with me. Here, it is like your American Express Card — 'Don't Leave Home Without It.' I have many others." Celo laughed and pulled a stainless steel Smith and Wesson from behind his belt.

She was silent as she stared at him, wishing the pistol away. Instead he set it down on the table.

"I *am* using you. I admit it to you freely." Celo shrugged. "Just as you are using me." He laughed loudly and then his expression turned serious. "If it helps the cause of my people, I do not mind killing the Turks or the Ustashe. But I did not kill the Americans. It was not in my interest to kill them. Someone else did that."

"Why didn't you talk to EUFOR or the United Nations about this, Celo? Why me?"

"EUFOR!" he scoffed. "EUFOR will want an easy person to blame. I am an easy target because I have been a nuisance to them, and I was there—because who did this wanted everyone to think that *I* am responsible. The UN is too lazy to investigate correctly, and the European Police . . . they are a joke. They are policemen without guns...nothing but a herd of eunuchs!"

"I'll keep that in mind," she, said, ignoring the crude remark. "They have a new commissioner from Ireland. He arrived yesterday. I know him. I'll talk to him."

"What is his name?" Celo asked.

"Mark Lyons. He's from Belfast."

Celo fell silent for a moment. At once, he seemed to rouse himself. She saw his jaw tighten and he straightened in his chair. In one swift, smooth motion, he grasped the Smith and Wesson from the table and returned it to its place behind his belt. He zipped his jacket, and looked over at her momentarily before standing up to leave the café. He was visibly agitated, perhaps even astonished.

"Does this mean our interview is over?" she retorted, refusing to react to his theatrics.

Celo towered over her. He was staring out the windows with a kind of abstracted intensity. Finally, he looked back at her. "I know him too. He is not from Belfast. *He is from here.* Don't report anything until I say."

CHAPTER 22

DISORIENTED AND UTTERLY EXHAUSTED, he struggled under Celo's weight, using the shotgun as a crutch. As Celo's strength waned, he became heavier to carry. On the verge of collapse, he heard the voices of his aunt and uncle in the distance, calling their names.

"Dear God," Maja gasped, rushing to them with her husband not far behind. She screamed Celo's name.

Their hair was matted with blood; and their faces cut and bruised, Celo's severely. Their clothes were ripped and bloodstained, covered with crumbled leaves and mud. The reek of fear and vomit mingled with the cold scent of human decay and excrement.

Only when they both collapsed, did the gunshot in Celo's abdomen reveal itself.

Milan took the shotgun from him and threw it aside, then picked Celo up and carried him inside the house. Maja hooked her arm under his and they followed closely behind.

There was a fire in the fireplace and it was warm inside. Seeing his reflection in the big mirror above the fireplace, he recoiled at his broken and bloodied face. He began to shake uncontrollably.

As Milan laid Celo on the bed, he looked back at him. "Marko, what happened?"

Celo gripped his father's shoulder. "No, it was my fault," he whispered hoarsely. "I took him hunting, and we ran into the soldiers. . . ."

"Don't talk, son," Milan ordered, holding a rag to his wound. He turned back to him, sitting beside him. He was sobbing quietly.

"Water," he wheezed. "I need water."

Maja brought him a cup of well water and he swallowed it greedily. He passed the cup back to her and between gasping breaths, he struggled to speak. His aunt and uncle listened in horror as he struggled to tell them what had transpired at the dam: the executions, the survivors, the guard he'd wounded, the officer who pursued them both, and who they assumed now to be now dead.

He saw his uncle turn to his Aunt Maja. "Get both boys cleaned up. Pack a bag for each of them, and for yourself."

"Where are we going? What about you?" Tears were streaming down her

cheeks. Looking down at her son, she began to visibly tremble. "Celo is in no condition to travel, and—"

Celo sat up abruptly, and immediately grimaced from the pain rocketing through his body. He coughed violently. Through clenched teeth, he blurted out: "No! I'm fine!"

Milan opened the door. Speaking deliberately in his deep, strong voice, his message to them was simple and precise. "Get yourselves ready. I'll be back soon."

A little over an hour later, he returned with a group of five people in two cars. When they entered the house, Maja nodded at them and politely greeted them, but looked at Milan with eyes that pleaded for an explanation. One of the people was a nurse from the Zvornik medical clinic. The third was a man he recognized as Goran Saric—the head of the organized crime syndicate in Eastern Bosnia. He could see the figures of the others, Saric's bodyguards, speaking in hushed tones outside, close to their window and smoking cigarettes. Saric's presence was unnerving, because it was confirmation that their situation was indeed desperate. They were now relying on the mafia for their safety.

Maja had finished packing and cleaning him and Celo just before everyone arrived. Celo had become listless and his complexion was an ashen white.

She turned to Milan. "Celo's worse. He's lost so much blood. I'm worried."

Milan turned to the nurse beside him, who immediately took charge of treating Celo's wounds.

He looked on from the bedroom.

"Maja," Milan said, "this is Goran Saric. He will help us."

She looked at him, but did not make an effort to shake his hand. "Yes, I know who you are," she said to Saric evenly, then directed her gaze toward the window. "Your friends can come inside if they like. We have coffee."

Saric smiled, shaking his head to both offers, and motioned to his bodyguards. "They're comfortable outside."

Milan motioned for her to sit down at the kitchen table. He sat at the end of the table, and Saric opposite her. She stared down at the peeling wood surface, and then up at both men with obvious anxiety.

Milan's voice remained calm and even. "We have to get you and Marko out tonight—"

She shook her head insistently. "But what about Celo? And you?"

Milan reached over to hold her hand pleadingly. "Celo is very bad. I'll take care of him at the clinic. When he is healthy enough to travel, we'll both join you. Mr. Saric has agreed to help us."

She looked at them both, the tears returning. "Where will we go?"

Goran Saric leaned forward. "To Budapest, first."

"First?"

Milan nodded. "And then to Ireland. You have the passports and relatives there. We have to get you away from the communists."

"But Marko? Marko doesn't have an Irish passport. And neither do you."

Milan squeezed her hand. "No, but he can use Celo's. It's several years old, and they look almost alike in the photo. When you arrive, you will send it back to Saric, and we'll join you."

"Why can't we go to your parents or to Sarajevo . . . or to Belgrade or Zagreb?" She asked imploringly. "We could wait for you there."

Goran Saric shook his head. His tone was authoritative. "Your son and nephew killed a soldier tonight. Not an ordinary soldier—he was an officer in the Territorial Defense Forces—Tito's own. They're searching for both boys now, and when they find them, they'll surely kill them, and both of you. The doctor . . ." Saric pointed at Milan. "Your husband told me you have two Irish passports. With these you have a chance to escape to the West. Without them, it would be much more difficult for me to help you and it would take more time than we have."

Milan abruptly stood and walked to the desk. He pulled out two envelopes from the bottom drawer, one large and one small. He placed them on the table in front of Maja. The large, sealed envelope was the one with their official identity papers. The small one lay open, filled with U.S. dollars, German marks and British pounds. The passports were also inside.

"Where—?"

Milan anticipated her question and waved it off. His voice became more insistent, more urgent. "I'll join you, Maja. Celo and I will be fine, I promise, but you and Marko must leave now. We'll meet you soon."

Both men pushed their chairs back from the table and stood up. Milan leaned over to his wife and whispered. "Get Marko. You must go."

His aunt's face was flushed from the tears streaming down her face. The nurse was carrying Celo out of the bedroom past him. She had placed a blanket over him to keep him warm. He followed observing, trying his best to understand.

Saric opened the door and as the nurse walked out with Celo in her arms, she turned to Milan and Maja. "He'll be fine, but we must get him to the clinic."

Milan walked to Celo and placed his hand on his forehead. "Put him in the back seat of my car. I'll be right there."

Goran Saric stepped forward and issued a string of very calm, concise orders to his bodyguards, who immediately took over and loaded Marko into the Citroën. Every movement made him wince.

As bags were being loaded into the cars, Saric turned to both parents. "You must say goodbye now. Time is short."

Maja knelt down in the Lada's rear seat where Celo lay. She kissed her son on the forehead, and caressed his badly beaten face with her hands. He opened his eyes slightly.

"Mama. . . ."

He watched as his aunt's tears fell silently. She kissed him and pulled the blanket up to better cover him. "Your father is taking you to the clinic, son. The two of you will join us in a few days, when you're better." She watched Celo swallow, then close his eyes, heavy with fever.

"I love you."

"Mama . . . don't leave. . . ."

Maja choked back her tears and shook her head. "We have no choice, son."

Celo grimaced in pain. "Please. . . ."

Saric placed his hand on her shoulder. "We must go, Maja."

Maja extended her hand to her son and stroked his cheek. "I love you Celo, you have to know that no matter what."

She stood up and Saric closed the car door. Milan walked her to the black Citroën. She was sobbing.

He climbed into the back seat and Milan looked in.

"I'm sorry, Uncle . . . it was all my fault." His voice seized up.

Milan kissed him, and held his head in his hands. "Listen to me. It was no one's fault, Marko. You and Celo did the right thing by helping those men. I'm proud of you. We can't stay here though, so you must go with your aunt. We'll join you when Celo is better."

He nodded, dazed. Alternating voices seemed to fill the air, all bleeding into each other. Outside, the night was immense and the stars bright. Everything seemed to envelop them and he suddenly felt as if his life was spinning out of control.

Milan stood, and guided Maja to the other side of the car. He kissed her, and whispered something in her ear.

Saric's bodyguard started the car, and Maja embraced her husband. Her body shook as she separated from him. She sat in the back seat and placed her arms around him. Before the car drove off, Milan passed a black case through the window to him. It was his father's violin.

"After they took you and your father away, I went to your house and found this.

Your father would have wanted you to have it."

Driving away from his home, he clutched the violin case in his arms, trembling, feeling vastly alone...at some point he slept.

JANUARY 25: ZAGREB, CROATIA

MARK SHIFTED on the futon, away from the gathering cloud of old nightmares and disembodied voices from the past. He felt as if he'd been thrust into a film, running rapidly, irrevocably in reverse. Not a single full day had passed since his return to Bosnia and he was facing the same demons he'd faced more than thirty years ago. In that time, he'd lost his family and Yugoslavia had imploded in a bloody civil war while he looked on, but those memories and ghosts—all from a distant and surreal past— were returning now with a vengeance, in a relentless and haunting whisper. *"You left us, Marko . . . but we have not forgotten you."*

He stared at several of the photos Sandy had taken at Oborci. It *was* Celo. Older, aged by experience and harsh conditions, but the eyes were the same—just as green and intense as he had remembered the last time he'd seen them that day at Brnisi Dam. And now they were looking back at him from an 8x10 photograph like an apparition. Celo was there, at Oborci . . . at the ambush. . . . He was certain of it.

His impulse was to interrogate Sandy as he would any witness to a crime, to ask if Celo was responsible for the carnage at the ambush site, but he knew she had seen his reaction as he stared at the photos of Celo. She could not understand it perhaps, but she'd seen it. He said his name and he'd betrayed too much.

Schauer, sensing the tension, had insisted that they all get some sleep. He welcomed Schauer's suggestion, quickly gaining respect for his insight and his obvious influence with Sandy. Without Schauer's presence and assistance, she would certainly have fled to The Hague. He now realized that they could not remain in Zagreb with these new revelations.

Reaching to the coffee table, he picked up Schauer's telephone and dialed. He guessed that they'd have gotten in at around 10:00 P.M., and it was now just after 1 A.M. Mike McCallister answered. He and Vladimir were staying at the Regent Esplanade Hotel in downtown Zagreb. Mike's voice was surprisingly upbeat, given the late hour. He muttered an apology for the late call, but quickly changed the subject to ask whether Mike and Vladimir

105

could have the helicopter ready to fly to Sarajevo at nine the next morning.

McCallister's response was immediate. "We'll be ready for you. To UN headquarters, I assume?"

"No," he replied after a brief, thoughtful pause. "To EUFOR Headquarters first, to see General Rose. Is that doable?"

He sensed a presence in the room before he heard the wood floor creak. He looked up from the futon to see Sandy dressed in gym shorts and an oversized, faded Harvard University tee shirt, standing in the shadowed doorway. She was petite yet athletic and had the legs of a long-distance runner. Her dark hair fell to her shoulders, freshly brushed. Seeing her there—arms crossed with her eyebrows raised—was enough to distract him from his thoughts of past demons.

"Consider it arranged," McCallister replied, continuing on about flight clearances into EUFOR Headquarters with no response from him. "And how is Miss Evenson, commissioner? Ye reckon she's now more inclined to stay on with us? *She's a looker!*"

He sat up, uncomfortably, still looking at Sandy with a look of embarrassment. He felt certain that his reply to McCallister only served to further betray his distraction. "Aye. She's fine. She's right here, so I'll tell her ye said hello."

He hung up the phone and an awkward silence followed. He started to explain, but she interrupted him.

"I came to get the phone so I could call my friend, Bob Childs. I'm glad I did, because otherwise I'm not sure I would have known we were going to Sarajevo." She paused for effect. And then in a semi-fierce tone, she said, "When were you planning on filling me in, Mark Lyons? As we got into the car? Or as we got on the helicopter?"

"I couldn't sleep," he replied quietly, handing her the telephone. "I just realized that we can't stay here in Zagreb. EUFOR is controlling the investigation, so General Rose needs to see your photos and hear your story. Aside from the forensics, your account and those photos are the only hard evidence there is."

Sandy crossed her arms, her green eyes straight and level, dubious. "Why? So they can cover this up more than they already have? So they can continue to call this a mine accident? I'm sorry if I don't share your confidence in EUFOR or in General Rose. Around here, you have to *earn* respect, but instead he's alienated himself from the whole effort. He hates the

UN and he's done nothing but obstruct the tribunal's investigations since he arrived here as a two-star general. Now that he's back with four stars, I can only imagine the havoc he'll wreak. Sorry, but we'd be safer if we were talking to the secret Serbian goddamned police!"

"They need to at least know what we know."

She moved around the futon, sat on the coffee table and leaned toward him. "What do we know? More to the point, what do I know about *you*? If it's full disclosure you want, tell me about yourself, Mark Lyons! Why, for instance, are you the only Irishman I've seen in ten years who can speak Serbo-Croatian fluently? Why is it that on your first day on the job you knew the British SAS team back there, and on a first name basis? And why do I get the distinct impression you know some of the people in those photos? What are you, some kind of fucking spy?"

He was disarmed. He shut his eyes momentarily, then sat fully upright to face her. "Okay. Full disclosure?"

"Full disclosure," she answered coldly.

Mark nodded in resignation. "I hate to disappoint."

She raised her eyebrows and leaned back on the table, awaiting his explanation. "Oh no, I'm sure you won't disappoint me."

"Well, the danger in me telling you anything about any of this is that you may not believe me."

"Try me."

He nodded in silent resignation. "Originally, I come from Yugoslavia, now what is part of Serbia. My father was a professor at the University in Belgrade. He was a prisoner of Tito's during the purges in the 1970s, when academics and others who denounced Tito's repression of minorities in Kosovo were harassed, rounded up and imprisoned. They executed him, or he died in prison—I don't know which. My mum died of cancer when I was a baby. So, I was alone. I lived in an orphanage here in Zagreb for a brief time, and then lived with my aunt and uncle in Zvornik."

"Bosnia?"

He nodded. "Aye, when it was all Yugoslavia. They had a son—my cousin—who was like a brother to me. Really the only friend I had at the time. One day, on the way back from school, we got into some rather terrible trouble . . .," he said reflectively, "the kind of trouble that changes ye forever."

"What happened?"

"We were only kids, but we saw something the Yugoslav army didn't want us to see, something they didn't expect *anyone* to see."

Sandy leaned toward him. "What?"

"A mass execution of prisoners. Dissidents, academics, I still don't know who they were. All under the guise of a military exercise."

Sandy was silent for a moment. "Your father?"

He shrugged. "I don't know if he was there or not. I tried to find out that night, searching through the bodies. A few were still alive. Wounded, but alive. There were so many of them. . . . Before we could help them, before I could find out if my father was among them, the soldiers came back. They saw us. We fought, just so we could get away. We fought one of them, hand to hand. Somehow we made it home, but my uncle knew it was only a matter of time before they would find us. My name then was "Marko," but it became "Mark" after my aunt and I escaped to live in Belfast."

"Belfast?"

He nodded. "My aunt was half Irish, half Croatian. She had dual citizenship in Ireland. Most importantly, she had a passport. My cousin was in no shape to travel from his wounds; he'd been beaten too severely.

There was a plan for my uncle and cousin to join us there later, but they never made it. I never saw either of them again until—"

"Celo . . . the guy in the photo . . . he's your cousin, isn't he?"

He paused, and nodded. "Yeah, I believe that's him."

She didn't immediately respond. She leaned back on the table to reveal a generous, attractive figure, and looked at him closely. "Well, when I saw him there at the restaurant, I can tell you he looked as shocked as I was to see what was happening. He was prepared, had his own guns, and from what I saw, he knew how to react, how to shoot back, but I don't think he intended to be there." She paused, studying Mark. "How does a juvenile delinquent from Bosnia become an Irish police chief?"

He smiled slightly and shrugged. "Funny how a few shattering hours can change the course of a lifetime, isn't it?"

"But Belfast? That's not exactly been an oasis of peace and stability either."

He was hesitant to broach the subject of what had happened in Northern Ireland. "I never said I was trying to escape it."

She nodded slowly.

He continued. "I never questioned it at the time, but looking back, perhaps it's why the transition wasn't too difficult. I never knew anything but that . . . *this* . . . kind of environment. I went to school, joined the British Army just to have a job, volunteered for the SAS and spent over ten years with them before joining the RUC."

"The RUC?"

"The Royal Ulster Constabulary. I was the Deputy Chief Inspector of the RUC's Special Branch."

"Fighting the IRA?" she asked quietly, matter-of-factly.

He was slow to respond. "Not only them. The RUC was renamed the "Police Service of Northern Ireland. I was the Assistant Chief Constable in Belfast."

"Why did you leave to come here?"

He sighed quietly. "I was sent," he said simply.

"By whom?"

"Another story, too long to tell. . . ."

He looked out the window and saw the lights of the city square outside Schauer's apartment. He felt he'd said too much already—far more than he had intended to tell anyone about himself. He didn't tell her about the days he'd spent putting bits of people into plastic bags after the IRA bombings, or of the nightmares that returned to him each night. They would not end however much he wished them away. Rather than becoming more abstract with the passage of time, the dreams had become far more vivid. Images of mutilated corpses with mangled limbs, blood seeping from the backs of their heads, bulging, milky eyes staring back at him—all of it mingled together in one recurring dream. He found himself avoiding sleep for fear of what it would bring; but insomnia only made them worse, more violent whenever sleep forced itself on him.

He pointed to the table where the photos were still sitting. "You know, if that is the Celo I knew, unless he has transformed himself into some kind of a self-styled terrorist, I can't believe he's responsible for killing those folks."

She reached over and touched his hand reassuringly. For the first time since they'd met, her smile was sympathetic, even warm. She leaned toward him. "Well then, we should find him after we talk to General Rose."

He smiled and nodded. He could still feel the warmth of her hand on his even after she'd withdrawn it. She stood up and began walking back to the spare bedroom.

"Wait," he said. "Full disclosure—that's a shared proposition, isn't it?"

She looked down, smiling faintly, circumspectly. "Good night, Mark."

Chapter 23

AS THE GIANT HELICOPTER emerged from the mountain pass leading into Sarajevo, Mark Lyons could make out the European Union Force Headquarters through the low-hanging clouds below. Ilidza stood as a suburb of Sarajevo on its western periphery. Before Serb armies ravaged it in 1992, Ilidza was a resort and health spa, famous for its hot sulfur springs and their healing powers. After the Dayton Accords were signed, it became a NATO base and was then abandoned when they withdrew. With the outbreak of the Ravno Crisis, EUFOR reoccupied the graffiti decorated buildings, painted and renovated them. The complex was surrounded by parks, bike paths and residential apartments.

As they prepared to land, he could see a fence surrounding the complex, covered with a green fabric screen to prevent drive-by shooters and potential sniper attacks. Storage containers, mobile trailer offices, and industrial generators dotted the compound. A courtyard with a meticulously groomed lawn and flower beds stretched between two brown stucco buildings, formerly the Serbia and the Herzegovina Hotels. At its center was an ornate fountain ringed by the flags of European Union member countries.

Wheeled armored personnel carriers guarded the single entrance to the base, their machine guns pointed in the direction of the gate to support the Norwegian, Polish and Danish guards who checked the identification and credentials of all who sought entry.

Vladimir pointed at the helicopter landing pad just ahead of them, enshrouded by a layer of steam from the hot springs. Mark turned around to see Mike McCallister doing his best to ignore the vibration of their descent and the characteristic steady drip of hydraulic fluid from the machinery in the ceiling above. Sandy Evenson was looking out the window port as the helicopter began its descent. She was calm, and poised, dressed in a creme silk blouse, navy slacks and heels. Her coat was devoid of the glass fragments that had clung to it yesterday. When the helicopter touched down, its rotor wash swept away the steam and a wall of dirt flew up to replace it. Stepping off the helicopter, Sandy slung her backpack over her shoulder and walked toward a boardwalk that stretched across the hot springs surrounding the helipad. Mark walked beside her. "You know the way, I assume?"

The distinct odor of sulfur bit at their nostrils.

She nodded her head forward. "This way. His headquarters is in the Serbia Hotel."

"You've been there then?" Mark asked.

"Yeah, but always in less conspicuous circumstances. I told you, I'm not a fan."

"That's two of us," he whispered under his breath.

As the thumping of the rotors slowed to a halt, McCallister turned to him. "Commissioner, if ye don't mind, I'll arrange for a car to pick us up and take us downtown when you're finished."

He nodded. "We'll be back soon, Mike. An hour—no more."

Mark felt a familiar sensation returning to him as they walked toward the EUFOR Command Headquarters, passing the makeshift Post Exchange, cafés, and hotel annexes. The architecture was predominantly French Colonial, and even with the shopping amenities, it had the feel of a place perpetually at war. Most of the buildings were still pockmarked by rifle fire exchanged by warring factions in the previous Bosnian war. The green nylon screen covering the fence line created a fortress-like environment, further advanced by the wide variety of uniforms worn by men and women from all of the EU member states' armed forces and police. Norwegian guards patrolled the fenced perimeter in pairs, each armed with an automatic rifle.

Through the clouds, the sun was attempting to come out again in Sarajevo, belying the previous day's winter storm. It was cool and breezy, yet temperate enough for soldiers to sit outside, drink coffee and eat lunch. He and Sandy passed by the outdoor cafés and entered the courtyard surrounded by the many flags of each EU member nation. Local Bosnian workers were planting brightly colored flowers along the periphery of the courtyard in well-manicured flowerbeds.

He turned to Sandy. "I don't suppose they know there's a war on?"

She looked at the workers, digging and planting. "Them? They're just glad to have a job."

He nodded. It was a cynical but realistic assessment forged by an experience few had the courage to endure. He was also aware it was precisely that kind of perspective she was trying to escape. Now, unintentionally, he'd brought her back to the heart of it all.

They approached the Serbia Hotel, a four story stucco building, and were greeted at the entrance by Italian soldiers with assault rifles who demanded to see their identification. They flashed their UN I.D. cards and proceeded up the white granite steps. The glass doors opened automatically and they walked into a slow-moving current of men and women in a wide variety of uniforms. In the corner of the smoke-filled atrium, a cappuccino bar was operating at full capacity with a Babel of voices swirling around. Two dining rooms, one dedicated to the officers and one for the enlisted soldiers, were serving lunch.

"His office is on the third floor. He lives on the fourth." She pointed toward a spiral staircase. "I understand they cater in lobster from Spain and caviar and wine from France for him every evening."

Mark climbed the narrow staircase behind her in silence.

She stopped, turned to face him, and whispered. "You think I'm joking, don't you? I'm not. The man's a megalomaniac. Thinks he's Napoleon."

He continued to walk. "That sounds like the Ian Rose I know."

"He's like a caricature of himself. He also has no understanding of Bosnia, but now he thinks he's a Balkans expert."

"But he's in charge," he responded matter-of-factly.

"Yeah, and he'll be the first to point that out to you."

"And so we have to deal with him," he continued, hoping to temper what was becoming a heated exchange.

"You can deal with him. I'm only here for the ride."

He opted not to respond. He knew she resented having to be back here after she'd just left.

They entered the third floor and found the air clear and fresh, devoid of the cigarette smoke that pervaded the floors below. The floor was white marble tile, decorated with teak office furniture and stained oak woodwork that was in need of polishing. They walked past the political advisor's office to an anteroom with two desks on opposite ends of the main entrance door to General Rose's office. A middle-aged secretary was at a desk on the right side. A uniformed British army major in a heavily starched, camouflage uniform sat next to her. Mark remembered seeing him get off the helicopter at Oborci, and guessed that he was Rose's aide de camp. He walked directly to his desk and the Major stood to greet them. Mark introduced himself and informed him of their appointment.

The major looked momentarily over to the secretary, who imparted an apologetic, knowing glance back to her colleague. "Commissioner, please accept our apologies. We've been trying to reach you for several hours, but I understand you were flying back from Zagreb." The major held up a paper filled with handwritten telephone numbers. One said "Jon Schauer" on it.

"The general won't be available to see you today. He asked that I reschedule your meeting with him, possibly for tomorrow or some other time this week that may be convenient."

Mark did his best to conceal his frustration.

Before he could respond, Sandy walked up to the aide's desk with a large envelope containing the 8x10 photos of the ambush at Oborci. She pulled them out and spread them out over his desk, handing him the photograph on top depicting the mine exploding beneath Ambassador Fulbright's black Suburban. In the far right side of the photo was the image of a man dressed in white coveralls, aiming an assault rifle at the damaged Suburban. The image was blurred, obscured by what appeared to be smoke or blowing snow, or both.

"If he's in, why don't you show him this...*right now?* I'm sure he'll find it compelling," she offered.

The major was speechless. His gaze alternated from the photos to Mark and Sandy. He regained his composure quickly, and picked up the photos to show General Rose.

Sandy grabbed his left wrist and pulled the stack of photos back from him, leaving the one 8x10 she had originally handed him.

"Sorry, without a good narrative to accompany them, more than one photo would lead the General to sensory overload—that one'll do."

"Yes, sir...ma'am," the major stuttered. "I'll show this to him now. I'll...I'll just be a moment."

Mark smiled at him and then at the secretary. "Good man."

He looked at Sandy. She was calmly placing the photographs back in the envelope. He smiled, impressed with her chutzpah.

"He seemed a bit rattled didn't he?" she whispered under her breath.

Within seconds, the office door opened and Lieutenant General Ian Rose stepped out with the photo in hand. His tall frame filled the doorway. He wore the British army's green dress uniform. Mark noticed the grey eyebrows, so full that they nearly joined together at the bridge of his nose. His high pitched voice had not lost its somewhat effeminate tenor. "Lyons, Miss Evenson. Come in."

Rose led them to a sofa and invited them to sit. He sat in a chair facing them, and placed the photo on the coffee table. His fingertips silently drummed the arm of the chair, but his face gave nothing away. "You have my attention, Lyons."

"I'm sure you know by now that what happened to the Fulbright delegation was not an accident as it's being reported in the media," Mark said, motioning at the television, which was turned to CNN International. "It was a deliberate attack...an ambush."

Rose was silent for a moment, glancing at Sandy only momentarily with eyes glazed. He shook his head reprovingly.

"You should both know that I haven't yet arrived at any conclusions regarding the incident at Oborci," he said smoothly. "At the direction of England's Prime Minister and the President of the United States, it's now being investigated by the FBI, and our troops are now securing the scene—"

"Yes, Ian, but I'm sure you must be interested to know what happened."

Rose shrugged. "Matters like these take time to resolve. In due time, you and I will both see the FBI's report."

"In due time...," Mark repeated, catching Sandy's glare. "Well, that's fucking great, Ian, but there's a problem with that. This report is indeed wrong, but *intentionally* so. When you have proof of a crime, you don't just ignore it. And you don't wait and see what happens." He took the envelope from Sandy and dumped the photos on the coffee table, spreading them out for him to see. "I don't understand how you can treat this as anything but what it is."

Rose blinked and countered with a tone of insistence and condescension. "We have witnesses to this incident. We are questioning them. Their testimony supports our preliminary theory that this was indeed a mine accident. When farmers find mines in their fields, they lift them and stack them on the roadsides. You will learn that, Commissioner, when you have more time here in Bosnia. If you are a witness as well, Miss Evenson, we will need to question you and take your photos into evidence, of course."

Sandy's eyes narrowed and Mark saw a sudden hardness in her face. Her tone was even, measured. "General, by all means, have your people come see me," she scoffed. "I'll be glad to talk to them."

115

Rose looked at her disapprovingly. The lights in the office flickered.

Mark stood up and spoke in a matter-of-fact tone. "Well, that's a load of bollocks, and you know it. I think we're all aware that if this incident *is* proven to be an ambush rather than an accident, it would force Washington and Ten Downing back into a wartime stance here—something I'm quite sure they'd dearly like to avoid." He lowered his voice. Sandy was looking at him intently. "You know, we came here in good faith. I brought a witness here to *help* you. It's obvious to me now that was a mistake. Maybe the New York Times is interested in the truth?"

Rose shifted in his seat with a fierce look of disdain. "Lyons, you would be well advised to issue your threats to the FBI, *not* to me. I'll ensure they're well informed of your intentions."

"I haven't issued any threats to you," Lyons said, looking away in exasperation. "Tell the FBI I'd be happy to meet with them."

Rose stared at him impassively. "I have no choice but to take these photos into evidence."

"Take them," he answered, his voice thick with sarcasm. "We have all of the digits." He opened the door and smiled thinly, amusement melding with irritation. "Goodbye, Ian."

Rose followed them to the door and addressed his aide. "Please see that the commissioner and Miss Evenson are escorted off-base and have transportation to where they need to go, outside the compound."

Before they were out the door, Rose called out to his secretary. "Get Roman Polko on the line."

MARK AND SANDY descended the stairs in silence several steps behind the major. Mark felt Sandy's gaze on him as they walked, and found it futile to try to ignore it. Despite his outward composure, he felt certain she could determine that he was seething. "Did I say something to upset ye?"

"Oh no. I'm just a bit surprised, I guess," she said, with suppressed glee.

"Surprised?"

"By the role reversal. I thought I was going to be the bad cop, and you the good cop," she whispered conspiratorially.

"Was that the plan?"

"You completely rewrote the script in there," she answered. "Was it just me, or was it getting a bit personal?"

"He's as thick as bottled pig shit," he muttered, realizing that Rose had pushed him over the edge. Too quickly. What she couldn't know was that more had been left unspoken during that meeting than had been said. Or that this encounter was a continuation of a complex decades-old dialogue. "The man couldn't write his name with his toes—" He stopped mid-stride. Beyond a packed group of Land Rovers and other military vehicles, he saw a woman walking toward them from the outdoor café next door. He recognized the gait of her walk before he recognized her face.

"What?" Sandy asked, confused.

"Kate Kamrath," he replied absently, glancing at Sandy.

The woman approaching them was smiling broadly, obviously surprised. "Mark? ...Sandy?"

Mark saw Sandy staring at him again in disbelief. *"You know Kate too? Christ! Why don't you just run for office?"*

He didn't answer. Again he felt the awkwardness of a chance-contact recognition he'd rather have avoided. Few non-Irish journalists knew about his past, but Kate Kamrath was one of them. The fact that she was here was a certain indicator of something serious brewing. Of what precisely, he didn't know, but now his alarm bells were ringing loudly.

Kate Kamrath was tall, blonde, thin, and an amateur triathlete. She approached, wearing well-worn jeans and a red and black North Face jacket. Her hair was short, her face long, narrow, and weathered—with a blithe set to her mouth. She flashed a broad, disarming smile that belied features that could otherwise be regarded as harsh, even intimidating by those who didn't know her.

"You're a ways away from Belfast, Mark Lyons," Kate said with a calm, rather coy brightness. "I heard there was a new sheriff in town."

He shook her hand and smiled at her. "As usual, you're very well informed."

She turned to Sandy, and he watched the two embrace. "Sandy, this isn't your typical police guy." Kate turned to face him. "Far more dangerous, a ton smarter, and way too handsome." She chuckled to herself, shaking her head in mock disbelief. "You know, I was beginning to worry that there wouldn't be much interesting to write about in Bosnia after the last war, but when I heard the legendary Mark Lyons was here, any fears I may have had were quickly eliminated...." She turned back to Sandy. "I thought *you* were leaving for The Hague this week?"

Sandy response was awkward and clipped. "I was...still plan to...but something else came up." She glanced at the major, who was watching the encounter with some interest. "Kate, this is General Rose's aide. He's been nice enough to escort us off-base."

There was a glimmer of acknowledgement in Kate's eyes. She walked over to shake the major's hand. "I was just coming over to your headquarters to chat with General Thorpe. They're picking him up at the airport within the hour."

"Is John here...in Bosnia?" Mark asked.

Kate nodded. "I wanted to see if he was available for an interview before he disappeared into thin air."

"That explains the convoy, doesn't it?" he answered. A blue armored Toyota Land Cruiser with a three-star placard on the bumper stood parked with several other Land Rovers near the gate.

"How long are you in town?" Sandy asked Kate.

Kate paused and looked at them both. "Until I can get some answers about what happened to the Fulbright delegation. They've placed a complete embargo on any information relating to yesterday's incident, except to say that it's a "mine accident." No one's willing to talk, and when that happens, my antennae go up."

"I'm not sure how far you'll get with this lot, but good luck," Mark said.

"Well, some things just aren't adding up," Kate said. She folded her arms. "Okay, so tell me what should probably already be obvious to me— why are you here *together?*" She glanced at both of them, again with her broad smile. "Never mind, I know...it's a small world...but since we're all in one place...let's all meet for drinks tonight at the Irish pub just outside town, can we? Say, eight?"

Sandy looked over at him. "Maybe. We're just getting back from Zagreb, so it might be a bridge too far. I'll call you."

He shook his head and smiled. "I'll have to pass tonight. You two go. Have one for me, though."

Kate nodded and smiled. "I'm at the Hilton, and you should have my cell number."

Sandy nodded, holding up her cellular. "Got it."

Kate started to walk toward the Serbia Hotel, but Mark turned to her in midstride, gently grasping her forearm. "When you see him, please give General Thorpe my regards, Kate, would you?"

Kate's expression turn serious again, melancholy even. "I'll tell him. I'm sure he'll want to see you while he's here. And some other people are also dying to see you too, I suspect."

As Kate continued to walk, Mark shook his head, amazed...still finding himself not immune to Kate Kamrath's incisive methods, which could often be charm and pure subterfuge. He turned to Sandy. "She already knows."

She nodded in agreement. "Of course she does."

CHAPTER 24

MARK LYONS WAS USHERED into Roman Polko's office as soon as he arrived. Polko was sitting at his desk, speaking on the telephone. The office was expansive and luxurious with a beige colored carpet, leather furniture and teak-paneled walls. Polko looked up, and silently stood to greet him, shaking his hand briefly before returning to his conversation.

Mark sat on the brown leather sofa and looked around the large office at the hundred-or-so framed photographs and plaques hanging on the walls around him in what seemed a mosaic of Polko's life. He recognized Polko as a younger man with luminaries that included Lech Walesa, Barack Obama, Pope John Paul II, Ronald Reagan, Mother Theresa, Henry Kissinger, and Princess Diana--with personal inscriptions in gold and silver metallic ink that concluded with phrases like, "in admiration," "with friendship," and "with great respect." Behind Polko's desk was the UN flag, and in a corner next to a full bookshelf, the flag of Poland.

In the center of the wall, there was a framed black and white photograph of a younger Polko in a winter jacket with a target rifle strapped to his back, receiving the Olympic Bronze Medal for the Biathlon in 1968. Beside it, there was a photograph framed in gold tinted wood that depicted the Berlin Wall lit up at night by construction lights. He walked over to it to get a closer view. A group of eight men and women were on top of the wall, surrounding a man dressed in jeans and a leather jacket, wielding a sledgehammer. The sledgehammer's obvious target was the wall's grey seam, colorfully spray-painted with yellow, blue and red graffiti. The crowd observing him below was cheering.

"It was a rather pitiful swing, I'm afraid," Polko commented, behind him. He was grinning. "I spent my entire life waiting for that wall to come down, and when I finally had the opportunity to help destroy a part of it myself, my performance, I am embarrassed to say, was...well...rather unimpressive."

Mark smiled and silently shifted to another photo beside it, more and more intrigued by Polko's life. The photo was contained in a black acrylic frame. It showed a thin, gaunt figure in front of a tourist bus, who only vaguely resembled Polko. His face was unshaven, and his eyes were sunken. He wore ill-fitting work clothes.

"This is you?"

Polko nodded as he sat down on the chair at the end of the coffee table.

"I was just released from three years as a political prisoner in Belgrade."

"Why did they hold you?" he asked, taking his seat on the sofa.

"It was the height of the Cold War. A friend of mine and I were captured, trying to escape to the West. We hitchhiked through Poland and East Germany to Czechoslovakia and Yugoslavia, thinking it would be easier to escape over the border into Italy." Polko shook his head and laughed. "It was a foolish, if courageous, effort. Two Poles, both of us naïve, 26 years old, walking around in a small border town at five o'clock in the morning, looking for some food. We did not know the language, and so we were not difficult for the Border Guard to spot. They arrested us based on suspicion, but knowing well our intent." Polko crossed his legs. "I refused to sign their confession or loyalty oaths, so I was rewarded with a sentence of seven years hard labor. All made particularly scandalous because Poland had never had one of their Olympic Medalists attempt to defect until then. My freedom was purchased two years into my sentence."

"Purchased?" he asked, surprised.

Polko nodded. "By Amnesty International, along with ten other 'hard cases'—those of us they could not reform." He pointed at the photograph again. "That is the bus that brought us to the American sector in West Berlin—Checkpoint Charlie is there in the background."

"It has been a long road here to Sarajevo for you."

Polko nodded thoughtfully. "And, I suspect, for you as well, Lyons."

He was silent for a moment. "It's the past...," he responded absently.

"Yes, you are correct. But do we ever really know the truth of what has happened in our past?" Polko's tone was lightly philosophical. "In spite of my bad swing, that is why these photos serve as a good metaphor for me."

Polko reached down to the coffee table beside him and picked up a palm-sized rock and handed it to him. The red and yellow paint was still visible, and he realized it was a piece of the Berlin Wall. He felt the coarse surface against his fingertips, as well as the irony of holding a piece of the very wall—the "Iron Curtain"—that had come to symbolize his separation from his family...while he and his aunt were in Ireland and Celo and his uncle were living in Tito's Yugoslavia. He smiled and handed it back to Polko, but the diplomat politely refused, gently pushing his hand back.

"No, it is yours, Lyons."

Mark shook his head. "I can't—"

"No, no, you must take it. I insist!" Polko was smiling broadly. "Don't worry, I have another much larger piece."

"Thank you." he replied simply, unwilling—unable—to release the piece of concrete from his grip. He sat down on the sofa, opposite Polko. "I'm sorry we held onto your helicopter for so long—as it happened; we had to use it to fly to Zagreb last night."

Polko laughed. "Zagreb! Yes, they have very good restaurants there! Don't worry, only the motor pool was in a panic, and I told them to relax. It's yours to use as you need it. And judging from how popular you have already become here, you may need it often!"

"Popular?"

Polko nodded, appearing amused. "I received a call from General Rose after your visit with him this afternoon."

"I'm not surprised. I was hoping to see you before he called. It wasn't the cordial, helpful visit we'd hoped for."

"Well, from my conversation with him, I had the very distinct impression that there is more to the Fulbright accident than meets the eye."

He nodded. "It wasn't an accident. The convoy was deliberately attacked." He removed the stack of 8x10 photographs from the envelope he was carrying, and handed them to Polko. "This is a second set. We left the other with Ian Rose."

"My God," Polko uttered under his breath, his eyes squinting periodically as he flipped through the photographs. "Who took these?"

"Sandy Evenson. From the ICTY. She witnessed everything from inside the restaurant on the roadside."

"Yes, I know her well...General Rose also mentioned her...where is she?"

"We arranged a room at the Holiday Inn for her. She's exhausted. And after our meeting with General Rose, I can't say that either of us was particularly encouraged."

"He is in a very difficult position right now," Polko said apologetically, still viewing the photos. "You are correct, he is not happy—he asked me to stop what he perceives as my 'separate' investigation."

"I hope I haven't blindsided you, Ambassador. I never intended—"

Polko waved him off. His expression was sober and focused. "Your job is to investigate, Lyons. Technically, he is right—I have nothing to do with it. General Rose mentioned photographs as evidence, but I assumed that he was telling me about photos taken *after* the incident had occurred. Seeing these, there is no wonder he wants to keep these out of the public eye!"

"I suspect we've made things more difficult for him."

Polko nodded thoughtfully. "You have, but only because you and Sandy were never part of his equation…until you came to his office this afternoon."

"That may have been a mistake—I didn't mean to put you in a bad situation."

Polko shook his head. "No," he said matter-of-factly. "You must stay engaged, Lyons. I knew Jack Fulbright and Joe Steinberg. They were great men, and great friends. I owe it to them and to their families to find out who did this."

Polko handed the stack of photos back to him.

Mark pulled out the photo with the clearest image of Celo, and placed it in front of Polko on the coffee table. "I believe this is Celo Mescic."

"The same Celo who is leading the Serb repatriations around Ravno?"

He nodded, and paused. "He was at Oborci also. I don't know why—"

Polko's expression was suddenly intense. "Someone like him does not show up without good reason! Do you think he did this?"

"Well, my instinct is that he had nothing to do with it."

"Why not?" Polko was standing now, pacing.

He sensed that Polko was several steps ahead in their conversation, whether it was because he had previous knowledge of Celo's role, or if he was driving toward a specific conclusion…as he had when they met. He would not make the mistake of underestimating Roman Polko again.

"None of the photos show him directing the ambush or firing at the convoy. He appears to be defending himself. And because—"

Polko started to interject; he apologized.

Mark inhaled. "Because, Ambassador, I know him…he's my cousin."

Polko's surprise was only evident in how he raised his eyebrows-- slightly, imperceptibly. He stopped pacing. "How close are you?" He asked directly, now in a tone that was markedly calm and subdued.

"It's been more than thirty years. I haven't seen him, or spoken to him since—but I do feel I know him."

"Men change, Lyons," Polko answered, and gestured toward him. "Look at yourself."

He nodded. "No, I don't deny that. But in this case—if you don't disapprove—I think it would be helpful if I find him…and talk to him."

Polko winced slightly and was silent as he considered the request.

"You should know that he's been indicted for war crimes. He's on the tribunal's black list."

"Black list?" Mark asked, unable to conceal his surprise. "What does that mean?"

"It means he doesn't know he's been indicted. He won't know until he's transported to The Hague for trial."

"Until he's arrested?"

"That's correct."

Mark nodded his head slowly, looking down at the carpet before looking back at Polko. "Why you are telling me this?"

"I am telling you in confidence, because you need to know as the Commissioner of the EUPM, but also, now, as a member of his family."

"Do we arrest indictees?"

"No, that is left to the military—with NATO and EUFOR. They decide the timing of the arrests. But typically you must deal with the aftermath."

"So many years after the war is over…. Why now?"

"There are many arrests still to make. The indictments are valid for as long as they live. Many others at very high levels, on all sides of the last war have yet to be arrested for their crimes, but their indictments remain. Until they are arrested, justice will not be served in Bosnia."

"But those indictments have been announced for over two decades! Why is Celo black listed?"

"It is likely that they feared if his indictment were announced, he would flee to Belgrade, or go underground, like Karadzic and Mladic did."

"What crimes do they want him for…may I ask?"

Polko looked intently at him for a moment and then walked over to his desk to retrieve a stack of papers from a folder inside a drawer. He leafed through them, and pulled out a single sheet and read from it: *"Ethnic cleansing near Stolac. Burning and demolishing Croat homes with explosives. Ordering the destruction of the Stari Most Bridge in Mostar.* Those are the specific charges."

"Not genocide?"

"No." Polko read from the page in front of him. "He has been indicted for 'violations of the laws and customs of war.'"

"How is this connected to Ravno?"

Polko sat down. "It's not; however, you are aware that he has been a central figure there. There are some who said he started the violence in Ravno. There is always a tendency to 'pile on' in these circumstances, and I have asked the Tribunal to resist such a temptation. In any case, it is not related to the indictment." Polko leaned forward in his seat toward him. "So, this is the question you must answer for *yourself*, more than for me—*can you sufficiently distance yourself?*"

Mark's thoughts rushed to his aunt who was now 72 years old, living on the Antrim coast of Ireland. She never wanted to leave Celo behind. For years, she'd tried to bring him to Ireland, through every means and contact available, but on each occasion Celo refused to leave Yugoslavia. He'd seen how the vitriolic letters Celo had sent her made her inconsolable, as if he were punishing her for abandoning him. And then, after a year, the letters stopped. While she never talked about Celo, he knew that she blamed herself for the circumstances that had separated her and her son. Through a family friend in Zvornik she learned that her husband had been executed by the JNA a week after the horror at Brnisi Dam, but they had said that Celo survived with the assistance of the head of a local crime syndicate that had successfully smuggled he and his aunt to Ireland on a merchant tanker carrying iron ore. Now Celo was wanted as a war criminal. The news shook him. His voice was low, and his tone was measured.

"Ambassador, my past has always been my burden to bear." He paused and considered how best to frame the question that now preoccupied him. "He's my cousin…my aunt's son. She raised me. She hasn't seen him since we fled Yugoslavia…with your permission, I'd like to ask him if he would voluntarily turn himself in, to avoid any further violence—to himself or others?"

Polko nodded his understanding. "Let me see what is possible. I will get back to you."

He stood and shook Polko's hand, knowing that the diplomat had overextended himself by telling him about the indictment. The information he'd given him was strictly privileged. As he approached the door, he stopped and turned to Polko.

"Can I ask you another question, Ambassador?"

"Certainly."

"With respect, I've wondered how you seem to know so much about me...about my past?"

"A fair question." Polko smiled and placed his hand on his shoulder. "When I was searching among many candidates for your job, you were on no one's list. Someone who knows us both, well, convinced me that you would be the ideal choice."

"Can you tell me who?"

Polko walked back to his desk, hesitating before he turned to face him. "John Thorpe."

He nodded. He wasn't surprised to hear Thorpe's name for the second time today. "A small world," he replied simply.

"Yes, it is." Polko answered.

"I understand he's here in Sarajevo."

Polko nodded with particular politeness. "He asked about you, and wants to see you. I told him you were away flying in my helicopter...he wasn't surprised," Polko said laughing. "He said to tell you he can give you a better ride."

He smiled knowingly and shook Polko's hand on his way to the door.

"Lyons," Roman Polko said as an afterthought. "Remember the children of Ravno...of the Balkans—they are the ones we should help first."

Mark nodded, absorbing Polko's comment.

Polko held the door for him, clasping his arm, relieving him of a reply. "Be careful—let me know how I can help you."

CHAPTER 25

THE CLOUDS HUNG HEAVY in the sky all day, threatening rain, but producing only fog. Bob Childs felt the cold, damp mist weighing on him. The condensation collected on his prematurely grey hair and began to run down his forehead to his nose and temples. He pulled his overcoat tight to his sides. His periodic evening walks through Gornji Grad, the hill in the center of the city where the seat of government was located, were what sustained him through this turbulent time. The region was in the process of imploding…again. He knew the language, the dialects, the people and the countless agendas. After two decades of living in the Balkans…in Belgrade, Sofia, Sarajevo, Bucharest and Zagreb, the CIA had chosen him to be the Station Chief for the Balkan region. When the job was offered, he had initially resisted, knowing that the specter of another Balkan war loomed. What he could not say was that he doubted his own ability to influence the steadily worsening situation in Bosnia and prevent it from spreading throughout the Balkan region.

Now, a year after taking the job, as he had predicted, the situation had worsened—incidents of ethnic cleansing, house burnings, rape camps, and mass graves—sporadic at first, were now prevalent, leading to another Balkan war.

Prior to the ambush, he had thought about how best to convey his concerns to key decision-makers. He contemplated sending the report to the CIA headquarters in Langley, Virginia but worried that it would be ignored. Ambassador Fulbright's mission to the Balkans as a Special Envoy had opened a new door to him. He knew Joe Steinberg well, from years past, when Steinberg was smuggling Hamid Karzai into Afghanistan as the newly installed President of the country only weeks after the attacks of September 11th.

As the Ravno crisis deteriorated, Childs became more and more anxious. Fulbright was the last best hope for a diplomatic solution to the crisis. If he was to have any success in stopping the hemorrhaging in the Balkans, Jack Fulbright had to walk into the Banja Luka summit armed with the same detailed intelligence he was privy to.

Conveying that heightened sense of awareness to Fulbright, however, would carry with it risks. The most significant risk was that Childs would lose credibility by painting a picture that many would see as alarmist. He turned to God for strength, finding that in times like this, his Catholic faith in God ultimately brought conviction and peace of mind. After a great deal of thought and prayer, he had assembled everything...assumptions and facts in a single memo. The resulting memo had the qualities of being both controversial and yet, incontrovertible. But it was also volatile.

Volatile, because it conveyed something separate and distinct from a fact or an assumption—a *rumor* that he had obtained from a single, direct source—someone whom he trusted—who had no reason to lie, and who had always been reliable in the past. It was rare enough to receive such information directly...but when he did, it was only possible because of the extensive network of contacts he had built up over time throughout Eastern Europe. The meeting occurred at a resort lake outside of Tuzla, over a fried calamari dinner. "They have smuggled in plutonium," the informant told him in fluent Serbo-Croatian, without specifying who "they" were. The word "plutonium," however, was the same in both English and Serbo-Croatian, and it echoed in his head at its first mention. South African plutonium, he'd said...stolen from the Koeberg Nuclear Reactor near Capetown, sold to an al-Qaida cell in Algeria, smuggled through Ravno and now still in Bosnia, near Bocinja.

Winding through Zagreb's cobblestone alleyways, he caught a glimpse of Saint Stephen's Cathedral through the granular fog with its soaring, distinctive twin Gothic towers ahead in the distance. They were an imposing presence, constructed with precisely that intention, Childs thought. There were many other churches in Zagreb, but it was Saint Stephen's that impressed him most, brought him closer to God and gave him solace in challenging times. One evening more than two years ago, he had wandered inside the massive Gothic cathedral. It was there, inside, with its extraordinary frescoes, sculptures and statues, where he began to pray and go to Mass every morning on his way to work at the nondescript nearby safehouse in the heights of Gornji Grad. In that time, he had met and struck up a friendship with the Archbishop of Zagreb, Vojislav Pijadje—or "Papa

Voyo," as he preferred to be called. Papa Voyo had become Childs' informal counselor over the past year—always available to him, someone he trusted and because of Papa Voyo's own high position in the church, he could talk to in confidence—who understood his challenges and help guide him—as if their conversations were occurring in a confessional.

During one of his weekly meetings, Childs agonized in veiled terms over whether he should put his observations in writing and send them to key decision-makers and to Jack Fulbright: *"when rumors overshadowed facts,"* he'd asked, *"...when it is probable that, if reported, those rumors would be dismissed as alarmist or unsubstantiated; and when the consequences of ignoring those rumors could be potentially catastrophic, what is a public servant's moral responsibility?*

The tall, thin prelate had listened carefully and smiled, pausing to stroke his dark grey beard. In his characteristic thoughtful tones, he finally replied in the timeless and reverent manner to which Childs had become accustomed. *"Peace is God's will, Robert! Any information that you can convey to achieve it* must *be shared."*

As a spiritual friend and mentor, Voyo injected a moral dimension in the midst of the gathering chaos; simple wisdom that offered him clarity and newfound resolve...a dispensation and cleansing of the spirit, much like absolution conveyed through the sacrament of confession. *"Iudica, Domine, nocentes me: expugna impugnantes me. Apprehende arma et scutum et exsurge in adiutorium mihi,"* he had intoned, crossing Childs in a parting benediction. "Judge Thou, O Lord, them that wrong me: overthrow them that fight against me. Take hold of arms and shield, and rise up to help me."

With the memory of Voyo's benediction fresh, he had flown to Sarajevo to personally deliver his report to Steinberg—a brief encounter, and somewhat rushed, but as Steinberg scanned his message, Steinberg's looked up at him with eyes that grew increasingly wide with worry: *"If this is true,"* Steinberg finally told him, *"it changes everything."*

Upon his return to Zagreb the next day, Childs received the frantic call from Sandy Evenson. Because of her call, he was the first to report the ambush at Oborci. He flew down by helicopter to view the scene. At first sight, it could have been an accident; but there was Sandy's call. The coincidence of all three cars destroyed, and all of the passengers killed—with none injured—was just too great. Upon closer examination, the signature blast patterns of six rocket propelled grenades slamming into the armored plating of the vehicles removed any possibility that it was an accident. The absence of anything inside the vehicles confirmed Childs' worst fear: that the attackers had managed to take all of the classified paperwork, including his own report about the plutonium. If assassination was not the main motivation for this attack, he reasoned, stealing top secret documents was a prime possibility.

SARAJEVO, BOSNIA AND HERZEGOVINA

AFTER RETURNING from the meeting with Roman Polko, Mark opened the door to the roof of the Sarajevo Holiday Inn and looked out over the city. The sun was setting behind the mountains ringing the city, packed with buildings, homes and graveyards with the signature obelisk posts for the Muslim graves and crosses and glossy headstones for the Croat and Serb graves. Below, streetcars screeched to their stops, car horns blared and dogs barked. He lifted the violin from its velvet case and then the bow. The polished wood and familiar weight of the instrument in his hands was calming. He pressed the violin to his cheek and ran the bow over its strings as if he were weaving silk. The somber tones emanated from violin, resonating and radiating from the bow in its own unique voice. It surrounded him like a cloak and he felt its remarkable, familiar echo run through his limbs, building, fading and building again. A sense of repose and innocence renewed steadied him. His father's voice returned to him, reassuring him that everything would be fine. *"When it is dark enough,"* he'd say as he lifted the bow, *"you can see the stars."*

In those moments, playing his father's violin, everything was restored. Like a man in a dream, time passed without his awareness of it. As the sun descended behind the mountains, he closed his eyes and the melody he heard was no longer his own, but his father's...playing the same violin to him as a young boy, beside his bed.

ZAGREB, CROATIA

A FREEZING RAIN had begun to fall on the cobblestone walk, making it slick and giving it a burnished pottery-like luster. Crossing the street toward the light blue stucco exterior of the Archbishop's Palace, Childs looked up at the water fountain with the Virgin Mary in gold at the top and four archangels below her on each side, as if keeping guard. He bowed his head as he walked past them, past the cathedral around to the Archbishop's Palace, or simply "the Residence," where Voyo lived. He knocked.

He was greeted by a disfigured, yet familiar, face—concave on one side where his cheekbone and jaw connected. The grey stubble did little to cover the deformity. Despite his facial appearance, Papa Voyo had a certain refined elegance. He was dressed in a scarlet cassock or *simar*. His ecclesiastical rank was indicated by the color or his simar, the large gold pectoral cross on his chest, a gold ring with a yellow stone on his hand and a square red cap, or *biretta* as it was commonly called. His frame was rail-thin, and his face was long and gaunt, but his eyes were active—alive and cunning, like those of an old lion. His voice was suffused with warmth and hospitality. "Robert! I'm glad you've come. I have been waiting for you."

Childs smiled as he entered, shaking Papa Voyo's hand. "I'm sorry to keep you waiting, Your Eminence...."

"Patience is the virtue of us Franciscans," Voyo answered good-naturedly. "Let me take your coat." His English was perfect, but his accent pronounced.

Childs removed his overcoat and handed it to the Cardinal, who hung it up in the hallway closet. As he'd been during their other late night visits, Papa Voyo was alone in the elaborate residence.

"I was very sorry to hear about your Ambassador Fulbright—a terrible, terrible thing," Papa Voyo offered. "Did you know him?"

Childs shook his head. "No, but I knew many of the others."

Papa Voyo shook his head slowly. "I am very sorry, Robert. It was a tragedy...senseless." Voyo turned and motioned him down the hallway. "Come."

He followed Papa Voyo into the large living room of the residence. It was lined with shelves and countless books. The room was in semidarkness, and it carried the unique scent of old tobacco, candles and the mustiness of old furniture. The lights were dimmed, and several candles were lit around the room. Leather chairs were positioned along both sides of a long, hand-carved mahogany conference table that Papa Voyo had once told him originated from Kenya. A crucifix hung on the far wall between a framed photograph of the late Pope Benedict XVI and another of Cardinal Alojzije Stepinac.

Childs sat down in the chair, and watched Papa Voyo walk; almost float, it seemed, into the kitchen. Since he'd known him, the Cardinal always seemed to be in motion.

"I made some coffee," Papa Voyo called out. "Would you like some?"

"Of course." The coffee, he knew, was Turkish. Powerful, thick as mud and super caffeinated.

Papa Voyo continued the banter, asking about Childs' wife and daughters. He finally came out with a wooden tray and set it down on the mahogany table. He poured the sludge-like brew into two small cups, and handed one to him on a small saucer.

"It wasn't an accident, you know," he said, stirring the thick brown coffee.

Papa Voyo was impassive, pausing only momentarily before returning to the kitchen with the metal coffee pot.

He continued. "They attacked his convoy—and they murdered them." He tasted the sweet, grainy mud-like coffee that he had learned to savor during his visits to the residence. Papa Voyo reentered the room with his pipe and a bag of tobacco.

"They?" He set the pipe and tobacco down on the end table next to him, and reached for his own cup.

"Actually, no one knows who did it. Until we do, they're calling it an accident."

"An accident…that is what they are saying on the news…in the papers." Papa Voyo motioned at the Zagreb newspaper, *Vercenji list* in front of them. It had an image of the wreckage on the front page.

"To prevent anyone from overreacting."

Papa Voyo grunted, and had begun to fill his pipe with tobacco, tamping it down with his right thumb. He lit a wooden match and sucked the flame into the pipe, finally exhaling the smoke in a cloud that surrounded him like a wreath. Voyo looked at him through the smoke before blowing out the flame. "Illusions are sometimes necessary, Robert."

"Yes, but this isn't an illusion. It was a deliberate attack. I was there—I saw the scene."

"You see things others do not," Papa Voyo replied. The ring of smoke twisted and folded, then dissipated.

"I'm crazy then?" he asked, with a tone of mild sarcasm and a smile. He leaned over to sip the coffee.

"No, Robert," Papa Voyo said. "You are enlightened."

Childs sighed. "I'm exhausted, Father."

Papa Voyo nodded. They'd had this conversation before. "Because you take your work as seriously as you should…you care when others acquiesce. Simple minds cannot easily relate." He struck another match to relight his pipe. "I'm sorry about the loss of your friend, Ambassador Steinberg."

Childs looked toward the stained glass window, dimly illuminated by a distant street light. "He was a good man…he had a family. He didn't deserve to die like that."

"He was a diplomat. He understood the risks of his profession," Papa Voyo replied softly. "God chooses when we depart this world. No one else." He stood up to go into the kitchen, and came out with two glasses of water, handing one of them to Childs. "Here—after the coffee, you need this."

As he sat down, Papa Voyo pointed at the photo of Stepinac. "He was a diplomat too—a diplomat of our church. He also understood the risks, and he died for us. Next month, he will be our Saint, you know—Croatia's first."

Childs felt the subject shift abruptly to Stepinac, and as he heard Papa Voyo talk about the plans for the canonization ceremony next month, he sensed this would be the topic of their discussion tonight. He was very familiar with Stepinac's legacy and was well aware of how controversial he was throughout the Balkans. He had included his concern over the canonization ceremony in his report to Fulbright, mentioning it as another impending flash point and catalyst for violence.

It was a topic he had wanted to broach to the Cardinal for some time, but hadn't knowing how emotional it could become. He knew Alojzije Stepinac was entombed inside the cathedral behind the altar.

He took a sip of water and set the glass down on the end table. "Can I ask…why the canonization ceremony needs to be in Medjugorje?"

"Because it is where his last miracle happened!" Papa Voyo replied enthusiastically. He paused and nodded, his tone now matter-of-fact. "It is the appropriate place." Voyo handed him a pamphlet translated to English.

He took the pamphlet, but shook his head in response. He knew the story, having met the Vatican team that had investigated the latest miracle attributed to Stepinac a year and a half ago. The fact that this had occurred in Medjugorje made it even more dramatic—and there were also those who said that such an unlikely story proved it to be more obviously contrived.

The first miracle at Medjugorje was said to have occurred in June of 1981. That afternoon, six children from the town were playing on a nearby hill when it is said that an apparition of the Virgin Mary appeared and spoke to them. Three of the six claim to continue to see the apparition of the Virgin daily, while the other three see her, they say, on special occasions. Twenty-five years later, four Canadian women who had been diagnosed to be in the latter stages of Hodgkin's and non-Hodgkin's lymphoma were attempting to make the steep and winding ascent up Mount Krizevac—the mountain above Medjugorje, overlooking the Hill of the Apparitions, where the Virgin Mary had first appeared that day in 1981.

Childs opened the pamphlet summarizing the miracles attributed to Stepinac that were required for him to advance from beatification to sainthood. Voyo had bookmarked and outlined the passage he wanted him to read...as if he'd prepared it in advance for this very discussion:

> Soon after embarking upon the long winding ascent, the women turned back. In their weakened state, they were unable to physically negotiate the uneven, rocky path or the formidable hike in the 95 degree heat of day. Descending, they met a priest in sandals, carrying a hickory walking stick. His home, he said, was outside Zagreb in a small town. On the side of the trail, he rested with them, talked to them, and laughed with them, telling them of his own battle with a rare blood disease that—like lymphoma—was also terminal. He gave them a blessing, and then he encouraged them to make the ascent with him, reassuring them they would take frequent rests at the Stations of the Cross. As they continued their climb, their strength returned and to their surprise, they found that they needed less and less rest as they approached the summit. They arrived at the top of the hill, where the priest led them in prayer to the Virgin Mary at the giant cross

overlooking the valley. Despite their secret hopes, there was no apparition, no vision. To quench their considerable thirst, the women purchased water from the concession stand on the opposite end of the cross. They searched for the priest hoping he would make the descent with them, but he was gone. Days later, all four of the women returned to Canada...later diagnosed to be healthy, with no trace of the cancer. The women attempted to contact the priest in the town that he had mentioned to them—Krasic—by telephone, but they did not know his name. When one of the women traveled to Krasic herself, she too was unsuccessful in finding the priest—until she had seen the photograph of him in the town's Catholic Church: the photograph of Cardinal Alojzije Stepinac, discovering that he had died in 1960.

Childs bowed his head and closed the pamphlet. "It will cause riots, Your Eminence. Surely the Vatican knows that—I *know* you do. It's too close to the fighting in Ravno. People will be hurt, even killed...."

Papa Voyo stood and pointed at the photograph of Stepinac. His voice was low and restrained, but Childs could detect an abruptness and ferocity that he had not previously encountered from the prelate. Yet he'd seen it before, when underlying hatred and indignant grievance suddenly erupt from an otherwise composed demeanor, exterminating and revising history as they recount it. It was most prevalent in those who had experienced the trauma of violence and were forced to suppress it, rather than effectively address it through psychological counseling. He had seen it make the faces of the most beautiful women appear ugly and even murderous when memory spilled over to historical revisionism and hallucination. His voice climbed defensively. "The Chetniks, the Turks cannot stop this, Robert. The United States cannot! He is *our* Saint. Two miracles happened at Medjugorje—it is hallowed ground!"

"It'll be a killing field." He sensed the circular argument he was being led into, and he resented the fact that he wasn't being given any choice. He had experienced the hateful soliloquies before from many others—Serb, Muslim and Croat—and he knew it was going nowhere constructive. Inexplicably, he had struck a raw nerve in Papa Voyo and he regretted it. It was not the reason for his visit. "Your Eminence, I am not denying that the canonization is justified—but you know the place you have chosen is on the edge of a war zone!"

Papa Voyo sat down, leaned into the chair and folded his hands together in a pose that seemed to indicate self-imposed restraint. He paused and inhaled. "Let me tell you so you understand: I grew up in an orphanage here in Zagreb. My parents were killed by the Serbs during World War II. I had no religion and I did not believe in God." He shrugged. "—I had no reason to! The state raised me and I eventually became an officer in the JNA. Tito had imprisoned then-Archbishop Stepinac. They assigned me as his guard during the last two years of his life. Because of our proximity to one another, we had many conversations together. I was the godless skeptic, and I suppose he viewed me as his last challenge. When I told Cardinal Stepinac my story, he asked me if I could forgive my family's executioners. I was infuriated at his suggestion! Those who could forgive such an act, condoned it, I told him. He disagreed with me, firmly but gently. I cursed him and told him that I wished him to die as my family had so he could understand their pain, and mine." Papa Voyo looked at him. "You never knew this about me, did you, Robert?"

He shook his head quietly, resigning himself to the impending exegesis. "No...no, I didn't, Your Eminence."

"Stepinac did not return my hostility. Instead, he prayed for me! I asked him to stop, but he continued. Despite my anger, we spoke more and more often. While I argued, he reasoned with me and sought to educate. Somehow we became friends. Grudgingly, I admired him. When the Pope made him a cardinal, Tito did not let him go to Rome. He remained confined. At the personal request of the Archbishop in New York, I smuggled his red robe in to him. But he would not wear it, he said, until he could baptize me. Three months before he died, I agreed."

Papa Voyo pulled a framed 8x10 black and white photograph from the drawer of a nearby mahogany secretary and handed it to him. It was Stepinac in the robe of a cardinal, and a young, beardless Papa Voyo in an officer's uniform. The contrast was vivid and dramatic. Voyo looked at him as he placed the photograph on the table. Since it did not elicit any reaction, Papa Voyo continued. "So you see, Robert, I owe my faith to the Cardinal. The fact that he appeared in Medjugorje is his sign to all of us, and to me. He loved the town well before the first miracles there. He said Masses in Medjugorje. It is no surprise to me that is where he chose to be seen. On earth, Zagreb was his prison. We cannot continue to keep him captive here for eternity."

"But Father, the reality is that you will bring the war to Medjugorje—you'll destroy that beautiful place. Is that what you want?"

"You worry too much," Papa Voyo said, simply, his face growing darker, his eyes implacable.

"Your Eminence, in fairness, you should know that I've asked my counterpart at the Vatican to plead the case for a change of venue."

A shadow crossed his face, and Papa Voyo stood again, abruptly, walking to the kitchen in silence as though he didn't want to talk anymore.

He could hear the sound of glasses being pulled from a cupboard. In truth, he was amazed by Papa Voyo's revelations. He had concealed this personal history from him for over a year, choosing to tell him now. He had no idea of his connection to Stepinac, and hearing it made him realize that Papa Voyo was a man of many dimensions, and very likely a prime force behind the effort to bestow sainthood on Cardinal Alojzije Stepinac.

Voyo returned with two glasses half-filled with red wine and handed one to him. "We should perhaps—as you Americans are fond of saying—'agree to disagree.'"

"Ignoring the problem won't make it go away." he said, taking a drink of the dry, red wine. "We now have no choice but to talk to the Cardinal Secretary."

Voyo set his glass down and folded his hands on his lap. "Of course, you are correct," he sighed. His demeanor had changed from what had previously been argumentative and confrontational to sad, even apathetic. The tone of his voice now had a wistful quality to it. "These problems must be managed proactively."

These problems must be managed proactively.

He stiffened in his chair. It was a direct quote from his memo to Fulbright—from the first paragraph. As soon as he heard it, he felt a chill go down his spine and a distinct tingling in his fingertips. He noticed his hands were shaking. A tightness gripped his chest and suddenly his bowels felt watery.

The passage of time seemed to stop. He looked around the room as if he were caught in a dream. Everything felt terribly misaligned and confused…the room began to spin around him. All the nerve endings in his body were becoming numb. His chest suddenly felt as if it were encased in lead. The wine glass fell to the floor in a shattering clatter. Red wine splashed on the oriental carpet and stone tile floor.

"I...I don't feel well, Father," he said, his voice wavering. "The wine...."

At that moment, he remembered Papa Voyo's earlier response: *"He was a diplomat."* It had been a direct reference to Ambassador Joe Steinberg. He struggled for clarity. He had never told Papa Voyo of his friendship with Steinberg; he had only mentioned that a friend was killed in the attack. Somehow, though, Cardinal Voyo knew of the memo, and knew Steinberg was the recipient.

He had read it. It was the only explanation.

He could barely make out Voyo's long, pale face, but was acutely aware of the sweet smell of his pipe tobacco burning, and the sound of the steam pumping through the radiator behind him. He heard the priest shift his weight in his chair. The panic that he should have felt did not come...only an icy blast of confusion and horror, like an extended electric shock. He wanted to run. In his mind he was running away...from the mistakes of his past...from the Balkan morass...from the madness that confronted him. He told himself to run, but his body would not respond. Numbness suffused his body. He sat, motionless. Paralyzed. Finally, he collapsed in the chair, but he'd been somehow propped up and restrained as he sat stock-still. And yet, the room seemed to revolve.

"No, I know you don't feel well, Robert. I'm very sorry," Voyo's voice responded tonelessly, laconically. "You should know about the miracle attributed to Cardinal Stepinac for which there is still no official record. For years, Tito was poisoning him. With arsenic, with ricin, and even cyanide in his food. But do you know? Through it all, the cardinal was unaffected by the poisons." Voyo laughed. "They were all quite lethal. You should know this, because you have consumed one of them, ricin, and you are experiencing the effects now." Voyo was now pacing elliptically in front of him. "Instead, Robert, the cardinal died of Vasques' Disease—a disease of the blood—not from any poison. It is the miracle no one talks about...and maybe the one no one knows about. I only know this, because as his guard, I was responsible for placing the poisons in his meals. When he did not die, when he continued to pray for me, he became *my* Saint."

At once, a searing, hot pain shot through his temples, creating a brilliant pyrotechnic display of orange and red shapes and electric blue flashes. Suddenly, everything blended together to create a swirling kaleidoscope of effervescent, variegated patterns.

Voyo's awful drone echoed relentlessly. "The pilgrimage to Medjugorje will be an extraordinary event for all Catholics, and for all Croatians. If there is more violence, it will be God's will. It is His will that we reclaim the legacy that was taken from us. You have been a great help to us with your report to Ambassador Fulbright and Steinberg. It is exceptional—well informed of what is at stake, the threats we face, and the measures you recommended to address them. But it was your mention of plutonium that surprised us and the possibility that they would target the Vatican that caused us to act. We had no information on this. If it is in Bocinja as your report says, the Turks have it, and of course, we have no alternative but to locate it and take it from them."

Voyo used the term *"Turks,"* a derogatory reference to the Muslims, who adopted Islam when Bosnia was under Ottoman Turkish rule.

"Why?" It came as a barely audible, rasping groan deep within his dry, constricted throat. He craved water. Mucous suspended from his mouth and nostrils.

He sensed Voyo behind him now, whispering in his ear. "Because, Robert! They killed Christ, and they will not stop until they kill us…. They seek revenge for the defeat we wrought on them in 1683. I am sorry Americans had to die. I am most sorry that you also must be sacrificed Robert…you are good and faithful man. You will be an unspoken martyr for the Church."

He heard Voyo transition to an Act of Contrition that he realized the priest was uttering on his behalf, administering Last Rites. He heard the words but they ceased to register.

The once-colorful mosaic receded into thick, mold-like shadows…grey, mucoid splotches that darted around like moths in the darkness, obscuring any view of Voyo and the nine-inch dagger that he had positioned above his first vertebrate, at the base of his neck below his cerebral cortex.

He could feel himself falling, his own spirit falling into an abyss. He hardly heard Voyo's solemn intonations, but he could smell his sour breath. His thoughts drifted to his two daughters, who would be asleep in their beds by now. His wife…Renee. Because he hadn't called home to tell her he would be late, she would be expecting him home in less than an hour. He vaguely remembered that they had argued that morning about changing plans for the coming weekend because he had to work. Because of their argument, he had left without kissing her or saying good-bye.

Voyo completed the sacramental prayers with the words, *"May you know peace, my son."* And with the prayer complete, he plunged the dagger downward. There was little blood as the spinal cord was severed. During his last moment on earth, Robert Childs heard the rain clearly outside. He felt no physical pain, only a profound sense of regret and sorrow.

CHAPTER 26

GENERAL JOHN THORPE sat alone at General Rose's desk with the STU-III secure telephone to his ear.

A voice on the other end answered. "General Thorpe, this is the Situation Room. Sorry for the delay. We expect the President momentarily."

He looked outside and watched the workers of Ilidza Base planting flowers along the ring of flags that surrounded the courtyard. The flowers were red, white and blue…a not-so-subtle statement. After a five-minute wait, and several other similar announcements, the voice came back: "General Thorpe, stand by for the President. Be advised that there's a slight echo on the line. SITROOM drops."

He recognized the President's voice on the other end just as the Situation Room communicator exited from the call. "General, glad you made it to Sarajevo. I wanted to catch you as soon as you arrived. I believe our folks have already told you about the plutonium found near Ravno. I've ordered a search and render safe team to your location. They should arrive within the next twelve hours—I want you to direct them."

He remembered his discussion with Jim Goodwin in the Rose Garden after the NSC meeting and then again during his transatlantic flight, informing him of the Presidential Directive to deploy a nuclear emergency search team (NEST). His conversation with General Rose had been rushed, centering on the basing requirements for the team, and on the absolute requirement for secrecy. The team, they agreed, would be based at a EUFOR base in an isolated corner of Mostar's airport to allow the two U.S. Air Force C-130 cargo planes to land and preposition themselves with all of the team's equipment.

Thorpe waited for the President to finish.

"Yes, sir," he answered. "I'm aware of the situation. We are setting up an operations center in Mostar to coordinate search and control teams. If we find anything, we'll call you."

"I just don't have a good feeling about this, General—I don't know if it's connected to the attack on Jack Fulbright, but we can't discount the possibility. We need to find out what it all means and I'm relying on you to do that." The president paused. He was about to respond, but the president continued. "And something else—our CIA Station Chief for the area, Bob Childs, has been missing for about fifteen hours now. He never came home last night according to his wife. They live in Zagreb."

As he held the phone to his ear with his shoulder, Thorpe scribbled notes on the pad of paper.

"Okay, I've got it, sir. We'll check on it."

"The embassy in Zagreb is expecting you." The President continued.

"Sir, there are photographs of the ambush on Ambassador Fulbright's convoy-- as it occurred. Up close, from a witness who was on the scene. And although I haven't confirmed it yet, I believe a reporter from the New York Times has a good idea that Oborci wasn't an accident. I thought you should know."

He heard only the momentary rush of static. "What's his name?"

"*Her* name…Kate Kamrath. On my way in here, she confronted me with lots of questions. I know her, so I may be able to get her to delay on submitting any story…but I can't say for how long. Eventually, she'll start playing hardball."

"And who took the photos?"

"A war crimes prosecutor from The Hague…Sandra Lee Evenson. That was her UN vehicle on the satellite feed we saw in the SITROOM. I understand she's still in Sarajevo."

The president paused and consulted with someone on his end of the line. "Okay, thanks. We'll handle the reporter on our end. Get those photos over here as soon as you're able, so we can see them"

"Yes, sir."

"General, you're my representative there—you have a direct line back to me. The folks in the SITROOM can reach me at any time, day or night."

CHAPTER 27

SANDY EVENSON TOOK A SEAT in a booth off to the side of the bar to wait for Kate Kamrath. Although she was early, the Dubliner Pub was beginning to crowd with Sarajevo's large expatriate community. She ordered a scotch, and ran her fingers through her hair. The last two days were a blur, and sitting at the bar of an Irish pub made it seem even more surreal. The constant state of change had been what had kept her in the Balkans for so many years, but it was now the reason that she wanted so desperately to leave. Places like Bosnia attracted people who sought challenges beyond the scope of the corporate or political world. It was a place where politics, promise, justice, injustice and war converged all at once. Her first experience with those dynamics came in 1992 in Vukovar, as the town was destroyed by Serb shelling, and thousands of its citizens were killed. Sandy remembered when she had met Kate Kamrath there. Both of them were investigating the execution of over 250 Croatian men. She was a Special Prosecutor for the War Crimes Tribunal, and Kate was a reporter for Time Magazine, stationed in Berlin.

During her years in Bosnia, she had come to know the majority of Western journalists who had responsibility for the Balkans. She admired Kate for continuing her coverage of Bosnia when it had slipped from center stage and when all other journalists had flocked to other global hotspots.

Kate's responsibility was Europe—and she knew it—better than any other reporter. She focused on it exclusively and consistently demonstrated the continuing relevance of the Balkan Region to Europe and the world. Their friendship was the rare kind that can only be forged in a war where you shared living space, risks, days of boredom, moments of terror, and uncertainty; and witnessed the extraordinary compassion, dedication and appalling inhumanity of people at war—or in the midst of war.

Theirs was the kind of friendship that didn't require a high degree of maintenance. Months could go by without seeing or hearing from one another; then they would catch up easily, as if they'd never been apart. Sandy admired Kate and she trusted her to deliver a balanced, accurate story—free of hidden agendas and sensitive to the ethnic and cultural nuances of the region.

In retrospect, the fact that Kate Kamrath had some knowledge of what had transpired at Oborci should not have surprised her as much as it had. She knew Kate's contacts in the Balkans were extensive, and in the past she'd been one of them.

She was less willing to admit to herself that the real reason she wanted to meet had less to do with catching up than with Kate's obvious familiarity with Mark Lyons, and her own desire to learn more about him.

Mark was different than any other UN bureaucrat she'd seen in the Balkans or anywhere for that matter. His appearance alone belied the fact that he was an Assistant Commissioner for the European Union Police Mission. His hair was too long, his face too young, and his demeanor too composed—but he'd also demonstrated that he wasn't afraid of confrontation when the situation called for it. What made her most suspicious from the beginning was that he was *way* too good looking. He had the physique of a professional athlete. He was different than the UN bureaucrats who masqueraded as policemen. She sensed a certain fatalism about him, a disregard for the politically correct, for his own career...and possibly, for himself. Not only was she intrigued by him, she was *drawn* to him. He broke every stereotype that she could apply. After two days in close proximity with him, he was *still* a mystery to her, and that only compounded the attraction.

She saw Kate Kamrath enter the pub wearing a brown suede jacket, a lavender blouse, and worn jeans carrying a large colorfully beaded purse. She waved at her and Kate smiled as she walked over.

"Sorry I'm late. I was trying to email a story back to New York, but I couldn't get a connection, so I had to fax it through the hotel."

"No worries," Sandy replied. "I was early."

Kate hung her coat on the chair and slid into the booth. "It was good to see you this afternoon. I thought you'd flown this coop!"

"I thought so too, but Sarajevo is like the Hotel California...you never quite leave."

"I didn't expect to see you with Mark Lyons."

She hesitated, took a sip of her scotch. "I didn't expect you to know him."

"I'd heard a rumor he was coming to Sarajevo. How do *you* know him?"

She set the glass of scotch down and grinned. "Would you believe me if I told you he swooped down from the sky just to meet me?"

Kate laughed. "I've heard stranger stories in this place, so why should this fairy tale be any different?"

She leaned forward and looked at her. "Is this an interview, Kate? Because if it is, it'll be a different kind of conversation."

Kate waved her hand to placate. "No, no interview! Sorry! Old habits die hard, and sometimes I can't help myself—."

"I can't figure him out," she said, leaning back in her chair. "For a newcomer, he seems to know a lot of people here."

"Mmmm," Kate nodded. She ordered a small Guinness Stout from the waiter. "That's true. He knows a lot of folks, and they know him...he's one of the more interesting personalities you'll meet around here these days."

"How well do you know him?"

"Outwardly, I suppose I know him well," Kate said. "But given his circumstances I'm not sure anyone can claim they really know him."

"What circumstances?"

Kate looked at her briefly yet thoughtfully, smiling and sipping from her glass. "Mark Lyons is one of the break-glass-in-case-of-emergency guys you normally only read about, Sandy. He's had to live through some pretty tragic events that most people could never relate to, or deal with quite frankly. He was a Colonel in the British SAS, and then ran the counterterrorist program in Northern Ireland for the RUC."

She nodded. "The Royal Ulster Constabulary...he told me."

"Really! It's amazing that he told you anything like that. He generally doesn't talk about himself—what else did he tell you?" Kate asked, suddenly interested.

"That he came to Ireland from Yugoslavia, to escape."

"From one hell to another," Kate commented. "I learned that about him just recently, but someone else had to tell me...not him. When peace broke out in Belfast a few years ago, the powers-that-be decided he no longer served their purposes. He was discarded, essentially."

"How do you know him?"

"I was covering the peace process in Northern Ireland. I had heard about then-Colonel Lyons and his campaign against the IRA. I interviewed him and shadowed him, but he was always elusive. I could never pin him down. It's what you never read in the papers about how the IRA finally agreed to come to the negotiating table. Mark was really the one responsible for ramping up the raids against the IRA cells, and the effect was so devastating that they really had no choice. I understand he participated in the raid against the terrorists who took over the Iranian Embassy in London and led the only successful searches for SCUD missiles during Desert Shield and Storm. He was well on his way to becoming a General, but he retired to take over the RUC's Special Branch."

"Why did he do that?"

"I don't know...it paid more, I suppose. But he'd also just gotten married."

"He's married? ...He didn't mention that part."

Kate paused and took another sip of her Guinness. "He probably won't, because he's not anymore. He's a widower. I'd imagine that's ultimately the reason he was finally sent here, away from Belfast."

"I'm not following you."

"Well..." Kate paused. "The first thing you gotta know is that Mark Lyons' story is a tragic one...to put it mildly. Several years ago, his wife was held hostage by the IRA, and *he* was the ransom. He was going through the process of turning himself over to the IRA, when the SAS launched their attack. Unannounced. The IRA killed her as soon as they realized what was happening."

"Good Lord...." She directed her gaze toward the window as more people entered the bar.

Kate nodded. "I'm simplifying it, but that's the short version. I'm sure he's still not fully recovered from it...how could you? In addition to blaming the IRA for his wife's murder, he also blamed himself and the SAS— particularly Colonel Ian Rose.

"You mean—"

Kate nodded. "Same guy—now *General* Rose. After his wife's death, he went right back to work. For the next year or so, he went on a personal crusade to bring the IRA to its knees without the assistance of the Army, who he essentially cut out of the entire picture. He was wounded several times, once severely. With the RUC Special Branch that he trained and organized, he conducted his own private war against the IRA that forced them back into the negotiations that ended up pretty successful."

She drank the scotch from her glass and felt a familiar warm sensation slowly creep down her chest and arms, settling to her fingertips. "So, he's not your normal, everyday UN bureaucrat."

"Nope," Kate said, shaking her head with a sardonic smile. "Far from it."

"Why is he here?"

"Some claimed he went too far. He didn't limit his attacks to the IRA. He went after the other side too—the Unionists—the Protestants. It was a violent time. Much of it happened behind the scenes. There was some publicity, but for the most part Mark's Special Branch cleaned up the messes they made. The Protestants began publishing large casualty numbers in the wake of Mark's raids. It was questionable whether all of the dead were combatants. After the IRA announced they were ending their terror campaign, he was promoted. He used his new position as Assistant Chief Constable in Belfast. He used the job to go after organized crime leaders who were perhaps coincidentally, former IRA. Eventually, he became a liability for the political leadership in Dublin and in London. So, I'm assuming that's why they sent him into this job. Here, he's in a prestigious position, but he's also effectively out of sight, out of mind—away from Belfast, where I understand he still has a price on his head...."

"And so they figured no one cared about or really knew about Bosnia anymore?"

"Something like that. But what they weren't counting on was that guys like Mark Lyons don't just fade away." Kate looked at her, concerned. "Why don't you tell me what happened at Oborci, Sandy?"

Sandy sighed. "I thought this wasn't an interview...."

"I'm asking you as a friend," Kate answered. "Not as a reporter."

"Kate, I can't...not right now."

"It wasn't an accident, was it?"

"Not now...later," she replied, her voice almost a whisper. "I promise you'll be the first I come to."

Kate leaned back in her seat. "I heard today that Bob Childs' missing...everyone at the embassy in Zagreb has an all-points bulletin out for him. Have you heard anything about that?"

She inhaled and shook her head. "No, I haven't. But it doesn't surprise me. Bob does that from time to time. It's his job."

"Yeah, but this time he didn't even tell his wife."

"I know Renee. It's not the first time for her either. He's under a lot of stress. He has more contacts than any diplomat. He'll show up. As an announced CIA Station Chief, his job dictates that kind of thing."

"That's my point," she said, a little disconcerted.

"I spoke to him two days ago. He's fine, Kate."

Kate nodded, finished off the Guinness and popped a few Tums in her mouth. "Okay, then…let's get drunk."

She smiled—*really smiled*—for the first time, she realized, in at least two days.

Kate ordered another Guinness for herself and a scotch for Sandy. She leaned back in her seat, clearly amused. "You like him, don't you?"

"Who?" She realized that her face was flushed.

"Sandy Evenson, I wasn't born yesterday. I saw you beside him this morning, and I saw the way you were looking at him. It was obvious—at least to me it was."

"I had no idea he had such a history."

"Yeah, well, everyone has baggage these days," Kate sipped her beer, and looked around the bar with a wry smile. "And at the end of the day, we're all baggage handlers, aren't we?"

She swallowed the rest of her scotch. "You mentioned General Thorpe to him during our encounter at Ilidza…."

Kate nodded again. "Mmmhmm."

"Kate?" she asked, sensing more to her answer.

Kate was silent for a moment as she considered her response. "John Thorpe was Mark Lyons' father-in-law."

Sandy's eyes widened with the sudden recognition. "His wife…who the IRA killed?"

"…was Thorpe's daughter. Yes."

"Good Lord…." She directed her gaze toward the window as more people entered the bar.

Kate was now contemplative. "Sandy?"

She glanced back at Kate. Her voice was subdued. "Yes?"

"Be careful with him, okay? For his sake and for yours."

She nodded imperceptibly, still trying to absorb what Kate had revealed to her about Mark Lyons.

CHAPTER 28

MARK LYONS HAD NOT SLEPT well in the small room at the Sarajevo Holiday Inn. There were the dreams...the image of the dead at the dam—piled in grotesque heaps upon one another, mouths wide open, seeping blood, their eyes unblinking—staring.... He saw the moonlit image of one man beside him, reaching out to him, gasping, cajoling, interrogating in the night, *"Why did you allow this to happen to us?"* The screams of the dying came back to him, over and over; and the fear, now so familiar, rose up in his throat. He awoke with a start, shivering, his face glossy with sweat. A dog was barking outside, continuously. He pulled the covers over his body. The room's temperature varied wildly from too-hot to too-cold depending on whether the fan was on. His sheets were soaked.

He blinked to make the dreams go away. This rays of light pierced the darkness through the curtains. He searched for some logical framework that would explain the surreal events of the past several days. However hard he tried, nothing made sense.

Taking a shower, he realized that he'd allowed Ian Rose to get under his skin. It had also caused Roman Polko to become an arbiter of an issue that, in retrospect, was entirely avoidable. He'd lost control for one reason only: *Celo was there.* It had been two decades since he'd seen him, and suddenly—on his first day back in the Balkans, Celo had found him, looking at him through a photograph with the same intense blue eyes he remembered from decades ago.

He stepped out of the shower and dressed, wearing black jeans and a thick, white Norwegian Wool sweater. He had made a pot of coffee and poured two cups before putting on his coat.

Walking from the hotel's atrium, he saw the lobby and restaurant ten floors below. He found the room number he knew to be Sandy Evenson's, knocked softly while still holding a cup of coffee in his hand, but there was no answer. Shifting the cup to his left hand, now holding both cups, he knocked again, more forcefully.

The door opened, and Sandy was wearing one of the hotel's white terry-cloth robes. She was holding the bridge of her nose as she looked up at him.

"Yes?"

"Rough night?"

"Jesus, what time is it?"

"8 A.M.....here, I brought some tea. I figured ye might need it."

"My head's spinning like a top," she said, taking the cup from him. She held it appraisingly, taking a sip before motioning for him to enter. She sat down on the bed, and ran her fingers through her hair. "Well, Kate knows that what happened at Oborci wasn't an accident. She knows it was an ambush. She wanted more information, but I managed to convince her not to publish a story yet."

"How did you manage to convince her?"

"There's a price...."

"What's that?"

"We owe her a story. After that fiasco with General Rose, though, I was half-tempted to tell her everything."

He nodded and paused, attempting to conceal his curiosity. "What else did you talk about?"

Sandy paused for just a moment before replying. "You."

He walked over to the window, looking outside. "Well, then, I'm almost afraid to ask."

"Why didn't you tell me?" Sandy was now looking up at him, holding the Styrofoam cup to her mouth.

"About what?" He felt the familiar discomfort return.

"About what happened in Belfast," Sandy answered. "I must say, I was fairly stunned."

He knew that Kate Kamrath had most likely given her many of the details of his past...at least the more dramatic pieces of it.

"There's a lot that happened there. I don't advertise it. It's the past...."

"Is that why you left?" Sandy asked

He turned to her and shrugged. "Aye, that would be quite a leap, I think."

"It's not the same." She turned away from him as she said the words.

"Flight is flight."

Sandy took another sip of her tea and set it down on the desk, she sat down. "In a sense we're all refugees here—everyone's running away from something and when you leave, it usually means you're ready to confront yourself again. You never escape entirely."

"Mmmm. " He sat down on the bed. "What were you running from then?"

"I don't know. Maybe reality."

"This isn't reality?"

"No, it's hyper-reality. Everything's compressed—intense. Everyone…all of us…we're all wearing war goggles. Things are larger than life, surreal—even when things seem normal to you, they're not…at least by anyone else's standards."

He smiled. "Why do you think that is?"

"Because it's one of the few places where you realize your own mortality on a daily basis …at least subconsciously…where you know that it could all be over today…they don't let you forget."

"They?"

"Ghosts."

"Oh, them." Mark smiled.

"No one *just decides* to come here," she added.

"What then?"

"You're lured here."

"By ghosts?" He immediately regretted his sarcasm, but it was too late.

Sandy held out her hand like a traffic cop and shook her head. "Alright, don't patronize me, Commissioner. I've been here too long to put up with it from anyone, you included."

He shook his head. "I'm sorry, I didn't intend—"

Sandy stood and walked to the window that looked out over Sarajevo's mosques and churches. "This place has a gravitational pull all its own," she said, explaining herself further. "For humanitarians, tyrants and warriors alike. Here, you don't have to look for problems to solve. They come looking for you."

"I see," he answered. "And when they're all solved? What happens then?"

"You declare victory and go home."

He smiled, suddenly enjoying the exchange. "That could take a while, couldn't it?"

Sandy shook her head, still looking out the window. "No, not really.

151

Everyone lives on dog time here—one year equals seven. Look at me; I'm the poster child for Balkan Lost Causes."

"So I take it you don't come here for the money."

"Nope."

"Why then?"

Sandy shrugged. "Deliverance...redemption...immunity...pardon.... It's one big happy confessional."

"And you?" he asked. "What were *you* seeking redemption from?"

She paused thoughtfully and turned around to face him. "I'm sorry about your wife, Mark."

He was at once disarmed, and he felt completely exposed. "Well, I certainly *was* the topic of conversation last night, then, wasn't I?"

"One topic, yes," she replied. "Before we got really drunk." She looked up at him, eyes large and sympathetic. "Kate told me what happened."

Mark nodded. "Well, that's not why I'm here...in case you're wondering."

"It would be okay if you were."

"I'm here for the job," he answered. "Not redemption."

"Of course not." she threw the Styrofoam cup in the trashcan by the desk.

Mark looked up at her. He was more and more intrigued. He'd never met anyone quite like her before, and it was her allure that surprised him...in fact, terrified him. "Why don't I wait for you downstairs in the lobby?"

"Where are we going?"

"I wanted to ask for your help in finding my cousin."

"Celo? The cousin who pointed the gun at me?"

"Are you still okay with that?"

She nodded and gave him a sardonic smile. "I have a few things I'd like to say to him."

He smiled and walked to the door.

"Mark—?" She was standing behind the bathroom door, holding it open. He turned to face her.

"I'm sorry for bringing up the subject of your wife—it wasn't my place to—"

"No—it's a fair question. It's just not something I talk about very often. Ever really."

She smiled. "I understand."

He opened the door, paused and half-smiled. "They do tend to stay with you, you know…," he said musingly.

"I don't understand."

He looked up, directly into her eyes. "Ghosts."

MARK RECOGNIZED John Thorpe reading the *Herald Tribune* at a table in the hotel restaurant, just outside the smoke-filled lobby. Seeing Thorpe there surprised him initially, but it also occurred to him that the Holiday Inn was where most diplomats and VIP's stayed in Sarajevo. Thorpe looked up as he approached.

"Don't you need reading glasses, General?" Mark announced, smiling.

Thorpe stood and embraced him.

He looked at John Thorpe. Even without his uniform on, he looked every bit a soldier: short brown hair, solidly built, well-dressed in khaki slacks and a darker khaki shirt. A dark blue jacket hung on the chair behind him. His eyes were discerning, and his face was weathered. John Thorpe was one of the few men he'd come to ever truly admire, but seeing him now was not something he could have been prepared for. He realized that he'd not seen Thorpe since Annalisa's funeral.

Thorpe stood several inches taller than Mark, and as the two embraced, their smiles were tempered with common understanding of each other's past.

"I heard you were staying here, Mark. It's good to see you."

"It's good to see you as well, John," he answered. "Really good."

Thorpe motioned for him to take a seat beside him.

"Coffee?"

"Tea, please…if they have it."

Thorpe nodded and signaled a waiter and ordered a pot of tea.

Several other official-looking men and women in blue jeans and khaki who Mark assumed were part of the FBI's investigative team were eating breakfast at the tables around them.

"I understand you were at Oborci after it happened?"

Mark nodded. "About a half hour after."

"I understand you believe it wasn't an accident?"

He slowly shook his head, stirring sugar into the cup of tea. "John, it was an ambush. Textbook. Whoever did it, planned it deliberately, and ensured there would be no survivors."

"But there were witnesses." Thorpe said in a matter-of-fact tone.

"Several."

"And photos too, according to Ian Rose," Thorpe answered.

"Yeah," he said, looking back at Thorpe. "He hasn't been helpful."

Thorpe nodded thoughtfully. "Obstinacy has always been a strong suit of his."

After a brief silence, he looked up at Thorpe. "Are you here because of that…because of what happened to the Fulbright Delegation?"

Thorpe nodded slowly. "That's part of the reason. Four of the dead were ours."

Mark nodded. "I'm sorry, John. They never had a chance, you know."

"That's why I'm determined to find the bastards who did it."

"I'll be glad to help."

"The photos?"

"I'll show them to you—tonight a good time?"

Thorpe nodded. "Tonight's fine."

"I want you to meet one of the witnesses, but after our meeting with General Rose, she isn't exactly high on generals at the moment. So, I need to a bit more time to tell her about you, if you don't mind."

Thorpe nodded and smiled in response. "I understand." He poured more coffee into his cup, and looked at Mark intently. "How are you?"

Mark paused and nodded. "I'm well. It's a bit strange to be back here after so many years, and then to be involved in an investigation so quickly. It's like a scene out of a bad movie, to be honest. But I'm well, thanks."

Thorpe looked at him. "That's not what I meant."

Mark paused again, understanding the question, but not knowing how best to answer.

"I miss her, John," he said finally. "I can't stop thinking about her." He looked away, toward the front desk as his eyes began to well up. "Sorry."

Thorpe nodded silently in acknowledgement and looked into his eyes. "I miss her too. We all do."

"I can't seem to get the thought out of my head that if she hadn't ended up with me, you'd still have her."

He could feel Thorpe's eyes bearing down on him. Thorpe's voice was low and his delivery even. "Well, that's nonsense, and you know it. There's nothing you could've done."

"I'm not so sure. It was my fault for dragging her into the mess. She had no stake in it. She was an innocent—"

Thorpe stopped him. His giant hand clamped down on Mark's forearm. His voice was stern. "I want you to remember this, Mark, because it's the only time I'll tell you. She was a grown woman. She made her own decisions, including the one to be with you. She made it with both eyes wide open. She understood the risks—I know that, because I raised her. If you don't believe that, you're patronizing her, and me, and you should reassess."

He turned his head and looked directly into Thorpe's eyes. "Not a day goes by when I don't think about that day. I should have stopped Rose. I knew better...I knew him! I knew what he would try to do!"

Thorpe shook his head slightly. "Ian Rose made a mistake—but he used his best judgment...say what you like about him, but you know as well as I that he's a good officer. The man did what he thought was right at the time. I can't fault him for that."

He contemplated what Thorpe had said, and chose not to respond. Releasing Ian Rose of all responsibility for Annalisa's death was noble perhaps; but it was like rewriting history. Even if the terrorists had killed him, she quite possibly would have lived.

Thorpe turned to him. His eyes were filled with tears. His voice was deep, and betrayed his own grief. "You gotta know that Annalisa was proud to be your wife...there was nothing she wanted more than that. And I'm proud to have you as my son-in-law, *still*. But she's gone, Mark. You have to realize that—Hell, there are times when I have to remind myself!" Thorpe paused, took a breath. "Nothing we can say, no one we can blame, will bring her back...."

The cold logic of Thorpe's words cut through him. "If I forget what they did to her, then I've forgotten her," he answered, searching for the right words.

Thorpe straightened, tapping the table resolutely. "You...we...have to move on. It's what she would want from both of us. And that's all I'll say about it to you."

"Okay," he answered. "Fair enough."

"I'm glad you're here," Thorpe said. "I'm sorry it took these events to make that happen."

"Well, it's mutual then." Mark looked over and saw Sandy walking out of the elevator toward the lobby. She did not appear to see him in the open restaurant with Thorpe.

"Is she the one with the aversion to generals?" Thorpe asked with a slight grin.

He nodded. "It is," he said, beginning to stand up. The transition was awkward, hurried. He did not want to introduce Sandy to Thorpe at that moment. "You'll have to excuse me for the brief encounter. She can be rather elusive."

Thorpe laughed and waved him off. "Go!"

He rose, and extended his hand to Thorpe. "By the way, why did you say that the attack was 'part the reason' why you were sent?"

As Sandy approached, Thorpe sipped his coffee and glanced back at him. "Branches and sequels," he replied simply.

Mark nodded slightly. He was familiar with the operational terms that described how one event could lead to or contribute to another in rapid succession. He also understood Thorpe's response was meant to be intentionally ambiguous, yet designed to clearly convey that now was *not* the time to discuss it.

SANDY STOOD outside the restaurant facing Mark as he walked toward her. She wore a denim jacket over a white cotton blouse. The several buttons that remained unbuttoned at the top of her blouse did not escape Mark's notice, nor did the worn khaki jeans and brown boots that she wore. He had assumed Sandy to be in excellent physical condition, and seeing her now—dressed as she was—confirmed that impression.

Mark realized that John Thorpe would be making the same observations from the table, where he was ostensibly reading his copy of *The Herald Tribune*. He wasn't quite ready to introduce Sandy to Thorpe. The "aversion to generals" comment was a subterfuge—a way to avoid even the perception from his former father-in-law that he'd found someone else after Annalisa. Now, even the thought that Sandy Evenson could be more than simply a witness left him with an awkward, if not altogether uncomfortable feeling.

"Am I interrupting anything?"

He shook his head, looking back at Thorpe for a moment. "Not at all. That's the commanding general for the Joint Special Operations Command. I'll introduce you to him later tonight."

"He's not wearing his uniform."

"No, he wouldn't be...," he said, smiling. "He's a different breed of general than any other you'll meet."

"After yesterday's encounter with General Rose, I hope so."

He paused thoughtfully, walking out of the hotel. "Aye, well, in many respects, I'd say he's the 'Anti-Rose'...."

CHAPTER 29

JIM GOODWIN WAS PERSPIRING as he rushed from the backseat of his chauffeured car into the ground entrance of the West Wing. He flashed his green White House access badge to the Secret Service agent at the control desk and ascended a narrow stairway to the left. Stepping aside for several people to pass by, he turned left and proceeded down the hall to the National Security Advisor's anteroom, where two secretaries and an executive assistant sat with computer screens on their desks, answering telephones. The executive assistant, an Army major dressed in a civilian suit, ushered him into the office, announced him to Rachel Cook, and shut the door behind him.

Rachel Cook was sitting at her desk and stood to greet him.

"This is a visit I'd rather have avoided, ma'am."

"Any visit from you is welcome, Jim. You know that." Cook said. She motioned to the blue and gold tapestry sofa. "What've you got?"

Goodwin spoke as they moved to the sofa.

"Amidst everything else that's happening in the Balkans, there's a separate situation that's developing there that I wanted to brief you on before we approach the President." He sat down and withdrew a folder marked with an orange coversheet that said, "Top Secret." He paused before handing it to her.

Cook read the two-page CIA Report without comment, but he could see her expression harden.

TOP SECRET UMBRA WNINTEL NOFORN
29 JANUARY
SUBJECT: MOVEMENT OF LEVEL 4 PERSONALITY

1. (TS) CONFIRMED MOVEMENT OF DR. AHMED NAZIR FROM ISLAMABAD, PAKISTAN TO SARAJEVO VIA PAKISTAN

INTERNATIONAL AIRWAYS ON 28 JANUARY. NAZIR'S PRECISE
DESTINATION AND PURPOSE FOR THE VISIT TO BOSNIA-
HERZEGOVINA ARE UNKNOWN.
2. (S) NAZIR PERFORMED AS THE DEPUTY SENIOR ENGINEER FOR
PAKISTAN'S MODERNIZATION OF ITS NUCLEAR ARSENAL. PRIOR
TO JUNE 2008, NAZIR WAS RECOGNIZED TO HAVE FULL ACCESS
TO ALL NUCLEAR PROGRAMS IN PAKISTAN.
3. (S) NAZIR GRADUATED FROM THE MASSACHUSETTS
INSTITUTE OF TECHNOLOGY WITH BACHELOR'S, MASTERS AND
DOCTORAL DEGREES IN THE FIELD OF NUCLEAR PHYSICS AND
ENGINEERING. HE SPEAKS FLUENT ENGLISH AND HAS WORKED
AT SEVERAL NUCLEAR POWER PLANTS IN THE UNITED STATES
AND SOUTH AFRICA DURING THE PAST DECADE.
4. (TS) THE U.S. TREASURY DEPARTMENT COUNTERTERRORISM
TASK FORCE HAS CONFIRMED THE WIRE TRANSFER OF 6
MILLION EUROS FROM DUBAI TO LIECHTENSTEIN'S CENTRAL
BANKING SYSTEM ON 20 JANUARY IN THE NAME OF AHMED
NAZIR.

Cook sighed and looked over his glasses at Goodwin. "So now we have a
disaffected Pakistani nuclear scientist in Bosnia?"

"It would appear so, yes." he said. "Normally it wouldn't be so much of
an issue, but when you consider it along with the stolen South African
plutonium that turned up there, it's cause for concern." He paused. "Quite
frankly, I'm worried."

Cook nodded her head slowly. "That's what they pay us to do, Jim.
Worry."

"Yes, ma'am," he answered. "But this is different—it's the kind of thing
that keeps you up at night—this may be the real deal."

Cook nodded thoughtfully. "I've never heard of Nazir. Who is he?"

"Essentially Pakistan's true Doctor Strangelove. By all accounts, he's
brilliant—soft spoken, humble, religious."

"Religious?" Cook asked, glancing back at the color photo of Nazir. He
wore wire rim glasses that emphasized his thin, nearly gaunt face and dark
complexion.

"To a fault, yes. Devoutly Muslim. Not someone we would typically
regard as hostile to the United States or dangerous, but he's credited for

bringing Pakistan's nuclear power system into the 21st Century. From constructing state of the art Pebble-Bed Nuclear Reactors there, to upgrading their nuclear arsenal to one that's hydrogen capable. India has no counterpart with his skills and level of intellect—and they know it—so there have been several attempts on his life—all unsuccessful. He was one of Pakistan's elite until he fell from grace a couple years ago.

"Why?" Cook asked, suddenly curious.

He shrugged. "No one quite knows—demands for money perhaps. He has a son and daughter—twins—both nearly college aged. Tuition to Oxford is expensive, you know, and I'm told Pakistan's Parliament may not have approved Dr. Nazir's requested raise."

"He's unemployed then?" Cook asked, with her head supported on one side by his thumb and index finger.

"Unemployed, desperate, with an ax to grind with the government—and it's the ax that he could potentially wield that concerns me."

"Where's the money coming from?" Cook asked, pointing at the message.

"From Afghan and Pakistani opium production. The Taliban is funneling the profits, $3.5 billion worth, through the ISI, Pakistan's intelligence service, and on to al-Qaida."

Cook shifted in her seat. "So we have a full equation here...expertise to construct a device, weapons grade plutonium, means of delivery, a safe area for planning and construction, financing—"

He nodded slowly. "And the motivation too."

Cook seemed to be considering his words.

Goodwin continued. "The girl in Ravno who died of radiation poisoning died from accidentally ingesting a tiny plutonium pellet...the size of a pea. The CDC recovered it during the autopsy. It and the other pellets we found in the barn had the Koeberg—the South African nuclear power plant's—symbol stamped into it."

Cook was silent as she reread the CIA report. "We sent a NEST team to Bosnia, didn't we?"

"It arrived in Mostar a few hours ago." He passed another paper to her. "This is the record of a six million euro deposit from Dubai to Luxembourg's Central Bank. The name on the account is Ahmed Nazir. The sender is listed as a construction firm in Riyadh, Saudi Arabia.

"So he's employed after all," Cook commented in a somber tone, handing the paper back.

"It would appear so."

"This report says that he's in Sarajevo now?"

Goodwin nodded. "We confirmed that he flew into Sarajevo aboard a Pakistan Airways flight eleven months ago. He hasn't been seen since. We've checked every major hotel in Bosnia, Serbia, Montenegro and Croatia and he seems to have just disappeared."

"Well, I don't believe much in coincidences," Cook said, her voice taught. "If they have a device—"

"They'll use it," he answered for her. "They won't sit on it."

"Okay Jim," Cook nodded solemnly. "Can you brief the President on this now?"

"Yes, ma'am," he answered. "This report is currently classified as 'POTUS/VPOTUS/NSA/NDI EYES ONLY.' With your permission, the one who needs this information the most, in my estimation, is General Thorpe. He's in the best position to influence the situation with his special mission units on the ground, and to find Nazir. Wherever we find him, my guess is that we'll also find the missing plutonium."

Cook nodded, and handed the folder back. "Okay, let's show this to the President. Have the Situation Room send a copy to General Thorpe right away."

SARAJEVO, BOSNIA AND HERZEGOVINA

"MR. LYONS!"

As he approached the glass doors with Sandy Evenson, Mark Lyons turned around in the direction of the young twenty-something concierge who was smiling, holding up a folded piece of paper. "A message for you, sir."

He walked over to the counter and took the page of hotel stationary. Thanking him, he unfolded it to see a typed note:

Message received via telephone
7:25 a.m.
To: Mark Lyons/Room 509

Message: FANTA LAKE, 3:00 p.m.

The sudden recognition of the term "Fanta Lake" revealed its source. Mark smiled faintly. He walked back to Sandy, who was pushing the glass door open.

"That wouldn't be General Rose's apology, would it?" she quipped.

CHAPTER 30

Bosnia: U.S. Envoy to the Balkans, Ravno Crisis in '11th Hour'
By Kate Kamrath
New York Times News Service

Washington/Sarajevo - United Nations High Commissioner Roman Polko said yesterday that the Ravno crisis had reached a crucial "11th hour." A United Nations Spokesman said Polko will deliver "a stark message" to the three Balkan Presidents that they must collectively agree to the peace deal or face the risk of air strikes on their forces deployed in Bosnia. The Pentagon followed up on Polko's warning by saying that any air strikes will be "decisive and overwhelming."

Chief NATO Peacekeeper, General Ian Rose in Bosnia, responded today to the possibility of NATO air strikes against Serbia and Croatia by saying NATO and the European Union will take whatever steps are necessary to keep the peace in Bosnia-Herzegovina. NATO troops remain stationed in Bosnia in accordance with the 1995 Dayton accords.

A spokesperson for the European Union-led European Force (EUFOR) in Bosnia said army and senior government officials in Belgrade have been unwilling to give assurances that they will not intervene in the Ravno campaign on the Bosnian Serbs behalf.

However, Celo Mescic, the popular, unofficial advocate for the Republika Srpska—the Serbian half of Bosnia—threatened to use his rising influence to reactivate the air defense systems in the Republika Srpska in order to defend against NATO air strikes. All air defenses in Bosnia have been switched off since the Dayton Accords were signed.

Although the Bosnian Serb Army was in shambles following the last war that ended in 1995, it is believed to have significantly rebuilt its military machine with assistance from Serbia and Russia and is beginning to advance toward the city of Dubrovnik on the Mediterranean coast. On the ground in Ravno today, the Croatian Army is continuing an offensive that has left several ethnic Serb villages in flames and sent more than 20,000 Bosnian Serbs fleeing their homes since Saturday. Croatian Prime Minister Milo Stanic has called the military action "purely defensive," designed "to preserve the historical integrity of the Croatian Republic in the face of Serbian aggression."

"People are terrified," said Dr. Jean Rene Lauvergeon, from Doctors Without Borders in Ravno. "The situation is dire, the suffering is immense, and people here are now only waiting to die."

MARK LYONS DROVE the UN Toyota 4Runner along the road leading into the city of Zvornik, listening to Sandy Evenson read Kate Kamrath's report.

"I'm sorry I asked you to stay on in the face of all this," Mark said after she'd finished.

Sandy shrugged. "Honestly, you probably couldn't have kept me away. I probably would've arrived home in Connecticut and turned around to come back."

The two hour drive from Sarajevo was an easy one and his conversation with Sandy Evenson was light, focusing on her home and family, the jobs and failed romances that led her to Bosnia a decade ago. He did his best to deflect attention to his own life story in very subtle ways, revealing only aspects of it when there were no other options—life in the SAS, school days, his aunt who lived in Antrim and her own accounts of life in Bosnia during the last fifteen years. He looked out his driver's side window, and she pointed to the Zone of Separation, or ZOS. He'd heard of it before. It was an artificial boundary created by the Dayton accords, abolished and since reinstituted after the Ravno Crisis to separate the Serbs from the Muslims and the Croats. Driving through it now, it was, still, a no-man's land of blasted concrete and clay cinder block homes and minefields.

"Every time I see it, it depresses me," Sandy said, pulling out one of his CD's, by the group "Chieftains." She opened up the case and read the inside description. Reviewing the song list, she found several songs written by "Mark Lyons."

"Whoa!" she exclaimed, pointing at the case. "Is this 'Mark Lyons" *you*?"

He looked over at her and smiled, continuing to drive. He nodded.

"Well, then, I'm impressed."

"You shouldn't be," he answered. "It's only a hobby of mine…a distraction. The band members are my mates."

Sandy put the CD in the player and fast forwarded it to the first song written and played by Mark with a fiddle, and with another playing the flute and a ship's bell. It was entitled "Camelot's Ashes"—an instrumental, sad and languorous, perhaps evocative of another time, Sandy thought. It reminded her of something that would come from him, given what she had come to know.

"Well, I'm impressed," Sandy said with finality. "So don't spoil it, okay?"

He nodded silently, a slight smile crossing his face.

As the ballad played, they approached the city of Zvornik. Passing through the ruins of an ancient brick underpass, the old aluminum plant was the first landmark he could readily identify—the same aluminum plant that Celo had shown him almost four decades ago as a shortcut to take during their afternoon walks from school. It appeared abandoned now. Long grass covered the fence, and the rust on the machinery was a reminder that life had changed here and jobs were scarce. He pointed to it. "This is where we would play when I was a boy. It was a fortress to us when we were kids. Always busy, night and day. We would sneak inside and climb the conveyor belts on Sundays when it was closed. It's a bit strange to see it like this now."

He pointed to the road that turned left in a north. "That's the way to Dulici and Brnisi Dam. The city of Zvornik is here on the right where you see the colored buildings." He checked the clock on the dash. "We have some time…you hungry?"

"Quite possibly," she replied.

He turned into the town center, with the crowded, winding streets and high rise apartment buildings stacked into the city center. They parked in the first available spot.

She stopped him before he opened his door. "I know you grew up here, Mark, but I have to tell you—Zvornik is the heart of darkness. I can't tell you how many mass grave exhumations I've been to around here. And many of the senior Serb officials—the mayor, police chief, and army commander who are now in power were responsible for them."

He nodded. "Until the day I was forced to leave here, it actually wasn't a bad place for a kid to live." He paused and pointed toward a pizzeria with a burgundy-painted wood sign over the door and a window decorated with red and black velvet trim. "Pizza?"

She smiled, knowing he was changing the subject. Inside, it was nearly filled to capacity with a bustling crowd of what he guessed were locals. The heat from the ovens provided enough heat to make it very warm inside. The distinct aroma of pizza dough baking and pasta cooking blended with their cigarette smoke and Serbian rock music played in the background. A waiter seated them in a corner by the window.

He looked outside and saw a group of boys, probably ten or twelve years old, clearly truant, running through the streets with toy pistols and rifles, attacking an invisible enemy. He saw one of them, and then another, realizing they looked all-too-familiar. He heard their voices through the glass.

"...Attack! ...Attack! ...Attack!"

Celo was leading the assault, and he was following him.

Sandy's voice interrupted and they were gone, like smoke.

"What's wrong?"

He looked back at her with an abstracted glance. "I'm sorry?"

"You're staring. Like you've seen a ghost."

He shook his head, leaned back in the booth, and gestured outside toward the small mob of boys, hunching behind cars, just below their window.

"I'm sorry. I was thinking...that was me, what I was doing thirty-some years ago."

"Mark Lyons, 'Boy Warrior'?"

"Something like that," he said, pulling his sweater off. He wore a black tee shirt underneath, with a red and yellow logo in the corner.

He saw her staring at him, intently. He realized that with the thick sweater off, his arms were exposed, as was the distinct outline of an athlete's frame—muscled yet lean and sinewed. The tendons and muscles stood out in his forearms. His left bicep was muscular and defined, with a large jagged ridge of pink scar tissue—like an arrow—running across its length.

"The Chieftains," he said, referring to the logo.

166

"Mmmhmm…as in the music we were just listening to?" Sandy asked, now grinning.

He nodded. "Aye, the same."

"I'd like to hear you play."

He laughed. "At yer own risk!"

After a moment, Sandy said, "Is this what you want, Mark?"

"What do you mean?" he asked, confused.

"To be here…you seem out of place here, that's all."

He looked out the window again, not prepared for the shift in the conversation. The boys were gone, replaced by two gypsy girls, begging passers-by.

"Are you ready for this?" she asked, noticing his lingering distraction.

"For what?"

"To see your cousin," she answered, glancing at her watch. "About an hour from now."

He looked into her eyes. They were kind, yet incisive—inquisitive. "I don't know—I'd like to know if he had anything to do with the ambush."

"I have a hard time believing that's the only reason you'd like to see him," Sandy said.

"Why?" he asked, absently.

"How many years has it been since you've seen him?" There was a glint in her eye. "Wouldn't that constitute probable cause?"

"Thirty…plus"

"Excuse me?"

"We last saw one another more than thirty years ago. That's why he wanted us to meet here, I suspect."

"I'm sorry," she replied, reaching out for his hand. "I didn't realize."

It was the lightest of touches. Once he felt it, he didn't want her to let go. He shrugged. "There's no way you could."

"What's the point of meeting at the dam?"

"Guilt. Symbolism. We Serbs are masters at it, you know," he said, chuckling. "And Celo—he was always one for high drama."

Sandy raised her eyebrows. "That's interesting."

"What?" he asked. "The symbolism or the guilt?"

"You said, 'We Serbs.'" Sandy replied. "So, what are you? Serb or Irish?"

He found himself once again temporarily without equilibrium. He shrugged. "Both...or neither—I don't know. I was baptized and raised Serb Orthodox while I was here in Yugoslavia. My family name was Mescic. When we moved to Ireland my Aunt Maja raised me in the Catholic Church. When she remarried, I was given the adopted name of Mark...so I suppose I'm a hybrid—a mutt." He paused to consider her reaction. Her eyes remained intent. "And what about you?"

"I'm American. No identity crisis there, but I've come to consider myself more of a global citizen, quite honestly."

"A good concept," he replied. "I could adopt it too, I reckon."

She took a sip of her Coca Cola. "Would you rather go to the dam alone?"

He shook his head. "I think you have a score to settle with him, don't you?"

"Well, that can be done in any number of venues, but I'm glad to accompany you, if you'd like."

He looked at her again. Her dark brown hair fell easily across her shoulders, and her eyes seemed to transition from green to a bright hazel. He could no longer deny that beneath her tough—acerbic—exterior, she had an underlying radiance and a compassion that he hadn't expected. It fascinated him, and he found himself smiling at the distraction she had provided him.

The pizza arrived. He released her hand, and as the waiter placed plates in front of them, he served her a piece.

"I'd like for you to come along."

Chapter 31

MARK LYONS TURNED the Toyota 4Runner onto the gravel road leading up to Brnisi Dam. Deftly shifting gears and weaving between potholes, he maneuvered the SUV past a farm house and newly planted corn fields on both sides of the heavily rutted dirt road. Ahead, the forest merged into the fields of deep, green grass and forests on dramatically undulating hilltops. Continuing their drive along the narrow roadway, a wall of rock appeared in front of them, forming the backdrop for an otherwise idyllic setting. The same forest that had hidden him and Celo that night concealed the masonry dam from the main roadway to Zvornik.

He stopped the 4Runner and studied the dam. The images of the dam returned to him in flashes as he'd remembered it that night with Celo. It looked much larger to him back then, but it was the same place. The guard shack was still on the top of the western-most edge of the dam as he'd remembered it that night, where the guards had started firing at him, and where Celo had fired back to protect him. Daylight made the whole scene seem surreal, as if it were all a distant dream.

Sandy looked up at the dam through the windshield. "It looks like a drive-in theater."

"Yeah, it does, I suppose." He smiled faintly, relieved at the interruption. "Problem is, they've only shown horror movies here...."

He continued to negotiate the SUV uphill. Turning a corner in the road, there was a red Jeep Cherokee backed into the forest, facing outward.

"Is that Celo's?" Sandy asked.

"Imagine so," he answered, parking alongside the Jeep.

He pulled the key out of the ignition and felt Sandy's hand on his arm. "Mark, I'll stay here. You go."

He paused and looked at her. Her expression was suddenly serious, and yet compassionate, empathetic.

He nodded silently, and leaned back into the seat with his head against the headrest. He didn't want to be here—it was a place that bred malefic spirits of decades, generations past. "I don't know why I agreed to come back."

"You came back to see your cousin again," she answered simply.

"Maybe…I'm not sure that's *his* rationale though."

Sandy placed her hand on his right forearm. "Go see him. It's been a long time for both of you."

He exhaled and leaned forward. "After what happened at Oborci—"

"I'll meet him, whenever it's appropriate, but in the meantime, you two need to catch up," she said, reaching in the back seat for her backpack. Unzipping it, she pulled out a book. "I brought homework, so I have lots to do while I wait for you. Take your time."

He bowed his head, smiling, and then glanced back at her. "You are very kind."

She smiled. "I know. Now, Go!"

He paused and smiled, shaking his head slightly.

"What?" she asked in a mock taunt. She smiled broadly, and pushed his shoulder. "You Serbs are all about dramatics, aren't you? Now, *Go!"*

The scent of pine and gentle wind belied the violence that had occurred at Brnisi Dam—not just that night long ago, but during the last war as well, when it was used to execute thousands of Muslim men and boys as Srebrenica fell to General Ratko Mladic's Serbian Army. The cold breeze, the smells of clay and dirt, the crunch of gravel beneath his feet, the guard shack above—were raw reminders that for thousands of people in years past, Brnisi Dam was a place to die. And yet somehow, miraculously, it was also a place where he and Celo had survived.

He felt his original anticipation to see Celo begin to approach resentment. He didn't want to be here. Sandy had been right…it was about the dramatics, and Celo was an expert. Symbolism was one reason for meeting here; but the real reason, he suspected, was Celo's way of levying blame in a symbolic way: blame for his insistence that they see the dead that night, and for his father's death soon after—ultimately ruining his life.

A cow grazing in the field nearby mooed. He looked up at the dam as he approached it. It was a simple design, but efficient enough for what it was intended—to create a needed dumping ground for the now-defunct Zvornik aluminum plant. He walked up a steep incline in the road leading to the top of the dam, and found himself momentarily surrounded by a dense forest of pine trees and scrub oak obscuring the view of the dam and the surrounding area. Makeshift steps of large rocks had been placed into the switchbacks to help with the climb upward. He stopped to listen. His heart was thumping.

It was dark, foreboding even—a quality unique to the forests of Yugoslavia, compounded by the widespread threat of land mines throughout Bosnia in the wake of the '92 civil war. Decades later, children and livestock were still falling victim to land mines despite the massive de-mining effort that the international community had undertaken long ago. He knew not to venture off established pathways and roads.

"Hello, Marko. It's good to see you again." The voice came from the opposite direction in Serbo-Croatian. It was deeper, more resonant than he remembered, but familiar to him nonetheless. It had the same tonality…the same underlying intensity. Full of authority. Mark could make out a large, broad-shouldered silhouette amidst the rock outcroppings in the forest, but his view remained obscured in the darkness of the forest.

"I'd like to say the same, but I can't see you," he answered in Serbo-Croatian.

Celo stepped out of the shadows. If he'd intended to create a powerful first impression, it had worked, Mark mused—to the extent that he looked like an urban version of Christ himself. The absurdity of the image nearly caused him to break out into laughter. And yet, Celo seemed to come by it honestly.

His hair was black and curly, extending to his shoulders—his face was angular, with broad unshaven cheekbones with at least a day's growth. A leather jacket, white Polo tee shirt and faded, starched Calvin Klein jeans covered his large, muscular frame. Rattlesnake-skinned cowboy boots concealed what he was certain to be a small caliber pistol in an ankle holster.

Celo stopped at the edge of the trail, a short distance from him. Both men looked at one another in what in any other circumstance would have been an awkward silence. The recognition between them was gradual, yet undeniable. Celo's eyes were deepset, blue and appraising.

Celo broke their silence. "So you remember me?"

"It's been a long time, Celo, but I would never forget you…."

"Yes," Celo responded, stripping the last remaining leaves off a nearby sapling. "Yes, it has been a long time."

Mark knelt down and picked up a handful of brown dirt and fragments of decomposing leaves and pine needles. "Why did you bring us back here, Celo?" He let the dirt fall from his hand to the ground.

A flock of ravens took flight around them, startling Mark for just a moment.

Celo smiled broadly and held both of his hands up to survey the surrounding area. "Why?" He laughed. "It's very simple, Cousin! Because we should not forget our past." He paused and turned to face Mark directly. "Those crows, they are birds of omen for us. You know this?"

Mark nodded. He was fully aware of the Serb defeat at the hands of the Ottoman Turks in 1389, called the "Field of Blackbirds." He felt a stab of uneasiness, unwilling to subscribe to the culture of superstition rampant in Serb folklore. "Yeah, I know that."

"After you left, the man who raised me brought me to see the museum at the World War II Ustashe concentration camp at Jasenovac. There, I saw the pictures of all the Serbs they slaughtered in cold blood…pictures so terrible, so horrifying that I could not comprehend. But the museum is gone. The Croats destroyed it in the last war here, but I do not forget the past. I still see those images in my head. It is what defines us, isn't it? This place defines our past—for you, for me." Celo paused briefly. "Those birds, Marko? They are free. We are not."

"Eventually we have to move on," Mark said, avoiding Celo's metaphors. "We can't be held hostage to the past." He paused and looked at Celo more closely. What caught his eye were the deep weathered lines in Celo's face, like wet, wrinkled parchment ironed smooth. The raw strength of his features was offset by the same deep, intense blue eyes he remembered. But he'd aged in a way that wasn't detectable in the photographs of him at Oborci. All of it, combined, gave Celo a very intimidating, yet captivating aura, and he suspected that his cousin's physical appearance was also what had contributed to his growing celebrity status in Bosnia.

"You look good, Celo."

Celo walked over to him and what started as a handshake quickly transitioned to an embrace. Celo maintained the grip on his hand. It was like clasping a thick leather work glove.

"You don't look so bad yourself, Irishman."

"I'm still Serb."

Celo half-nodded, half-shrugged. "Yes, well, at least you still speak our language. I was worried that you'd forgotten. That is good."

"I haven't forgotten anything."

Celo removed his hand from his shoulder, and gestured in the direction of the dam, barely visible through the trees. "You know, I've come back here every year and every year it is not pleasant for me. But it's how I remember. It was thirty-five years ago, Marko...do *you* remember?"

Mark was stripping a twig of its leaves. "Yeah, I remember, but I'm not nostalgic for it."

"I do not forget the past," Celo continued. "Others do, but I do not. After what happened here, after I lost everything, all I had left were my memories." Celo paused and looked up the road and then back to him, resolutely. "I will not forget."

Celo started up the hill and Mark followed beside him.

Both men were silent—the crunch of gravel beneath feet their only exchange as they crested the dam. The orange body of water was fully in front of them, close up. Thick industrial pipes surrounded the head of the lake where the dam was situated in a kind of half-moon. A white powdery residue covered the pipes and the banks of the lake.

"Fanta Lake," he announced quietly.

Celo grunted and squatted to pick up some stones. "So, you do remember." He threw the stones in a sideward pitch. They skipped, creating black streaks across the polluted water.

"I have nightmares about that night, still."

"Coming back here will help, then," Celo answered.

"I'm not so sure."

"I am," Celo said decisively. "It helped me."

"The advantage of proximity, I suppose."

Celo threw the rest of the rocks in his hand at the lake, making no attempt for them to skip. A series of small splashes caused the orange film on the lake to momentarily separate where they made contact with the water, only to quickly converge upon itself...as if it were quicksand.

"Why have you come back, Marko?"

He reflected on the question briefly, not fully expecting it. "I thought I knew, but I'm not so sure anymore."

"Things are so bad in Ireland that you would come back to Yugoslavia?" Celo had turned to him with a quizzical expression that quickly transitioned to a sardonic, pitiless smile.

He nodded. "Things were bad, yes. Improving now."

"They are no better here," Celo replied softly, matter-of-factly. "We are still dying."

He shrugged. "Maybe that's why I came then...to help."

Celo scoffed and began to laugh loudly as he backed away from him. "You? You came to help? *That's* why you came back? You're too much for me, Irish Cousin!"

He shifted impatiently, and crossed his arms, gazing across the lake, over the undulating swells of terrain carpeted in various shades of deep, lush greens. After a moment, he squatted, digging a small trench in the dirt with a stick.

Celo continued. "Do you know why the fighting...the violence here keeps going...why the peace treaties don't work?"

He shook his head, unsure of what Celo was getting at.

"Because here in the Balkans, killing means something!"

"I don't know what you mean," Mark answered.

"All the death! All the violence! It isn't like anywhere else," Celo said in a carefree tone. "Here it *defines* us."

"Why were you at the ambush site, Celo?" he said, changing the subject.

Celo shrugged. "Bad luck."

"I see...."

"Why did you bring *her* with you?" Celo asked, gesturing down the hill where their vehicles were parked.

"Because she's part of my investigation —."

"That's right!" Celo responded, holding his index finger up with mock realization. "You're here to help!"

He ignored his sarcasm. "And because you were in the photos, in plain view."

Celo's tone changed to disbelief, anger. "Because I was there, *I was responsible?*"

"That's not what I said, or what I asked," he answered softly, looking at Celo directly. "Why were you there?"

"Everything is not always as it appears, Marko, especially here."

"Well, then, maybe you can enlighten me."

"I was lured there...and she was there taking photos. I almost shot her, but I let her live." Celo shrugged indifferently. "I don't know...maybe I was framed."

"Is that what you believe?"

Celo exhaled, and his exasperation was now more evident. "You're the investigator, not me. You tell me."

"Who lured you?"

"I have many enemies—that should not come as a surprise to you, should it?"

"Well, if that's the case, your enemies didn't want to kill you. They only wanted to see you take the fall for the murder of an American ambassador."

"To discredit me...to see me suffer. I was their fish...what do you call it? Their herring.... Yes! *I was their herring,*" he repeated, savoring the phrase.

"Whose?"

"Someone who knew about my plans to build a Catholic and Orthodox church in Derventa."

"Why—"

"They said the bid depended on me meeting there with the Archbishop's representative."

"You didn't think it was a trap?"

Celo smiled. "Of course. That's why I came with men and guns."

"Why go?"

"If I didn't go, someone else would be given the contract."

"You didn't question the caller? Who called you?"

"Someone from the Archbishop's office in Sarajevo—look, if you ask too many questions, they give the contract to someone else, and you lose. Then no money"

"I see."

"Two of my men were killed there. It was chaos. Ask your UN woman. She'll tell you."

"Then you were framed."

"Possibly, yes."

"You must have an idea of who would want to do that to you."

"And to the Americans."

He nodded. "That would seem to narrow the possibilities." They walked toward the dam's decline. "Who, then?"

"I have an idea," Celo said, turning to look at Mark.

Mark was silent.

"It's too early for me to say right now."

"Will you let me know?"

"Possibly. But only if you're truly here to help."

"Well, I am," he said simply.

"Why are they saying it was an accident? It wasn't."

He shrugged. "Politics. I don't know. It's not clear to me. But it's a lie." At that moment, he caught a glint of sunlight reflecting off something metallic in the wood line, across from the dam.

"Are those your people in that wood line watching us?" Mark asked, his voice now just above a whisper.

"Where?"

He turned to his cousin, speaking in a soft conversational tone. "Celo, you gotta level with me! If you came alone, then we're under surveillance of some kind. And it's likely that they're either British or American special mission units."

A quick look of understanding crossed Celo's face and he grunted warily. "You mean a special operations team?"

He nodded. "Delta, Seals or the SAS."

"Why would they be here watching us?"

"Several reasons come to mind."

"Can they hear us?"

"Yes, they probably can."

"Why are they here, Marko? *Did you bring them?*"

"No. Do you know that you've been indicted for war crimes?"

Celo's jaw tightened. His surprise was veiled by a tone of controlled fury. "War crimes? Ridiculous! For this war or the last?"

"The last."

"And they want to launch a special operation to capture me and bring me to The Hague?"

"I suspect they won't do anything as long as I'm with you."

Celo stopped and turned to him.

Celo was taller by three to four inches, but in their proximity he felt Celo towering over him.

"I've done nothing wrong," Celo insisted. "Then or now! I fought for my country, *for our survival*. You must tell them that! How do you know this?"

"I was told," Mark answered. "That's all I can say."

"Tell them that they don't have to launch a special operation to capture me. I have a wife, Marko. And a son. He's six years old. Another on the way. If they want to talk to me, they can call me on the telephone. I will come in."

He nodded. Celo's emotional but rational response took him by surprise. He didn't know about Celo's marriage or the fact that he had a son.

"Will you tell them?"

Mark nodded. "I'll tell them."

"After you and Mama left, Papa was killed. Did you know this?" Celo asked, walking alongside the lake.

"I know what you wrote in your letter," he responded, recalling the first letter his aunt had received from her son six months after arriving in Belfast. It was an angry, hysterical, rambling note that was barely legible in its script or comprehensible in its content. He condemned them both—his mother and he—for abandoning him, but he would never forget the first sentence from his cousin's letter, after finding it under his aunt's bed: "They killed Papa today...."

"They hunted us down the next day," Celo said in a monotone, as if talking to himself. "I was at another house nearby. Papa was at home collecting some last minute things before we would leave for Stolac. But I heard the shots...they had the pistol we left behind, and knew it was Papa's."

Mark felt like he'd just been kicked in the stomach. His chest tightened and his eyes welled up. Suddenly, it was difficult to breathe. "I left the pistol behind."

Celo shook his head. "No. I did. It was my fault."

"None of this would have happened—."

Celo gently struck him with a large fist to the chest. "It is past."

Mark shook his head and smiled. "Will you see your Mother? She's older now. She has always blamed herself for what we did. She talks about you...prays for you every day. She hasn't stopped."

Celo turned away from him. When he turned to him again, his face had a single streak down the cheek.

"She is fine?"

"She loves you."

"But the things I said...what I wrote?"

"Meaningless. You're her son, Celo."

Celo nodded. "I would like to see her again."

"I'll tell her. She'll love to know that she's a grandmother."

"It is complicated now. Someday...."

He saw the glint of metal again, and caught movement in the woods to their left, across the dam, in the distance.

"You see them?" Celo asked quietly.

He nodded. "We should go."

CHAPTER 32

GENERAL IAN ROSE watched Celo Mescic's red Jeep through his binoculars, following some five hundred meters behind the white Toyota 4Runner. He knew that a CH-47 "Chinook" helicopter holding a team of Special Air Service, or "SAS" commandos was circling in a holding pattern over the horizon. As the 4Runner turned left onto the main road leading to Zvornik, the order came over the radio to another SAS team that had been pre-positioned in the woods the night before.

"*Stand-By…Stand-By….*"

After learning through audio surveillance that Celo would be at Brnisi Dam, a meeting at Ilidza Base had been hastily convened in Sarajevo the previous afternoon. The mission of capturing and arresting Persons Indicted For War Crimes, commonly called "PIFWiCs" in Balkan parlance, was nothing new to the 22 SAS. They had been doing it successfully for years since the Dayton Accords. Occasionally, they were forced to kill the arrestees in self-defense when they resisted with deadly force. It was never the preferred outcome, but the Special Operations men executing the raids knew that it was always a possibility.

The CH-47 flew "nap-of-the-earth," hugging the terrain at low altitude, over the tree tops and masked by the hillsides. Within seconds, the sounds of its rotor blades were beating nearby. The pilot's voice came over the radio.

"*Delta One, Uniform Six is in position.*"

The announcement was succeeded by a series of further radio announcements.

"*…Alpha Three Zero in position….*"

"*…Alpha Three One in position….*"

"*…Target in site….*"

"*Estimate sixty seconds to intercept…fifty…forty…. Intercept imminent….*"

He inhaled briefly. As the commander, he had the option to abort the mission now if anything appeared out-of-the-ordinary, anything that threatened to adversely affect the operational plan, or if he felt their mission had been in any way compromised. He saw the jeep's left turn signal blinking. He knew that he had to make the call now if the mission were to be a success.

"Roger all stations, this is Delta One...Go!"

With his execute order, two .50 caliber sniper bullets tore through the jeep's front tires and axle, causing it to skid in the gravel road and come to a complete stop. In an instant, the CH-47 catapulted over the hilltop, flared overhead, and hovered above the jeep. The wind generated by the rotor blades beat down on the ground, lifting up a tornado of dust and dirt below. Simultaneously, three long thick ropes fell to the ground from the rear and side doors of the helicopter. Men with helmets, dressed in black and armed with submachine guns emerged from each of the doors and slid down the ropes. Before they hit the ground, two black Land Rovers had positioned themselves in the front and back of the damaged jeep. When all of the SAS soldiers were on the ground, all three ropes were released from the CH-47, dropping to the ground in heaps.

A loudspeaker in the rear Land Rover screeched on as the massive helicopter flew off into another holding pattern, circling the raid site. The voice was deliberate and slow in unaccented Serbo-Croatian.

"Celo Mescic, you are surrounded by a NATO Special Operations team. We are authorized to use deadly force if you resist. If you are armed you must open the door of your vehicle and dispense with your weapons immediately by placing them on the ground. Do so now!"

The door to the jeep did not open.

"Roll down your window and place both hands outside, in full view. Do so now!"

A moment passed with no discernable movement from the jeep. The only sound was the CH-47 circling overhead. The stench of burnt rubber surrounded the jeep. Six SAS soldiers trained their HK MP-5 submachine guns on each door—some kneeling and others standing—surrounded the jeep in an inverted "L." Red laser dots danced around the sides of the vehicle and on the windows.

The driver's window rolled down, slowly. Two hands emerged from inside. Two soldiers approached carefully, their weapons at the ready. The voice came over the loudspeaker again.

"We will open your door and you will step out of the vehicle, your hands

exposed to us and visible at all times."

One of the soldiers opened the car door, and a man stepped out—shorter and leaner than they had expected, less imposing than the man whom they had profiled.

The patrol team leader was the first to realize the disparity...that something was not quite right about this man. It was confirmed when he spoke—in English...with a distinct Irish accent.

"Bloody Hell, Lads! Was all this necessary? A siren or warning light on one a yer' Hotspurs would've done the trick!" Mark Lyons looked around the scene, with his hands up, smiling broadly. "Are you boys from Two-Two?"

As the true identity of the driver's identity became clear, the team leader lowered his rifle to his side, and assumed a relaxed posture that indicated exasperation, even a tinge of professional embarrassment.

Mark waved his hands at the assault team. "Is Ian Rose here? Can ye tell 'im Mark Lyons would like a word with 'im?"

"Colonel Lyons?" The team leader asked in obvious disbelief.

Mark grinned again and nodded apologetically, his hands still up in the air.

The team leader turned away and spoke into the whisper-mike attached to his helmet.

"Delta One this is Alpha Three Zero, I'm afraid we've got the wrong man."

Rose paused. "Who is he?"

"Well, Sir, shall we say...a rather illustrious member of our own regiment."

He issued a curt order. "Hold him there."

THE TEAM LEADER turned to Mark. "The General will be here momentarily, Colonel Lyons." He extended his hand. "It's a privilege, Sir. I apologize for any inconvenience—a case of mistaken identity."

Mark shook his hand and slapped the young officer's shoulder. "Well, I fear that it was I who inconvenienced you lads."

A third black Land Rover raced toward them. A small crowd of local residents were forming at a farmhouse across the road. The Land Rover stopped short of where they were standing. Rose stepped out, dressed in a green patterned camouflage uniform, tan beret and a holstered pistol. His eyes squinted through dark aviator's sun glasses. As Rose approached, he glanced at Mark but made no effort to greet him. He only surveyed the scene around them.

"Ian, could I ask ye for a lift back to Sarajevo?" he asked, pointing to the disabled jeep beside them. It was covered with dirt, and was dug into the ground with its front tires shredded. "This was my only transportation, I'm afraid. It's my cousin's ye know…I was test drivin' it."

Rose still refused to look at him. His voice was subdued, but could not conceal his anger. "You switched vehicles with an indicted war criminal, and deliberately obstructed his capture."

Mark smiled calmly, feigning amusement. "Bollocks, Ian! If Celo Mescic was a war criminal, he was on the black list, wasn't he? It wasn't announced, and no effort was made on your part to coordinate with the EUPM prior to this fabulous ambush your lads have pulled off here—*we* are responsible for international justice. Not the SAS. I'm certain that if you wanted to arrest him, Celo would come in willingly. Would ye like me to arrange it?"

Rose was silent, but his jaw was clenched tightly. Ian Rose's impatience was his weakness, and he had exploited it fully. It had saved Celo from what likely would have been a violent exchange that would have resulted in his death, but he knew the long-term cost was the rekindling of a rivalry that was hostile when he'd left it.

"So, how 'bout that ride, back to Ilidza?"

Rose turned to the team leader. "Put him on the chopper and transport him to base."

He watched the team leader turn away from them, speaking into his whisper mike. Rose glared at him, and chewed on a stick of gum.

"I'm obliged for the ride, Ian," Mark said.

Rose's light green eyes betrayed his fury. "Stay out of my way, Lyons. This isn't a game."

He nodded as he looked up to see the CH-47 come to a hover above as it prepared to land in the field beside them.

"No," he said, turning to face Rose, all levity gone. "No, you're quite right. It isn't."

CHAPTER 33

MARK LYONS HEARD the knock on the door to his hotel room echoing through a fog of fatigue that had swept over him during the helicopter ride from Brnisi Dam to Ilidza Base. He looked at the digital clock on the bed stand beside him. It was 5:43 P.M. He still had his clothes on. The room was dimly lit through the drawn shades. The message light was blinking on the telephone, but he hadn't heard it ring.

The burst of adrenalin he'd experienced at the dam after subjecting himself to the receiving end of an SAS ambush sustained him for most of the flight to Sarajevo. It was the adrenalin that sharpened his senses acutely, and inoculated him against stress. In the most dangerous situations he encountered he would feel the world slow down around him, and his perspective and range of awareness took on a disembodied quality. He became aware of everything around him—as if he were watching a 3-D movie being shown in slow-motion. He was one of the actors—and in every case he was the only one moving at full speed. Somehow, it allowed him the opportunity to react an instant sooner than he would otherwise be able to respond. Whether it was instinct or an innate sixth sense, he didn't know, but he was certain it had saved his life on several occasions.

He experienced it all for the first time at Brnisi Dam more than three decades ago...the out-of-body perspective, and the kind of extrasensory awareness that came to him involuntarily. For a twelve-year-old boy, it made no sense to him. In fact, it frightened him—so he tried to repress it, along with the thoughts of his father, his uncle, Celo, the officer they'd killed on the hilltop, and the mass executions he'd witnessed at the dam. But the nightmares would not let him forget. They haunted him almost four decades later, and were joined by more recent memories so vivid, so intense that they often awoke him; and he would find his heart racing, lying in a pool of sweat.

He pulled himself off the bed. The knock on the door came again. He opened it to find John Thorpe standing in front of him, wearing the same clothes he had seen him in hours before at breakfast.

"I'm sorry if I woke you."

He shook his head and smiled as he opened the door. "I dozed off."

"You look like hell." Thorpe said, stepping inside the room.

"It's been a day...."

"I can come back."

"No, that's okay," he replied, opening the minibar refrigerator

Thorpe sat down at the table in the corner of the room. "I just got back from Ilidza. Ian Rose is on the warpath after picking up the wrong guy at Brnisi Dam. Know anything about that?"

He pulled out a Coca Cola from the minibar. "Something to drink?"

Thorpe shook his head. "No, thanks."

"Well, I think Ian may have significant psychological issues," he said, twisting the cap off. "He's completely unhinged."

"Be careful with him, Mark," Thorpe said. "He's the one with the guns and ammo now. Not you."

He nodded and drank from the bottle. "Hardly the basis for a peaceful occupation though."

Thorpe was silent for a moment and finally looked up at him. "I need your help."

He detected the sober urgency in his voice and sat down opposite him. "What is it?"

"It's hard to know where to begin," Thorpe commented, handing him a folder with two messages he'd received from Jim Goodwin via the White House Situation Room. "But this is start."

He saw the classification of "TOP SECRET— CODE WORD" on top, and understood the urgency. Documents like this were typically read in an approved facility—and the Holiday Inn, he knew, definitely did not qualify. John Thorpe wasn't one to take unnecessary risks, but he was clearly violating all of the established regulations and protocols since he did not have the formal security clearance that would allow him the access to view such a document.

He began to hand it back to him. "Are you sure—"

Thorpe nodded. "You're cleared."

He read through the first message on the subject of Ahmed Nazir and the stolen South African plutonium. The second message reported the disappearance of EX2 Robert Childs, the CIA Station Chief for the Balkans…missing for two days now, last seen at the U.S. Embassy in Zagreb. Of special significance, the message stated, Childs had been warning the Balkans Desk at the CIA Headquarters at Langley, Virginia of an ominous, but unspecified threat that was developing in Bosnia. A search of Childs' classified hard drive at the embassy in Zagreb revealed one document that he'd addressed to Ambassador Jack Fulbright the day prior to the ambush at Oborci.

"Do you have this document that's referenced here? The memo he wrote to Fulbright?"

Thorpe nodded and handed him another folder with the recovered memo. "If there's a smoking gun, this is maybe it."

He opened the folder and read Childs' memo to Fulbright regarding an ongoing Islamist effort to construct nuclear devices in Bosnia near Bocinja.

He looked up, half-way through. "Good Lord…."

Thorpe was silent as he continued to read.

"A nuclear threat against the Vatican! *Is this report reliable?*"

Thorpe shrugged. "We're investigating. If it is, it provides a viable motive for the attack on Ambassador Fulbright's convoy."

He stood up and walked over to his black nylon backpack. He took out the photos of the Oborci ambush and handed them to Thorpe.

Thorpe flipped through them. His surprise was evident. "Who took these?"

"You saw her this morning in the lobby. She works for the UN and happened to be there when it all occurred. We gave Ian Rose a copy of them, but he wasn't exactly appreciative."

"I knew it was an ambush," Thorpe said quietly. "Any ideas who did it?"

"I'm not sure, but whoever it was, they were very sophisticated to manage so many moving parts…the wounded horse deception, the daisy chain, the anti-tank munitions, the communications…some impressive capabilities. You know they had to rehearse it dozens of times for it to work."

Thorpe held up one of the photos. "This is Celo?"

He nodded. "I hadn't seen him in over three decades, John…since I escaped from this place."

"Three decades?"

He nodded slowly as he sipped his Coke. "I was meeting with him at Brnisi Dam to ask him what happened, when Ian's SAS team moved in to arrest him." He paused when he saw Thorpe's eyebrows raise. He could detect a faint smile on Thorpe's face. "They just missed him. It was a rather close-run thing."

Thorpe nodded and his slight grin betrayed his understanding. "I voted against that operation when I learned they were planning it, but some other folks here insisted." He pointed to the photos on the table. "Was Celo involved with this attack?"

He shook his head. "I don't think he was. He was in the wrong place at the right time. He says he was set up, and I believe him. When you consider it, it goes directly to the motive of who wanted to kill the ambassador."

"And the method…." Thorpe nodded. "Okay."

"John…," he said, reviewing the first message again. "This other business…the material from South Africa…do you think it's *here?*"

"There's a strong possibility. They found the pellets in Ravno with the girl who died there and they don't know that we discovered it. The rest of it's somewhere, and that's what I need your help with. It's the figurative needle in a haystack."

"No one's found this fellow, Childs?"

"No, not yet."

"All right then." He leaned back in his chair and looked at Thorpe. John Thorpe had a reputation as a soldier's general. He'd been wounded, nearly fatally in Afghanistan and in Somalia. His relationships with heads of state were well-known, and rivaled that of many ambassadors. He was greyer now than when Mark had first met him fifteen years ago at Hereford, England with his daughter, Annalisa. Thorpe was a Colonel then, commanding Special Forces Operational Detachment Delta, or simply "Delta Force."

Annalisa had been a student at Oxford, on a Rhodes Scholarship. While he was passing through England enroute to an exercise in Scotland, Thorpe had brought her along to Hereford for a private tour of the SAS facility that most civilians were never allowed to see. At the time, Mark was a lieutenant colonel commanding one of the SAS squadrons, and had been tasked to be their guide for the day. Although they did their best to hide it at the time, the attraction between he and Annalisa Thorpe was immediate, and also quite obvious to her father. He always wondered how it happened that their one-day trip was extended two additional days for "operational reasons" known only to the Delta Force and SAS Regimental Commanders. Within six months the two were engaged, and three months after that they were married in a chapel at Fort Bragg, North Carolina.

It was another, better time. Over the years, Thorpe had become one of his mentors. After Annalisa's death, he never had the opportunity to really talk to him about what had happened. He'd chosen to wait, knowing that he too was mourning her loss. The closest that they'd ever come to a meaningful discussion was in the hotel lobby that morning, but it was rushed and awkward, not at all the conversation he wanted.

"John, whatever I can do, you know I will."

Thorpe returned the classified document to the folder and placed it in the envelope. "Well, Mark, right now we're at the center of the universe."

"What can I do?"

"It's your good instincts we need. I have resources...troops, aircraft...anything that will assist."

"What military units...Muslim, Croat, Serb...are located near Oborci? Do we know?"

"No, not yet...but we're in the process of finding out."

There was a knock on the door. He stood up and walked over to open it.

Sandy Evenson stood in the doorway with her backpack. She had changed her clothes and was carrying a large purse. He felt a rush of relief to see her after making the switch between him and Celo. He smiled and greeted her warmly, inviting her inside, but she did not return the smile and when she spoke her tone was low and even.

"Aside from the fact that he's your cousin, *maybe* now you can explain why I aided and abetted a war criminal's escape from capture? And then *maybe* you can help me come up with a strategy to save my job as a prosecutor for the *War Crimes Tribunal*—"

In the midst of her diatribe, he opened the door all the way and invited her inside, where Thorpe was sitting, in the corner.

"Sandy Evenson—John Thorpe."

Thorpe stood and shook Sandy's hand.

Mark handed Sandy a bottle of Perrier from the minibar. Glancing down at the table, he saw that Thorpe had retrieved his notes and put them away.

Sandy sat down on the corner of the bed and saw the photos of the Oborci ambush stacked on the table. For a moment, there was an awkward silence.

"Sandy was gracious enough to give Celo a ride from Zvornik while I met with the boys from Hereford."

Sandy forced a smile, and drank the carbonated water as she glared at him. "It was an interesting ride...to say the least."

"I hope he was grateful for it?" he asked.

She smiled. "Well, he didn't point a gun at me this time, so I'd say our relationship is improving."

Mark nodded and returned the smile.

"He was a bit shocked that I spoke his language. I grilled him on his role in all of this all the way back into Zvornik, so he was more than ready to get out of the car. I figure if I can classify the encounter as an informal deposition, I just may be able to avoid being fired."

Thorpe was observing their exchange.

"He told me he was framed," he answered.

"That's what he told me too," Sandy said in a doubtful tone. "I know he's your cousin, Mark, but that's a pretty common response from a PIFWiC."

"You don't think he was set up?"

Sandy shrugged. "I don't know, but that's not my place to say one way or the other. He was the picture of indignance. It's difficult to distinguish between bravado and terror."

"Aye, well, that's always the trick," he commented, pitching his empty Coke can in the waste basket.

"What?"

"Striking a balance between the two...."

Sandy leaned back slightly and nodded in the direction of the photos on the bed before turning to Thorpe. "What do you think, General?"

"I think it took a lot of courage to do what you did." Thorpe's baritone voice and calm eyes exuded quiet authority.

"Well, I didn't have time to really think about it—I just don't understand why they're covering this up."

"My take is that they're in a Catch-22," Thorpe said. "If word gets out about an ambush, I think they're afraid they won't be able to contain the situation from Washington. So they've made the classic trade-off: secrecy for time. Your photos should force the issue."

Sandy nodded her understanding. "I'm famished...why don't we get some dinner?"

"What would you recommend?" Mark asked.

"Vinoteka is quite good. It's Italian—my friend Nermin owns it. It's across the river in the old town."

"Can you join us, General?" Sandy asked Thorpe.

Thorpe nodded as he stood up. "Yes, I'd be glad to, and please call me John."

He was relieved at Thorpe's willingness to have dinner with them, and yet he harbored some apprehension about the potential direction the conversation could take. "Let's meet in the lobby...say in twenty minutes?"

CHAPTER 34

SANDY EVENSON OPENED the door to her room finding an envelope on the floor with her name handwritten in neat cursive script. Inside the envelope, a handwritten note on a yellow sticky said simply: *"Sandy, this should answer your questions about our mutual friend. An article I wrote several years ago. -Kate"*

She unfolded the papers and found a faxed copy of a Time Magazine article with two photos on each side of the title:

Does Northern Ireland's Future Rest with These Two Men?
A Tale of Two Colonels
Kate Kamrath, Time Magazine (April 1, 2004)

Today, two men stand on parallel tracks of an undercover war against Northern Ireland's most deadly terrorists. One man is a policeman, the other a soldier. Their history is as intriguing, controversial and violent as the mayhem that has euphemistically become known throughout Ireland as "The Troubles."

Two of the most colorful figures in this history, Lieutenant Colonel Ian Rose and Superintendent Mark Lyons, nominally allies in this shadowy war, share an altogether separate history that, over time, has also made them archrivals. Two decades in the making, Lyons and Rose share a rivalry that is intensely private, but is nonetheless woven into the fabric of the ongoing covert war of police and SAS commandos in the most dangerous of wars.

The saga of the Lyons-Rose connection began in Hereford, England when Mark was assigned as the instructor-evaluator over then SAS Officer Candidate-in-Training, Lieutenant Ian Rose. After observing the student team Rose was leading target and attack the wrong house occupied by civilians, Lyons recommended that Rose be recycled through the course and retrained. Several SAS sources interviewed for this article say that Rose never forgave Lyons for what he viewed as a personal insult over a simple mistake.

Fifteen years later, on March 6, 2000, Major Ian Rose led Operation Oleander, a British SAS and MI5 operation that resulted in the public street side executions of three unarmed IRA operatives in London. Sanctioned by the Prime Minister himself, the operation set off a cascading chain reaction of violence in Belfast and a series of judicial inquiries that exposed another more extreme and little known dimension of the SAS—its mission to operate covertly, hunting down suspected terrorists, ambushing and killing them without warning and without the possibility of surrender.

Lieutenant Colonel Mark Lyons was commanding an SAS Squadron that was operating within Northern Ireland when the events in London transpired. After learning of the order to execute the IRA members, he urged the senior SAS leadership to reconsider the methods they were adopting as counter to the basic tenets of the Geneva Convention. Lyons' protests were ignored— he was told that the order had come from 10 Downing Street and was therefore irrevocable. Lyons' organization bore the brunt of the violence in Belfast sparked by Rose's operation in London. In all, the violence claimed eight lives, and several young men were imprisoned for life, falsely accused of murders they did not commit. Two weeks later, in a form of silent protest, Lyons resigned his command and departed the SAS for a position in the Royal Ulster Constabulary's Special Branch. Lyons relinquished command of his SAS squadron to a newly promoted Lieutenant Colonel Ian Rose.

Lyons' move, while not publicized, sent shockwaves through Britain's Special Air Service. He was alternatively seen as a hero and visionary by his men and a faithless opportunist by the SAS brass who Lyons had confronted with his decision to resign. The personal attacks on Lyons were relentless. A whisper campaign pointed to his Yugoslav heritage as a key indicator of his lack of loyalty to the United Kingdom. His critics were effectively silenced by a series of dramatic arrests and raids he planned and led. During the course of the several years, Mark Lyons' became something of a legend in the RUC's Special Branch.

In 2004, the Regional Major Investigations Team ("REMIT") was established as a replacement to the Special Branch. The Royal Ulster Constabulary was renamed the Police Service of Northern Ireland (PSNI). REMIT was placed under the command of newly promoted Detective Chief Superintendent Mark Lyons.

Lyons and Colonel Ian Rose were again fatefully drawn together when Lyons' wife, Annalisa, and an SAS undercover operative, Captain Harry Donovan, were taken hostage by a group of five IRA terrorists in a farmhouse on the outskirts of Belfast. In an open standoff with the police and SAS that lasted two days, the IRA demanded the release of ten IRA members held in Armagh Prison with life sentences. After the first imposed deadline passed with a refusal from the Ulster Government, the IRA executed Captain Donovan and dumped his body in front of the house. Another deadline of six hours was announced, with the IRA again demanding the release of its fellow members. At Mark Lyons' insistence and following intensive negotiations with the IRA, the gunmen agreed to exchange Annalisa Lyons for her husband. Lyons agreed to be hooded and bound prior to being delivered to the farmhouse in exchange for his wife's release.

Lyons accepted that by changing places with his wife, he would likely suffer the same fate as Captain Donovan. The IRA knew Lyons was a retired SAS Lieutenant Colonel and knew of his position within REMIT. The exchange was to be simultaneous. They were to be guided by a lone individual on either side. The exchange was to occur during the evening hours, at 9:00 P.M.

Mark Lyons was not kept fully informed of the plan, except that the possibility of the release of prisoners from Armagh was being "looked into." He was not informed that immediately after Captain Donovan's execution, the British and Irish Prime Ministers agreed upon a transfer of operational authority from the PSNI to the SAS, placing Colonel Ian Rose as the on-scene commander. Lyons had not been informed that an elaborate, secret planning process had already commenced in preparation for a full-scale raid on the farmhouse.

According to one source within the SAS, because Annalisa Lyons was the lone remaining hostage, Mark Lyons was judged by Colonel Rose to be "too emotionally invested" in the situation to be fully apprised of the SAS operation. Unknown to Lyons, the hostage exchange was planned to provide the needed deception for the SAS raid to occur successfully with minimal friendly casualties.

The uniformed PSNI officer walked Mark Lyons toward the farmhouse as a C-130 cargo plane filled with SAS commandos was flying high overhead, circling at 10,000 feet. In close succession, the team jumped off the C-130's ramp into the night sky.

Several steps into the walk Lyons sensed something was terribly wrong. Later he would attribute that feeling to the distinct fluttering sound of a HALO (High Altitude, Low Opening) parachute infiltration.

In a short, clipped conversation that ensued, Lyons learned that his escort was, in fact, the team leader of the SAS team overhead. Lyons protested vehemently, requesting an immediate "mission abort" in order to save his wife. The team leader, expecting Lyons' reaction, firmly denied his request and informed him that they had learned that the IRA gunmen intended to kill his wife *and* him during the hostage exchange, without regard to the agreement. At that moment, Lyons' handcuffs on his wrists were released and a Browning High Power 9mm pistol was slipped in his right hand with instructions to run to his wife on his orders. When the fluttering sound had stopped, Lyons knew that the team's canopies had opened.

As the team landed, a single shot rang out and Lyons' hood was removed. He saw his wife to his left front, also blindfolded, screaming his name. The IRA gunman who had been escorting her was at her feet in a heap. Lyons ran to her and saw the SAS team landing and surrounding the house, amidst a sustained barrage of gunfire. The team leader who had been his guide had been shot and lay motionless on the ground where he'd left him. Annalisa Lyons was shot a moment later by a sniper's bullet. Lyons picked her up and ran to a culvert for cover.

Annalisa Lyons died in her husband's arms. The SAS killed all six of the IRA members in the farmhouse, and despite the deaths of Captain Donovan and Annalisa Lyons, and the near fatal injury to the Team Leader, the operation was declared a success by Colonel Ian Rose, who eulogized the two hostages for their courage and praised the SAS team for their extraordinary skill in executing the daring mission. He made no mention of Mark Lyons in his remarks.

She dropped the papers to her lap. She could feel her heart pounding. Even after talking to Kate Kamrath the previous night, she had not heard the full account of how Lyons' wife had died. But this—it was too much information to process at once and only compounded her original impression that there was much more to Mark Lyons than met the eye.

She made her way to the bathroom, refreshed her lip-gloss and curled her eyelashes.

Why was he here?

As she read the rest of the article, she brushed her hair, and wiped away tears that had just begun to form.

> ...Mark Lyons took a week's leave to bury his wife on the Northern Ireland Coast. In the wake of the tragic incident, he refused to levy blame on either the PSNI or the SAS, placing responsibility instead solely on the IRA.
>
> Lyons' rise in the Police Service of Northern Ireland was meteoric. In a dramatic and controversial move, within a month of Annalisa Lyons' murder, the PSNI Chief Constable appointed Mark as Assistant Chief Constable for PSNI's Belfast Urban Region.
>
> After assuming his position as Assistant Chief Constable, however, Lyons extended this mission to apply equally to Protestant and Catholic paramilitary groups. Over the next several months, he launched a series of high profile raids on command and control headquarters belonging to the IRA and Orangemen in Belfast, who he claimed had transitioned from terrorism to organized crime.
>
> Lyons' defensive strategy has come under sharp criticism for its decidedly offensive methods. Electronic and human surveillance, infiltrating undercover agents, relentless raids and ambushes — often violently executed — have instilled fear in many quarters of Northern Ireland, but Lyons rebutted the criticism by insisting that "only terrorists and those who support them have anything to fear."
>
> Citing the imperative for "civilian control" and the preeminence of civil rights, Lyons announced his concern that Northern Ireland not be allowed to become a "police state" under any circumstance. At his urging behind the scenes, the British Army was forced to draw down its large scale presence from Northern Ireland, and maintain only a few small outposts.
>
> Lyons' tenuous balancing act was alternately applauded and condemned by civil rights activists, political leaders, and military officials alike. Colonel Ian Rose, the commander of the SAS contingent in Northern Ireland decried Lyons' methods by stating "at best, he is guilty of appeasement and cowardice. But at its

worst, it is obstructionism and open collaboration with terrorists." The new Assistant Chief Constable dismissed Rose's characterization and stated that he is aware that no one will be fully satisfied with the changes, but warned all parties in the coming days "not to confuse impartiality with neutrality."

Blending civil police reform with his extensive Special Operations experience, Lyons points to a system of intelligence and a kind of "predictive analysis" that he admits is "appealing and desirable in concept but difficult to achieve in execution."

There are, however, indicators that he has achieved just that, and in record time. Numerous IRA and Ulster Loyalist weapons shipments have been interdicted, and countless explosive stockpiles have been discovered and destroyed. As a result, the political leadership on both sides of the conflict hastily agreed to a general cease fire and the acceptance of conditions for peace negotiations. When asked about his role, Lyons' response is: "We set the conditions for peace; the parties themselves must do the work to achieve it."

She finished reading and looked up, realizing that she was in the elevator, going down to the lobby. It was a particularly slow descent. She folded the article and placed it in her purse. Exiting the elevator, she saw Mark standing near the concierge desk, talking to General Thorpe.

She approached both men, and watched Mark smiling as he listened to Thorpe. He had a serene quality about him that seemed to contradict what she had just read in Kate's article.

That explains a lot, she thought. Behind the calm façade, she had sensed his anguish and the linkages between Mark Lyons, General Rose and General Thorpe. Now, with a starkness she for which she was not fully prepared, she suddenly recognized the depth of these relationships and the history they shared.

She felt a deep sorrow for Mark, for what he had been through, and for General Thorpe—for the loss of his daughter. Understanding the tragedy they both shared, she suddenly felt like an intruder...and distinctly out of place. The urge to turn around and walk back to the elevator and return to her room was overwhelming. At that same moment, Mark looked over and smiled at her. It was a broad, quiet, warm smile that drew her toward him. Her impulse to flee dissipated.

It disappeared altogether when General Thorpe extended his hand to her, smiling. He gestured to the lobby entrance where a distinctly military-looking younger man was standing in wait. Through the glass doors she could see a SUV running outside.

"We'll take my Land Cruiser...my aide has agreed to drive."

CHAPTER 35

MARK SAT BESIDE Sandy opposite John Thorpe as they ate a combination dish of Italian antipasto. The walls of the restaurant were covered with frescoes of Europe's wine producing areas. They were greeted by Sandy's friend, Nermin, who was also the owner of the Vinoteka Restaurant. Sandy performed the introductions, and in short order a full array of dishes was served. These two people were managing to provide him with a measure of stability in all of the turbulence in the week since his return to Bosnia. With the influence of some good wine, he found himself more and more grateful for and comfortable in their presence.

Mark refilled Sandy's glass with the Cabernet.

She held the glass as he poured and immediately took a sip as he refilled his own glass. Thorpe was nursing a Czech-made Pilsner beer--his calm and humility belied the fact that he'd been handed an Executive Order from the President of the United States, and that he had the world's best Special Operations capabilities at his fingertips. In the years that Mark had known him, he'd never heard Thorpe raise his voice or curse. If there was anything in Thorpe at all that pointed to a penchant for violence, it was his deep hazel eyes that could focus intensely on the person to whom he was speaking. For someone with the build of an NFL linebacker, John Thorpe's reserved, comfortable manner endeared him both to the common soldier in the trenches and the most powerful politician or pundit.

Mark looked at Sandy Evenson and saw through her easy smile, how she leaned forward in her chair toward him, that she was not immune to Thorpe's frontier-style charm either. If he were not a Green Beret, Mark had often mused, John Thorpe would most likely be driving cattle at his family ranch in Montana.

Sandy's formidable knowledge of the Balkans challenged both men. She spoke eloquently on the root causes of the Ravno Crisis and related personal experiences that he would have otherwise attributed to a battle-weary soldier. He didn't know if it was the influence of the wine, or perhaps it was Thorpe's unique penchant to inspire confession, but Sandy had begun to reveal the compassion that drove her to spend two decades of her life in the Balkans when others had long ago left it behind.

Mark found himself at odds between what he now recognized was a strong visceral attraction to Sandy Evenson, and what was advisable or prudent, given their roles—his as investigator and hers as witness. John Thorpe's presence reminded him of Annalisa. Even after the years since she died, and he knew he'd still not fully recovered. She was a constant presence, even now. His sudden attraction for Sandy Evenson was tinged with guilt, made more acute by having his former father-in-law at the table.

It had begun to drizzle outside, and Thorpe was telling Sandy about the herd of buffalo he kept on his ranch in Montana, and his plans to expand it when he retired. At her prodding as to when that would happen, he responded, "soon."

Seemingly on cue, Mark leaned forward and spoke in the most serious, intellectual tone he could muster. "*Completely* inadvisable, John!"

"Excuse me?"

"It would be doomed to failure from the start...simply doomed." He shook his head and sipped his Cabernet to prevent himself from smiling. "*Especially* in the State of Montana!"

Thorpe rolled his eyes slightly.

Sandy leaned back in her chair with her eyebrows raised. "It seems perfectly fine to me!"

Mark shook his head again, exchanging a wide, complicitous grin with Thorpe. "Nay, let me explain," He continued in a much more exaggerated, extended, didactic lilt. "Because, ye see, real men, well...," he explained in an apologetic tone, "...they raise sheep."

Inadvertently, the comment had caught Sandy in the midst of a full sip of Cabernet. She struggled to place the glass back on the table without spilling it, and holding her free hand to her lips as she stifled a laugh.

"In Ireland, it is true that the sheep has always been man's best friend," Thorpe responded matter-of-factly.

"In fact, they are friendlier than the dog or buffalo," he retorted indignantly, raising a finger.

"So I've heard," Thorpe answered dryly.

"Stop it!" Sandy pleaded loudly, hands aloft in a gesture of surrender, still struggling to keep the wine down.

Nermin approached their table with another plate of food. "Gnocchi!"

"Dare I ask?" Mark said, smiling.

"Very, very good," Nermin announced. "It is homemade and it is prepared with a white wine crème sauce. It is our specialty. You'll see. You will love it!"

"I'm sure we will," Sandy said, smiling.

As Nermin placed the platter on the table, Sandy's cell phone rang. She reached inside her purse and answered it. After a moment, Mark heard her response.

"Jon? Wait...wait...I can't hear you. Let me step outside." As she stood to go outside, he could see her expression begin to change.

Thorpe turned to Mark, concerned. "Who's Jon?"

"Jon Schauer...in Zagreb, I think," Mark said. "He was the one who printed the Oborci photos for us."

Detecting the possibility of bad news, neither man served themselves the food in front of them. Sandy had disappeared out the door into the restaurant's foyer. She returned to the table, holding her cell phone to her side. She was wet from the rain outside. From the blank, stricken expression on her face, he realized that something was terribly wrong. Something had happened. Both Mark and Thorpe stood. Mark reached out to steady her, but she shook her head absently.

"Sandy?" he urged, holding her shoulders, gently but insistently. *"What is it?"*

She did not answer. She was shaking her head in disbelief, her eyes fixed on the ground. She brought her arms up to her chest and finally allowed herself to be held.

"Sandy!" he said, over and over. *"What is it?"*

Her hair was wet and he could smell the faint scent of her perfume. Mark repeated his plea to her, and felt her body shake.

"They found her in her apartment...in Zagreb...."

"Who Sandy," Mark asked again.

Finally, her eyes finally connected with his. She had gone pale and her words mingled with shock and disbelief. "Kate...Kate's dead...."

He pulled her face into his shoulder, and could feel the heat of her body and beat of her heart, pounding furiously. Suddenly, the meaning of her words sunk in and for a moment, everything went still.

CHAPTER 36

MARK LYONS OFFERED to bring Sandy Evenson back to the Holiday Inn, but she'd shaken her head insistently and told him in no uncertain terms that she wanted to get up to Zagreb without delay.

The shock in learning of Kate Kamrath's murder had still not worn off by the time he arrived at the Sarajevo airport with Sandy. Mike McCallister and Vladimir were waiting for them with the rotors of the giant white helicopter turning.

He felt an awful, familiar sensation of helplessness. He realized there was little he could say or do to ease her pain. Since their first encounter at Ilidza Base, he sensed that she and Kate were friends, but even then, he was not sure how close they were. Until now.

The helicopter lifted off the ground from the UN compound in Sarajevo. The lights of Sarajevo flashed through the windows as the helicopter banked to the northeast around a snow-covered Mount Igman enshrouded in clouds. The flight to Zagreb would take about an hour.

He closed his eyes. The whine of the helicopter's turbines and the steady deep vibration of the whirling rotors had a sleep-inducing effect on him. But the images and voices that came to him now were haunting.

Kate Kamrath.

When she was reporting on the Troubles in Northern Ireland, he'd gotten to know her well professionally and he respected her reporting. At the time, she struck him as fearless—and he remembered how that impression alone concerned him. In her drive to finish a story, she often ignored her own safety—and his warnings. He had seen her confront the most hardened IRA leaders and Orangemen on their own turf, and she had borne the brunt of their resentment on numerous occasions—having been run off roads at high speed, having her flat in Belfast ransacked and receiving numerous death threats in the wake of her published stories.

Through the publicity she had created around him, Kate had also played a role—albeit indirect—in his transfer out of the Special Branch to the Balkans. Of all the news reports about him Kate's were the only truly accurate accounts of his counter-terror campaign in Northern Ireland.

Kate Kamrath had sources that were deeply embedded on all sides of the Troubles—there were many occasions when it seemed she had her own vast intelligence network at her fingertips. She had a way of turning up at the scene of the bloodiest raids and ambushes—well prior to the police, who were also sometimes the targets. Precisely because of that tendency, there were those in the Police Service who sought her arrest for collaboration with the terrorists. But he always admired her for her tenacity and professionalism. She had first asked him for an interview—not to exceed an hour and he countered by inviting her to stay with him for a week to shadow him. Coincidentally, it had been the week that his wife had been held hostage and killed by the IRA. Kate's stories had vaulted him through the ranks of the RUC, making him legendary throughout Ireland and Great Britain as a police enforcer—a status he'd sought to avoid.

He awoke as the helicopter began its descent. Sandy had fallen asleep during the flight too. One of her hands held his forearm. She stirred, and as she awoke, she gripped his arm to lift herself upright. They both looked at one another in the red light that dimly illuminated the cabin, and he could see her attempt to smile as she rearranged her hair.

When the helicopter touched ground, the side door slid open and Jon Schauer stood with his hair blowing under the turning rotors. He helped Sandy off the helicopter's aluminum platform. Mark followed them toward Schauer's car parked on the tarmac with his hazard lights flashing. Suddenly, McCallister appeared rushing toward them with the two carry-on bags that both he and Sandy had hurriedly packed at the Holiday Inn.

"Don't forget these, Commissioner!" McCallister shouted over the whine of the helicopter's engine.

He slapped McCallister on the shoulder and squeezed with an appreciative, yet sober smile.

"Don't mention it," McCallister shouted. "Let me know what we can do to assist. She's been through a lot, I reckon."

He nodded. "I'll call you tomorrow."

"Aye! We'll be here!"

Mark threw the bags into the backseat and sat down beside them. Schauer pulled away from the tarmac, passing a guard as they drove through the gate. He looked at Sandy sitting beside him. Her eyes were already closed and her head was leaned back on the seat's headrest. Schauer had glanced over at her with a silence that conveyed both empathy and an understanding derived from what he knew to be a longstanding friendship. The trip to Schauer's apartment was a blur. He felt his personal sense of direction, too, growing confused in the course of events—he nodded off as they drove the rest of the way through the Zagreb city center in silence.

PART III

INVESTIGATION

CHAPTER 37

THE RAIN POUNDED heavily against the BMW's windshield. In any other conditions, Captain Dan Irons enjoyed driving on Germany's autobahns—they were well-built and *fast*. He'd spent the last week on leave, skiing in Zermatt, Switzerland, and wasn't too concerned that he had to be back at work at his unit—an air cavalry squadron just outside Frankfurt—early the next morning.

He had departed Zermatt well after peak hours to avoid the heavy traffic, calculating an eight hour drive that would put him back home by 4 a.m., perhaps 5:00 with the poor weather. Just after the Baden-Baden exit, large red and yellow neon signs indicated construction ahead. He slowed to 40 mph.

A large Mercedes sped past him in the left lane, spraying his windshield, and Irons knew it was traveling too fast—too fast for the road conditions and entirely too fast for the construction ahead, where the road narrowed and curved.

He swore to himself as the rear of the Mercedes began to swerve, slightly at first, and then more dramatically, until it hydroplaned out of control into the flashing barriers and the parked road machinery. It hit a bulldozer first, causing the Mercedes to spin and then flip wildly in the air, landing in a pool of sparks, shattered glass and torn metal. Somehow it had landed back on its wheels. The scattered flashing yellow and orange lights illuminated the smoking wreckage in spasms, like a defective strobe light low on power.

His heart was pounding. He pulled over on the shoulder of the road behind the construction, and ran to the Mercedes lying in a broken heap adjacent to a large, unhitched trailer. Its roof was dented severely, but remarkably had not collapsed. He attempted to open the driver's door, but it was jammed shut. Inside, the driver's head was against the window. He was an elderly man, with a dark complexion characteristic of an Indian, Bangladeshi or Pakistani... middle-aged he thought. He was badly cut and covered with shattered glass.

He ran to the passenger door and managed to open it nearly half-way. He squeezed himself into a kneeling position on the passenger seat. The man still had his glasses on, and one lens was cracked. He removed them from his head and noticed that he was bleeding heavily from a large cut to his forehead. His hands were splintered with glass. When his eyes blinked, Irons sure that he was still alive.

"Are you okay?" Irons asked in English, then switching to German—at once realizing the absurdity of the question.

The man's head slowly turned to face him, and Irons could see that most of his facial bones were broken. The left side of his head was severely lacerated and bleeding. Somehow, the airbag had not deployed.

"You are American?" The man asked in a rasping, heavily accented English.

He was struck by the man's response—with no apparent concern for his injuries, but instead, *"Are you American?"*

"Yeah, I'm an American, and you're a goddamned mess."

"I cannot breathe…."

Irons pushed the release on his seatbelt and started to pull it carefully away from his body. Before he was able to finish, the man interrupted him in a hoarse, barely audible voice.

"Do not worry about that…please…do you see a case in the back seat?"

He looked behind the seat and found an aluminum briefcase covered with glass, with a large dent on one side of it.

"Yeah, it's back there."

"Take it, bring it to your President…," The man's voice was now a guttural barely audible whisper. "…They will kill everyone." He knew that the man needed help soon or he would die.

"Yeah, okay, fine, we've got to get you to a hospital though."

"No!" The man's bloodied hand was now gripping Irons' shirt, already drenched from the rain outside. His eyes conveyed an intensity he'd never before seen. His voice was hoarser still, but as close to a desperate shout as he could muster. "Take the case and go, give it to your President…before it is too late…before they kill you too."

Realizing that he was staring at the man in disbelief, he reached for the briefcase and pulled it out of the back seat, wondering what could be so damn important about it.

"Take it and go," the man said, releasing his grip on Iron's arm.

Through the broken rear windshield, he could see the dim outline of people approaching the wreckage in the rain, like ghostly visages. His own car parked only twenty yards away, its hazard lights blinking methodically.

He swore in resignation, admitting that his better judgment had been compromised. He squeezed himself out of the Mercedes, briefcase in hand. Running across the field of broken glass back to his car, Irons opened the trunk and threw the briefcase inside. He was reaching for his first aid kit when he looked up to see the flashing lights of a Police van approaching.

Suddenly, he was awash in floodlights. Orders he could not fully understand were being broadcast in German. The Polizei stepped out of their van wearing white and yellow raincoats. One walked to the group of people assembled a distance from the wreckage, urging them back into their cars and to move on. The other was walking toward the accident site when a German lady pointed at Irons, shouting. The policeman diverted in Irons' direction, away from the wreckage.

"Were you involved in this accident?" the policeman asked in German.

Irons shook his head and responded in English. "No, I saw it happen and I tried to help. No one else was involved...there's a man inside, he's badly injured and needs a doctor now," he explained urgently.

The policeman switched to accented English. "Has anyone been close to the car?" He asked, pointing at the battered Mercedes.

He shook his head, not comprehending the intent behind the question. "No, only me."

"May I see your identification, please?"

He felt his frustration building. *Where was this leading?* He pulled out his wallet and handed his military ID card to the policeman who studied it under a flashlight and made several annotations with a grease pencil on a whiteboard without comment. He handed the ID card back. "You are an American soldier?"

He nodded, but his frustration was emerging. "Yes...I am. Look, the man in that car is dying! Do you understand?"

"*Ja*, I understand you," the policeman replied in a tired, routine tone. "An ambulance is coming." He pointed his flashlight at the license plates of Irons' BMW. "This is your car?"

"Yes," he answered, suddenly realizing that in his haste he'd forgotten to close the trunk. He caught the dull glint of the metallic briefcase lying against the spare tire where he'd left it. Irons felt sure that the policeman would check the open trunk next.

Irons tossed the first aid kit into the trunk and closed it.

The policeman stepped back. "Captain Irons, you may go now. We will care for the victim." The dismissal was not an invitation. It was a directive.

He was relieved, yet distressed at the policeman's apparent indifference. He got back into his car and drove off slowly, still glancing at the wreck in his rearview mirror. The lights of an ambulance were approaching in the distance. When he could see it no more, he looked at the clock. It was 1:15 A.M.

The rain had begun to subside, but a thick shroud of fog had replaced it.

CHAPTER 38

THE TINY ISLET of Vanga sits off of Croatia's Istrian Peninsula on the Adriatic. Part of the Brijuni Archipelago, Vanga is so isolated that most Croatians are not aware of its existence. While he was in power, Tito constructed three palaces on the larger of the Brijuni Islands, Veli Brijun or "White House." One of them—Bijela Vila—became widely known as the place Tito greeted foreign visitors whom he sought to impress. The island of Vanga was where he sought seclusion. Covered with Pine trees, wildflower meadows and beaches, Tito saw the island for what it was—a natural refuge from Zagreb, only a thirty minute flight away. He built a one story villa on Vanga, along with an airstrip to land his airplane. The island became his permanent summer retreat. Decades after Tito's death, despite sustained efforts to open it up for tourism, the public is still not allowed on the "Outside Island," as it is called today. Croatian Border Police continue to guard the island from hikers, wildlife photographers and other assorted would-be trespassers.

A rough asphalt road from the villa's driveway winds through an isolated wood of pine trees to a hidden red stone monastery run by the small cloister of Franciscans—the only authorized permanent inhabitants of Vanga. The church, also constructed as an annex of red stone with a rectangular stone bell tower, dominates the monastery. The road ends in a cul-de-sac in front of the church.

The black Ford SUV parked in front of the church kept in the hangar at the airfield. It had picked up the occupants of the military C-130 cargo plane a week ago, and delivered them to the villa. Each of the men had short, closely cropped haircuts and were dressed in military fatigues with a tiger stripe camouflage pattern. Their gear had been transloaded to a waiting truck that followed them to the villa. In the coming days, explosions and the sound of gunfire would occasionally be heard on the opposite side of the island. The men would return from training to the villa late at night.

One week later, Sunday, the fifteen uniformed men knelt in the front pews of the church in uniform, their heads bowed and faces blackened. After a short wait, Archbishop "Papa" Voyo entered the church quietly and slowly walked to the altar. Each of the soldiers turned his gaze toward Voyo. The scene reminded him of a medieval painting. Tinted blue and orange light from the stained glass windows illuminated the spot where he stood. He wore a black cassock with a gold pectoral cross. An oversize purple sash surrounded his waist. Voyo's long, narrow face—concave on its side—was expressionless as he walked down to them. He silently looked into each soldier's eyes before he delivered his benediction to them in their native Croatian. He spoke slowly, but loudly in deliberate, reverent tones—his voice resonating against the walls of the church.

"Centurions! Yours is a mission from God! Like the Archangel Michael with his interventionary sword, your sacred mission is to protect the rest of us from those who wish us harm and who seek to stand in front of Saint Paul's vision of the only true Roman Catholic Apostolic Church. Each of you has been hand-selected to be the guardians of our nation and for our church on behalf of the Holy Father. In the history of our church, there have always been warriors who serve in the shadows without fear or regard for their own mortal lives. In the history of Croatia...in the history of the South Slavs, our people have been the defenders of our faith. You are the direct descendents of the Knights Templar. As such, your mission is crucial to our collective survival.

Centurions! The day of honour you have tirelessly trained and waited for has arrived. You will step into the fires of hell to release us from the scourge of the Anti-Christ. As he roams this earth and seeks to destroy us, we will deliver final retribution."

He looked around and stared at each soldier intently with his deep, sunken eyes. They were young...late twenties to early thirties. Each of their jaw lines was sharp and defined. They were world-class athletes and marksmen, chosen for their piety as much as their courage—all trained to kill as a member of a team or alone, as a singleton operative. Each of them gazed at Voyo with a calmness that conveyed confidence, but clearly too, admiration for their archbishop who had personally selected them. They were aware of him only by reputation and the undercurrent of rumors that ran throughout The Legion...the *"Gabriel Team"*—in which they now served.

He grasped a palm branch, dipped it in holy water and scattered the water onto them. They, in turn, crossed themselves as he continued to speak.

"I have served in your ranks, Centurions. As your Grand Master, I am proud to see in you a new generation of legionnaires who, like us before you, are prepared to martyr themselves for the most noble and holy of causes."

He began to raise his voice, speaking with increased fervency. *"In this effort to defend us from our enemies, you cannot fail. Our enemies do not share our God. They seek our annihilation. You are the Legion of the Archangels Gabriel and Michael. They dwell in you! On this day—as you prepare to face our enemies in battle, I induct each of you into the Order of our Cardinal Saint Alojzije Stepinac."*

He walked back to the altar and returned to them holding a rectangular box covered with a violet silk sash. He placed it on the stand in front of the pew, and held each end with both of his hands.

"The honor of being a member of The Legion is manifest. Your induction into the Order of our nation's most holy servant accompanies that honor. It is a responsibility you inherit from the Knights who have gone before you."

He removed the sash to reveal a deep mahogany box that was hinged on one side. He opened the box. A white satin cloth covered its contents. He folded the cloth back partially and pulled two items from the box, grasping each in a separate hand. He held them up, as if in sacrifice.

"To each of you, Centurions, a rosary, blessed by the Blessed Virgin herself in Medjugorje, and a relic from the mortal remains of Cardinal Stepinac, bestowed upon you to safeguard you and to guide you when you face of the Satan."

Papa Voyo walked to each soldier kneeling before him in the pew, and performed a blessing by holding their head in his left hand and crossing them with his right, which bore the emblem of his ecclesiastical rank, a large ring with a deep red ruby stone. At the conclusion of each blessing, each man dutifully opened his hand to the cardinal, who took a shiny platinum knife and sliced the meaty part of their right palms, at the base of their thumbs. As the blood flowed freely from each wound, he placed and closed their hands around a rosary made of lapis lazuli and a tiny silk sack containing a relic from the remains of Cardinal Alojzije Stepinac.

CHAPTER 39

GENERAL JOHN THORPE walked up the short flight of steps and pressed the intercom button next to the door of the *Bundeskriminalamt*, or BKA, Headquarters.

Germany's *Bundeskriminalamt*—or literally translated, "Federal Criminal Division"—is the equivalent of the FBI in the United States or Great Britain's Scotland Yard. It is situated on Thaer Strasse 11, a dead-end street in an isolated residential district of Wiesbaden. The building is yellow painted stucco with a series of long oblong windows bordered in white. At every angle, there is a camera emplaced to observe those who approach and depart. Barbed wire fences surround the entire building except the entrance. He had the distinct feeling he was entering an office complex that had been transformed into a makeshift fortress.

He had received a late night call from Jim Goodwin to inform him of an incident involving a "person of interest" that was directly linked to the situation in Bosnia. After extensive coordination between the CIA and FBI, further details were to be provided by BKA Deputy Director Heinz Lohman. Thorpe made it into Heidelberg two hours later by jet. He was met by his Aide de Camp with the keys to a BMW 750i with the address to the BKA Headquarters in Wiesbaden already programmed into the car's GPS system.

The lock was released with a quiet buzz, allowing him to step inside. He announced himself and handed his military identification card to the security guard, who compared it to a list that was fastened nearby on a clipboard.

"Do you have a sidearm, General?" The guard asked.

He shook his head, somewhat surprised at the question. "No. No, I don't."

"Please have a seat in the waiting room, Herr Lohman will be down momentarily," the guard said.

He turned and entered the waiting room to his right. He sat down in one of the cushioned chairs and picked up the "Frankfurter Algemaine" newspaper on the table in front of him. The lead story on the front page concerned the Ravno Crisis and the NATO preparations for air strikes. His German was fair, but not sufficient to decipher the entire story. He heard a door open in front of him and looked up to see a man of modest height and a heavy, powerful build enter the waiting room. He recognized him from the photo he had seen at the entrance as Heinz Lohman, Deputy Director of the BKA. His hand was extended.

"General Thorpe? I am Lohman. I have heard much about you." Thorpe stood immediately to return his handshake. Lohman was dressed in dark wool pants, a white shirt with rolled up sleeves and red suspenders. His head was bald, but he had a thick moustache that nearly covered his upper lip. He estimated him to be in his early fifties, and in remarkably good shape. His English was also superb.

He put the newspaper down and was led through a metal detector. He answered Lohman's inquiries about the comfort of his flight from Sarajevo. This lead to a light-hearted rib about the advantages of flying Lufthansa over the American flag carriers. He responded that *his* American flag carrier was a U.S. Air Force jet. Lohman laughed and nodded.

They walked down a hallway and turned into Lohman's office. It was comfortable enough and large; but he noticed that aesthetics had taken a back seat to function. A large, distinctive secure voice encrypted telephone sat on the corner of his desk. The walls were filled with red hard-bound files. Lohman beckoned him to the oak table at the center of the office, sitting down opposite him, pipe in hand. He lit it and took in several puffs.

"General, last night, there was an accident on the Autobahn near Baden Baden. Only one car...it went out of control in the rain, and killed the passenger. These things happen quite frequently, you know, but it was the identity of the passenger that was so interesting to us." Lohman opened the hardbound folder in front of him. "We did not know he was here or we would have detained him." Lohman pushed the folder across the table to him. "His name is Dr. Ahmed Nazir, also well-known as the Stepfather of Pakistan's Nuclear Program. He's an unsung hero in Pakistan who has lived in the shadow of A.Q. Khan."

He knew the name A.Q. Khan well. He was the public face of Pakistan's nuclear program and since internationally reviled for selling secrets to other third world dictatorships like Iran and North Korea—but he had not heard of Nazir. He studied the file photo of Nazir. He was an older man, probably in his seventies, with grey hair and a dark moustache. In the photo, he was wearing medals that were awarded to him by the government of Pakistan. Another photo on the opposite end of the file showed an accident photo of Ahmed Nazir—his lifeless face severely lacerated and bruised.

"Why was he in Germany?" Thorpe asked.

"He has been importing nuclear technology for years. It is our guess that he came to purchase equipment components from European manufacturers."

"What components?"

Lohman shrugged. "Vacuums, Zirconium rods, titanium heat exchange tubes...many things."

He continued to read the dossier on Nazir. Turning to the photo of the wrecked car, he looked up at Lohman. "May I ask, Herr Lohman...what did you find in his car?"

Lohman shook his head. "His luggage...clothes...nothing of significance. His passport was in his pocket, and he had an airplane ticket from Sarajevo through Vienna to Zurich, with a return ticket to Islamabad through Damascus. But it is the fact that he was here, without our knowledge that worries us. We are investigating now."

"Was the car a rental?"

"Purchased with cash at a dealership in Zurich. And we are still looking for where he was staying. General, you should know that this is a worrisome situation for us...."

Thorpe nodded his acknowledgment, handing the folder back to Lohman. "And for the United States as well, Herr Lohman. It's why I'm here."

"I will keep you informed, and I would most appreciate it if you would do the same for us."

He nodded and extended his hand to Lohman. "Of course."

As they stood, Lohman walked over to his desk and returned with another red folder. "That's the file we have on Dr. Nazir, translated to English. It is your copy." Lohman paused and then transcribed a note on a 3x5 card that he pulled from his shirt pocket. "General, there may be something you can do." Lohman handed the card to him. "This is one of the witnesses to the accident—the first to arrive at the scene. He's an American soldier in Hanau...an Army Captain, I believe. Our police dismissed him, but maybe he saw something?"

Thorpe took the card from Lohman and promised that he would talk to the Captain. Ahmed Nazir's appearance in Germany, or anywhere in Europe for that matter, was troubling—more troubling given the intelligence report on Nazir that Jim Goodwin had given to him. He read the name on the card with Lohman's handwriting:

Captain Daniel Irons,
1st Squadron, 1st Cavalry Regiment
Armstrong Kaserne
Buedingen

CHAPTER 40

MARK LYONS and Sandy Evenson stood in the door of Kate Kamrath's downtown Zagreb apartment. The Zagreb detective escorting them stood aside after opening the door. It stank faintly of vomit, used kitty litter, and fear.

Mark stood for a moment, assessing. In his debrief the detective had informed them that Kate was found in her bed and had died of a massive coronary, likely while she was sleeping. The coroner had set the time of death at approximately 2:30 A.M. He'd seen the post mortem photos of Kate in the folder. She appeared peaceful and serene, face up—as if she were asleep.

Kate's apartment was small, yet comfortable. He scribbled the layout in a notebook, noting the location of the guest bathroom, combined guest bedroom and office, living room with a kitchenette, master bedroom. The furniture was contemporary rosewood, and the rooms were decorated with ornate red and black oriental rugs from Southeast and Southwest Asia.

Sandy raised the blinds in the living room to allow more light in.

"Have you been here before?"

Sandy nodded. "Many times."

"Is it as you remembered?"

"She switched the position of the sofa and the chair, since I was last here, but beyond that no change. She was always rearranging things like that."

Sandy turned around toward the guest bathroom. She walked into the bathroom and checked inside the shower and returned to the living room. "The cat...."

"Pardon me?" he asked, surprised.

Sandy shook her head. "She had a cat." She turned to the detective. "Where's the cat?"

The detective shrugged his shoulders dismissively. "We found no cat."

Sandy looked back at Mark with a remarkable intensity, and walked back into the bathroom. She pointed at the box with cat litter. "You see! She had a cat...a male Siamese...his name is Buster."

"You're sure he's not hiding around the apartment?"

As they searched through the apartment, looking for the cat, he could see no sign of a struggle or any overt signs that her apartment was searched.

Inside the living room, he saw the framed photo of Kate and him at the RUC Headquarters in Belfast among a line of others on the windowsill. He picked it up, remembering the time he'd spent with her, just days before Annalisa was murdered. Sandy picked up the photo as he walked away toward the master bedroom.

"Is this you?"

He nodded. "'Tis. I was surprised to see it."

"I haven't seen it before—were you close?" Sandy asked.

"Not close, but I think we shared a mutual respect for one another. She was quite a journalist. Not afraid to take risks, or extend herself."

Kate Kamrath's bedroom was cramped. He continued to sketch its layout. In its entry way, there was a small bathroom immediately to the right, and a closet to the left. The bathroom carried the astringent reek of Pine-Sol. An iron frame queen-size bed with a red oak dresser dominated the room. A small flat screen television and a single white fabric chair were positioned in the corner. Metal and glass nightstands were situated on both sides of the bed with the usual accoutrements: alarm clock, lamps, TV remote, books. The nightstand with the alarm clock had a tea pot with remnants of used tea leaves, and a pack of Tums.

The bed was not made—left in the same state that it had been found. Kate's black and grey striped comforter was folded back somewhat neatly. A long, rectangular pillow sat on top of it. He stepped back to survey the scene. After several minutes, he turned to the policeman and pointed to the lamp on the nightstand. "Was it turned on when you found her body?"

The policeman shook his head. "No, it was off. All the lights were off."

He opened the police folder with the photos of the scene when Kate had been found. There was no evidence of blood on the bed. Further studying the photos, in one of them he noticed the dull outline of an object in the shadows under the bed. He knelt and found an open book on its face, with several pages folded indiscriminately. He picked it up with both hands and turned to its cover. The title of the book was "Vatican Resistance." The subtitle read "How the Vatican Waged War against Nazism and Communism." The author was listed as *Brother Nicola Milesevic, Minister Provincial Dubrovnik.*

The top edge of the book was stained a light brown in spots. Still kneeling, he handed the book to the policeman.

"I can't find the cat in here," he called out to Sandy in the other room. He ran his hand along the rug below the end table and found shards of glass stuck into it.

He reached up to turn on the lamp but it failed to light. He unscrewed the bulb and shook it, and heard the loose filament rattle. The policeman handed him his flashlight and he noticed the cord for the telephone was disconnected. Looking down at the rug, he found remnants of dried wax at the base of the bed post…and at the base of the other posts as well.

He scraped up samples of the wax and put them in a loose envelop.

He straightened, returned the flashlight to the policeman, and walked out to the living room. Sandy was on her knees looking under the sofa for the cat.

"No sign of him," she said, standing up. "I don't know where he could be."

He walked into the kitchen area. The telephone against the wall was also disconnected. He opened the refrigerator door and searched inside, finding a half-full bottle of wine. He opened the chrome trash can and searched through its contents. After a moment, he gingerly pulled out the aluminum cork wrapping for the wine bottle and sniffed it, carefully…delicately. In a drawer, he found several Ziploc bags and placed the aluminum wrapping inside, along with the shards of china from the rug and the crushed tea leaves left over in the tea pot.

The policeman looked on incredulously, but in silence. Mark cast him an occasional thoughtful glance, raising his eyebrows, and knocking on the kitchen counter while he collected his thoughts. After a moment, he took the book from the policeman and placed it beside the Ziploc bag.

He found Sandy sitting on the daybed in Kate's combined guest bedroom and study. It was the only room that was slightly in disarray, but what one would expect of a reporter's study he thought…a glass and metal table with a laptop computer positioned between stacks of newspapers and reporters notebooks. The laptop was plugged into an outlet underneath the table. Multiple bookshelves surrounded a daybed against the wall. She had a bulging maroon fabric bag at her feet.

"What's in the bag?" Mark asked.

"Just stuff," she shrugged, pulling out the contents onto the daybed: a notebook, several magazines, a series of stapled pages from a variety of internet sites, and a Yoga instructional manual. The magazines and internet articles were all fitness and nutrition related. He pointed to the notebook, and Sandy handed it to him. It was like the others stacked on the table, but had the previous week's date hand-written on the cover. He flipped through the notebook and found only several pages written on...the text was mostly illegible, written in a pseudo-kind of shorthand that he could not decipher-- abbreviations, arrows and circled text, interspersed with some long-hand cursive that annotated locations and names...names of people she had spoken to, a few telephone numbers and addresses.

It was these names, written in Kate's script, which quickly caught his attention:

> *Bob Childs*
> *Renee C.*
> *A. Stepinac*
> *V. Pijadje*
> *St. Stephen's*
> *Medjugorje*

There were several telephone numbers...and at the very bottom on the final page, the marginal note: *"Opus Dei?"*

"What do you make of this?" he asked Sandy, pointing at the page.

Sandy studied Kate's annotations. "She was investigating Bob Childs' disappearance."

"Whose?"

"He was the CIA Station Chief for the Balkan Region, based here in Zagreb—a good friend. Renee is his wife. I know her," Sandy explained. "Kate told me he was reported missing, but I figured he was off on CIA business or something else double-secret. He never told me where he goes until after he comes back."

Mark nodded. "I remember. John Thorpe mentioned the situation to me yesterday afternoon."

She sat down and her eyes widened in a silent plea. After a moment her voice seemed to crack. "What's happening, Mark? My friends are dying or disappearing. I feel like I'm under siege...."

"I'd say it's well beyond the realm of coincidence," he answered, his tone serious. "Sandy," he said finally, then pausing again. "I'm not at all convinced Kate died of natural causes."

"That makes two of us, then," Sandy answered. She was standing near the enclosed bookshelf in the study, staring at the displayed photos of Kate with her family and friends, to include one of her with Sandy and Jon Schauer—laughing arm-in-arm at a water fountain in Zagreb. Sandy stepped back and looked up and down, canvassing the book shelf, still holding the photo. She stepped over to the other bookshelf on the adjacent wall.

"Mark?"

He walked over to her, and could see that she was troubled.

"Kate had a photo of her with her parents at their home in Vermont. It was always here...but it's gone. She wouldn't have moved it, it meant too much to her."

He watched as Sandy walked in and out of the bedroom and office. He looked over at the policeman assuming that he didn't speak or understand English, and could not comprehend their discussion.

Sandy returned, shaking her head. "I'm not being paranoid. I'm *not* imagining this."

"Okay then, this is important, Sandy. Can you describe this photo? What it looked like?"

"It was a basic 8x10 color photo of her with her parents—her mom on her right and her dad on her left, all three of them arm-in-arm. Their cabin was in the background. It was framed in pewter. Nothing fancy, but it's gone—did they take it?"

"It's possible. It's not uncommon for a killer to take a souvenir from someone he's murdered."

"Why?"

"To give them solace, sexual gratification, nostalgia...any number of things, but a photo of the victim in happier times would be fairly typical of that tendency."

"That's what I wanted to bring back to her parents. And it's gone."

He paused to consider what he'd just seen in Kate's apartment. He turned around and lifted a copy of the previous Sunday's New York Times from the pile on the table, and found another notebook with the previous week's date. He handed both notebooks to Sandy and then returned to the kitchen, where he pulled a large butcher knife from one of the cabinets. Proceeding to the master bedroom, he began to cut out pieces of the rug and the bed sheet that had several purple stains. The policeman stood away from him, eyes wide with shock.

Sandy stood in the doorway visibly surprised. "Mark?"

He continued to cut the carpet, placing the pieces into baggies. He stood and faced her. "It's just a theory, but I think Kate was poisoned."

"What?"

He nodded. "It's the only good explanation. She was in Olympic shape. Athletes like her don't have coronaries unless there's something else in their system that causes it."

He turned to the detective speaking in Serbo-Croatian. "I need your help," he said, holding the police file up with the bagged evidence. "I believe Kate Kamrath was murdered."

CHAPTER 41

GENERAL JOHN THORPE drove into Armstrong *Kaserne*, the isolated Army outpost nestled in the foothills of the Vogelsberg Mountains at 5:30 in the morning. Above the entrance to the Army barracks, a gold sign with black letters read: "Home of 1st Squadron, 1st Cavalry Regiment Dragoons." An American guard checked his military identification card and waved him through.

As he drove through the gate, he passed a Military Police station constructed of stone on the right. A cold mist enshrouded the buildings ahead of him. The streetlights were refracted by the fog, providing a dull glow that barely illuminated the cobblestone street below. Along the narrow road, he saw a small post exchange, medical and dental clinics, a bank, and a child care center. At the end of the road close to the rear gate of the Kaserne, a driveway connected into a large parking lot that served a series of two-tone brown stucco buildings. He pulled his car into the U-shaped drive and parked it in front of the more prominent two-story building to the right of the others, guessing it to be the squadron's headquarters.

Thorpe walked into the foyer. The history of the 1-1 Cavalry was captured in numerous framed photographs, paintings and prints of battle scenes dating back to the Mexican War of 1846 and extending to Vietnam, and Operations Desert Storm, Enduring Freedom and Iraqi Freedom. Another photo showed the squadron crossing the Sava River from Croatia into Bosnia in 1995. Photos and paintings of all 37 Medal of Honor Recipients and members of the 1-1 Cavalry lined the hallway along with their award citations.

"We hold the record for Medals of Honor, Sir," a deep baritone voice called out behind him.

Thorpe turned around to see a very large yet muscular black man with graying, closely cropped hair. He was in an Army warm-up suit and running shoes.

The man held his hand out to Thorpe. "I'm Mike Kancir, the Squadron

Command Sergeant Major, Sir," he said. "Can I help you?"

Thorpe smiled and shook his hand, immediately impressed with the unit's senior non-commissioned officer. "Sergeant Major, I'm General Thorpe...I need to see your commander if he's around."

"Yes, sir. He should be in his office. The squadron begins its physical training at zero six."

He glanced at his watch. It was 5:45 A.M. He followed Sergeant Major Kancir down the hallway into an office with large, basic brown faux leather and oak government furniture on the left and a large conference table on the right. At the other end of the room, a man in his early forties with a blonde crew cut and a long, wiry frame sat behind a desk reading the military's "Stars and Stripes" newspaper.

"Sir, you have a visitor," Sergeant Major Kancir announced with a subtle urgency. "*General* Thorpe."

The battalion commander, an Army lieutenant colonel, looked up and immediately stood at the sight of Thorpe's imposing frame entering the room, introducing himself as Lieutenant Colonel Brian Gaddis. It was rare to have a general officer at Armstrong Barracks or in his headquarters, with no aide and in blue jeans. Lieutenant Colonel Gaddis expressed his professional embarrassment for not extending him the requisite military courtesy by meeting him outside the building and calling the headquarters to attention.

Thorpe attempted to allay his concerns by telling him that he was arriving unannounced, and that the purpose of his visit was to speak to one of his officers about an accident that he'd witnessed the previous evening. Lieutenant Colonel Gaddis confirmed that Captain Dan Irons was an officer assigned to the Blackhawk Squadron as a Kiowa Pilot in their "Executioner" Troop... recalling that he'd just returned from a week's leave, skiing in Zermatt, Switzerland. Thorpe told him that rather than have Irons summoned, he preferred to walk over to see him personally.

Lieutenant Colonel Gaddis quickly threw on his Army warm-up jacket and escorted Thorpe to the troop's building, bordered on one end by a series of aircraft hangars. Thorpe saw a group of soldiers assembling for their morning formation, just as the sun began to come up. Gaddis walked over to one of the men standing behind the formation and pulled him away toward Thorpe. The young man, dressed in an Army warm-up suit, saluted Thorpe.

"Sir, Captain Dan Irons reports."

He returned Irons' salute. "Captain, I'm sorry to interrupt your PT this morning, but I need to talk to you about the accident you witnessed the other night, if you don't mind."

Irons nodded in response. "Sir, I tried to help him, but he wouldn't have any of it. Is he okay?"

"No," he replied. "He's dead."

Irons was quiet for a moment and looked at him and then at Gaddis. "Sir...the Polizei...I tried to get them to help him too, but they sent me away."

Thorpe watched Irons carefully and quickly gathered that he didn't realize the significance or the gravity of what he'd witnessed. "Son, don't worry about any of that. You did all you could for him. He died of internal injuries. He wasn't gonna survive no matter what you or the police did for him." He paused and looked at the young captain, and placed his hand on his shoulder. "Now, I need you to listen carefully...this is important: was he conscious at all when you tried to help him?"

Irons nodded slowly. "Yes, sir. He was."

"Did you talk to him?"

Irons nodded again. "He was delirious, Sir. He kept telling me to get his briefcase and to talk to the President...that they were going to 'kill us all'...crazy stuff really."

"He wanted you to get his briefcase? Did you?"

"Yes, sir. He wouldn't stop telling me, so I did. It's in my trunk. I was rushing to get back here on time for our morning formation...things got so busy here, I forgot about it, to tell you the truth."

He paused for a moment and looked at Gaddis and then at Irons. "I need you to get it for me, Son."

Irons seemed to hesitate and Thorpe smiled, remembering what it was like as a junior officer to be in the presence of a general.

"Now, please."

CHAPTER 42

MARK LYONS SAT inside the coroner's office and closely examined Kate Kamrath's autopsy report. Jon Schauer and Sandy Evenson sat opposite him at a conference table, quiet and emotionally exhausted after formally identifying Kate's body in the antiseptic cold of the morgue.

For friends and relatives, the process of identifying a body was emotionally draining, if not devastating. As a soldier and a policeman, he came to regard death as a frequent, unwelcome presence—but also an inescapable one. He quickly learned that in order to maintain his own humanity and perspective, it was often necessary to sometimes step into another room…to create some separation between the living and the dead.

From his own experience, he knew that there was a tendency in an investigation for detectives to imperceptibly reverse their deductive reasoning by arriving at conclusions that supported random and often erroneous "facts." By searching the apartment and piecing together evidence previously not considered or deemed significant, he was certain that Kate Kamrath had been murdered.

Over the course of his years with the SAS, killing had become yet another skill set, and he'd even come to regard it, however morbidly, as an art. As a police investigator he realized the act of killing another human being, no matter how one performed it—whether with a bullet, a knife or a syringe—was an inherently violent act—a final imposition of one's will against another. For that reason, there was an established relationship between the killer and the victim, not just a motive—that the killer often attempted to hide. He knew that identifying that relationship, no matter how subtle, was the key to unraveling such a plot…and in this instance, the identity of Kate Kamrath's killer.

The coroner's notes on the autopsy report described Kate as a 38-year-old female, brown hair, brown eyes, height in centimeters, weight in kilograms, scars "none," wounds "none," "red/inflamed gums--gingivitis," "mucosal inflammation/erosion of small intestine, lymphatic hypertension/ edema," "shock," and "dehydration." Lab results indicated a urinalysis with results pending. At the bottom of the page, the cause of death was listed simply as "Heart Block, Third Degree" exhibiting symptoms of "infranodal block... arterial blood clotting... pulmonary edema... bradycardia... and hypokalemia... compounded by pneumonia and severe dehydration." He copied the diagnoses and statistics on a notepad. Her white blood cell count was listed as 32,200mm/per ml. The normal healthy count for a person was 4,000 to 10,000. Further down on the form, he came to a technical term and bold font heading that he could not understand in Serbo-Croatian that with the coroner's assistance ultimately translated to "Full Spectrographic Chemical Analysis." He copied the handwritten annotation beneath it: "trace residue of olive oil, cinnamon, calamus, cassia on forehead, palms, ears, eyelids, nose, lips and feet."

He closed the folder and his notebook and looked over at Sandy. He handed the autopsy report back to the coroner who sat at the head of the table, adjacent to them.

"Doctor, she did not die of natural causes."

The coroner did not respond immediately, except to run his fingers through his thinning hair. He answered Mark quietly in English. "Of course, then, I am surprised. What is your theory, Commissioner?"

"I believe Kate Kamrath was murdered," he answered. "I'm no doctor, but I've seen this before. She was poisoned. The detective who accompanied us to her apartment has new evidence that should confirm it: the tea leaves, the pack of Tums, and a bottle of red wine. Either could have been the source of her poisoning. The piece of rug beneath her bed where she spilled the wine and tea may reinforce that theory. He's submitting all of it for analysis at your lab."

"Poison?" The coroner asked incredulously.

Mark nodded. "The clotting, edema, pneumonia, the bright red tinge to her gums...her white blood cell count and the inflammation in her organs—"

The coroner shrugged his exasperation. "Yes, but these are also symptomatic of severe dehydration or anorexia."

Mark nodded. "It's consistent with poisoning," he answered quietly.

"If your assumption—" the coroner continued. "If this was the cause of death, what type of poison was used?"

"A chemical toxin of some sort—something you will have to determine with tests of her tissue samples, a blood toxin screen and urinalysis," Mark answered. "Have you done those?"

"We are awaiting the results from the lab," the coroner replied nervously, on the verge of embarrassment.

The coroner continued. "If what you say is true, we have missed something terribly important."

Mark nodded. "It's not always obvious. Until you consider the evidence in her apartment and the outcome of the tests, these signs can easily lead to the wrong conclusions, but I believe the toxicology tests will confirm it."

HEIDELBERG, GERMANY: CAMPBELL BARRACKS

JOHN THORPE WATCHED on as a joint FBI and CIA investigation team inventoried the contents of Ahmed Nazir's briefcase in the U.S. European Command's tightly controlled office used for storing and handling highly classified information. He sat, waiting for the rough initial "field translation" of its contents from Urdu and Arabic to English. After reporting the discovery of the briefcase to Jim Goodwin at CIA Headquarters, he requested the field survey prior to sending it to Langley for detailed translations and forensic tests, which he knew could take days. At first, Goodwin had resisted the idea, but he'd insisted.

"I don't need a map to find them, Jim, I need an address," he replied in his Montana drawl. "And I need it quickly."

Goodwin finally acceded with the goal of harvesting any immediately useable intelligence from the briefcase and handing it off to Germany's BKA and their national counterterrorist force, GSG-9. As a condition, Goodwin asked that the briefcase and its contents be shipped to Langley by the most expeditious means possible. Several minutes away on the Heidelberg Army Airfield, a Navy F/A-18 Super Hornet was standing by to fly the briefcase to Langley with a single air-refueling stop enroute.

The team of three FBI agents and a female CIA analyst worked in silence, interrupted by occasional low tones of English mixed with Urdu and Arabic. Thorpe had met the Team Leader who introduced herself simply as "Nazzi," a bespectacled, unassuming, prematurely grey CIA analyst of Pakistani descent who he guessed to be in her early forties. In handing her the briefcase, told her it was imperative to translate anything providing names, addresses and telephone numbers. Everything else could wait.

He sat across the room drinking from a cup of coffee. In less than an hour's time, Nazzi approached him with a paper in her hands, and a distinct smile on her face.

"I believe we've found that address you're looking for, General."

CHAPTER 43

PAPA VOYO WATCHED the man and woman accompany the Zagreb police and detectives into the reporter's apartment building. From their dress and gait, he concluded that they were not Croatian, but Americans. Her apartment was along the same route he used for his morning walks, near Ribnjak Park, directly behind the Archbishop's Palace. Every day for the past four days, he had stopped to observe the scene around her building. On each occasion, he prayed for her. He was, after all, now responsible for her soul—just as he was responsible for Robert Childs' and Cardinal Stepinac, and all the others. They were good people who did not fully understand the common enemy they faced and the extreme measures sometimes required to defend against those who sought to destroy or undermine the church. Because of their ignorance of the threat, and their potential to obstruct his efforts, he reasoned that God had willed their sacrifice. His own words confirmed it....

And he seized the dragon, that ancient serpent, who is the Devil and Satan, and bound him for a thousand years....

Now the Satan had been released, and he'd been given no choice but to act to zealously defend the church and her faithful.

He'd entered the reporter's apartment that evening after hearing the commotion outside her door, and was alarmed to find her on the floor, still fully conscious in her nightgown. The telephone receiver was in her hand, but he'd disconnected it that afternoon. The convulsions and delirium from the dried, crushed Foxglove he'd mixed into her tea had set in. He picked her up and placed her back on her bed. There was a murmur from her throat, and realized that she was trying to speak to him. He'd seen the look of terror in her eyes as he lit the candles at the head and foot of her bed, and he sought to reassure her that she would soon be in the presence of God. God, he promised her, would accept her into his Kingdom. He had spared her the quick death he had given to Robert Childs because as a reporter, he reasoned, she had to be made to understand fully the reason for her sacrifice—that her death, like Christ's, would not be in vain.

One of the unique characteristics of the Foxglove plant was that it caused heart failure. When ingested in sufficient quantities, it produced all the clinical symptoms of Digitalis: dizziness, nausea, burning in the stomach, heightened heart rate, convulsions, shock, coma and because she ate Tums regularly as a calcium supplement, the effects of Foxglove were accelerated and amplified, causing death to come in about an hour's time.

Just as he'd done for Robert, he administered the sacrament of Last Rites to Kate Kamrath with the chrism, the consecrated oil he had made from scratch. As she took her last breath, he was overcome by an intense joy, knowing the eternal life he was bestowing upon her soul.

...Also I saw the souls of those who had been beheaded.... They came to life, and reigned with Christ a thousand years.

He'd watched the police come and go from her apartment the next morning after she died under his hand. He'd picked up the mess she'd made before he left to erase any signs of foul play. As near as he could tell, his efforts had produced the desired result. It was what one would expect of a routine investigation for a death that had diagnosed as occurring from natural causes. As he'd intended it to be. There was no need to alarm the authorities.

This visit was different from the others he'd seen, though. He watched the man and woman with some degree of fascination, and dismay. They were outsiders, friends of the reporter's perhaps. After they left her apartment, a crime scene van arrived at the house, indicating that they were launching an expanded investigation into her death.

As he walked casually by, he got a closer look at the man and woman. He remembered the framed photos on the reporter's bookshelf, and then recognized the man from one of the photos—standing beside the reporter on a cobblestone street.

He continued to walk along the winding pathway. His calm had been shattered. His daily devotional prayers for these departed souls were interrupted by a deep resentment over this couple's arrival. They were intruding. A shiver overcame him without warning, and a sharp, visceral fury overcame him.

They too would have to be stopped.

MARK LYONS WALKED with Sandy Evenson out of the Coroner's Office. As they stepped outside, a breeze caught the door, shutting it.

"We'll find who did this to Kate, Sandy, I promise," he said.

Sandy nodded silently and then turned to him. "Who would do this to her?"

He escorted her to a short brick ledge leading up the stairs and motioned for her to sit. He sat down beside her. "I don't know yet. But I believe Kate did, and the notes she left behind may help." He put his hands in his pocket and pulled out a digital memory chip. "And this...," he handed it to her. "I kept along with her reporter's notebook. It was in her camera. The police have everything else."

Jon Schauer walked out of the doors and approached them. Sandy put the chip in her pocket, her voice more steady now. "Jon can download it at his place."

Mark squeezed both of her arms. "Are ye okay?"

Sandy nodded and smiled faintly. "Yeah, aside from having to deal with a homicidal maniac, I'm fine."

As they approached Schauer's car, Mark's cell phone rang with a different tone than he was accustomed to. Pulling the phone out of his pocket, he discovered a text message waiting for him:

THE BEST-Jarunska 5 -9 SAT...C

"The Best?" he asked Schauer.

"A discotheque near the university," Schauer answered. "One of Zagreb's hot spots. Who sent that to you?"

Mark glanced over at Sandy. Her eyebrows were raised. Both knew the "C" was Celo.

Chapter 44

CARDINAL VOJISLAV PIJADJE looked down at his congregation assembled in Saint Stephen's Cathedral for the Vigil Mass. As before each of his sermons, he began by canvassing the pews and staring intently into expectant faces of his parishioners. In turn, old and young alike fixed their gazes toward him with anticipation. With the exception of the tourists who also attended his Masses, he knew each of his congregation well, and they knew him. Over the years they were buoyed by his strength and they routinely sought solace in the confidence and faith he conveyed—forged over decades of experience as an army officer under Tito, sustained by his conversion from agnosticism to Catholicism, and then further reinforced in his role as the unlikely protégé of Croatia's beatified Cardinal and soon-to-be-saint, Alojzije Stepinac. Indeed, it was Papa Voyo, they knew, who was quietly leading the path to his sainthood. To the thousands who adored him, Papa Voyo was nothing short of the Apostle Paul incarnate—a sinner, converted to the priesthood by Christ.

Voyo glanced at his watch. It was 5:00 P.M. By now, the Team would be flying from Vanga Island to its target in Northwestern Bosnia. Even now, he was confident that he was fulfilling his duty to defend Croatia and the Church from those who were planning its demise. Ultimately, the responsibility to unleash the wrath of the Archangel Michael was his alone. It was a sacred rite bestowed upon him in an enigmatic, ritualistic ceremony years ago by Stepinac himself, reserved for only a select few, hand-picked through the ages—from the Knights Templar and from a small cloister of saints martyred at their hour of death. He had invoked that sacred power in the secrecy demanded of him, armed with the exemptions of Pope Innocent II's papal bull, *Omni Datum Optimum*: to fight against Satan in his most inviolate form, to rescue the faithful from the power of the enemy, and to deliver their souls to judgment swiftly and silently, answering only to the authority of the Pope.

His voice resonated through the Cathedral.

"According to the Gospel of Saint John, following the Incarnation of our savior, Jesus Christ, Satan was imprisoned and cast to the fires of Hell; but in a symbolic expression, John tells us that after a thousand years he is destined to return. And then!" He raised his voice and his hands in front of his silk crimson vestments. "The final battle between good and evil will come to pass, crowned by the return of Christ and his final judgment upon the living and the dead...."

BOCINJA, BOSNIA AND HERZEGOVINA

MAJOR SAVO HELETA, Commander of the elite squadron of ecumenical guardians, known only by a few as the "Gabriel Team," looked down from the helicopter flying over the Bosna River that meandered toward the Muslim village of Bocinja, nestled deep in the mountains of Northwestern Bosnia. Bocinja was unique to other Bosnian Muslim settlements in its strict Islamist orthodoxy, and the rare incidence of outside visitors to the village. Men and women in traditional Arab dress, and women with burkhas covered their heads. The minaret of a large white mosque overlooked the town below, marking it distinctly as a Muslim enclave. The smoke emanating from chimneys created a haze that blanketed the valley like a vaporous shroud. Both helicopters followed the winding path through the valley to the outskirts of Bocinja and veered off dramatically to the right, tracing a narrow loggers' road upward. The road finally stopped at a large camouflaged warehouse, barely visible among the pine trees.

SAINT STEPHEN'S CATHEDRAL: ZAGREB, CROATIA

"...BUT THE THOUSAND YEARS has passed, this battle has already begun," Voyo announced, lowering his voice. "And if we are to cast off Satan and achieve our own redemption in the eyes of the Christ, we must fight against the evil forces arrayed against us." He threw his arms above his head in a dramatic sacrificial pose. His tone was resolute. "On the day of the

Apocalypse, we will all be judged as Soldiers of Christ. Order of the Templar! Defend our church from the faces Satan has arrayed against us. God wills us to succeed! This battle has presented itself in certain terms. Allied with the Archangels Michael, the Angel of Mercy; Uriel, the Angel of Justice; and Gabriel, the Angel of Judgment—just as you defeated Saladin, you will defeat the evil now in our midst. Your armor is your faith. You need fear neither men nor demons."

BOCINJA, BOSNIA AND HERZEGOVINA

THE FIRST FRENCH-MADE Super Puma helicopter landed in the semi-circular dirt drive in front of the warehouse. The other helicopter circled high above. The team of commandos, dressed in white camouflage fatigues, jumped from the skids of the first aircraft, and fired their HK MP-5 Submachine Guns with pin-point precision. Bearded mujahideen streamed toward them, screaming *"Allaahu Akbar!"* and *"Allahu Al-Kabeer!"* and wildly firing AK-47 assault rifles and RPG-7 Grenade Launchers toward the helicopter. But the Gabriel Team had achieved the element of surprise. In teams of two, the commandos fanned out in well-rehearsed, controlled movements to surround the warehouse—each soldier knelt with his rifle pointing toward the warehouse while his teammate pointed his rifle outward into the forest.

The second helicopter landed to the rear and offset from the first. A five-man team rushed off and stacked themselves against the side doorway of the warehouse. The lead man on the team attached a plastique framed charge against the doorway. With the blast, the door flew open and the team rushed in through the smoke. Inside, sporadic bursts of gunfire and small explosions ripped through the aluminum and broke glass windows. The assault team moved through the maze of rooms. When they finally emerged on the opposite end of the warehouse, four men holding a stretcher struggled to haul a large smooth-surfaced stainless steel container resembling an industrial garbage can onto the hull of the second Super Puma. When they'd finished securing it to the floor, the team leader gave a prolonged blow into his whistle and the commandos began to retreat back in alternating echelons to the helicopters.

The Super Pumas' turbines spun in high-pitched whines that preceded the rush of dirt and snow to their rotors. Once they had accumulated sufficient power and thrust, the helicopters lifted vertically upward. Above the tree tops, they angled their noses downward in a final maneuver before flying over the mountain range toward the Croatian Coast and across the sound to Vanga Island.

CHAPTER 45

MARK LYONS STOOD outside "The Best" Discothèque, carefully considering the prudence of entering a club with a clientele that had an average age at least half his own. He wore a pair of worn blue jeans, a black turtleneck shirt, and a black leather jacket—sufficient, he'd thought, to help him at least partially assimilate; but the nouveau riche, extra-wealthy businessmen, the city's star athletes and the women they attracted contrasted sharply with the image he presented as he awaited entry in the long queue.

He was about to walk away; when he felt a hand softly grip his arm above his elbow. He heard Sandy Evenson's voice before he saw her. "Wondering if you blend?" She was smiling broadly, waving her hair from her face, and holding a bottle of water in her other hand.

"I actually was, and I've concluded I don't," he replied, attempting to conceal his surprise.

"Well then, you need a woman to go in there with you!" Sandy answered, placing her arm in his. She wore black leather pants and a colorful, tight-fitting knit sweater. Her chest brushed against his arm as she walked him toward the entrance.

He smiled. "Thin cover, I'd say,"

"Perhaps, but I'm all you've got, Commissioner," she said. "Unless...."

"Unless?"

She took a final sip from her bottle of water and deposited it into a nearby trashcan. She nodded and looked at the queue. To their front, a group of tall, leggy blondes and brunettes fashionably dressed in short, tight fitting skirts were waiting to enter. "Unless you'd like to take one of them?"

"I was just going to leave."

"I know, but you can't. He's your cousin."

"That's the thing about family—ye can always see 'em again, right?"

She placed her free hand on his wrist and held it as they walked. "Mmm Hmm, even if it's three and a half decades later."

"A cheap shot."

"Maybe, but you *have* to see him." She paused and smiled. "That's the thing about family."

"What's that?"

"They're the friends you don't choose."

"I find it hard to believe he'd want to meet me here," he said shaking his head. "With everything happening in Ravno, how can a Serb nationalist feel at all safe in a place like this—in the middle of Croatia's largest city?"

"Connections, I'd say," she answered. "Heavy ones— and he can blend, you can't."

At the entrance, he could feel the vibrations of the European techno and turbo rock inside pulsating. He pulled the EUPM badge case from his coat pocket and handed it to the bouncer standing outside the door.

"Are you carrying any guns?" The bouncer asked. "If you are, you must leave them with me."

He suppressed the urge to laugh and shook his head. "No, I'm not armed."

The bouncer handed the badge back to him with apparent disinterest. He noticed him staring rather intently after Sandy as he waved them through.

"I think he likes ye," he joked.

"I...*think not*," she replied directly, elbowing him in his ribcage. "Try to focus, okay? We're working."

He smiled, grateful that she'd found him. "Do ye think they'd have a daicent cup of tea?" he shouted over the noise.

She turned to face him, smiling. "I think not."

The area inside was illuminated with black light and a white, pink and blue strobes and lasers that bounced against mirrors. The crowd generated its own heat and he could already feel himself begin to sweat. He led the way, as Sandy followed close behind. They weaved through the crowd, around the bar toward the opposite corner of the room. It was here, he guessed, that he'd find Celo—with his back against the wall, and the entire room visible from where he sat.

"Marko!" He heard Celo's shout over the music. He looked back at Sandy who was pointing to a group of tables to their right. Celo was sitting, as he'd expected, against the wall. Several other rough-looking men, who he guessed were bodyguards, sat in the tables around him. "Over here! Come! Sit!" The bodyguards dispersed, giving up their seats for them.

Celo looked dramatically different than he did four days ago at Brnisi

Dam. There, he'd been the consummate outdoorsman, but here, dressed in a cream-colored linen shirt, buttoned only half-way, and exposing heavy gold chains that adorned a powerful, well-defined physique, he'd taken on an entirely different persona tailored to the environment. His eyes were bright from the stimulation of alcohol and the pounding turbo rock. He stood and extended the chairs to them. "Sit!"

Mark held the chair for Sandy and shook Celo's hand, who pulled him in and hugged him. "Cousin! I knew you would find me!" He returned his embrace and smiled, embarrassed by Celo's animated welcome, and certain that the bottle of *schlivovitz* on the table was contributing to the display. He was well-familiar with the plum brandy from his childhood, and knew it to be a timeless Balkan tradition, similar to grappa in taste. "I have a toast!" Celo announced with a flourish. He poured the *slivo* into an empty shot glass and refilled his own glass. He looked at Sandy. She was smiling at him, her eyebrows raised with obvious amusement.

"Here is my toast!" Celo bellowed with his wine glass in the air.

"Wait!" Sandy interrupted. "Are you going to pour me a shot too?"

Celo turned to her, obviously taken off guard. He lowered his glass. "You want to drink *slivo*?"

"Of course!" she answered. "Why wouldn't I?"

"Yes! The *slivo*—it keeps the trigger finger loose!" Celo poured another shot of *schlivovitz* and turned to him. "Marko! I like her!"

Celo raised his glass again. "To my long-lost cousin! May God protect you!"

Mark laughed suddenly, remembering it as the same way he'd introduced him to his classmates after he'd come from the orphanage. *My long-lost cousin....*

Celo pushed his glass into the others, raised it in unison, and swallowed the *slivo* in a single gulp. He slammed his glass on the table triumphantly and smiled broadly. He reached for the bottle and poured another round. "And now, Marko! You! You too must give a toast!"

Mark glanced over at Sandy, her half-smile and eyes crinkled at the corners conveying no pity, only amused anticipation. "All right then..." He hesitated only for a moment before standing up and raising his glass. He looked into his cousins eyes, directly. "Celo—may the angels protect you, and may heaven accept you."

Celo laughed loudly, infectiously. "Yes! That is good! May the heavens accept me!" He guzzled the *slivo,* and again slammed his glass down on the table.

Mark leaned over to Sandy who had only managed to take a sip of the brandy. "How was that?"

"Mmm," she nodded. "One for the ages. Good theatrics."

He leaned back in his seat. "I didn't expect you to want to meet here, Celo."

Celo laughed again. "No, and neither did they!" He pointed at the people in the crowd, many of whom were now staring at them as they stood around or danced. Mark saw some of them looking in their direction further away near the bar.

"You asked to see me," Mark replied. "That's why I'm here."

Celo's smile faded. "I wanted to meet so you could tell me who killed the reporter—Kate Kamrath."

"You knew her?"

Celo was canvassing the discotheque, as if searching for prey. He nodded absently. "We were meeting again this week. Here, today."

"How did you know she was murdered?"

Celo shook his head. "It doesn't matter. I'm told you're investigating this."

"So is the Zagreb Police Department," he answered. "She was a friend. We're here to find out what happened."

"What happened?" Celo replied abruptly.

"I'm not sure exactly. They're saying she had a heart attack, but I believe she was poisoned."

Celo leaned back in his chair. "Do not worry. I'll find who killed her," he replied confidently. "And who killed the Americans at Oborci."

"You told me in the car—as you, we, were evading the SAS—that you already knew," Sandy replied.

Celo shifted in his seat and leaned forward again. His gaze was steady, intense, and for the first time, entirely sober. "I have a good idea."

For a moment, the words just hung there. "I don't understand your linkages, Celo," Sandy replied finally in Serbo-Croatian. "If you know who did this to her, tell us."

"I'll tell you when I'm ready!" Celo shouted, pounding the table publicly. Glasses spun wildly and one tipped over, crashing to the floor. The bodyguard sitting at an adjacent table shifted to a ready-position facing them. "Not until then!"

"Have it your way," Mark answered, unable to conceal his frustration. "This isn't a game. What happened at the dam wasn't a game. They were there to capture you or kill you. Right now, you could be in The Hague, Celo, you should know that."

"I'm not afraid to go there. I've done nothing wrong! I've committed no war crimes. I have only protected myself and my people! I won't allow them to hunt me down like some animal...like some wild dog!" Celo was now shouting at them and pointing at Sandy. "Tell them this! You work for them, do you not? If they try to arrest me, tell them I will defend myself! And people will die!"

"I wouldn't tell them that," Sandy replied, trying to remain calm.

"There at the dam, I dare say such an attitude would not have served you well," Mark replied.

"You led them to me!"

Mark shook his head and reached across and took hold of his cousin's massive wrist. "Celo, listen to me! They believe you were behind the ambush on the Americans. You were there!"

Celo shook his head resolutely, speaking in English. "I was...how do you say in your movies? ...Framed." He pointed at Sandy. "And so was she there! It is too much coincidence! Why is she not a suspect too?"

She began coughing as if clearing her throat, and then burst out in laughter. "Why?" Her surprise was only matched by her sarcastic tone as she leaned forward, pointing with both hands toward the center of her chest. "Brandishing an AK-47 was never my style. Maybe that had something to do with it?"

Celo scoffed. "You were lucky I didn't shoot you!" His bright blue eyes held a spark of amusement.

"Obviously," Sandy replied, now provoked and exasperated. She turned quickly to Mark. "Can we dance?"

It wasn't a question.

"I don't—"

Sandy took Mark's hand firmly in hers and looked pleadingly into his eyes. "Yes, *you do*," she whispered in his ear. She stood up and gently tugged his arm.

"Stop, Marko" Celo directed with some asperity. "Sit...please."

Mark looked over to Sandy and they sat back down.

"I remember what happened at the dam, Marko, four days ago," Celo paused and reached for his jacket. "And too, I remember what happened there nearly four decades ago." He pulled out a black oil cloth from his jacket pocket and placed it on the table. "Do you remember?"

Mark shifted and looked away and caught his reflection in the mirror. In that split second, he saw a young pre-teen looking back at him. "Yeah, I do, but I've moved on, Celo. That was a long time ago."

Sandy reached for his arm and squeezed. "Should I leave you two?"

Mark shook his head. "No, it's okay."

Celo shrugged and smiled, a bit grimly. "Yes, you are correct. It was a long time ago. Maybe, but you know it's made both you and me what we are today. It's led us both back here. This, you can't deny."

Mark was silent as he looked at the cloth framed by his cousin's hands. He looked back up at Celo.

"I have carried this with me since that night, to remind me. So that I would never forget what they did to us," Celo said. He unfolded the oil cloth to reveal a shotgun shell, a small caliber bullet casing and a Serb Orthodox cross attached to a small bundle of leather string. "Do you recognize these?"

Mark felt his heartbeat quicken and his mind raced as he struggled to maintain composure. They lay there, strewn across the table, like relics of an ancient holy war. He felt Sandy Evenson's eyes upon him and for a moment, he wondered what she could be thinking now. A chill passed through his body…Celo's shotgun echoed against the hills above him…the Makarov recoiled in his hand as he fired it into the soldiers who pursued him on the dam's steppe…the cold, gritty hand of the man from the grave, slipping away from him as they climbed through the scrub oak.

He nodded somberly and paused. "The cross?"

"My Father's." Celo picked it up and handed it to him. "I took it from around his neck after they executed him. I watched them murder him in cold blood from the forest. They shot him in the back of his head. His hands were tied behind him. His blood is on the leather."

"Celo, I—" He handed it back to his cousin, now seeing Celo's clear resemblance to his Uncle Milan. It was his uncle's eyes, he now realized, that he'd recognized in Sandy's photos at Oborci.

"It is past," Celo waved his hands abruptly, as if to end the discussion. He refolded the oil cloth and returned it to his pocket. He switched to English. His tone was nonchalant. "How do you say? What's past is past."

240

At that moment, he felt precisely the opposite. The past was the present, and try as he might, he realized he could not escape it. Ever. "I'm sorry, Celo." He felt his heart sink, and his eyes well. "If I could do it over again...."

"You know that my mother was Catholic," Celo said. "My Father, Orthodox."

Mark nodded.

"Did she raise you as a Catholic?"

He nodded again. "I didn't much practice it though."

Celo rubbed his father's cross between his fingers. "The Catholics killed your wife, did they not?"

He felt his sorrow transition to anger at his cousin. "How do you know—?"

"You see, Marko, this is the difference between us. For you, the past is forgotten. Until you are reminded. But for me—for the rest of us, we do not need to be reminded of who our enemies are. The past defines us. It is the past, but *it is who we are*. We don't run from it."

"I try never to look back, Celo," he answered, now fully exasperated. "It never leads anywhere good."

Celo shrugged and smiled thinly. "As you wish." He stood and put his jacket on without any further comment. He walked around the table, over to Mark.

He stood to meet him and could feel his cousin's warm breath against his face, then the sudden grasp of his massive hands on his shoulders. Celo reached into the inside jacket pocket and slipped Mark a folded rectangular road map. "Meet me in nine days, at the place I've circled. At noon. Not before." He glanced over to Sandy. "You come too, if you want."

He gripped the road map and placed it in his jacket pocket. He looked up and could see his cousin passing through the crowd toward the exit, surrounded by his bodyguards. An excited stir filled the dance hall, and he finally disappeared from view.

Sandy rose from her chair and shook her head. "Elvis has left the building," she uttered, her voice barely audible in the raucous discotheque. "And I didn't even get to dance."

Mark smiled as he helped Sandy with her coat. "We're working, remember?"

"Your cousin has issues, Mark."

He shrugged, now facing her. "He thinks he's the bee's knees, I'll say that about 'im. Better to experience him piecemeal, rather than all-at-once."

Sandy shook her head. The music was loud and pounding. "He's gotta be the bride at every wedding and the corpse at every funeral," she shouted.

As they turned to walk toward the door, three men suddenly stepped in front of him—large, muscular men with crew cuts and tight black tee shirts and leather jackets. They had brutal, uncompromising expressions with cold, wild eyes. The man in the center was the largest, in his mid-thirties, he reckoned. His face was heavily pock-marked and dominated by a nose made even more considerable by an excess accumulation of cartilage. Inside, his eyes still squinted. The other two men standing beside him were unshaven and menacing in their stances and expressions. Mark attempted to excuse themselves, when the man in the middle placed the edge of his hand on Mark's chest. Mark stopped and looked at the man's large hand and then into his narrow eyes. He squeezed Sandy's hand, who half-whispered into his ear.

"Maybe we forgot to pay for the *schlivovitz*?"

He shook his head. "Doubtful." He turned to look at Sandy and could see that she was obviously not frightened by the three men standing in front of them. "You may want to run back to the ladies' WC and call the police on your cell phone if these blokes aren't inclined to negotiate."

Instead, she stepped forward. "Can I help you gentlemen?" she asked in English, looking into the eyes of all three men in succession

"You were with the *Chetnik*," The man in the middle said pointedly, entirely in Serbo-Croatian.

She waved both of her hands in front of her "I can only *hope* that you aren't going to act like a bunch of thugs," she shouted in fluent Serbo-Croatian. "Why ruin our evening?"

Mark pulled his badge out into full view and spoke in their native tongue. "I am the Assistant Commissioner of the European Union Police Mission. I'm here on official business, and that discussion was official, not personal. Certainly, you gents can understand—"

He heard Sandy shout at the same time he saw the man's arm swinging in the direction of his chest. He blocked the swing with his left arm and grasped the man's right hand with his free hand. Twisting it hard to the left, he felt the man's body slam against his side and back. In a fluid, controlled motion, he slipped both of his thumbs to the front of the man's hand to grip the end of his palm, twisting it hard until his body reeled downward onto the floor. In a swift motion he slammed the elbow forward, and felt it splinter. His shoe made contact with the man's large nose before he fell to the floor in a heap. He looked for the other two men, expecting them to resist as well, but was confused for an instant when he saw them lying on the floor, splayed on their backs. Two other men, whom he immediately recognized from his encounter with the SAS at Brnisi Dam, were standing in front of him, grinning broadly.

He smiled with the sudden recognition, brushing himself off. "I didn't expect to see you lads here, but perhaps I should've."

"Don't mention it, Colonel. Glad to be of service to ye," the tall thin Sergeant replied, his foot on one of the thugs' head. He pointed at the larger man groaning in pain on the floor. "You laid him up rather well. Textbook!"

"Aye, well, I'm a bit rusty." He stepped around to shake the commando's hands, motioning to the hulk lying motionless on the floor. "Luckily, this one was too quick by half."

The Sergeant leaned over to whisper in his ear. "Now, Colonel, for General Rose's benefit, you understand, we weren't ever here. That's the orders."

Mark nodded, still smiling. "Course not. My thanks to ye. Well done." He was grateful to them, knowing that the real reason for their presence here was to continue their surveillance of Celo. And yet, they'd compromised themselves by involving themselves in his fight.

He looked back and saw Sandy standing there, looking stunned. "We should go," he said, distracted.

She only nodded and held his hand as he negotiated their way through the crowd, outside. After walking a distance toward Jon Schauer's apartment, they found themselves in Zagreb's city square. Sandy finally stopped midway near the statue of Ban Jelacic, the Croatian patriot for whom the square was named. She stared at Mark.

"I didn't have any choice, Sandy, I—"

She shook her head. "No, I've got that part. I suppose I should've been prepared for it."

He shrugged. "It was a simple wrist lock. That's all."

She paused and nodded. A spark of humor appeared in her eyes. "Oh."

He detected the sarcasm as they walked through the city square. He was eager to change the subject, and when his cell phone rang, it was a welcome distraction. He answered the call still looking at Sandy and recognized Mike McCallister's voice...anxious...urgent in its tone and delivery.

"Terribly sorry to call at such a late hour, Commissioner, but I thought ye might want to know about an incident I just heard word of in the village of Bocinja."

"Bocinja?"

"West of Banja Luka, and just below Bihac."

He thought for a moment and mentally placed the location in northeastern Bosnia. "That's in the Federation, then, isn't it?"

"It's Muslim, in its entirety, yes. Fundamentalist, actually...closed to us 'infidels'."

"What happened?"

"Well, a bloody massacre," McCallister answered. "The local police are reporting a bloodbath—twelve shot dead at a warehouse just outside the town, in the forest. All men with assault rifles. Possibly mujahideen, but that remains to be seen. All shot to death."

"Do they know when it happened?"

"All the signs say sometime early this evening. A couple kids found the bodies after they heard the shots."

Mark winced, remembering when he and Celo had come upon the same kind of ghastly scene at the dam.

"Any idea who did it?"

"No, not yet. But it was efficient, deadly, and professionally executed. They left no casualties, only fatalities...."

McCallister's delivery had transitioned to distinct urgency. He continued. "I think we should fly down there, Commissioner. They're saying everything's in an uproar, men in Arab garb with Kalashnikov's are everywhere, patrolling the roads, making threats. They won't let EUFOR in the town. It's rather, well...tense, ye might say."

He looked at his watch. It was a little after 9:00 PM. "Vlad can fly in there at night, with the weather in the mountains?"

"He assures me he can do it."

He thought for a moment. All hell was breaking loose, but it was in disparate pieces, with no logical connectivity. Ravno, Oborci, Robert Childs' disappearance and Kate Kamrath murdered in Zagreb...and now this, in Bocinja. But he trusted Mike McCallister's judgment. In the several days they'd been together, he knew Mike wasn't one to claim the sky was falling, unless it truly was. He exhaled.

"Okay. Have the local police secure the site until we arrive." He glanced over at Sandy, now looking at him, concerned. "I'm on my way to the airport now."

"We'll be ready for ye then." The line went dead.

"I assume dinner's off then?"

He nodded and related McCallister's report.

"I know Bocinja, Mark," Sandy replied. "The entire town is populated by Arab expats—the mercenary variety. Mujahideen. They've been there since the last war—former extremist Islamic whackos who've shacked up with any poor Muslim girl who'll have them. They go off and find jihads to fight and if they live through them, they come back to mama. They're armed and they're goddamned psycho. Don't go in there without a EUFOR escort."

"They aren't letting them in, as I understand it."

Sandy stopped and faced him with a determined look. "Well, then, I'm going with you."

CHAPTER 46

GENERAL JOHN THORPE sat with Heinz Lohman in the light blue and white Bormann Construction van on the cul de sac at the end of Kaspar Merian Strasse. Two large cranes and a large bulldozer were there, with stacks of rebar grates and cinder block to construct a home on the remaining open lot. All of the material and equipment had been moved to the site four days ago, on Lohman's order. Both men wore the coveralls of the Bormann Group, one of the most well-known construction firms in Europe.

The specially equipped van was packed with state-of-the-art surveillance electronics, radios, cameras and video screens. Against the back wall of the van, a weapons rack held four submachine guns and four pistols. The van was crowded. In addition to him and Lohman, two other GSG-9 operatives sat on metal stools with ear phones, monitoring the house across from them at 23 Kasper Merian Strasse.

Thorpe studied the blueprints in the dim light. Periodically, he compared them to the television screen images that provided full 360 degree coverage of the house. It was a large, elegant home—three stories, three balconies, white and brown stucco, with more than ten rooms and an indoor swimming pool—all on a hilltop overlooking the Main River Valley. Only minutes after he had given Heinz Lohman the address, Lohman was able to tell him that the house was owned by the Deutsche Bank and leased to the Organization of the Islamic Conference eleven months prior. Sitting in his Wiesbaden office, Thorpe watched Lohman give the order to begin surveillance of the house.

Within two days, the BKA's surveillance team reported sightings of two persons of interest issued "Red Notices" by Interpol—the closest instrument to an international arrest warrant that is used by the global community. On day three, Lohman called him in Heidelberg to tell him that he had secured a sealed warrant to raid the house and arrest its occupants. Lohman thanked him and before hanging up, had asked him if he would observe the raid with him.

MTG   184000   1948 ⁰⁶

LOC   163000   350 ⁰⁰

C.C.   12000

MR + Co.   9900 ⁰⁰

K + S   3250 ⁰⁶

Dunaee   2384.00

                    10,534 ⁰⁰

1319 Duval Street | Key West, FL 33040
P. 305.296.6577 | f. 305.294.8272 | southernmostresorts.com

SOUTHERNMOST
HOTEL COLLECTION

Four additional Bormann Group vans turned onto Kasper Merian Strasse at 5:59 A.M.. In the sixty seconds that it would take them to reach the house at the end of the street, a helicopter hovered above, and two additional vans occupied their positions on the street below. At 6:00 A.M, six GSG-9 commandos exited the helicopter by sliding down a thick ninety foot rope onto the sundeck in the rear of the house. Seconds later, the roar of door charges exploding and glass shattering interrupted the serene quiet of the Saturday morning. In quick succession, muffled cracks of silenced gunfire inside the house and more explosions could be heard from the street.

Over the radio, he heard clipped commands issued in German as the commandos cleared the rooms.

Lohman translated with each transmission. "They have killed everyone inside...*all* of them were armed...all of them resisted."

Another exchange in German prompted Heinz Lohman to motion him outside. "Come with me, General. It is now safe."

As they approached the house, the commandos forming the security perimeter closest to them rose from their kneeling positions and escorted the two older men. Smoke was pouring outside several windows. He noticed frightened neighbors peeking outside their windows and front doors. A policeman with a bullhorn made a series of official announcements in German, which he concluded were meant to inform them of the police action and to urge them to stay indoors until the site had been secured.

The front door to the house had been blown from its hinges, and was lying splintered in the entryway. The glass windows around the door had completely shattered from the force of the explosions, leaving shards of glass inside and out. A blanket of black smoke hovered on the ceiling.

The team leader—tall, muscular, with closely cropped blonde hair— greeted them inside the closed foyer and led them through another adjacent doorway into a large living room. He saw the body of a man on the sofa wearing a blue cotton robe, slumped over with his arms grotesquely extended toward them. His eyes were open. Three bullets had been fired into his chest, causing a deep crimson stain to his robe. A pistol and several magazines littered the floor in front of him. As the team leader spoke in calm, deliberate tones, Lohman translated for him.

"This is the first of the men wanted by Interpol. He is a Yemeni." Lohman compared a file photograph to the dead man, holding it beside the lifeless face. "Sheikh Saeed, also known as Mustafa Mohamed Ahmad. He is known to us as Osama Bin Laden's closest financial advisor, his paymaster." Lohman picked up the stack of folders on the coffee table and set them back down. "These papers will be of use to you, I believe." The GSG-9 team leader and two other commandos approached Lohman and handed him another photo while they briefed him. Lohman initially looked surprised. He pointed at the spiral staircase outside in the foyer and handed him the color photo with the Interpol identifier. "Upstairs, this man, Ijaz Shah, was found attempting to escape from the kitchen balcony. He is a Pakistani, a former high-ranking official within their ISI." Thorpe instantly recognized Lohman's reference to the ISI as Pakistan's military secret service, the Inter-Services Intelligence. He knew them to be deeply involved with the Islamic fundamentalist groups that were most closely associated with al-Qaida. "These men...they are not trivial personalities," Lohman paused and pursed his lips before continuing. "My men report something they have discovered downstairs. Please, follow me, General."

He followed the GSG-9 officer and Heinz Lohman down the staircase and into the room containing the indoor pool. The pool had been drained. Inside the pool's deep end, blue plastic tarps were pulled back to reveal long, thin aluminum pipes neatly stacked in open crates on the pool floor. The crates were marked "KOEBERG" in black spray-paint, with the universal symbol for radiation hazard marked in red paint. Lohman's expression was somber.

"General, you know what these are?"

Thorpe nodded, and inhaled deeply before attempting a reply. "Yes, I'm afraid I do, Herr Lohman. They're zirconium rods." He pointed to the shallow end of the pool. "And those, over there, the thick ones appear to be heat exchange tubes made of titanium alloy—critical components for a nuclear fission device," ...and in this case, judging by their quantity, he concluded, "several of them."

CHAPTER 47

NAZZI LOOKED AT THORPE directly. Her tone was matter-of-fact, like that of a doctor to the family of a patient, announcing the need for emergency surgery. "General, the terrorist cell occupying that house was operating under the thin cover of Islamic Reconstruction, a non-governmental organization running rehabilitation and redevelopment projects in Afghanistan with very close links with the Taliban and al- Qaida."

Thorpe nodded. "The bodies in the Wiesbaden morgue seem to confirm that." He handed her photos of the empty pool filled with boxes of rods and tubes. "What worries me is that they had enough of these to build ten bombs, or more. Some were missing from their crates."

Nazzi shuffled through the papers in the file she held. "We found this manifest in Nazir's briefcase. There was a shipment of Iron Ore drill bits transported by truck from Wertheim, Germany into Frankfurt, and then flown by an air cargo jet into Sarajevo on December 20th—nearly two months ago." She handed him a single page that was written in German. "Here's the invoice. If there was anything that would approximate the size of those rods and tubes, drill bits would be a logical choice, I think."

He nodded. "No one except an expert in mining would know the difference. My guess is that the shipment flew through customs."

"According to these papers, the shipment was received on January 7th," Nazzi said.

"Five days later," he answered thoughtfully. "Do we have any idea who signed for it?"

"A construction company in Tuzla. We've checked it out and it doesn't exist. But-" Nazzi paused, digging into another file. She passed him copies of Lufthansa boarding passes. "We found these—"

He studied them.

Nazzi continued. "Those are airline tickets routing from Islamabad, Pakistan to Damascus, Syria, with a final destination of Frankfurt, Germany.

There were also copies of boarding passes for each connection."

"This name on the ticket...isn't that—?" he began to ask.

"Sayed Yatama?" Nazzi said, rhetorically.

"We're talking about the same guy...the architect of the 9-11 attacks?"

"Yes," she said. "One in the same. He slid right through German Customs. Normally they're quite good, so I don't know how he managed to slip through their system. This alias was listed in our State Department and Customs databases, but not Germany's. Odd, because Interpol has him covered too."

Thorpe inhaled. He knew about Sayed Yatama-having supervised several operations in Afghanistan and Kenya, with the goal of capturing or killing him. Each had been unsuccessful with Yatama eluding them on each occasion by just hours or minutes. In the personality profiles, Yatama was often described as a bright, friendly, highly intelligent, British-born Pakistani who had morphed gradually into one of the most deadly and wanted terrorists in the world.

Nazzi continued. "If there's a major operation in the works, he's certainly the one in charge of the planning and execution."

"Is there any way of telling where he is now?" he asked.

"Anyone's guess," she replied. "But German Customs provided us with this security photo of a clean-shaven man with a thin face, olive complexion, round spectacles and black hair, wearing a tweed sports jacket. Thorpe leaned forward into the desk as he studied the photo. In the corner, printing on the photo read:

> Munchen Bahnhof
> Sayed al Masery (Pakistan National)
> Abfahrt (Munchen): 29.01//2235
> Ankunft (Sarajevo): 30.01//1315

This convergence of incidents—the stolen plutonium from South Africa, and the shipment to Sarajevo of other nuclear precursor materials required for the construction of a sophisticated nuclear device—was, by itself, cause for great alarm, but the confirmed arrival of a known high-profile and high-ranking al-Qaida operative into the same area, *and* only days after the Fulbright assassination was cause for immediate action if they had even a vague idea of where he was.

"So he's in Bosnia," Thorpe replied quietly—so quietly that Nazzi asked him to repeat.

He continued to flip through the papers, very worried.

Nazzi took a step toward Thorpe and lowered her voice. "But there's something else I think you should know about, General...."

CHAPTER 48

STEPPING OFF the Russian-made helicopter, Mark Lyons was enveloped in a blast of wet snow and exhaust. The helicopter's floodlights illuminated the images of Bosnian Policemen near the warehouse and a handful of local men who appeared to be dressed in traditional Arab-Islamic garb. All of them were facing him, their hands and arms in front of their eyes to shield themselves against flying debris. He turned around and helped Sandy Evenson off the platform and to the ground.

The whirl of the helicopter's blades and the whine of its turbine engines echoed loudly against the adjacent hillsides. He walked Sandy toward the warehouse, heads ducked to avoid the rotors. He glanced up to see an inverted bowl of leaden, dark grey clouds gathering and converging upon one another like gobs of steel wool.

More snow on the way.

Enroute, Vladimir had advised him of the worsening weather conditions and had struggled to find a clear path through the clouds. On three separate occasions, he was forced to turn the helicopter around to find a better route. On his final attempt he succeeded, but Mark sensed his growing concern about the weather conditions ahead. In minutes the low clouds would force them down and prevent them from lifting off again. Recognizing the dilemma and the imperative to investigate the incident, Mike McCallister provided the solution by radioing to the EUPM Station in Zenica nearby to send a separate car under police escort to Bocinja for Sandy and Mark so that they could drive to Sarajevo if necessary. McCallister and Vladimir would fly back to Zagreb in order to avoid the coming storm.

"Off you go!" He shouted back at McCallister.

The helicopter lifted off, blasting Mark and Sandy from behind as they approached the warehouse. A group of five policemen, toting flashlights and armed with pistols, were standing together near white and black police cars parked near the wood line, turning away to protect themselves from the massive gust of wind. When they turned back to face him, he recognized one of the policemen as the police sergeant from the Oborci ambush. He extended his hand and spoke his name, but Sergeant Maric looked away. He recalled that they had not departed on good terms that day. He placed his hands in his coat pocket, while facing the group of policemen.

"Who's in charge of this scene, may I ask?"

There was no answer. The wind gusted, swirling snow around them.

He turned to Sandy. "Do you have your camera with you?"

She nodded. "Here in my backpack."

"Does it have a flash?"

"Yeah, it does."

"Okay, start taking photographs. No matter what happens, don't stop."

He switched to Serbo-Croatian and pointed at the bodies that littered the area around them. "Who's in charge?"

Again, silence. He looked over at Sandy, now feigning amusement. He walked past the group and raised his voice a decibel.

"I see. No one's in charge, so that leaves me, doesn't it?"

Sandy began to snap photos of the area, and a policeman ran forward, waving his hands excitedly, as an umpire would announce a foul ball. "No! Access to the warehouse is forbidden, and there can be no photographs!"

He recognized the rank of lieutenant on his collar. "Ah, so, Lieutenant, is it?"

The lieutenant nodded and repeated himself. "Entry to the warehouse is forbidden...no photographs."

He fully recognized that his authority as the EUPM Commissioner was being challenged and understood the precariousness of their situation—it was only he and Sandy. Their helicopter was gone and their car had not yet arrived. He heard the sound of EUFOR helicopter blades beating in the distance. He couldn't yet determine the precise intent or motivation of the police, but he also knew that he would need to act quickly and boldly, or that authority would vanish in an instant. He remembered Mike McCallister's report that locals had stopped EUFOR from entering the village of Bocinja. Sandy was looking over at him expectantly.

Opting for a well-staged bluff, he reached into his coat pocket and pulled out his ID wallet, flipping it open to display his EUPM badge. "Lieutenant, before flying up here, EUFOR positioned themselves on the outskirts of this village. Now, they will stay there unless I call them forward. All it takes is a call to the EUFOR Commander, General Rose, and they will drive through the town and occupy it in force…tanks, helicopters and hundreds of soldiers. Tell me if that's what you want."

The lieutenant stood silent and expressionless.

Again, he nodded. "Okay… Sandy?"

Sandy nodded with only the trace of a smile conveying her understanding of his intent. Acting was not her strong suit, but their success now depended on it. She pulled out her cell phone and pushed the speed dial for Jon Schauer's apartment in Zagreb, and after a few rings, she heard his answering machine pick up.

"Yes, Commissioner Lyons for General Rose, please?" After a moment, Sandy spoke again. "General Rose, please stand by for Commissioner Lyons." She passed the phone to him, and suddenly the helicopters they'd just heard flying in the distance were directly…fortuitously…overhead, above the darkening sky, descending.

The lieutenant held up his hands. "No! Please! EUFOR cannot occupy this village! It will be very bad for everybody!"

He glanced at the number she had dialed and handed the cell phone back to her. "I dare say Jon should find that call highly entertaining," he whispered. Sandy bowed her head as much to conceal her smile as to protect herself from flying snow.

The sergeant approached Sandy and asked to hold the camera. Sandy handed it to him with a terse, stern warning that she wanted it returned in the same condition.

As they approached the warehouse, they encountered the scattered and frozen bodies of mujahideen that littered the ground.

"Dear God in heaven," Sandy uttered.

Mark surveyed the scene with dispassionate eyes. The blue tarps that the police had placed over them had been partially blown away by the blast of the helicopter rotors. He knelt by each body. Each of the men appeared to be in his thirties. All of the faces had thick beards. Some were dressed in camouflage fatigues, others in traditional Middle Eastern Arab garb. The shots that had been fired into them were well-aimed to the head or to the center of their chests. He tried to turn the bodies over, finding each of them to be pinned to the ground by frozen blood emanating from massive exit wounds.

He looked up at Sandy who was standing directly above him, closely observing. Conventional bullets were incapable of producing wounds of this magnitude.

This is no ordinary killing spree...

He walked through the front door of the warehouse, broken glass crunching under their feet. The lights that still worked flickered on and off, dimly illuminating the interior. The air had a peculiar feel to it...damp and musty. Airless. He saw Sandy shiver, wiping the wet hair out of her face. Sergeant Maric and the Lieutenant followed closely behind them. Work tables lined the concrete walls on the far end of the warehouse with metal parts bins on the opposite end. Approaching the work tables, Mark nearly tripped over two bodies. Two AK-47 Rifles lay beside them. On another wall, there was a large, black banner emblazoned with red Arabic script that he could not decipher.

He leaned down and pushed the selector switches on each weapon to "safe" before stepping around them.

Machinist tools, piles of metal shavings and large chunks of stainless steel lay scattered on the tables. He picked them up and carefully set them back down, contemplating the purpose of the warehouse and considering how it could be linked to the carnage around them.

He came to another draft table in the corner of the room. On top, there was a copy of the Koran. Underneath it, he leafed through a stack of blueprints in English text with hand-written subscripts in Arabic. The blueprints portrayed the design for a machined device, two and a half meters in diameter and height, roughly the shape of an hour glass. The next blueprint showed an internal view, using cut-away depictions of the various components that resembled Russian nesting dolls with one layer fitting inside another. The core component, in the center of the schematic was labeled, "Tritium/Polonium." Surrounding it was the name of a spherical component that he immediately recognized: "Plutonium 239 (8 Kg)."

He felt a sense of dread overcome him; and yet his own internal denials were met with further confirmation of what he already suspected...the next layer was "Beryllium Powder, Neutron-Reflecting, wrapped in micro foil" and the larger massed layer was simply "C4 Explosive"...

"What is it, Mark?" He vaguely heard Sandy behind him.

He looked back at her, but did not respond. He began flipping— frantically—through the rest of the papers on the draft table. They were filled with complicated equations that did not make sense to him, page after page of them....

$$10 \ Kg \ Pu \ 239, \ (d = 19.86 \ gm/cc$$
$$N= (8.4 \ x \ 10^{13} \ j)/3.2 \ x10^{-11}j/f) = 2.6 \ x \ 10^{24}$$
$$^4He_2 + \ ^9Be_4 \sim \ ^{12}C_6 + \ ^1n_0$$

At the bottom of the pile of papers he came to what he thought were invoices and receipts—mostly in French, some in German, one in English from Capetown, South Africa…with shipping dates all to Sarajevo dated a year to a month ago:

Moronvilliers

Direction des Applications Militares (DAM)

CEA

Phillips

Bruveres-le-Chatel Lessond

Koeberg.

His eyes searched the warehouse, scanning until he saw the bins on the opposite wall. He rushed over to them.

He heard Sandy's voice again, more insistent. "Mark? What is it?"

He glanced at her in silence, his concern immediately apparent.

There was an occasional clicking sound, but he could not determine its origin. At the entranceway, he saw the Lieutenant was leaning casually against the wall. The policeman who he'd recognized, Sergeant Maric, was following them, holding Sandy's camera and taking photos as he followed him.

The bins were filled with stainless steel bolts, screws, fittings and thick rolls of foil and cheese cloth. He sifted through them, but found nothing out of the ordinary…nothing that couldn't be found in an ordinary machinist's shop. He stood up straight and looked around. At the far end of the warehouse, through the shadows, he could make out a large jagged space where a door had once been. He walked over and found a light switch. Turning it on, a single light illuminated the narrow room. It was lined with cheap metal shelving and cabinetry of different sizes, and a bank of technical machinery: Gamma detection cameras…hydraulic presses…balancing machines…and a grouping of shielded glove boxes for handling hazardous material.

Searching the cabinets above, he found the bottom shelves to be locked with a single heavy duty padlock and extended clasp. He gave a cursory sweep of the room and went back into the main area of the warehouse, over to the bodies of the men under the tarp. One of the men was dressed in fatigues, and appeared older, taller and heavier than the others, and his beard was longer and greyer. He searched the pockets of his uniform and in one of his cargo pants pockets found a ring of keys. He pulled them out and went through the series of keys until one fit the padlock. He placed the lock on the bench above the drawers and opened the clasp to provide access to the drawers.

Numerous zip-lock type plastic bags filled with a fine white powder were scattered at the bottom of the first drawer. The adjoining one held self-contained glass bowls half-filled with what appeared to be metal shavings. The other drawer had a hard rubber-like container inserted. A cover slipped over it, extending from top to bottom. He put his gloves on and withdrew the container from the drawer. The container was heavy, and even through the leather gloves, he could feel how hot the metal was. He gently shook the container once and heard the dull sound rattle inside.

Now, with the clicking sound and flashes from the camera in Maric's hand, his heart pounded. He looked up at Sandy and Sergeant Maric, cautiously sliding open the top of the container to expose nearly fifty silvery metallic pellets, some tarnished yellow from oxidization, and of various sizes ranging from small marbles and ping pong balls to baseballs.

On the inside lid, there was another stenciled label… *Pu*

Jesus God!

For the first time in recent memory, since Annalisa had been taken hostage, he recoiled with alarm and an overwhelming sense of dread. His heart seemed as if it would pound out of his chest.

Written in longhand, underneath the stenciled acronym "Pu" was the translation of the chemical symbol:

Plutonium

CHAPTER 49

FEBRUARY 4: BOCINJA, BOSNIA AND HERZEGOVINA

MARK STRAIGHTENED HIS COAT on his shoulders and locked his eyes into Sandy's. He felt the knot in his stomach tighten, and his heart was pounding like an Olympic runner's. Despite the freezing temperatures, he was soaked with sweat. Sandy held his gaze.

"Dear God—what do we do?" she whispered again.

The Lieutenant was approaching them through the blown-out doorway inside the warehouse. He quickly returned the lead container containing the plutonium pellets to the drawer, refastened the steel clasp, locked it, and stood up. He doubted whether the Bosnian Police had any idea of what they were sitting on, aside from a simple murder scene. And he doubted further whether they could ever predict the overwhelming and lightning-fast response to come.

"For now?" he asked rhetorically, feeling his pulse begin to slow down. "We let their ignorance work on our behalf."

"Like mushrooms…."

"Mushrooms?"

"Kept in the dark and fed only shit," she whispered.

Mark smiled as the Lieutenant walked up to the doorway of the room.

The lieutenant looked around until he saw Sergeant Maric behind them, and only then did he appear to relax. "Your people from the police mission are here. You may go now, Commissioner, if you are ready. My men will escort you out of the village to assure your safety."

Mark nodded. "Very kind of you." He looked at her and then glanced down at the drawer containing the plutonium to verify that he had properly locked the metal clasp. He could feel the key ring in his pocket. Across the room on the draft table, in full view, were the blueprints for the device. He stepped out of the room with everyone in tow. When they walked out of the warehouse, they found themselves surrounded by snowflakes descending in the darkness. They felt hot as they landed on his face. Two white Toyota 4Runners with UN markings were parked on the dirt road to their front, engines running and lights on, their windshield wipers struggling against the accumulating snow. They were greeted by an American EUPM officer, who handed him the keys to the second vehicle and invited them to follow him to Zenica.

As they prepared to depart, they could see a figure approach on the driver's side through the blizzard of snow. He rolled down his window and saw Sergeant Maric holding the camera close to his chest. He handed it to Mark without speaking a word.

Mark thanked him in English for returning the camera, and for taking the photos. He started to drive off, but stopped himself before calling back for Sergeant Maric. "Why?"

Maric turned around to face him.

"Why did you help us, Sergeant?" he asked.

The policeman looked away toward the warehouse and to the bodies outside. The snow now covered the blue tarps. "We are Muslims, Commissioner, but we are not like these mujahideen. *That* is why I helped you."

Mark looked at the policeman and nodded his understanding.

Driving down the path, sliding occasionally on the light blanket of snow, he turned the car's GPS system on and waited until it displayed a grid coordinate. He pulled his cell phone from his pocket and searched for John Thorpe's speed dial number. He heard the static as it struggled to make the connection. Finally, there was a distant ring answered by Thorpe's familiar voice.

"John-Mark here. Quick, copy these grids down and I'll explain."

He repeated the letters and numbers of the map coordinates several times phonetically to confirm that Thorpe had an accurate copy, and explained in detail what they had just witnessed… about the bodies, the plutonium pellets, the lead box, where he could find it…the fact that although they had not found a nuclear device on site, they'd clearly seen a capability and the materials to build one…and if the blue prints were any indication, perhaps several. He continued with a description of the police force at the warehouse and the fact that a EUFOR contingent was halted outside the village. He concluded with a brief summary of the weather conditions in the area, mentioning that he and Sandy were now driving back to Sarajevo and would meet him there.

He finished and there was a long pause. For a moment he thought he'd lost their connection. Thorpe's reply, when it finally came, was terse and simple.

"Mark, make sure all of your people are away from there. I'll take care of it from here."

He ended the call and struggled to keep the 4Runner on a straight and controlled path down the hill. The other UN vehicle they were following was nearly invisible ahead of them in the blizzard.

"Why do I get the impression that you knew about stolen plutonium from Capetown before we arrived here?" Sandy asked.

He paused. "I knew what John Thorpe told me, but I had no idea this is where we'd find it."

"What am I missing here?"

"There are two things you can use plutonium for—as a fuel for nuclear reactors, and to construct nuclear weapons. Really nothing else."

"So they weren't trying to solve the energy crisis back there?"

"No, I think we can rule that out."

She was silent for a while as she looked out the window at the falling snow. "Do you know it's Saturday?" The wipers grated on the windshield. "Back at home, people are living normal lives, shopping at malls, going to the movies, spending time with their families...friends. And here we are in Bosnia dodging ambushes and chasing after Doctor Strangelove! *Does this seem at all normal to you?"*

He searched for the best response. He felt a profound sense of guilt for drawing her into a growing, violent morass that he was struggling to understand.

She shook her head and laughed, as if amused by a sudden revelation. *"That's it!* It *is* normal to you, isn't it? All of this is!"

He continued to drive in silence. He glanced over and saw her looking at him, her expression now intense. He shrugged.

"No," she said with a resolute tone. "This *isn't* normal, Mark. It's why I wanted to leave here in the first place."

He nodded. "At this point, I can't say that I blame you."

"But the difference between you and I," Sandy continued, shifting toward him. "Is that despite it all, I can still tell the difference."

"And I can't?"

She shrugged. "If you can't, your soul is damaged and you're living in a dark, dark fog."

Mark navigated the SUV through the snow, downshifting and struggling to keep it from bogging down in the snow. Her words, he sensed, were derived from a past profoundly different from his own. She knew very little about his life. While she was motivated by a visceral desire for justice, he realized he was probably fed by a deeper undercurrent of vengeance...an essential distrust of the human condition. More than most others, he suspected, he'd seen up close what other human beings could do to one another, often without provocation.

How could he make her understand?

He remained silent, unsure how to respond. Along the narrow roadway, a green British Army Land Rover came into view on the roadside. A British soldier was walking around outside—the front tires to the vehicle were buried, having spun deep into the ground. Rolling down the passenger window, he found himself looking at General Ian Rose.

From his expression, it was apparent that Rose, too, was caught off-guard by the encounter. He glanced quickly at Mark and then turned his head awkwardly, straight ahead. Mark was amused by his reaction.

"Ian! I had no idea! It's rather a mess here, isn't it? Ah, let's see...we have a winch—we'll pull you out!"

Rose scowled. "Don't bother, Lyons. We have people on the way."

"Oh, no bother at all! Glad to help!"

Mark backed their 4Runner directly in front of the Land Rover, and extended the winch line to its bumper. Rose's driver turned the ignition and gave it some gas as he activated the 4Runner's winch line. The Land Rover was soon set free. Rose exited the vehicle and walked up to Mark, who had already unhitched the winch and was now rewinding it.

"Lyons, I don't know why you're here," he said flatly. "But my advice is for you to leave before things get worse for you."

Mark felt a fleeting wave of anger pass over him as he continued to maneuver the winch. He looked over at Rose, dressed in freshly starched brown, black and green Army camouflage uniform, and wearing a black beret with the SAS emblem and insignia.

"Ian, I think you know why I'm here. I was sent here. Despite what you may think, I'm not the enemy. We're on the same team."

"You deliberately aided and abetted the escape of an indicted war criminal, Lyons. I would consider that 'cross purposes.'"

Mark nodded. "You mean, Celo, don't you?"

Rose was silent.

"Yes, well, I can see how that is your view, but things are not always as they seem."

"He's your cousin and you helped him escape capture. I think it's *perfectly* clear."

"It doesn't mean a damn. You should know that he's willing to surrender peacefully. Unfortunately, now that you've tried to capture him by force, he's unwilling to surrender to you, Ian." He finished rewinding the winch and stood upright to face Rose. "All things considered, I can't say that I blame him."

"You will come to regret your approach, Lyons," Rose seethed. He pointed at the 4Runner. "And you should know that your friend is wanted for questioning by the FBI as a witness to the ambush at Oborci."

Mark nodded at Rose and smiled. "I *thought* it was an ambush." As he walked back toward the 4Runner, he turned around to face Rose and pointed up the hill in a sweeping motion. "One last thing…a friendly word of advice: you may want to vacate this area. My guess is that it will be swarming with our American compatriots from Fort Bragg very soon…the lads from Delta Force." He looked at his watch. "In minutes, actually."

Mark began walking back to his vehicle and turned around. "'Who Dares Wins', remember that motto, Ian?"

Seething, Rose closed his mouth tightly. His eyes were red, and his expression was as cold as the snow falling around him.

"Cheerio then!" he said again, smiling.

Mark got back into the 4Runner and looked at Sandy. Her eyebrows were raised with a mingled inquisitiveness, waiting for him to speak. He put the vehicle into first gear and waved at Rose's driver, who was grateful for the assistance. And yet, as they departed he found himself breathing more rapidly and felt his heart pounding hard in the wake of his encounter with Ian Rose. Now, he realized, the visceral rage he once felt toward this man for what he had done and for what he failed to do that day in Belfast had not yet dissipated.

He continued to drive in silence, and turned his wipers on "high."

"Are you okay?" she asked finally.

He glanced over at her and nodded, pointing toward the progressively heavier snowflakes collecting on the windshield. "It's rather difficult to see in this stuff…yeah, I'm okay."

"You may want to slow down then." Her voice betrayed a mounting concern over how fast he was driving in the current weather conditions.

He downshifted forcefully. "Sorry about that."

"Okay, Mark...," she exhaled and shifted in her seat to face him. "*Look,* I'm here. I'm not one of your soldiers or your policemen, so I hope you feel like you can talk to me." Sandy paused for a moment, looking out at the forest blanketed in white. "Kate told me about you and General Rose before she died...*so, can you please talk to me?"*

"Sandy, I'm sorry...I—" He stopped himself as he considered how to respond. "It's the past. Going back to it is an exercise in futility."

"So how do you cope with it all?"

He shook his head, and turned to her briefly, looking into her green eyes. "I don't know." He shrugged meditatively. "You just do. You muddle through, you compartmentalize...internalize...."

"That's all?"

"You don't approve?" he asked abruptly.

She shrugged. "It's not my place to approve or not. It's your method, so it must be fine for you. I'm just not sure it would work for anyone else."

He looked away from her, and focused again on the road ahead. His stomach was in knots. This was not the conversation he wanted to have, not a conversation he'd ever had before, with anyone, but she had drawn him into it. "I don't expect you to understand."

"I understand," she answered quietly, "but despite it all, despite the cruelty I've seen, I haven't completely given up on humanity...I still believe in the good we're capable of." She paused. "That's why I wanted to leave— before it was too late."

"Why did you stay?"

Sandy looked out the window for a moment before she answered. "Because I'd almost forgotten. And you helped me remember...." She looked over at him with emotion-filled eyes. "Not to give up."

Overhead, there was a sudden loud roar and the chassis of the 4Runner shook as if they were sitting at the epicenter of a powerful earthquake.

"What—?" she exclaimed, holding the armrests, while looking up through the windshield.

Three large grey airplanes with their props turned strangely upward were skimming the tree tops...in the snowstorm. He recognized them as U.S. V-22 Osprey's—ultra-fast troop transports that flew like airplanes, but were capable of taking off and landing like helicopters. Their state-of-the-art avionics allowed them to fly in the very worst conditions. Along their flight path above the forest, the jet stream lifted the snow off the ground in a brief, swirling white-out.

"That would be General Thorpe's lads, I reckon," he answered quietly.

He started the engine back up and turned the 4Runner back on the snow-covered path behind the other vehicle. After a few hundred meters, they came upon the main road leading from Bocinja to Zenica. The sky was lightening as dawn approached.

CHAPTER 50

MARK LYONS and Sandy Evenson drove through the city of Zenica on the winding road toward Sarajevo, passing a large group of boys—a dozen of them between the ages of 8 and 10, he estimated—standing alongside a burnt-out car, milling around on the roadway.

"What are they doing?" Sandy asked.

Mark looked in his rearview mirror and saw them throwing stones into the adjacent field, and then ducking behind the car's chassis. He understood what they were doing. Shaking his head and cursing quietly, he abruptly stopped the 4Runner on the opposite end of the road. He looked at Sandy.

"They're trying to detonate mines from the roadside—an interesting demining technique, but a bloody dangerous one." He looked back at the boys. They had since stopped throwing stones into the field and were now facing the 4Runner. "Let me see if we can stop the madness before someone gets hurt."

She smiled at him and nodded, wished him good luck.

He approached the boys and greeted them in their native Serbo-Croatian. They were all dressed in ragged blue jeans, Chicago Bulls hats and Michael Jordan sweatshirts and sneakers. One of the younger boys was dressed in a set of American Army camouflage fatigues, complete with velcroed patches, folded in the sleeves and legs several times so they would fit him. The boy was smaller than the others and held a toy AK-47 rifle in both arms, at the ready. Underneath an oversized U.S. Army Green Beret, his face was sprinkled with freckles and his eyes were wide.

He fought back the urge to laugh. The boys' expressions turned from shock to genuine happiness when they discovered that he spoke their language, and suddenly he found himself mobbed by the boys, pointing at the field, shouting, "*Mina! Mina!*" It translated directly to "mines."

He waved, finally silencing them. "I am the United Nations Police Chief for Bosnia!" His voice was stern, but he smiled, looking from one boy to another, his eyes coming to rest on the youngest. He pointed at the field, threatening the loss of life and limb, pantomiming the loss of his own leg to further illustrate the consequences. "I'm too busy to take you to the hospital! Now go!" The pack of boys howled in laughter and walked off—still rambunctious, but sufficiently chastened, he thought. The young boy in the camouflage uniform trailed behind the rest of the boys, throwing backward glances, smiling broadly. The final time the boy turned around, and for an instant, he saw himself as a boy...*Marko*...waving back.

Blinking hard, he called UN Headquarters on his cell phone and reported the minefield so that it could be cleared by a UN demining team. He returned to the 4Runner and found Sandy talking on her cell phone with Jon Schauer.

"Which carrier? When is it scheduled? I'll catch a flight tomorrow morning...afternoon latest... Okay... Okay... Thanks...Bye."

She finished the call and held her cell phone in her lap with both hands. She looked at him with a taught expression.

"They're flying Kate's body back to her home in Vermont tomorrow evening. I'm going to escort her back, Mark."

He nodded and looked into her eyes. She'd made up her mind, and, he knew intuitively, it was the right thing to do.

CHAPTER 51

FROM A DISTANCE, against an unnatural lavender sky, Mark Lyons saw the man's face…his profile…in the crowd of people milling about in the open air market. It was a vague recognition at first, but as he drew closer and saw the man smile, he was certain.

It was him.

The compelling sense of familiarity mingled with the man's ethereal obscurity. But it was the same grin that had taunted him, and which he had seen that grey, cold morning after Annalisa had slumped in his arms, after his hands had been soaked in her blood. …*After they'd taken her from him.*

Closer still, he could hear the man's thick northern brogue, and his laugh winding its way through the market stands around him. It was not possible, he told himself.

They'd killed him that day, hadn't they?

The SAS had told him there were no survivors. But he was there…in front of him, very much alive.

They'd lied.

Ahead, he saw with clarity this man who had, in an instant, destroyed his entire world.

He approached him from behind, slowly, purposely, deliberately, shouldering past people, but all-the-while keeping his eyes on the man—*only him*. He was leaning casually against a white BMW, talking and laughing with a coterie of men around him. The man's clothes were the same as he remembered…the black leather jacket, the worn blue jeans and black leather shoes, the cigarette always hanging from his lips, and the cloud of smoke wafting around his head…the greasy, dark brown hair…but it was the profile that convinced him. It was seared into his memory.

But why was he here?

He felt his adrenalin surge. Like a predator stalking prey, he could sense the people around him, their voices, the pungent smell of fish and herbs from the market stands, the cobblestones under his feet. He could not discern any other threat. If he maintained the element of surprise, he knew, it would all be over in seconds. The images of that day flashed before him like a strobe...of Annalisa, lifeless and heavy in his arms...of the SAS Commandos—men who he'd once commanded—dressed in black, descending upon the farmhouse, like a flock of bats.

He felt his heart beating wildly, and under his jacket the cold sweat rolled off his skin, but he was careful to keep his movements calm and measured. He skirted the BMW from the rear, walking on the sidewalk along its passenger side.

The kick he delivered to the man's right knee elicited the clean snap he'd expected. Before he could resist, he thrust his hand into the man's throat and gripped it tightly. Squeezing further, he slammed his head in reverse onto the hood of the BMW, placing a large dent in its center.

The crowd of people had quickly dispersed and he realized that the man was attempting to talk. He maintained the grasp on the man's neck and watched as he fell into unconsciousness. As he tightened his grip, he knew he was dead.

Another separate image of Annalisa's killer standing casually beside him caused him to release his hand from the man's throat. The man was laughing, taunting him with his cigarette still hanging loosely from his lips. He realized, with an eddying awareness, that he'd just killed the wrong man.

How...?

Looking down at the man lying on the hood of the car, he now recognized, fully, the colorless, lifeless face of Ian Rose staring back at him.

MARK SAT BOLT UPRIGHT in bed, breathing heavily, overcome with a surreal sense of the past racing against the future. He found his pillow and tee shirt drenched in sweat. His sheet and comforter were on the floor in a twisted heap. His eyes surveyed the pitch black hotel room. The digital clock on the bedside table glowed. It was 3:22 A.M.

He shivered and ran both of his hands through his hair, closed his eyes and commanded the ghosts of his past to shut up. "Bloody Hell...I must be fuckin' mad."

He pointed the remote and turned the television on to the BBC. The room glowed with a faint, fluorescent blue light. He closed his eyes and began to drift in and out of sleep. Just as the commentator made reference to "the impending war in Bosnia," Mark forced his eyes open. Footage of houses being blown up, graffiti on the ruins of schools and hospitals, rampant militias firing upon the other, and roads filled with refugees flashed on the screen before a map of the Balkans and then Southern Bosnia appeared with arrows pointing from various locations all in the direction of Ravno and the city of coastal city of Neum.

Ravno. An obscure town in Southern Bosnia near the Mediterranean coast. Unknown to the world. Heretofore a place insignificant to the rest of the world, but now, ironically perhaps, the strategic epicenter for a war that threatens a fragile Balkan peace....

...Three armies face one another, along the borders Ravno intersects. Croatia, Bosnian Muslims, and Serbia. Combat between all factions in and around Ravno has become more fierce, the toll on the civilian populace heavier, and the atrocities more numerous and brutal. The massive scope of this violence has not been seen since the last war here, but the true origins date back to the days of Ancient Rome and the Ottoman Empire. Today, the stated goal of each faction is to protect their own people from extermination at the hands of their enemies. But those most familiar with the crisis point to Ravno as the crossroads for the three factions, and threatens to cut off the long Herzegovina corridor extending from Split to Montenegro...land historically dominated and populated by the Bosnian Croats, but through the intensive resettlement efforts of Celo Mescic, the ethnic balance around Ravno has tipped to the Serbs....

...The change was transparent to outside observers, but was a source of great consternation by the other long-time Croat residents. Their cries went unnoticed until Serbs won all of the opstina elections. Croatian President Milo Stanic intervened on behalf of the Bosnian Croats in Herzegovina and declared the elections "tainted," and therefore "null and void" in the eyes of Croatia....

...When UN observers validated the results, the violence began....

...Roman Polko, the UN High Commissioner for the region was in Ravno yesterday. "It has been a charade, really. Anytime a single event causes such violence, there is a deeper, more profound problem. Bosnia has suffered from our long-term neglect, and that is why we find ourselves, again, today, in this very bloody conflict...over a small farm village. It's senseless."

In fact, the European Force—EUFOR—had assumed a passive role in this mounting crisis, apparently hoping that it would resolve itself. But today, without waiting for German or French approval, the U.S. President and England's Prime Minister authorized their forces to begin air strikes and full scale defensive ground operations against all factions who were found to be in violation of the Dayton Accords....

...The EUFOR Commander, General Ian Rose, in Ravno, defended the action: "The UN mandate already exists. Our goal is simply to enforce the existing peace accord, implement an immediate ceasefire and push the warring parties into negotiations. As soon as that happens, we will have completed our job here."

...Despite General Rose's optimism, and given the current desperate conditions here, that, it would seem is easier said than done....

Xenia Dormandy, for the BBC World News Service, in Ravno, Bosnia.

He got out of bed stiffly and made his way to the bathroom. He turned the light on, and saw an envelope protruding under the hotel room door. It had the blue and red "Holiday Inn-Sarajevo" logo in the upper left hand corner, and his name was typed in the center as "Mr. Mark Lyons." He opened the envelope and found a pamphlet in Serbo-Croatian that had been folded in quarters so that it would fit inside. He unfolded it, and realized that it was a Sunday church bulletin—for Saint Stephen's Cathedral in Zagreb. He brought it into the bathroom and scanned it. On the front page, he saw the schedule for next week's masses neatly boxed in with a yellow highlighter. Inside the box, a light blue highlighter outlined Sunday's 10:00 A.M. Mass. He opened the bulletin, and a piece of folded hotel stationery fell out. He picked it up. The handwriting was in a distinctively European, neatly crafted cursive script written with a blue fountain pen:

> *-Attend this Mass. Sit on the furthest left end of the front pew.*
> *-Revelations of the past reconcile the future.*
>   *Lazarus*

Lazarus? Another crazy evangelical trying to claim another soul in desperate times.

He set the bulletin and note aside on the sink countertop.

He relieved himself, washed his hands and again caught site of the signature...*Lazarus*...the distant memory of the name he'd heard over and over again in his dreams as a young boy suddenly rushed forward. He shuddered at the memories he'd tried so hard to forget.

It was not possible…. Was it?

He splashed his face with cold water and then switched to warm, savoring the contrast. Looking into the mirror, his eyes seemed distant, and his face only vaguely like his own.

CHAPTER 52

PAPA VOYO STUDIED the large oddly-shaped stainless steel device, gleaming under the bright lights in the center of the hangar. Major Savo Heleta stood rigidly with his hands clasped behind his back. Heleta's warrior physique was entirely compatible with his hand-selection by Cardinal Vojislav Pijadje to command the Gabriel Team. Like the Ecumenical Guardian before him, Papa Voyo had chosen his own successor; early-on, watching the young orphan's impressive performance in school and overwhelming dominance in sports, Papa Voyo knew Savo Heleta was "The Chosen."

And yet, to any outside observer, the physical contrast between the two men was stark. Heleta was an intimidating figure, tall, thickly muscled and defined, with an intellect that was equally as formidable. At the age of only twenty-one he had been granted the status of "supernumerary member" in the Opus Dei sect of the Catholic Church. Under his maroon beret, Heleta's head was shaved and tanned. His face was striking and angular, freshly shaven. In conjunction with the starched tiger stripe-patterned military fatigues, Heleta was a head taller than Papa Voyo and his body-builder's physique cast a wide shadow over the elder cardinal. Papa Voyo's rail-thin frame was covered in a black habit. Perhaps the most dramatic difference between them was their facial appearance. Heleta had clean, tanned and perfectly contoured features, while Papa Voyo's face was seamed, concave and hollow, and covered with a thick blanket of whiskers.

The device rested on a small circular iron-framed table. Papa Voyo placed his hand on the device tentatively as he walked around it, feeling its cold surface. It was perfectly constructed, flawlessly crafted, and smaller in size than he'd expected. And yet, he knew well the destructive power it contained. He stopped beside Major Heleta, and placed his hand on the flat glass top of the device. Papa Voyo's graveled whisper was inaudible to everyone else in the hangar, but Heleta.

"You have done well, Savo."

"My men, Eminence. They have done well."

"A team is a reflection of its leader, and you reflect well on them."

"We are flattered then," Heleta responded, doing his best to redirect the subject of their conversation.

"It is God's victory, but his work for you is not finished, my friend."

Heleta chose not to respond, intuitively understanding that he was about to receive another mission.

Papa Voyo unfolded a piece of paper and handed it to Heleta. He waited as his protégé read.

TOP SECRET
UMBRA/NOFORN/WNINTEL
FM: ROBERT CHILDS, CIA STATION CHIEF, ZAGREB, CROATIA
TO: AMB JOSEPH STEINBERG, AMB JACK FULBRIGHT
"EYES ONLY"
1. (S) A GROUP OF ISLAMIST MUJAHIDEEN TRAINED IN AFGHANISTAN ENTERED BOSNIA-HERZEGOVINA ON 12 JANUARY OVER LAND THROUGH THE BRCKO DISTRICT AND ARE CURRENTLY IN ISLAMIC MILITANT CAMPS NEAR ZENICA (CENTRAL BOSNIA) AND TUZLA (NORTHEAST BOSNIA).
2. (S) THE GROUP OF MUJAHIDEEN IS LED BY ABU-HAMZA, A KNOWN WAHHABI TERRORIST ACTIVE IN AFGHANISTAN, CHECHNYA AND IRAQ. ABU HAMZA IS OPERATING FROM THE LARGEST OF THE TERRORIST TRAINING CAMPS IN BOCINJA.
3. (TS) CUSTOMS DOCUMENTS CONFIRM THAT TWO PAKISTANI NUCLEAR SCIENTISTS, DR. BASHIRUDDIN MEHMOOD AND AHMED NAZIR, ENTERED BOSNIA-HERZEGOVINA THROUGH SARAJEVO ON THREE SEPARATE OCCASIONS OVER THE PAST YEAR. THEIR VISITS WERE SPONSORED BY YASIN AL-KADI, THE OWNER OF VAKUFSKA BANK, ALSO A PERSON OF INTEREST SUSPECTED OF FINANCING MUSLIM FUNDAMENTALIST ACTIVITIES AND AL-QAIDA NETWORKS IN EUROPE.
4. (TS) EMBASSY SARAJEVO HAS OBTAINED CUSTOMS DOCUMENTS THAT CONFIRM THE ARRIVAL OF VARIOUS MACHINISTS COMPONENTS AND TOOLS FROM FRANCE, GERMANY, PAKISTAN AND RUSSIA TO SARAJEVO AND BIHAC OVER A ONE YEAR PERIOD.

5. (TS) A HIGH PROBABILITY EXISTS THAT PLUTONIUM PELLETS NOT ACCOUNTED FOR AT THE KOEBERG NUCLEAR POWER PLANT IN CAPETOWN, SOUTH AFRICA WERE SMUGGLED INTO BOSNIA-HERZEGOVINA BY ABU-HAMZA THROUGH RAVNO IN DECEMBER WHEN HOSTILITIES COMMENCED THERE.

6. (TS) SOURCES EMBEDDED IN THE VAKUFSKA AND ILAMSKA BANKS REPORT AN INTENT TO CONSTRUCT MULTIPLE HYDROGEN NUCLEAR FISSION IMPLOSION DEVICES AND TO TARGET UNSPECIFIED UNITED STATES AND VATICAN INTERESTS.

7. (TS) ACCORDING TO THESE SOURCES, ALL ACTIVITIES ARE BEING CONDUCTED WITH APPROVAL GRANTED BY MUSLIMS AT THE "HIGHEST LEVELS" IN BOSNIA AND WITHIN THE AL-QAIDA NETWORK. EMBASSY SARAJEVO REPORTS THE PROBABILITY OF PROLIFERATION TO ISLAMIST TERRORIST ORGANIZATIONS TO BE EXTREMELY HIGH. STATION CHIEF ASSESSES THE SITUATION TO BE "GRAVELY SERIOUS."

//END//NOTHING FOLLOWS//CHILDS SENDS//

Heleta finished reading the report and handed it back to Papa Voyo, and pointed at the top of the page.

"Of course, I recognize these names—Steinberg, Fulbright—they were the Americans in the convoy at Oborci. Did this come from the briefcase we seized?"

"Yes," Papa Voyo responded. He knew Heleta had not seen the contents of the charred aluminum briefcase before now, because he'd given the team explicit orders to deliver all documents obtained from the ambush without reviewing them. He had not wanted to predispose them to a conclusion prior to their operation. When it was delivered, he had been gratified that it was still intact given the vast destruction at the ambush site.

"So there are two devices?" Heleta asked. "How reliable is this report?"

"We should be certain of it." Papa Voyo paused and remembered the final conversation he had with Robert Childs in the Residence. His sacrifice, as well as the reporter's, was necessary to ensure their success. "Everything else reported by the American in this message has turned out to be true. I have no reason to doubt he was correct about this as well."

Heleta pointed at the paper now folded up again in Papa Voyo's hands.

"It was not in the warehouse. I personally checked every room, every closet. Do we know where it is?"

"That is what you must learn," Voyo said sharply. "I know these people and what they are capable of. They have sought to destroy us. But now, after we have defeated them in their lair—"

He looked away, toward the doors of the hangar where the rest of the Gabriel Team was assembled and placed both of his hands on the device as if he were offering it in sacrifice. "They will seek to use the other instrument against us in retaliation. They will detonate it in the Vatican."

Heleta's expression was contained. Controlled. His intense blue eyes met Voyo's. "We will find it, Eminence."

Papa Voyo nodded at his protégé. "Savo—whatever the cost, whatever corner of the earth they are keeping it, you must go. Because finally, we have met them—they are what has been prophesied by the Apostle Luke: '*The Day of Wrath may catch you unexpectedly, like a trap; for it will come upon all who live upon the face of the whole earth. Be alert at all times, and pray that you may have the strength to escape all these things that will happen....*" His eyes had not left Heleta's. He drew closer to him. "Find it and destroy it. *Destroy them.*"

"Certainly, they are Satan's offspring," Heleta said somberly. "We will find them."

Papa Voyo's piercing black eyes stared at Major Heleta. Voyo crumpled the report and handed it to his protégé. He turned and gazed at the Gabriel Team in silence. What he could not tell them was that in their efforts to eliminate the Islamic threat against the Vatican, he knew that ultimately their sacrifice too would be required.

CHAPTER 53

FEBRUARY 5: SARAJEVO, BOSNIA AND HERZEGOVINA

SANDY EVENSON SAW John Thorpe and Roman Polko sitting at a corner table in the hotel restaurant. She finished checking out and left her bags with the concierge before walking over to their table.

"Do you always wake up so early, gentlemen?" Sandy asked with a smile.

Both men looked up and rose. Thorpe pulled the chair out for her. "Sandy! Join us!"

Polko had a broad smile and gestured to the chair. "Please, Sit!"

She set her coat on an adjacent chair and sat between both men. John Thorpe was in impressive shape for a man in his fifties, she thought…good skin, hard-looking, like he still ran and made regular visits to the gym. He had an air of quiet authority and confidence—a trait she also saw in Mark Lyons. Roman Polko was, as always, dressed impeccably in a tailored suit. His hair was a distinguished grey. He had the aura of a professional diplomat. Within UN circles he was nothing less than a rock star. During her time in the Balkans, he'd fully supported the war crimes tribunal and her own efforts during trying times.

"Can I order you some breakfast?" Thorpe asked, looking over at Polko. "You see, it's rare to find a place in Europe where you can get a genuine American breakfast, so I try not to miss it!"

Polko shook his head. "The American breakfasts are too heavy. Here in Europe we know better than to burden ourselves with so many calories, general!"

She smiled as she declined the offer, accepting a cup of coffee instead. She looked at Thorpe. "I understand those were your planes flying overhead yesterday in Bocinja?"

"You were with Mark at the warehouse, then, I take it?"

"I was," She answered.

Thorpe nodded. "Where are you from, Sandy?"

She was momentarily caught off-guard. "Connecticut."

"Then they were *our* airplanes," Thorpe answered, with a wry smile.

"Mmm hmm...well, they were very impressive, but you should tell them to be careful when they are flying so close to the treetops."

Thorpe laughed as he took a bite of his toast. "I'll be sure to tell them."

"Well, I'm relieved."

Thorpe had a confused expression. "Relieved?"

"Relieved that you're both here after the warehouse episode—I figure you must not be worried if you're eating breakfast."

Polko smiled and shook his head. "We were just discussing this. It's very serious."

Thorpe nodded his agreement. "There's plenty to be concerned about. It was a very good thing you and Mark found that place."

"We wouldn't have gotten in there without Mark's insistence, and wouldn't have made it into the warehouse without his sheer force of personality, really. The natives weren't at all friendly, and I'm sure your arrival sufficiently chastened them."

Thorpe nodded and she saw a trace of a smile flash across his lips. "They found themselves a bit outgunned I think."

"Is that your baggage I see over there?" Polko asked, pointing at the front desk.

She nodded at Polko. "I'm flying to Zagreb for Kate Kamrath's Memorial Service and then to Vermont to escort her body home."

Both men nodded. Thorpe refilled her cup with coffee.

"I'm very sorry about Kate, Sandy," Polko said. "And all of the circumstances."

She shook her head slightly. "What did she do to provoke that?"

Thorpe shook his head. "Nothing. It's senseless."

Polko folded his newspaper and looked at her. "With Mark running the investigation, we'll find who murdered Kate. I'm confident of that."

"You both have many other things to worry about. I was there yesterday at the warehouse. I saw the plans, the materials...your planes flying over us. When you consider what's at stake in the grand scheme of things, there's no comparison."

Thorpe sipped his coffee. He pointed at the newspaper on the table. "Oborci, Bocinja, Robert Childs' disappearance, Kate's murder...I don't believe any of these are random incidents. They've been too well-planned and flawlessly executed."

"But how could Kate have been connected to all of this?"

Thorpe set his cup down and pursed his lips as he considered his response.

Polko looked up and answered before Thorpe. "Ms. Kamrath was investigating Jack Fulbright's assassination. She came to my office to interview me two days ago. When I sat down with her I discovered she knew essentially what I knew."

"None of us told her," Sandy interjected.

"Yes, I know," Polko answered. "She was a remarkable journalist."

Thorpe nodded his agreement. "She got close enough to make some folks feel threatened."

"So they killed her?"

Thorpe shrugged slightly. "Quite possibly."

"If it's all connected...if it turns out that way," Sandy said, looking at both men. "Will you help find whoever did this to her?"

"I will, Sandy," Thorpe answered. "Whatever I can do to help, I will."

"Yes," Polko said. "Of course. It is our responsibility."

"And will you take care of *him?*" she asked, pointing at Mark, who was walking through the hotel's glass doors in a light blue Gore-Tex running suit.

Polko smiled. "Of course, but you should know that he is taking care of us!"

"He's human, like the rest of us, Mr. Polko." She waved to catch Mark's attention.

Mark looked over and approached their table smiling. She could see he was covered in sweat and condensation from an early morning run. He shook hands with Thorpe and Polko, and smiled at her.

"How far?" Thorpe asked.

"Not far enough," Mark answered, standing over their table. "Rather pitiful actually. Did Sandy tell you we saw your planes overhead yesterday?"

She reached over to grasp Thorpe's forearm. "They're *our* planes."

"Oh, I see, this is an American thing then, isn't it?" Mark laughed, glancing over at Polko and winking. He paused and pointed over to the front desk. "Are those your bags?"

She nodded. "Yes. I have a 10 A.M. flight."

Mark seemed to be quietly considering his response as he sat down beside them. Sandy moved her coat. He turned to Roman Polko. "You know,

I called Mike McCallister this morning and asked that he and Vlad fly down from Zagreb to pick us up." He turned to Polko. "Sir, with your permission, I'd like to use your helicopter to fly us to Zagreb so we can also attend the memorial service." He paused, looking at Sandy intently. "We also have some unfinished business to attend to there."

Polko nodded. "Of course. As I told you, it is yours to use freely."

"I'll take you up on it, thanks," she replied.

Mark wiped the sweat from his eyes. "Good."

CHAPTER 54

FEBRUARY 5: SARAJEVO, BOSNIA AND HERZEGOVINA

ROMAN POLKO PAID the bill over the objection of the others. When the waiter left he turned to the others as he stood up to leave. "If you need anything...if there is anything I can do to assist, you must not hesitate to contact me."

Polko shook everyone's hand at the table.

Mark turned to Thorpe. "A rather interesting place, that warehouse, wasn't it?"

Thorpe nodded. "We've been able to determine that the cells in Bocinja and Germany were connected. Most of the mujahideen who were killed in Bocinja were in our databases. They were Afghan and Pakistanis—all confirmed members of al-Qaida. And there were two Yemenis. The preliminary information we have on them is that they're metallurgists, and good ones...MIT-educated."

"So why the raid?" he asked. "Was this a case of the chiefs killing all the Indians? Or what?"

Thorpe nodded. "It may, but as you really look at it, it doesn't make sense. They left all that plutonium, the plans for the devices, the other materials to construct several more if they wanted to. Why leave all that behind?"

"So there's a third party at work," he concluded.

"Yes," Thorpe answered. "We think so."

"And the plutonium?"

"The same pellets missing from the Koeberg Plant in Capetown."

"Were they able to construct an actual device?" Sandy's eyebrows shot up in alarm.

Thorpe's voice was somber. "All of the evidence leads us to believe they made two of 'em. Sophisticated designs, not crude ones like you'd expect. Comparatively, these are light weight and very efficient."

"Jesus...." Mark muttered under his breath. "And where are they? Do we know?"

"No, we don't," Thorpe answered. "We have a NEST team surveying freighters in the Atlantic sea lanes and we have another one at the airport in Mostar searching the ground here, but without anything more specific it's much like finding a needle in a haystack."

"And so it's possible we may have not just one group that has a nuclear bomb, but two competing ones?" Sandy asked.

"Yes." Thorpe said after a momentary pause. "That's our assumption."

Mark looked at Sandy who was obviously concerned.

"Mark?" Thorpe said softly. "I don't have to tell you—"

He wiped more sweat from his forehead and eyes with the cloth napkin from the table. He knew Thorpe was referring to the gravity of the situation they were facing. "No.... No you don't."

CHAPTER 55

MARK LYONS ESTIMATED that they had been airborne in the back end of the Russian Helicopter for about 20 minutes, when a deafening roar came overhead and then another. He saw Sandy Evenson's eyes widen and look over at him, clutching the aluminum seat tightly. In that instant, the helicopter shuddered violently and heaved hard to the right. He felt as if he were in a high-rise elevator that suddenly had its cable cut. The floor seemed to be taken out from underneath them. They were a dead-weight falling. He could feel the rush of air and the rotors biting the air in an uncontrolled descent. He reached over and placed his arm around Sandy's shoulders and pressed their heads down to their knees, holding her hand tightly.

The bastards've shot us down.

And yet, as he glanced around, he could see no structural damage to the helicopter, no holes…no smoke. Inside, the hull was rocking and vibrating violently…hydraulic fluid was pouring out from the ceiling, and then a loud grinding noise. He struggled to look up at the windows, and through each, he saw a flashing blue and green…sky, earth, sky, earth…like a camcorder that had inadvertently been left on in movement. They were spinning, fast, and the ground was rushing up at him. He knew they would hit the ground in seconds. After everything he'd been through…everything still left to do, it angered him that he would have to die this way. He felt a stab of guilt that he'd selfishly kept Sandy here with him.

Now she would die too.

He tightened her seat belt for her; then his own. He heard Sandy curse as the hull shook and rattled. She started to sit back up, but he pushed back hard on her shoulders, and yelled for her to keep her head down. He could hear the terrible sound of the gears grinding harder, faster, high pitched — like hundreds of children's finger nails scraping against a chalkboard. It was accompanied by the distinctive, sweet smell of hydraulic fluid in the cabin, and he found himself praying to a God he no longer fully believed in.

The impact he'd anticipated did not come. A moment later, the helicopter's rotor blades were turning again, haltingly at first, and then at full speed. The grinding and shaking had subsided. Vladimir regained control of the helicopter, with little room to spare. He released his tight grip on Sandy's shoulders, unbuckled his seat belt and looked out the window. Sandy joined him. It was only then that he realized they were within 100 feet of the ground, and climbing steadily. He looked at Sandy wide-eyed.

"I think we're okay," he shouted. "We're climbing again now."

"What *happened*?" She asked, shaken

Mark shrugged, and placed his hand on her shoulder. "I don't know. I'll ask Vlad."

Sandy nodded, not saying a word. She seemed unsure whether it was best to be relieved or wait for the next blow.

He made his way up to the cockpit and stuck his head in between Vladimir and Mike McCallister. McCallister's face was an ashen white and his expression blank.

He squeezed his arm. "Mike! Are you okay?"

McCallister turned his head to Mark and nodded slowly. "Jesus, Mary and Joseph...."

"Pray for us!" He finished in the most cheerful tone he could muster, and unbuttoned the top buttons of McCallister's blue uniform shirt. "You'll be fine, just take in a few breaths! We're just fine."

"I'm as sick as a seagoing parrot," McCallister gasped. "This is my last flight in one of these bloody contraptions!"

He looked at Vladimir, who was still checking gauges and adjusting instruments with one hand and steering with the other—all the while, focusing on the horizon. He could make out the Roman castle in Jajce outside and below them. After a moment, Vladimir looked at Mark with a determined expression that still conveyed a measure of residual distress.

"Vlad? We *are* fine, aren't we?" Mark asked. It was more a plea than a question.

Vladimir glanced over at him, eyes raised, and then returned to the instruments, without responding.

"What happened?" Mark asked simply.

Vladimir looked forward momentarily, adjusted their direction of flight, and turned back to him. "It was an American jet, Commissioner—an F-22, I think, judging from the tail. One of their new fighters. He flew too close to us, and stole our air. His jet stream almost knocked us out of the sky. He *had* to know he would do that."

"Why? Did he reach you by radio?"

Vlad shook his head. "No warning.... None. We are lucky...very lucky to be in the air."

"Is he coming back for us?"

"No sign of that...yet." Vlad answered. "I don't think we could survive another like it."

Mark remembered the BBC report he'd seen only several hours prior in his hotel room about the American decision to launch air strikes...today. And still, it didn't make sense. Their helicopter was clearly painted white, with black UN markings. The weather conditions were clear and could not have obstructed their view. No good American, British or other NATO pilot could conceivably mistake it for anything else. *Unless it was a deliberate act, to intimidate.* If they had meant to kill them, they wouldn't have relented until the helicopter had been downed.

"Are you still able to fly this thing?"

"Nothing's damaged. She's still airworthy."

"Okay, hug the landscape as best you can. Stay in the valleys where they can't fly, but get us to Zagreb, safely. Okay?"

Vladimir nodded his understanding.

Mark stepped back into his seat and joined Sandy. She turned to face him.

"Well?"

"Well, apparently one of *your* airplanes decided to invade our space."

"Well, then they're not one of mine. I disown them," Sandy said matter-of-factly.

"But who would do that?"

"There's just the question," he answered curtly. He knew that it likely did not occur by accident and the thought that it could actually occur *by design* quickly led him from a state of disbelief to sudden anger and resentment against the one person who could have given the order.

He sensed Sandy's gaze. He looked away from her, but she reached for his arm and squeezed.

"Mark?"

He looked back at her. His expression was somber. "There are times when you can't help but feel as if you've met the *real* enemy."

"Our own Air Force?" She asked incredulously.

He shook his head. "They just announced on the news that they've approved air strikes throughout Bosnia. As the EUFOR Commander, General Rose controls the Air Force."

"I've gotten the impression that he isn't exactly a fan of ours."

He shook his head. "He's a bloody ingrate is what he is."

She leaned back against the webbed seating, and turned her head to him. "Yeah, but that's still no excuse. The order could've come from the White House too."

"We've met the enemy," he added dryly. He tightened his jaw for a moment and looked up at the ceiling. The hydraulic fluid leak had slowed to a steady drip. "And he's us."

PART IV

RECONCILIATION

CHAPTER 56

JIM GOODWIN KNOCKED softly on the door to the National Security Advisor's West Wing corner office. Rachel Cook looked up from her desk, stood and walked over to shake his hand. She shut the door and motioned for him to take a seat at the glass-covered oak conference table, and sat opposite him. Goodwin saw the dark rings starting under her eyes, her effort to cover them up with makeup, and instinctively understood the pressure she was under. Between the non-stop intelligence reports, the Oval Office threat briefings, the interagency meetings with the deputy and principal members of the National Security Council, the constant barrage of phone calls, and the precautions now underway to ensure continuity of government in Washington and in New York and Boston, he guessed she was getting only a couple hours of sleep a night.

She greeted him with a warm smile and a calm, steady voice. "Jim, my folks in the SITROOM tell me you were up late last night," she scolded, lightheartedly.

Goodwin offered a wry smile in response. "Funny, they said the same thing about you!"

"Touché. Well, you could have at least come up to visit me. The Secret Service are great guys, but they aren't always the most stimulating company," she teased. "What have you got for me?"

"On a hunch, last night I had our folks scrub everything that had been coming in during the past six months from Zagreb—every document Robert Childs wrote or commissioned that wasn't sent to us at our Headquarters." He paused and looked at the National Security Advisor before continuing. He pushed two files toward her, both with bright orange "Top Secret" cover pages. "We received these by diplomatic pouch from Zagreb last night. I wanted you to see them."

She scanned both documents quickly, and then looked up at him with her eyebrows raised.

"He knew about the plan to construct the devices?"

"Apparently so, but what's so remarkable is that from reading the second document...the notes that were found in his desk...he also may have had an idea of what was being targeted."

Cook picked up the second document and flipped the cover page open. "What's the connection?" She appeared only semi convinced. "I'm not sure I understand his notes—they're not that specific."

"No, they're not, but they demonstrate a pretty sophisticated thought process *and* prior knowledge of a threat that we've now confirmed. It's not hard to connect the dots."

"Okay, help me...," She pointed at the first hand-written annotation on the paper. "Who's Cardinal Stepinac?"

"The late Archbishop of Zagreb during World War II who was jailed during Tito's reign and later died under house arrest. He's loved by Catholics and hated by the Serbs and Muslims...they accuse him of abetting mass executions by the Nazis."

She moved her finger to the next line. "And this? ...Medjugorje? Isn't that like Lourdes?"

Goodwin nodded. "It's the Catholic pilgrimage site in southern Bosnia—where a group of kids saw apparitions of the Virgin Mary."

She nodded. "What's so significant about this date, May 1st?"

"The Pope is canonizing Stepinac on that day. In Medjugorje."

"That's only a week away...."

He nodded. "That's why I'm here."

"What are you saying?"

"We know that the Vatican has always been one of their targets. Looking at his notes, I believe Childs was theorizing that Medjugorje was a compromise target."

"It seems like an obscure place to detonate a nuke," she said.

"On the surface, yes...," Goodwin answered.

She nodded, now understanding his implication. "I see...because the Pope *is* the Vatican—why target him in Rome when you can bring the Vatican to the Balkans?" She paused. "It's a plausible theory, I suppose, but it doesn't tell us where the devices are. We still don't know—all we have are assumptions."

"I spoke to General Thorpe last night. We know that the construction was taking place in Bocinja. We've scoured the place. From all the forensics, we can say with reasonable certainty that they completed two of them—a gun-type device and an implosion device. Over time we estimate they had the capability to build about eight of either kind. All indicators…everything we translated and analyzed from both raids in Wertheim and Bocinja point to the completion and delivery of the gun-device over three weeks ago to another cell that we haven't identified yet. The implosion device was probably completed a week ago, but no one had taken delivery of it. It sat in the warehouse, waiting for pick up."

Cook leaned back in her chair. "Why the raid?"

"It depends entirely on who was responsible. If it were an inside job, the intent would be to keep it all a secret. That would be a good assumption if they hadn't left all the material and bodies behind. But if it were an outside job, as we suspect it was, their sole intent would have been to steal the devices, direct from the manufacturer."

"But you think they only got one?"

"That's our assumption."

"Who *was* responsible?" she asked in a worried tone. *"Cui Bono?"*

After a brief pause, she repeated the English translation: "Who Benefits?"

"Either the Serbs or the Croats, would be my guess. I can't say which at this point. Both groups would have their own motives—self-defense prime among them."

"Or retribution." She leaned back in her chair and folded her hands in her lap, directing her gaze out the window to the north lawn of the White House and Pennsylvania Avenue beyond it.

"The Sword of Damocles," Goodwin answered.

She looked at Goodwin, but did not immediately reply as she considered the proposition. "It's a theory."

"But a plausible one…*and* it's backed up by the notes of the CIA Station Chief on the ground," Goodwin answered.

"Who was Childs' source, do we know?"

"We don't. But whoever it was, we know now that they were reliable. In one of his papers he makes mention of 'Lazarus,' whoever that is. If it's a codename we have no record of it."

She sat up straight. Any previous signs of her fatigue were now gone and her tone was serious. "Okay, Jim, based on this I'm convening a twenty-four-seven CSG." Goodwin recognized the acronym "CSG" as the Crisis Security Group—a high-level interagency crisis response cell that met in the

White House Situation Room and via secure video teleconferences.

She stood, opened the door and addressed her executive assistant. Goodwin could hear her clearly. "I need to talk to both General Rose and General Thorpe as soon as possible. Also, find out the name of our ambassador to the Vatican—I'll need to talk to Secretary Stone before calling him." She walked back to the table and lifted both reports in her hands, as if presenting them back to him. "Okay...are you free for a couple minutes to brief the President?"

Goodwin understood it to be a purely rhetorical question.

CHAPTER 57

MARK LYONS' CELL PHONE rang as he and Sandy Evenson approached the security area in the departure terminal. It was Mike McCallister. He listened as McCallister informed him of a EUFOR warrant that had just been issued for Sandy Evenson's arrest.

"What?" Mark asked, bewildered.

"They want her for obstructing a EUFOR investigation, fleeing the scene of an accident, obstructing the capture of an ICTY indictee."

"I didn't know they could do that," he said, looking over at Sandy with a concerned, surprised expression. She was listening, and intrigued by his reaction but was unaware of what Mike McCallister was telling him.

"Neither did I," McCallister replied. "But General Rose signed it."

"It's not worth the paper it's printed on," he answered.

"Nonetheless, I thought you should know."

He thanked McCallister and hung up. He turned to Sandy. "It seems that General Rose has crafted an arrest warrant for you."

Sandy shook her head in disbelief. "What planet is that guy from?"

He glanced at her, amused at her words, and shrugged. "Well, that's precisely the problem."

"And what would that be?"

"When they give foolish men bombing authority."

"No, it's what happens when someone is missing their intelligence gene," she said. "Will they be pulling me off my plane in shackles?"

"I rather doubt it," he answered, smiling. "I don't think they're that efficient."

They arrived at Customs and he found himself staring at the gate, suddenly at a loss for words.

"Sandy, I—"

She placed a hand on his forearm and smiled.

He nodded. "What can I do?"

"You've done all you can...all I could ask," she answered. "I'm not in a position to ask you for anything else, Mark…but—"

She paused.

"What is it?"

"In case they have G-Men waiting for me on the other end, do you think you could talk to General Thorpe, and let the White House know I'm not the enemy here?"

He nodded and grinned. "Absolutely. I'll do that."

"Mark…." she looked up at him as she pulled out her ticket in preparation to go through the gate. "I'll miss you."

He nodded. "And I you."

Something in her eyes disconcerted him. "I'm worried."

"Don't. We'll get all of this sorted out."

She placed her backpack on the floor beside her. "I feel like I'm abandoning you."

"You've done far more than you had to. Well beyond the call of duty," he said, shaking his head. "You know you have to do this for Kate."

She nodded, threw her head back to reveal a disarming, luminous smile. "You know the funny thing? If Kate were here, she'd be telling me not to worry about her."

After a brief, awkward moment, she stepped closer and quickly reached up to embrace him. He reached around quickly and held her head tightly against his. Her hair felt like silk against his face and in his hands. He could smell the light fragrance of her perfume. She clung to him tightly and he could feel his carefully emplaced barriers suddenly being reduced to rubble. He hadn't expected such a reaction, deep within.

She pulled back slowly and nodded. Wiping the tears from her eyes, she mustered a smile and laughed. "I'm rather pitiful, aren't I?"

He shook his head. "You're doin' the Lord's work."

He squeezed her arms to reassure her; then released his grip. "Go carefully then."

She picked up her backpack and slung it over her shoulder. "*You* be careful," she said directively, hesitating for a last moment to look at him; she drew back and then turned around.

He watched her pass through the Customs station. Despite the compelling urge he felt to wait, he forced himself to walk away, not wanting to prolong a farewell he now knew he hadn't been fully prepared for.

CHAPTER 58

MARK LYONS ENTERED Saint Stephen's Cathedral and was immediately taken by the cavernous, elaborate interior.

He looked around and contemplated the ideas that had inspired the interior design. Gradually, the pews were filled—mostly with elderly men and women, along with the occasional group of younger tourists. The organ began to play softly and he realized that he, too, was a tourist of sorts, albeit an unlikely one.

He walked past the gold framed oil paintings depicting the Stations of the Cross, and a large oil painting of an enthroned Byzantine Christ, one hand holding a scepter and the other outstretched in blessing. He found the front left corner pew as the handwriting on the invitation had instructed. Sitting down, he remained incredulous about the note, but was reminded that it was the mention of Lazarus that had led him here. In his lifetime, he'd only met one man who called himself by that name—but that had been three and a half decades ago.

He was torn from his thoughts by a soft tapping on his shoulder from behind. He looked back to see an altar boy, not more than twelve years old holding an oversized book out to him.

"The man asked me to bring it to you," the boy said gesturing back at the entrance to the church.

Mark turned and looked back, but saw no one he recognized. "Is he still there?"

The boy shook his head. "He left after he pointed to you."

He thanked the boy. The cover was worn, brown leather with embossed gold Cyrillic script that identified it as a Serb Orthodox bible. The smooth texture of the leather seemed familiar to him, as were the bound tissue-thin pages.

Outside, the church bells rang and the organ began playing at full volume. The congregation stood, and he followed suit. He looked over to the aisle and saw an altar boy carrying a large crucifix of silver and gold leading the procession of Mass celebrants to the altar. At the end, the Archbishop of Zagreb, a tall man with a narrow, heavily whiskered face followed, with his hands held together and pointed toward the ceiling in prayer.

Mark looked down at the bible in his hands, and opened the cover to the first page—an icon of Christ held out a large, narrow hand in blessing.

As he studied it, it became more and more familiar. The look…the feel of the soft leather binding.

Could it be?

An impulse shuddered through him and suddenly, he knew. It was the very same bible…his father's. The page seemed fragile and the colored ink was faded with age, making the Cyrillic print difficult to read in places. The scent from the old pages was also familiar and even strangely comforting, reminiscent of his childhood when his father would read biblical passages to him before his bedtime.

On the opposite side of the altar, a choir had begun to sing in a classic Gregorian-like chant. When they finished, the priest stood at the altar and welcomed the congregation in both Serbo-Croatian and English and then, in what he termed as the "tradition" at Saint Stephen's, he proceeded to say the Mass in Latin.

Studying the bible further, Mark noticed the gap in the pages, roughly in the middle of the binding. He opened it and found a small pile of old black and white photographs and a newspaper clipping underneath them. He picked the photos up and examined them closely.

It took several moments for him to realize that the photos depicted the field execution of a man who was kneeling down and facing a wide dug-out trench. The executioner was in a military uniform, holding a pistol to the back of the man's head. The second photo was taken right after the trigger had been pulled, and as the man was falling into the trench the executioner was still holding the pistol out in front of him, aiming it at him.

He turned to the third photo and the recognition was immediate and jarring. It was the photograph that he kept by his bedside as a child. It was a tangible thing that had reassured him and allowed him to sleep at night. He flipped back to the previous two photos, and studied them more closely. A sharp, painful spasm shot vertically along the back of his head, causing him to wince. He opened his eyes, and the statues, the candles the ornate walls of the church seemed to liquefy and shrink around him. He bowed his head to make it stop. A chill ran through his body with the inescapable realization that the man being executed in the photo was his father.

Lyon's struggled to maintain his composure. He forced himself to take a deep breath...and another. He shut his eyes in an effort to see things more clearly. Finally, he placed the photos back in the bible and closed it. He held his head with both hands, and ran his fingers through his hair. The chanting started again, and he willed it to stop. He didn't want to be here anymore, but his position in the front pew removed any opportunity for an anonymous exit. He felt trapped, and the grief he felt for his father quickly shifted to anger...anger at who brought him here—at this man, Lazarus, for not confronting him directly, for choosing this church to reveal the fate of his father to him, anger toward his father's executioner, and at the communist dictator Tito, for taking him from him when he needed him most.

The emotions seemed to cascade upon him with an unrelenting force. An old lady sitting beside him leaned forward and put her hand on his shoulder and shook him, asking him in Croatian if he was okay. He nodded and quietly thanked her.

He held the bible tightly in his hands and shut his eyes to block the Mass out. The choir had stopped chanting, and he opened his eyes. His hands were tightly clenched around the bible. At the top of the bible's spine, the newspaper article that had accompanied the photos was sticking out.

The Cardinal began his homily, speaking again in Serbo-Croatian to the assembled congregation—his voice thick and graveled, but also jovial, if not buoyant in its tenor. Mark was vaguely aware that he was speaking about the canonization of the cardinal from Zagreb.

"...Alojzije Stepinac...died in captivity of the Communist regime...to be canonized a saint next Sunday at the site of his last miracle...in Medjugorje...the Pope will officiate...."

"...his legacy as a Saint of Croatia honors us all...it is the place where we all should be...buses will be available in the city square to take you and your families to Medjugorje and bring you back to Zagreb Sunday night...."

He looked up at the Cardinal, and saw the cross held by a chain around his neck, and the ring on his finger. Underneath his dark grey beard, he could detect that the right side of his face was disfigured—his jaw and cheekbone flat, if not concave. The beard was successful in concealing only part of the deformity.

"He was my friend...But Cardinal Stepinac was also my inspiration...

responsible for who I am today…for who we are…an example and an enduring symbol for all of Croatia."

Mark pulled out the fragile piece of newspaper and carefully unfolded it on the front cover of bible to reveal an article no larger than his hand. It was taped on the seams where it had been folded, creased and yellow with age. The script was Cyrillic, and to the right there were two narrow, grainy photos, side-by-side—one of a young Yugoslav Army officer in dress uniform, and the other of a priest with a severe facial deformity. His curiosity was heightened by the article's headline.

Former Bodyguard for Tito Ordained Catholic Priest

<u>Sarajevo</u>. Yesterday, Vojislav Pijadje, a former trusted bodyguard to Marshal Tito and political officer within the Yugoslav Communist People's Army, was ordained a Roman Catholic priest in Sarajevo. Pijadje began studying for the priesthood in 1977.

He was released from service in the Yugoslav Army after suffering severe injuries from a military accident in Dulici, a small village near Zvornik, where he reportedly saved the lives of two boys who ventured into a training minefield. In an interview with him following his ordination ceremony, Pijadje confirmed that this incident proved that "God had other plans for me," but that the near fatal accident also firmly established within him a "healthy fear of the Lord."

Pijadje's service in the army spanned fifteen years, where he was assigned as a personal bodyguard to Tito, and was then hand-selected by Tito himself to guard the Archbishop of Zagreb, Alojzije Stepinac, who he had placed under house arrest following his trial for collaborating with the Nazi's during World War II. In that capacity, he found himself more and more isolated from the population, and he rediscovered his Croatian identity.

"It took me 15 years to make up my mind, but the call from God was always present. My long conversations with Cardinal Stepinac and much prayer reinforced the calling," Pijadje said.

Pijadje was ordained in the Franciscan Order and has been assigned to the diocese of Medjugorje, Bosnia and Herzegovina.

Tito offered no comment on Pijadje's decision to convert to Catholicism and ordination to the priesthood.

Mark remembered that at the beginning of the Mass, the priest had introduced himself as "Papa Voyo."

Short for Vojislav.

At that moment, he understood why Lazarus had brought him here.

There had been no "mine accident," as the article claimed. The man depicted in the newspaper photographs was the same army officer he'd confronted at Brnisi Dam more than two decades ago. He had caused the injury to his face on the hill.

Now, he was Zagreb's Archbishop!

A Cardinal of the Catholic Church…the church he'd been raised in…and the officer who had summarily executed his father.

CHAPTER 59

AT THE MOMENT their eyes met during the Mass, Papa Voyo felt a stab of panic run through him. For that fleeting moment, as he looked at the man in the front pew, he could discern an intensity of purpose in his eyes. Wearing a brown leather jacket, navy blue shirt and white slacks—his appearance was distinctly *not* Croatian—or European. He held a large book in his hands. It was at the beginning of the Eucharistic prayer when Papa Voyo recognized him. He was the one who had accompanied the police into the reporter's apartment the day before. Now, he was there, standing in the front row of pews! He could still hear his footsteps echoing throughout the cathedral as he walked toward the doors.

He realized that he'd faltered in his delivery. The deacon assisting him caught his attention by holding the gold-plated chalice even higher in the air.

"Through him, with him, in him...."

As he resumed the prayer, his initial panic was soon replaced by bewilderment. He'd gone to great lengths to make the reporter's death look like an accident. He cleaned her thoroughly and gave her Last Rites. He wanted her to be found that way. He had left no marks on her—no blood, no wounds.

One of the unique characteristics of the Foxglove plant was that it actually caused heart failure. When ingested in sufficient quantities, it produced all the clinical symptoms of Digitalis: dizziness, nausea, burning in the stomach, heightened heart rate, convulsions, shock, coma and finally, in several hours, death.

He'd ground the rootstock into a fine powder and mixed it into several items he found in her refrigerator: the half-used bottle of wine, her coffee creamer, and the bowl of fruit. He had watched her enter her apartment and knocked on the door thirty minutes earlier. She didn't answer, so he let himself in with the duplicate key Savo Heleta had made for him. Within several minutes, he heard her vomiting and moaning in her master bath. She tried to make a telephone call only to find the line dead. He'd made a point to cut it. He'd listened to her condition worsen, and then walked out to the kitchen counter and had taken her cell phone out of her purse so she could not use it.

Because Foxglove was a natural substance that quickly dissolved, he knew the poison was largely undetectable—unless the coroner specifically looked for traces of the plant's extract.

So how could he know?

The vestments he wore were heavy, and even in the cathedral's cool interior he realized he was sweating profusely. They stuck to his damp skin and he desperately wanted to remove them. He craved the fresh cold air outside, but at this point he had no choice but to finish with the Mass. He mopped his brow before continuing. He chastised himself for allowing himself to be so profoundly affected by this...a single, isolated incident.

A coincidence perhaps?

Privately he was intrigued by this man who had appeared and just as quickly, disappeared. Inside the vestuary, he opened a drawer and pulled out the framed photograph of him and Robert Childs, and then another framed photo of the reporter...who was this stranger that had appeared and just as quickly disappeared? After so many years as a soldier and as the *Guardian*, had he finally found a worthy adversary?

He would not wait to find out.

CHAPTER 60

SANDY EVENSON WALKED out of the bed and breakfast with her suitcase in tow, and breathed in the fresh, clean air. An intermittent breeze drifted through the porch. She heard the crunch of gravel on the driveway and saw a middle aged man with a pronounced limp approaching. He was neatly dressed in jeans and a white corduroy shirt. A Silver Chrysler 300 Hertz rental car was parked in the drive.

Jim Goodwin extended his hand, introducing himself as the Deputy Director of the Central Intelligence Agency.

Without making the effort to step down from the porch, she shook his hand, the other buried in her jeans' pocket. "Are you here to arrest me, Mr. Goodwin?"

"No," Goodwin laughed, shaking his head. "We don't arrest people—"

"Of course, not. You kill them, don't you?"

"Sandy, General Thorpe sent me."

At the mention of Thorpe, she walked down the steps and smiled at Goodwin.

"Okay, if you're with John Thorpe, then I'll freely confess."

He shook his head and laughed. "No need for confessions. John suggested that I meet with you while I was in town. I know what you've been through and if you have the time—"

She pushed her hair back. "I have a plane to catch in three hours. I was waiting on a shuttle but if you can you take me to the airport we'd have some time to talk."

He nodded. "I'd be glad to. That's where I'm heading too."

Sandy dialed her cell phone and cancelled her shuttle as Goodwin helped her with her luggage. She followed him to the car.

"Were you at Kate's funeral yesterday?"

"I was," he answered, loading her suitcase into his trunk.

"Did you know her, or did you come all the way up here just to give me a ride to the airport?"

"I knew Kate, yes."

"I never heard her talk about you, Mr. Goodwin."

"Jim—please, call me Jim," Goodwin said, shutting the trunk. "I don't suppose she would have talked about me that much."

Sandy had opened the passenger door and was in the process of sitting down in the leather seat when she sprung up to face him.

"What does that mean?" she asked tentatively. "Were you one of her sources?"

Goodwin was silent. "Not exactly," he said, finally.

Sandy looked at his card. "Kate didn't *work* for you, did she?"

"In a limited capacity, yes, she was," he answered quietly.

"That's like being almost pregnant, isn't it, Jim?" she answered, her voice thick with sarcasm.

"She was a reporter, but worked for us in exceptional circumstances, when we needed her."

She gaped at him. "What does that *mean*? She was working deep undercover or something?"

"Something like that."

Her head was spinning. Kate had never given her any indication that she was a CIA agent. Suddenly, inexplicably...she felt a profound sense of betrayal.

"I thought I knew her," she said bitterly. "Obviously I didn't."

Goodwin's expression was sober. He placed his hand on the car door. "Kate was exactly the person who you knew, Sandy. She gave us very strict parameters on the assignments she was willing to take or information she was willing to receive. She was still a reporter, and a very good one," Goodwin motioned inside the car. "I'll explain as we drive."

She relented and sat back in the car. Her mind raced as she tried to put the pieces together.

He shut her door and stepped around to the driver's side. Once in the car, he turned to her. "Sandy, I'm sorry if this is too much for you—"

She shook her head. "It's not. I'm just trying to sort it all out."

He started the ignition and they drove in silence for a few minutes.

"What assignments was she willing to take?" she asked finally.

He nodded. "She stipulated that she would only get involved in cases where the lives of other operatives were taken or at risk."

"I still don't get it."

"Her father was a CIA agent on our operations side of the house," he said. "He died in East Germany during the Cold War—in the line of duty."

"And whose lives were at risk recently, may I ask?"

"Our Station Chief for the Balkans disappeared two weeks ago. I—"

"Robert Childs," Sandy interrupted. "He was a friend of mine."

He paused. "We believe he was murdered."

Her heart sank. Kate had voiced the same concerns about his disappearance. "I spoke to him right before Ambassador Fulbright's convoy was attacked at Oborci."

He nodded. "You were one of the last people to talk to him then."

"And Kate's murder was related to his?"

"We can only guess—we haven't found his body so we can't compare the forensics. We found his car in downtown Zagreb in the *Kaptol* district. But I'd say there's a good possibility that's the case. After we received word from General Thorpe about Kate's death, and the information from you and Mark Lyons that pointed to murder as the cause of death, we took the case over from the Croats, did our own autopsy, and sent the blood and hair samples back to our lab in Quantico and the National Capitol Poison Center in Washington for analysis."

"What did they show?"

"They confirmed she was poisoned."

"But with what? How?"

He was silent for a moment. "Foxglove."

Sandy's eyes widened in confusion. "Fox-*What?*"

"More precisely, Digitalis--or Digoxin. It's derived from the Foxglove plant…it's prevalent in Europe. It's a drug that strengthens the contraction of the heart muscle and slows the heart rate. It's used to treat congestive heart failure, but in excess, it can also *cause* it. The Foxglove plant is as toxic as any plant out there—the whole plant is extremely poisonous. It attacks the cardiovascular system, and any digitalis in an otherwise healthy person can be ultimately fatal, and administered without a trace. The poison is relatively easy to make and easy to deliver. She ingested it, most likely from the tea she drank, and the calcium from the Tums she was taking only enhanced its toxicity. Her electrolytes were thrown into complete havoc and she went into full-blown cardiac arrest. In the veterinary world, it's known as a 'poor man's' euthanasia."

"Did she suffer?"

Goodwin hesitated before answering. He flipped the car's sun visor down and adjusted it. "Yes, she did," he said simply.

Her stomach tightened and suddenly she felt ill, and somehow responsible. "Who would do that to her?"

"Whoever she was investigating, would be my guess," he answered. "But we're dealing with someone who poisons to kill. That's a unique method of killing with a unique personality profile all its own. According to the profilers, they're normally the last people you'd expect to be capable of killing. They're usually devious, calculating people with no sense of remorse. Poisoners are psychopaths —'depraved indifference' defines them."

"But you don't know *who?*"

He shook his head. "No, not yet."

As he drove, she searched for answers, but found none, except the revelation that her friend wasn't really a reporter—at least not in the purest sense—but a CIA agent. "Why did you pick her?"

"Because I knew her from years past. She was the best I've seen, hands down."

"The best what? The best reporter or the best secret agent?" She was aware that her tone was becoming confrontational, but didn't care.

"Sandy, let me be clear. Kate Kamrath was a journalist, but she was also a patriot. We weren't paying her to do undercover work, it was solely her decision. She took both roles very seriously, and when we needed her most, she volunteered. Our operatives aren't the mysterious, sophisticated ones you see in the movies. They're human beings, like Kate."

"Quite honestly, I don't know how she reconciled it. At the very least, I'd say it's a conflict of interest. And most journalists would tell you the same thing."

"She had full rein to write whatever she wanted. *The New York Times* was paying her, we weren't. She could also have stopped helping us at any time. She, more than most, knew the risks."

"Does the CIA accept any responsibility for what happened to her?"

"We didn't kill her, Sandy. Someone else did. And we want to find out who did this to her as much as you." Goodwin's tone was even, and his pace measured. And yet there was an unmistakable, yet subtle softness in his voice that caught Sandy by surprise. "You should know that she was a friend of mine too."

She nodded tentatively. "How can I help you?"

"Tell me everything you can about what happened at Oborci…what you saw at Bocinja…."

She breathed deeply as she looked out at the winding, tree-lined road. "I'll be glad to tell you everything I can. But do you want to know my best advice?"

He nodded silently.

"There is one person who you should be relying upon over there. Who you should be supporting. But rather than supporting him, he's being obstructed at every turn."

"Who?"

"The Assistant Commissioner of the European Police Mission for the Balkans, Mark Lyons. He speaks the language, he knows the people, the country, all of the cultural nuances. Since I met him, I've seen him work, and in my opinion he's your last best hope."

Goodwin nodded. "I know Mark. I was surprised to hear he was in the Balkans. He's a legend in Ireland, you know." He paused. "Are you aware of his relationship with General Thorpe?"

She nodded. "You mean the former son-in-law thing? I am. Kate told me. She also gave me an article she wrote about him a while back."

"Well, John Thorpe and Mark Lyons are the very best at what they do. It's more than fortuitous that they're there—in one place—together."

"I think they must have a lot to talk about."

"They've been avoiding the subject of Annalisa since she was killed…avoiding one another," Goodwin said. "How have they seemed together?"

"As far as I can tell, fine. They laugh, they joke together. The subject has never come up, in front of me at least."

Goodwin nodded.

She began to shake her head and laughed nervously. "Just tell me you and the CIA have this all under control now. You know, I have a pretty good understanding of what you're up against—the political-assassination-turned-mine-accident that I *happened* to witness, the loose nukes, the plutonium, Bob Childs' disappearance, Kate's murder…." Sandy shifted in her seat so she faced Goodwin, fully aware that she was talking louder and more rapidly, but she no longer cared. "So, just tell me when you reach sensory overload, okay? Because with two of my friends now dead, I'm about there…."

Goodwin turned off at the exit pointing to the airport. They reached a stop sign. When he spoke, his voice was so quiet that she strained to hear him.

"Honestly, it scares the daylights out of me."

Sandy studied Goodwin. His eyes were expressive, which combined with his sympathetic, raw response made it all the more disarming. She liked him, and she admired his honesty. The fact that he had come up to Kate's funeral spoke volumes about him. *And* as the Deputy Director of the CIA, he was making time to listen to her in the midst of a full-blown crisis. He genuinely seemed to be interested in hearing her perspective, and he seemed to care. "Well, then, that makes two of us...but that doesn't solve anything, does it?"

He continued to drive in silence.

"Why do I get the impression that you're more worried than I am?"

"I'm worried that Mark may be trying to do too much, alone...," he replied pessimistically. "Without our help.

She listened and absorbed the comment. She apologized absently as she reached over to turn the car's heater down a notch. Her heart sank with the thought of losing him and she felt the creep of panic.

"My guess is that he'll figure out who killed Kate," Goodwin continued, "but in doing so he may be putting himself in precisely the same kind of risk that Kate and Bob Childs unwittingly put themselves in."

Abruptly, a wave of dizziness passed through her as the blood rushed to her head. She leaned her head into the seat and closed her eyes. She dug out her cell phone and dialed the United Nations switchboard. While waiting, she took out her Palm Pilot and ran through the address book.

The operator responded and she requested an immediate connection to the UN cell phone number assigned to the EUPM Commissioner for the Balkan Region.

"Mark Lyons, please," she repeated into her cell phone. "It's urgent."

A minute passed as Goodwin parked the car in the rental returns area of the airport. Sandy watched him get out of the car and close out the bill with the attendant. He was unloading luggage from the trunk when she heard Mark's voice on the other end of the line through the static. Although it was not a good connection, she felt a wave of relief pass over her.

"Mark, it's Sandy, I'm—"

Mark repeated her name several times as the connection faded in and out. Sandy heard the sound of traffic and an occasional car horn in the background and realized he was outside.

"I'm here at the airport with Jim Goodwin. I understand you know each other?" Sandy continued.

There was a brief silence on the other end. "I do know him—well, actually. He's a friend of John Thorpe's. We've worked together," Mark answered. The tone of his voice was tentative, distant. "But I don't understand. Why is he there with you? Is everything okay?"

She searched for a way to convey her message to him over a cellular telephone line that was already broken and echoing badly. She raised her voice in an effort to be heard over the static. "He tells me he was also a friend of Kate's, and that *she worked for him*."

"He told you that?" Mark replied matter-of-factly.

"He said she was working under some kind of deep cover," she said impatiently. "And he's fairly certain that the reason she was killed was because she was investigating the Fulbright assassination and Bob Childs' disappearance."

She waited for Mark to respond, but it didn't come.

"Are you still there?"

"I'm here. Just trying to digest it all," Mark answered. "How are you?"

She heard him try to change the subject, and felt her frustration building. "I'm fine," she responded curtly. Did you hear what I said? You're in danger. If Kate was too close to those incidents, so are you! Don't you understand?"

"Sandy, please. Don't worry about me. I never expected for everything to become so bloody complicated, for you or for me." Mark continued.

There was another long silence that she finally broke. She felt her heart beating rapidly as she struggled to breathe in a normal cadence. Everything was so matter-of-fact. Gone was his affectless charm, warmth...his clarity. She was confused and at her wits' end. "Of course it's complicated. Everything's complicated there! But don't you understand? It's also dangerous. Not vaguely and not possibly, but *definitely*, dangerous *to you*! Christ! That's why I'm calling you—to warn you! Don't you get that?"

"I do. And I appreciate you doing that. But you gotta know that I'll be okay over here."

"What do you want me to do? Just agree with you? I know these people, and I *don't* agree with you. They're not the IRA thugs you're accustomed to—they're far more dangerous and unscrupulous. They'd just as soon kill you as look at you. I've prosecuted them at The Hague. I've seen what they can do. Human life doesn't mean a *thing* to them."

"You can't worry about me, Sandy," Mark answered, his voice distant, disembodied.

"I'm sorry, Mark," she replied evenly, sarcastically. "I'm not sure I understand exactly what it is that you're really asking. Am I missing something?"

"You gotta trust me...." Mark voice trailed off.

There was a long silence before Sandy finally answered. When she did, there was a distinct edge to her voice. "Maybe I shouldn't have called"

"Sandy, please—let's not...that isn't what I meant."

"Well, then, please translate for me," she replied. "Because I think I hear you loud and clear, Mark. Don't worry about you. Don't call you. After everything we've been through."

"Sandy, I—"

"No, please, just tell me." She was seething. "I need to know."

There was another extended pause on Mark's end, long enough for her to reach a conclusion.

"Never mind," she replied coldly, her throat tightening, her voice trembling with intensity. "You make perfect sense.... Goodbye, Mark Lyons."

She ended the call and dropped her cell phone in her lap. Her chest felt tight and her head was pounding. She swallowed, closed her eyes and laid her head back on the car's headrest. None of this made any sense. Not his responses. Not even hers. She remembered the lines in Mark Lyons' face, his scent when he had held her at the airport. It wasn't a fleeting hug, but a tight, extended embrace that she didn't expect but desperately needed at the time. She wondered how she could be so wrong.

She let her head fall back on the car seat. This was a different person than the Mark Lyons she knew—not the same man she was falling in love with. Something had happened. Something was dramatically wrong—she knew it. She felt a desolate foreboding, as if the entire earth were disintegrating around her.

Her door opened. Jim Goodwin was extending his hand to her.

Chapter 61

MARK LYONS STOOD a while longer and then ducked into a nearby coffee shop in search of equilibrium. He sat down, placing the bible on the table in front of him and holding both hands to his head. In the wake of the call with Sandy Evenson, he felt as if he were unraveling.

A rush of guilt passed through him. He had not wanted to end their conversation the way he had, and now he found himself fighting an entirely new wave of emotion.

He wanted to talk to her, to explain what he knew....

About the Cardinal at the Cathedral, and the revelation that had been forced upon him there by the man from the Brnisi Dam who called himself Lazarus.

He wanted to tell her that Kate Kamrath's association with the CIA didn't surprise him. All along, he'd suspected something like it as an explanation for her murder. During the time he'd gotten to know her in Belfast, her stories were consistently too well-informed *and* her analysis was always impeccable. It also explained how she managed to show up at many crisis spots immediately after they occurred, before any other journalist would. Her investigative skills alone were formidable enough, but he guessed that an association with the CIA, if discovered, could have tipped the balance and contributed directly to her murder.

Sandy's concern that he could be their next target was not lost on him, but how... without sounding like a bloody lunatic...could he tell her that he actually *welcomed* a confrontation with Kate's killer?

He sensed that he was close to identifying whoever had murdered her.

What he hadn't expected was seeing his father and uncle's executioner in church. It was the only possibility. He glanced down at the church bulletin in his hand and read his name again out loud.

Vojislav Cardinal Pijadje, Archbishop of Zagreb.

And now, there could be only one response.

The photos he'd seen in the church, now in his coat pocket, were the voice of his father from the grave speaking to him.

An eerie resignation came over him. He'd last felt this way after Annalisa's murder. There was the confusion, the self-blame, the anger and the sadness, and then finally, the transformation and separate level of consciousness induced deep within, brought about by the recognition that no one else would take the action required but him.

During these moments, he felt as if he were back in Belfast, walking along the periphery of a mob, deliberately studying it and judging it with each ebb and flow, identifying its organizers and determining its personality, deciding at what place and time he would enter the fray and who he and his men would target in order to neutralize it to cause the mob to disperse.

Then, as now, he cast aside those things around him that could divert him from his purpose or soften his resolve—meetings, previous plans, coworkers and friends, and any instinct for self-preservation. In situations like these, they only served to distract and cloud one's judgment.

How could he tell Sandy Evenson that he actually liked being so close to it all? That he preferred the darkness and the solitude that came with it? That the fear he'd felt as a boy at the dam was gone?

He'd erected façade to keep others out. He'd made it impenetrable, in part to hide the fact that the fear had gradually been replaced by rage and an enduring sense of vengeance.

He started to call her back, but then stopped himself. He stared at the bible on the table in front of him. His heart was still racing with the recognition that it was the same one he'd held as a child.

He carefully opened it to a separately bookmarked page and found a highlighted passage from John, Chapter 11:

> *Our friend Lazarus sleepeth; but I go that I may awaken him out of sleep…*
> *Lord, if thou hadst been here my brother had not died. But I know that even now whatsoever Thou wilt ask of God, God will give it Thee.*
> *Thy brother shall rise again.*

Who the bloody hell was Lazarus?

He fought to make sense of the verse's meaning. *Was it Celo?* All of the cryptic notes he'd received so far had come from him. "Lazarus" could be a derivative of Prince Lazar, whose death in 1389 still represented the death of the Serb nation, to be resurrected when Lazar was raised from the dead. Through the centuries, Lazar had come to embody the coming resurrection of Christ.

Who else could it be?

He pulled the map out of his pocket that Celo had placed on his windshield several nights ago outside the discotheque after their meeting and their encounter with the Croat thugs. He studied the notation Celo had hand-written in Cyrillic.

"Meet here at noon, 12 February."

The circle on the map wrapped around the village of Stolac, just outside Ravno in southern Bosnia. An arrow intersected the circle and pointed directly toward a map symbol for a church.

It had been over a week since he'd seen Celo at the discothèque. So much had happened, that now it seemed like an eternity. He looked at his watch. February 12th was tomorrow.

Even if, by some stretch, Celo wasn't Lazarus, he deserved to know that his father's killer was still alive.

CHAPTER 62

"THIS IS WHERE you're heading, Commissioner—along this route," the flight engineer yelled above the combined high-pitched whine of the turbines. He was kneeling with the visor of his helmet up, pointing toward the town of Stolac in the lower left corner of the Digital Moving Map Display. "We'll drop you off here, in this clearing behind the hilltop, overlooking the town."

Mark nodded and gave him a thumbs-up sign. He counted six U.S. Air Force crewmen in the Special Operations MH-53J Pave Low IV helicopter, each dressed in olive green Nomex flight suits and dark-visored helmets—looking like neo-high-tech knights. One of them manned the .50 caliber machine gun on the tailgate and, on the side doors, two other crewmen sat behind immense ultra-fast mini-guns with clear plastic ammunition belts, gleaming with large caliber bullets, undulating and feeding into them from different directions like the whiskers of a fire-breathing dragon.

With the heat radiating from the helicopter's engines, Mark was grateful for the cool breeze that flowed from the side doors through the cabin. After he learned that they'd nearly crashed on their way up to Zagreb, John Thorpe dispatched a Pave Low up to Zagreb from Mostar to use at his discretion.

A second Pave Low was flying offset beside them as an escort.

"Is there a way I can contact you after you drop me off, if I need you?"

The flight engineer nodded, dug into his vest pocket and pulled out a small radio with an assortment of dials on its face, top and sides, painted flat-green.

"Here you go. It's one of our survival radios. It'll reach us wherever you are. We won't be far away, but even if you can't get voice reception, it'll send out a transponder signal that will cut through just about anything." The flight engineer pointed at the LED window with an assortment of digital numbers displayed, and the walkie-talkie-like transmit key. "It's set to our primary and alternate frequencies. Just push to talk."

Mark thanked him.

"Better buckle up," the flight engineer said. "We're heading into the mountains now, and we'll be flying fast and low to avoid any Triple-A."

He felt the helicopter take a sudden, controlled dive. Out the tailgate he could see the flat terrain drawing closer and gradually become more and more rugged. The roads were filled with people, horse-drawn carts, bicycles, automobiles and trucks. Broken-down trucks and cars were parked on the side of the road. Men and women looked up at the helicopter, while a group of boys were pointing up at them with toy AK-47 automatic rifles, pretending to shoot them down. He saw the tail gunner aim his machine gun down at them, and then abruptly lift up when he realized they posed no threat to the aircraft.

However fleeting the image, its effect on him was profound. They were only boys, caught up in a culture of war that was uniquely characteristic to Bosnia...boys too young to know its true cost or the terror it brought, but eager to act out what had been romanticized for them in movies or by television. He saw himself in them...and he saw Celo. He remembered their excitement at the army trucks driving in convoy through the town center that fateful morning...the guns they carried that afternoon to go hunting...the terrible scene they'd witnessed at the dam and the cascading events that followed, changing their lives forever. They too were only boys then, not unlike the boys on the ground below.

"...the source of this war is hatred. It is the adults who perpetuate it. ...It is the children who we must reach, so they can end it."

Roman Polko's words returned to him with a resonance that surprised him. He realized that it was Polko who had been the first to see it all so clearly, and express the problem in such simple terms—and yet at the time, he remembered that he had dismissed Polko's words out of hand. Now, they had a special force and meaning.

"I knew you would be the reluctant warrior...."

If there was any reluctance then, it was gone now. He now understood that his enemy was something much larger than he'd ever before envisioned—more formidable than any one individual or group. Everything that he'd seen as a soldier, as a policeman, and as a peacekeeper—the horrors of war and the terror it indiscriminately wrought against the guilty and innocent alike was as Polko had described—derived from hatred and handed down from generation to generation. Here and in Northern Ireland, he'd seen the consequences. It was the kind of hatred that exploited religious and ethnic differences evolving over generations—passed on from parent to child in their most formative years. Over time, it created a foundation for the politics of hatred that would follow. Polko had been right all along, he realized, and he'd refused to listen.

Roman Polko's request for a new Commissioner of the European Police Mission in the Balkans came at precisely the time when the negative reports about him in the print and broadcast media were at their worst, branding his tactics as "unnecessarily extreme," "brutal," and "wholly indiscriminate." When confronted by a reporter asking him to respond to the media reports, he responded that he "respectfully disagreed" and preferred to instead think of his operations as "thoughtfully measured, proportionate and well-planned."

Only days after one of his successful, yet bloody raids against protestant paramilitary groups in Belfast leaving twelve dead, he was informed that his name had been submitted by Ireland's Prime Minister to be the EUPM Commissioner. He resisted at first, knowing that he'd become a political liability to those who once supported him, but he finally acquiesced when he'd been told that both sides of the Troubles in Northern Ireland had finally agreed to reenter into negotiations under the condition that the police raids against them cease.

The helicopter was now passing through the dramatic rising and falling terrain south of Sarajevo, flying low through the deep gorges, hugging the mountain sides with will little room to spare. At times, the helicopter would bank fully at a ninety degree angle and Mark would feel the G forces pushing him against his seat. Whoever this American pilot was, Mark mused, he was very good indeed.

Out the tailgate, he could see the burnt-out ruins of houses below nestled among the massif of rugged peaks. Some of the homes were still burning with thick, black plumes of smoke pouring out from rooftops and windows, and rising into the clear sky. The blackened hulks of cars were strewn about the roadsides, and there were no discernible signs of life.

"Six minutes! Get Ready!" The flight engineer shouted.

Mark nodded and gave him the thumbs-up sign. The helicopter banked aggressively to the left and to the right, just above the tree tops, dipping below the ravines and valleys along the way. His heart beat more rapidly as he anticipated the landing. He unbuckled his seatbelt and slung the backpack over his right shoulder as he gripped the webbed seat with his other hand.

"One minute!" The flight engineer shouted, holding out his index finger.

Mark stood and held the anchor line cable that was stretched across the helicopter's roof. He felt the aircraft descending rapidly and at treetop level he saw only dense forest and rugged, mountainous terrain passing beneath them. One of the crewmen was laying prostrate on the tailgate peering out to spot the landing zone. The tail gunner was on one knee, methodically swiveling the .50 Caliber machine gun to acquire any potential targets on the ground below. The other crewman pulled himself back into the helicopter holding his thumb and index finger close together.

The flight engineer nodded. "Okay! Thirty seconds, Commissioner!" The Flight Engineer took hold of his arm and held him firmly in place as the helicopter touched ground. He felt himself being moved firmly and deliberately toward the tail gate. At once, debris from the ground lifted up around them under the powerful rotors and combined with the jet exhaust to form a translucent wall.

When the helicopter's ramp met the ground, he heard the flight engineer yell, slapping him on shoulder. "Go!"

He walked quickly off the ramp and onto the landing zone. As soon as he stepped foot off the ramp, the helicopter lifted vertically off the ground and disappeared in less than a minute's time. The sound of the rotors faded away in the distance.

He shivered in the cold, crystalline air. He pulled his map out of his pocket and oriented himself. It looked different than he had at first visualized, but it always did. It was one of his first lessons he'd learned in SAS training. *You have to adapt quickly.*

The church that Celo had marked on his map was about a mile away if he followed the ridgeline of the mountains to his east along a dirt road.

He varied his pace, zigged and zagged, walked and ran—to make himself less of a target if he was being watched from a distance. As the wind changed, the freshness of the cold air mingled with the smell of burning wood from the valley below.

The road became a track and then narrowed to a pathway. A hawk was gliding in a circular pattern above, it seemed to follow him as he walked, a presence like that of a patient hunter.

A volley of artillery shells screamed above him and a minute later, rumbled in the distance like thunder from Olympus.

Through the cedar and sycamore forest, he saw the houses—all destroyed, their roofs either burned or blown off. Some of the houses were still smoldering with gaping holes in their walls from the tank shells fired from hilltops and roadsides. Thick, acrid smoke rolled low on the ground, blanketing the ruins.

He consulted his map again, and saw the church in pristine condition across a field scattered with rock outcroppings and boulders in a grove of sycamores. *How could it have escaped the fate of the homes below?* It was a hauntingly beautiful place. Ornate religious designs were carved into the granite walls, and a separate belfry stood along its left side. It was an old church, he guessed—three hundred years or so. And it was without the traditional dome or "third cross" of the Serb Orthodox churches or the narrow minaret that was unique to the Muslim mosques. It was a simple parish church that had been spared by Croat militias because it was Catholic.

Why would he want to meet here?

"Stop there. Don't take another step."

He heard the voice behind him in Serbo-Croatian, and realized it was Celo's—loud, clear and distinct. It came as an order and sounded threatening. He turned around and saw Celo sitting on a boulder to his left at the edge of the cedars.

"'Hello' would be a better greeting, Celo. Friendlier, ye know?"

Celo smiled. "Yes, well, we can get around to that as long as you turn around and walk back to the gravel road back there. You are walking into a minefield. The Ustashe put it there to protect their church after leveling the rest of the village a week ago. We retook the town, but nothing's left of theirs except their goddamned church." He pointed toward the road behind him and then lowered himself from the boulder. "Just walk back to the road along the same path you came. I'll meet you."

"Bloody Christ!" he muttered. *A minefield...he led me to a bloody minefield and he let me walk right into it ....*

In an instant, he could feel a prickly hot sensation run through him and his heart was pounding. He slowly turned to follow his footsteps. He stopped and inhaled deeply.

"Go ahead! You're fine!" Celo yelled back at him.

He looked around him. At first it looked like a weed—directly in front of him, but it was too straight...too symmetrical to be anything organic. It

315

was metallic, like a sprinkler system outlet. He saw another several meters away, identical to the first. He'd seen them before. They called them "Toe Poppers" in the Regiment. Italian-made, shaped like a hockey puck, encased in black rubber, but filled with plastique explosives and tiny pellets, powerful enough to take a grown man's leg off at the knee or hip.

"Is this why you brought me here, Celo? To lead me into a minefield?"

Celo laughed. "Why would I want to do that? You're family, Marko. And you're not in the minefield yet. One more step and you would have been. But I stopped you."

"Yeah," he muttered in English, now concentrating on the original path he took from the road. "Thanks for saving me."

Slowly, deliberately, he followed his steps back. He looked up and Celo was on the road in front of him, his arms outstretched wearing a U.S. issue camouflage uniform with the black subdued rank of Colonel on both collars. Mark began to regret his decision to come.

"No commandos this time?"

"None that I know of," he answered absently.

"You came by helicopter?"

Mark nodded. "I did."

"An American helicopter, wasn't it?"

He was faintly impressed. Somehow he knew about the Pave Low, whether he'd seen it himself, if it had been reported to him, or whether it was just a guess.

"Ye, they offered me a lift from Zagreb."

"Ha!" Celo laughed accusingly. "You *are* in bed with them, then, aren't you?"

He reached the road and walked up to Celo who was dressed in black fatigues. "I'm not in bed with anyone. I was grateful for the ride to be quite honest. After seeing what's happened here from the air, I dare say I wouldn't have made it any other way, so I hope you have a good reason for bringing me all the way down here."

Celo belched loudly, not bothering to stifle to sound, and nodded. He slapped both of his giant hands against his shoulders. His voice was jubilant. "Oh, yes! I think you won't regret it! Come with me!"

He followed Celo along a narrow dirt path that first led away from the church and then turned back toward it amidst the grove of cedars. Walking behind Celo, he saw clearly now what an imposing figure his cousin was. He

316

was also a chameleon, able to transform his appearance dramatically to fit his surroundings and the situation. At the discothèque in Zagreb, he appeared the playboy, but here looked like the prototype of a commando-mercenary: muscular just to the point of being muscle-bound, with thick legs that resembled tree trunks and a back that was the shape of a "V"... black, shoulder-length curly hair—all of this, combined with the black uniform and an Israeli-manufactured Galil Submachine gun that was strapped to his right shoulder completed a distinct paramilitary image. One that Celo had undoubtedly sought—and had achieved.

"This is the only way in or out. The forest is also mined, so stay on the pathway," Celo warned.

"Right behind you," he answered. He looked up and could see the church through the trees. It was beautifully constructed, its façade a white stucco. At the front of the church an embedded archway surrounded a single wooden door with a statue of the Virgin Mary and a round rose-tinted window above it. The path led to a courtyard overgrown with grass, lavender and weeds. A figure appeared around the corner of the church, armed with an AK-47 Assault Rifle slung over his shoulder, and dressed in black fatigues.

Celo turned to face him with dense blue eyes. "This is my Deputy, Ivo Bostic."

Bostic nodded at him absently as he lit a cigarette, and replaced his lighter in his front shirt pocket. Celo proceeded down the slate walkway and pushed the doors, already canted on rusty hinges, open. He felt cobwebs against his face as he entered. Wiping them away, he stood inside the church and saw fugitive rays of orange light beaming down at angles from the stained glass windows overhead, intersecting one another. Prismatic images reflected on the adjacent walls. Above the altar, a large wooden crucifix hung overhead, suspended from the ceiling by three thick ropes. The air was cold, musty and acrid. He touched one of the concrete pillars at the entrance with his hand, and felt its dampness. Their footsteps echoed on the stone floor.

"The Ustashe say this is God's home!" Celo announced loudly, holding his arms and hands up. His voice echoed off the walls. "Before they incinerated the Serb homes in the valley below, all of the people were rounded up and told by the Ustashe militia leader that this church was to be respected as a 'Holy Place'." Celo laughed in disgust. *That's what he said! Can you believe this! That's what they were told...."*

Celo's voice drifted off as he continued to walk. Halfway down the aisle, he turned and faced him, his blue eyes cool and speculative.

"But! If this is the case, the same would be true of our churches, would it not?" Celo shrugged his shoulders in mock perplexity. "Would not our churches be looked upon in the same way? Would they not be treated as holy places too?"

Mark chose not to respond. He looked around at the churches walls. There was a colorful 18th Century fresco of the Apocalypse. To his left, another similar fresco, but this one depicted Christ's assumption into heaven.

Celo's gestures became more theatrical, and his voice louder and more dramatic. *"Of course!* That *is* what you would think! It's what I would think! War or no war. Their church. Our church. They are God's home! *But that isn't what happened,"* Celo said in a lower voice, walking now through the pews. "A week ago on Saturday, our Sabbath, the priest was executed in the middle of his service. Everyone was forced to watch. The doors were locked. Everyone was told that their homes were being burned, but the Catholic Church would be spared because it was a 'Holy Place.'" Celo turned into another row of pews and faced him as he approached. "And then the women and children were brought outside. The remaining men, young and old, were also executed. I was told you could hear their screams from inside the church. When they finished, our church was burned to the ground. Twenty-three men from the town were shot in their heads and left to rot in the streets. The women and girls were brought into the woods and raped before they were set free. Many of them also died. Those who survived told me what had happened. They told me that in the Church, the militia leader, kept asking where I was...where their 'Great Protector" was!"

He felt a dull headache forming in his temples. He didn't want to hear this, and he now regretted that he'd come. He'd been given no choice, except to listen. He desperately wanted to leave, but could not.

"I'm sorry, Celo, I—"

Celo held his hands up, shaking his head. "That's not why I brought you here. But you needed to know before I show you."

"Show me what?" he asked.

Celo nodded and led him toward the altar. They stepped up to the altar. Bostic opened the double doorway that led inside the vestuary. It was in disarray. The closet and cabinet doors were opened. Books, chalices,

Eucharistic hosts and papers were scattered on the floor. Celo continued to the other end of the room and pulled a badly charred box-like container from the counter and placed it on the small table beside the wall. As Celo turned it he saw that it was a briefcase.

Mark was confused at first. "What's this?"

"Open it!"

He popped the snaps open. He lifted the lid of the briefcase and saw the yellow coversheet marked:

TOP SECRET UMBRA NOFORN/WNINTEL

Underneath the security classification there was another blurb:

NATIONAL SECURITY INFORMATION
UNAUTHORIZED DISCLOSURE
SUBJECT TO CRIMINAL SANCTIONS

The memo under the coversheet had been crumpled. On top there was the signature blue eagle and office letterhead.

CENTRAL INTELLIGENCE AGENCY
AMERICAN EMBASSY
ZAGREB, CROATIA

He noticed the typed names on top of the memo next—"From Robert Childs, CIA Station Chief for the Balkan Region," and one line below, it was addressed, by name, "To Ambassador Jack Fulbright." He scanned the rest of the memo quickly and immediately recognized what he was holding. If this was indeed found here in the church, as Celo claimed, the implications were clear.

"Good Lord—"

"You see! I told you! They blamed me for killing the Americans!" Celo bellowed, alternately pointing at the memo in Mark's hands and the charred briefcase sitting on the counter. "But *they* did it!" He pointed at the back door to the church. "You must tell the Americans that the goddamned Vatican is responsible for the ambush, *not me!*"

Mark was shaking his head.

"You still don't believe me?"

"It's not important what I believe," he answered. "There are problems with this. Significant problems—"

Celo began pacing frantically. In front of him, he held his assault rifle in one hand and a gold chalice in the other. Finally, he stopped and faced Mark. "What are your fucking problems?" Celo screamed, pointing the chalice at him. "Everything is here! This proves it!" He threw the chalice at the bank of glass candles against the wall, shattering some of them, and sending others flying.

He was jarred by Celo's display, but made a conscious choice not to respond to his theatrics. He shook his head, and leaned against the counter. "Unfortunately," he began slowly, "it doesn't prove anything. You conducted the raid, you led me here, and they know we're blood relatives. They'll say you planted the evidence here, in a Catholic Church, that I was a co-conspirator." He paused and studied Celo. "And what's this theory of yours about the Vatican being responsible?"

Celo stopped pacing, glanced over at Bostic and nodded. "It is a great victory for us! Unfortunately, we arrived down there too late to help our people. Everyone in the town was gone. Even the Ustashe scum who lived here, but their houses remained untouched—only the Serb homes were burned! When we arrived, one of our people informed us that the Ustashe militia was camped out at this church. And we found them here, emplacing the mines. For two nights we watched them through binoculars and our night vision goggles. On the third night…last night…we attacked while most of them were asleep." He saw Bostic unlock the door. Celo walked over, opened it and threw it open to reveal the back courtyard of the church.

He first noticed the white and blue UNHCR plastic sheeting, and underneath, the soles of boots facing him. Celo was already outside standing there beside the sheeting, one hand holding the corners, and the other gripping his submachine gun. In a sweeping motion, he lifted the tarp and threw it away from the bodies.

The bodies were neatly lined up in rows. He glanced at each of them, and counted twelve in all. They were clean shaven and wore fatigues with computer-generated pixel camouflage patterns, black leather goggled radio helmets, survival knives and expensive brown Gore-Tex boots. Their wounds were mostly from gunshots—well-aimed—to the head or chest.

He felt nauseous.

In a separate pile, were their rifles, M-4 Carbines—the more compact version of the M-16, with a much shorter barrel and a retractable stock, but just as lethal. All of them were equipped with laser aimpoint systems, and several with M-203 Grenade Launchers.

"All of their equipment is the best on the shelf—they're professional soldiers—"

"Yes," Celo replied casually. "And I must give them credit, they fought well, even as they were dying…they fought, but the element of surprise was ours. So now, you've seen this. It explains much, does it not?"

"I'm afraid it leaves me with more questions than answers, Celo," he answered.

Celo was walking in circles around the line of corpses. He walked over to a freshly covered grave on the edge of the cemetery, marked by a grey granite cross tombstone that appeared to be newly emplaced. It was engraved with the inscription, "*Sigillum Militum Xρisti.*"

"Whose grave is this?"

Celo shrugged. "No one has been buried in this cemetery for at least a year…until now. We found this in the vestuary…."

Celo took out a wallet and threw it at Mark. It fell open on the ground, displaying a U.S. Embassy Identification Badge for "Robert Childs."

"It is a coincidence, isn't it?"

It was more than a coincidence, he knew.

"But there's something else!" Celo continued in a loud voice. "Something we did not expect!" He proceeded to rip open the dead soldiers' uniform shirts one after the other.

He looked up at Celo with a vacant expression. Here was his cousin, showing off his quarry, like a big-game kill. It was senseless and grotesque, and it sickened him.

Celo held up his index finger and then pointed at Mark, grinning widely. "You're right, Marko! These are *not* just militia or even Croat Army! They may be Croatian, but they answer to someone else."

"I'm afraid I'm not following you."

Celo was already shaking his head and waving both of his hands violently. "The Pope sent them!"

"That's ridiculous," he replied. "In every war there are lots of stray cats and dogs—militias, mercenaries, soldiers, civilians, refugees…."

"You do not believe me?" Celo asked in a strident voice. He leaned down to an additional corpse and ripped open his uniform shirt. "Look!"

A silk rope encrusted in blood hung around the soldier's neck, attached to a large white satin cloth that portrayed two knights on a single horse with red crosses on their shields, embroidered elaborately in red, encircled with the Latin inscription:

Sigillum Militum Xpisti

"Do you see, Marko?" Celo threw the vestment at him. "This is from Rome!" He proceeded down the line of bodies and tore the same vestment from each soldier's chest. "They're the Pope's personal fucking mercenaries!"

He ignored Celo's outburst and knelt down to study the cloth. It had the same inscription as the gravestone, but he still could not arrive at the same conclusion that the vestment was from the Vatican—anyone could have produced it as a special unit decoration. He'd seen plenty; and yet, among them, this one was indisputably unique.

He nodded slightly and looked up at Celo. "Can I keep this?"

Celo shrugged dismissively. "Do what you want. What will take you weeks to learn, I already know. This is why I brought you here. So you could see the enemy for yourself. Tell your United Nations that!" Celo was now shouting and his voice was hoarse. "You can tell them our enemy is the Pope!"

"It's quite a leap to blame this on the Vatican. Those vestments could be anything—tokens of good luck, special insignia, who knows? It's not exactly proof to build a case against the Vatican."

Celo shook his head in exasperation. "*This* is what I must deal with every day. No matter what evidence, what proof, I bring, we are ignored, and still they want to bring me to The Hague! I will not be the carcass for the Vatican's vultures." He pointed at Bostic, who was now standing outside, near the door to the Sacristy. "Bring them here."

He watched Bostic disappear into the sacristy and come back out with two medium-size black nylon bags. He set them on the ground at his feet and stepped aside, deferring to Celo.

"There!" Celo announced with a flourish. "Now you are rich, Marko!"

"What's this?"

"See for yourself!" Celo walked over to him, unzipped both bags and stood up.

He hesitated, increasingly uncomfortable with the situation Celo had placed him in. After a moment, he knelt down to open the first bag. He inhaled deeply and struggled to maintain his composure when he looked inside—bundled stacks of Croatian currency—Kuna—500 and 200 notes, all uncirculated and in pristine condition. He opened the second bag and found it brimming with stacks of American $100 and $50 dollar bills. Several stacks of bills fell out onto the ground. He looked up at Celo in disbelief.

"Celo, how—? Why is this here?"

"Take it." Celo's voice was now subdued and Mark could sense his resentment. "Take everything. It is the proof you wanted, is it not?"

He looked around and attempted to make sense of it all: Robert Childs' memo to Ambassador Fulbright...five bodies of well-equipped soldiers, all wearing special vestments...the grave with the tombstone...Bob Childs' identification card and wallet and these bags of currency—all in an isolated Catholic church in southern Bosnia that was surrounded by mines.

"I don't know what you expect me to do with it," he answered. "I shouldn't have come here. You shouldn't have asked me to."

"Why, Marko?" Celo shouted in feigned disbelief, waving his hand toward the church in a sweeping motion. "*This* is too much for you?"

"No. By asking me to come here alone, you've tied my hands. They know that we're cousins, and so they'll accuse me of being complicit in this—with you. You've placed me in a bloody untenable position," he said, looking intently at Celo. "But I think you knew that."

"Fuck-you!" Celo spat, and pointed at him. "Don't tell me about 'untenable' positions! You left! I stayed here when you and my mother ran away—like rats—to another country! Now you come back! I disowned you both, and now you come back with another name, you're a different person—you're not one of us! And you tell me I've put *YOU* in an untenable position? Fuck-you Marko! You're not one of us. You're not here to help us. You're a goddamned fraud."

"What the bloody hell do you want from me?" he asked, switching to English.

"Nothing—and I can do no more for you," Celo answered. "Now leave. Take those bags with you and give the money to the fucking United Nations—they need it. Ivo will lead you out of here."

He shook his head. "Is this the way you believe you can save your people?"

"By dying, I can save them," Celo answered. "Now get the fuck away from me."

Instinctively, he knew it was no use to further engage Celo in conversation. Everything was too close to the surface for him to consider anything calmly or logically. Leaving now was the wisest option he could settle on, but if there was any time to tell Celo, it was now.

He might not get another chance.

"I'm not your enemy, Celo," he heard himself utter. "I didn't want to leave. Neither did your mother. She cried every night for you, you know. She tried to arrange for you to join us, but you wouldn't come. I read your letters to her. It broke her heart. Ever since, I've felt responsible for that, and for what happened. You told me not to go down to see the bodies at the dam, but I went anyway. I've had thirty-five years to think about it, and I know that none of it would have happened if I'd listened to you…I'm responsible."

He felt tears streaming down his face. Celo was facing away from him toward the forest, and he couldn't determine whether he was even listening to him. He waited for a response, but Celo continued to look away in silence. Finally, he felt a tapping on his arm, and he looked up and saw Bostic. He mumbled in Serbo-Croatian that it was time to go. He was holding both bags in his hands. He handed Mark one of them, and began walking toward the trail they'd come from.

He looked back to see Celo on one knee, throwing his oversized Bowie knife into the ground directly in front of him—repeatedly—again and again.

Bostic accompanied him down the gravel road with one of the bags slung over his shoulder. He held his AK-47 at the ready as they walked. Arriving at the edge of the field where the helicopter would land, he stopped and dug into his backpack for the survival radio that the Flight Engineer had given him. He pressed the transmit button and requested pickup at the same spot, as planned. After a moment, he heard the pilot's acknowledgement over the radio's static. Mark slung the backpack over his shoulders. Bostic handed him the second bag.

"Don't spend it foolishly."

He shook his head. "It's not mine to spend."

"Your choice," Bostic replied evenly. "Celo gave it to you. I advised him against it, but he insisted." He looked into Bostic's eyes. They were the cold, dark, emotionless eyes of someone who was accustomed to killing and seeing people die violent deaths.

Mark nodded and proceeded into the wood line with the bags in hand. The sound of the Pave Lows approaching could be heard in the distance.

"Commissioner?"

He heard Bostic's voice calling out as he walked away, and he turned around to face him. He was shaving the bark off of a long stick with a knife.

"Your cousin...he is a difficult man, but a strong man, and he thinks much of you."

He did not know what to say after this exchange. Celo's accusations, however emotional, had an effect on him. A profound one. He nodded and hoisted both bags to his shoulders.

As he walked along the rough terrain, he struggled to balance the bags. Occasionally he stopped to rest. The sound of the helicopters' rotors grew louder. He stopped just short of the clearing, and at that moment he heard an explosion from the same direction he'd just come. A deep, reverberating thud that he could feel under the soles of his boots. Almost simultaneously, he could hear the roar of the Pave Lows approaching at high speed.

One of the helicopters came to a hover overhead to provide security for the helicopter that was landing to his front. The whine of the engines drowned out all other sounds and the wind generated by the rotors swept debris around him. The trees in the clearing leaned away, as if trying in vain to escape. He ran toward the back of the helicopter, stumbling occasionally under the weight of the bags. The rotor wash that initially forced him away, suddenly sucked him in. He saw the Flight Engineer waiting for him, motioning him on-board.

He stepped onto the tailgate and the Flight Engineer took one of the bags and grabbed his arm. He was moved forcefully to the front of the cabin. The other bag landed on the floor beside him.

"Welcome back, Commissioner!" The Flight Engineer's voice was genial but professional.

The engines went from a steady roar to a higher pitched, sustained wail. The massive aircraft lifted like a high-powered elevator, and they were airborne again. He leaned over to the Flight Engineer and shouted. "There was an explosion back there—did you see it?"

The Flight Engineer nodded. He squeezed the transmit device on the long wire connected to his helmet and held his hand up to his right ear. He realized that he was speaking to the pilot.

"We're diverting to see what it was. Should see it out the portside window now."

He leaned against the side window, and saw the Flight Engineer pointing.

Flying overhead, he saw the smoke first—thick grey and white smoke billowing upwards from a demolished structure...and beneath the smoke, the roaring orange flames consuming the ruins of the Catholic Church, swirling skyward.

Suddenly, it came to him with a ceramic clarity. Instantly he knew. The reason he'd come back. It was a revelation that he'd been running away from since he'd left Yugoslavia so many years ago.

All this time, it was a deep, yearning need to meet head-on the evil that had caused all of this hatred and turmoil...to confront the one ultimately responsible for the pain and anguish that was, thus far, his life.

Ultimately, confronting his father's executioner was the reason he'd been brought back here—and it transcended mere coincidence or the vague feelings that had previously haunted him in his dreams.

But all this time...for so long, he'd been a ghost.

Until now.

CHAPTER 63

MARK LYONS STEPPED onto the tarmac and shook his Flight Engineer's hand, thanking him for the flight.

As he walked away from the helicopter, one of the pilots issued a salute, which Mark returned in crisp, distinctive British fashion.

He walked past an iron gate manned by an airport security official. He dug into his pockets for the keys to the official UN Toyota 4Runner dispatched to him by the UN motor pool.

While he was pulling his keys from his pocket, his cell phone rang. The Caller-ID listed the call as "PRIVATE." He answered the call as he approached the 4Runner.

"Marko, this is Lazarus.

He stopped in his tracks. "Who are you? How do you know me?" he demanded.

There was a long pause on the other end. "Listen to me carefully. They have rigged your vehicle to explode when you start the engine or when you sit down in the seat." The voice came in fluent Serbo-Croatian. It was muffled and garbled, as if underwater, and slow in its delivery. "You are in grave danger. They are trying to kill you."

"Who are 'They'?"

"The priest, and his executioners." Lazarus replied. "But I think you must already know that, do you not?"

"How do *you* know that?"

He thought he detected a laugh on the other end. "Because I believe you should keep your friends close and your enemies closer, Marko."

"Why should I trust you?"

"You really do not know, do you?"

"No, I'm afraid I don't."

There was another long pause. "Because you saved my life," Lazarus said simply.

"When?" Mark asked. "When did I save your life?"

"When you were a boy, Marko…at the dam."

The memories--indelible visions of searching for his father in the pit of executed bodies again at Brnisi Dam…helping the men, helping them out of the stacks of bodies… the one had died in his arms, the other who he'd left for dead…*could he possibly have survived?*

"Tell me who you are, Goddammit!" he yelled into the phone.

But the line went dead.

CHAPTER 64

MARK LYONS WATCHED the Finnish army explosive ordnance disposal team remove the charge from the Toyota 4Runner and countercharge it in a nearby field. When they'd swept the parking lot to confirm that none of the other vehicles were booby-trapped, the Finnish lieutenant offered him the SUV's keys.

"You are lucky, Commissioner," the lieutenant said matter-of-factly, and in perfect, unaccented English. "Twenty kilograms of plastique were fit snugly under the driver's seat."

He took the keys from him. "It was a viable charge, then?" he asked quietly.

The lieutenant nodded. "Fully viable and quite effective too, as you saw. It was an advanced design, actually. We were very impressed. A redundant detonation capability, two Mercury switches, very compact, and magnetically bonded to the undercarriage, not tied. Nearly undetectable. If you hadn't told us it was there, we'd have had some trouble finding it...it takes a special skill and devotion to one's work to construct something like this. Would you have any idea who might have done this?"

He nodded at the lieutenant. "I may have some idea."

"I hope you are able to find him then. Let me know if we can assist you further."

He thanked the lieutenant and shook his hand. Mike McCallister drove up with a white Toyota Land Cruiser and stepped out.

"Bloody Hell! Now it's personal, Commissioner," McCallister said excitedly.

He shook his head and cast a sober glance at the tall policeman from Manchester. "It's been personal for some time now, Mike...."

CHAPTER 65

AFTER ARRIVING at Jon Schauer's flat and finding it unoccupied, Mark Lyons dropped off the duffel bags and went for a walk through the tight cobblestone alleyways of Gornji Grad. It was not yet dark, but the stores were closed and the cafés were only lightly occupied. He ended up at a corner café-restaurant across the street from the Archbishop's Palace and Saint Stephen's Cathedral.

From his vantage point outside the café's veranda, he had an unobstructed view of the front of the Archbishop's residence...an imposing stone building with a large turret that dominated the landscape. He watched the black Audi sedan with dark tinted windows and antennas drive out through the gate. He swallowed the last of his beer, dug out a five euro note and dropped it on the table.

The air was cool and the streets were still wet after the afternoon rain. He placed his hands in the pockets and crossed the street. At dusk, the cathedral looked somehow different than did in the morning light. The statues atop its twin spires seemed to glow giving them a rather surreal, lifelike appearance.

He rang the doorbell to the side gate, between the cathedral and the residence. No one answered. After several more attempts, he pulled the black nylon case from his inside coat pocket, unzipped it and pulled out two thin stainless steel instruments. He locked one of them into a larger handle, and then inserted each into the lock to the gate, one on top of the other. With the top pick, he scratched the top of the lock and in several seconds, he felt the pins in the lock give way, allowing him to turn it open with the other tool—just as easily as if he had possessed a custom-made key.

There were several cameras overhead, but he guessed that no one was monitoring them...security guards were expensive, even for a city archdiocese, and he was betting that there were none dedicated to task. He walked purposefully to the nearest door and repeated the procedure. Within seconds, the door to the residence opened. Stepping inside the elaborate marble floored hallway, the smell of pipe tobacco saturated the stale air. There was also the musty scent of old furniture and dust that, combined with the tobacco smoke, seemed more a natural habitat for a reclusive old monk than a Cardinal of the Roman Catholic Church.

He removed the mini flashlight from his coat pocket and turned it on to illuminate the hallway as he walked. There were no other sounds. No lights. The entire building seemed empty. The first room on his left was an office, elaborately furnished with a large intricately hand-carved desk, two tapestry upholstered sofas and a half-reclined easy chair. Persian carpets covered the floor. The shades, also a dark tapestry, were drawn on the windows. Behind the desk there was a large framed oil portrait of a man in a maroon and black Cardinal's robe with a rosary weaved between his fingers, seated with a reverential half smile, like the Mona Lisa's. He shined the flashlight on it. On the bottom of the gold frame he saw the brass plate with the engraved name: Cardinal Alojzije Stepinac.

He remembered that the subject of the Cardinal's sermon at the Mass that morning was the Stepinac Canonization. The ceremony was scheduled in Medjugorje next Sunday.

Six days away…in the middle of a war zone.

Casting aside the stated spiritual imperative of choosing Medjugorje as the site to canonize such a controversial figure, it was—by any measure— insanity, driven by rabidly nationalistic goals and personalities. Judging from his sermon and this life-size portrait in his study, he was reasonably certain that Cardinal Vojislav Pijadje—"Papa Voyo"—was the primary force behind it.

He directed the flashlight to the bookcases built into the far wall. Stacked on the top shelves, he saw the file boxes and cloth-bound photo albums. He stepped onto a stool and pulled one of the boxes out, stirring up a thick layer of loose dust. He suppressed a sneeze. Masking tape on top of the square box was marked "1960-61" in thick black marker. He removed the lid to reveal piles of photographs and papers bundled together with rubber bands. They showed a much younger officer with post-adolescent looks, a crew cut, proudly wearing a Yugoslav Army uniform, standing with arms akimbo alongside several fellow officers. He wrapped the rubber band around the stack of photos and placed it back into the box. He turned the desk lamp on.

Perhaps because they were in color and larger than the others, the last bundle of photos he pulled out caught his eye. He removed the rubber band

and spread them on the desk. Again, they showed the same young uniformed officer, tall and thin, unsmiling, standing at attention in front of a two-story crudely constructed brick house, holding a Kalashnikov rifle in both hands. There were several photos of the officer with an older man in a black cassock. The older man's face was thin, even gaunt, and his eyes deep set. The white collar clearly indicated that he was a priest. In some of the photographs, they showed with his hands held together, wearing a large ring on his right hand. In another photograph he was wearing a pectoral cross hanging around his neck from a gold cord and a red calotte on his head, indicating that he was either a bishop or a cardinal.

He looked behind him at the oil painting. The artist's rendition of Cardinal Alojzije Stepinac showed a very different man than the one in the photographs—strong and upright in posture...fit and in his prime, but the resemblance to both men was unmistakable, and confirmed his speculation that they were one in the same.

He pulled the albums out. On the front cover of each, the year was handwritten, "1982"... and another, "1977." He pulled several other albums out, searching for a single one that could corroborate once and for all what he'd seen yesterday in church. He found the album marked "1971," and stepped down. He set the album on the desk. He paused before opening it, and finally, still standing, he began to flip through its Cellophane covered pages. They were a mix of black and white and color photos...many of them had begun to deteriorate and were discolored with mildew.

Voyo was there in all of them, just as he remembered him that day at Brnisi Dam...wearing his utility uniform and a pistol belt, holding a swagger stick, towering above the other officers posing with him. Other photographs were taken at a city café and showed him in his dress uniform with another officer, accompanied by two attractive women in summer sleeveless dresses, smiling broadly and offering a toast to the camera.

He sat down at the desk. He flipped the pages, prying them apart when they stuck to the Cellophane. At the end of the album there were two pages with four photos that showed a man lying in a hospital bed with his face heavily bandaged. In one of the photographs, an older man, stocky and impeccably dressed in a three piece suit, stood beside the bandaged man, posed with his arm around him. The older man looked familiar to Mark, and the realization of the man's identity came as he positioned the photo directly under the desk lamp. *Could it be?*

332

Marshal Tito...himself!

It was all the confirmation he needed. The officer in the photos was indeed the priest who now called himself Papa Voyo—and he was now certain Voyo was also who he and Celo had fought at Brnisi Dam. Before returning the photo album to the shelf, he removed several of the photos and shoved them into his jacket pocket.

He realized that he'd lost track of time. It was 9:35 P.M., but he'd forgotten what time he'd entered the Residence. *Had it been ten or twenty minutes...or an hour?* He had no way of knowing for sure. Nor could he know when the priest or one of his people would return.

There was more he needed to know—the other linkages that were now only conjecture or rumor...Celo's insistence that the Vatican was involved in the ambush on Ambassador Fulbright...the CIA memorandum that had already proven to be correct in its theory of an Islamic effort to construct nuclear devices...John Thorpe's revelation that the Vatican was their target.

What was Papa Voyo's involvement in all of this?

He privately wondered if his discovery of what the Voyo had done to his father was somehow clouding his judgment—knowing that he was now facing the man who more than three decades ago was responsible for sending his life into a tailspin? What if it was all a coincidence? Could the photos in the church all have been fabricated by Celo? Only Celo knew the details of what happened at the dam that night. Given what he'd seen at the church in Stolac only several hours ago, Celo was the only one capable of generating such an illusion. And yet, the ambush at Oborci was not an illusion, nor was the murder of Kate Kamrath, or the disappearance of Robert Childs. The raid on the mujahideen camp in Bocinja and what he'd seen there was not an illusion.

Like the pieces of a puzzle that had spilled into the box of another and reopened years later, they were disparate pieces that produced an incoherent picture whenever he attempted to assemble or separate them.

Heart hammering, he rose from his seat at the desk and as he stood up, he knocked over a stack of papers and folders that had been on the corner of the desk. A Siamese cat that had been hiding behind the curtains jumped out and raced out the hallway, causing him to jump back as well. He took a deep breath and returned the photo boxes and albums to the shelves.

As he picked up the papers off the floor one of the folders that lay open caught his eye with the documents it held that were written in Arabic script...typed and handwritten. One of the documents was a map with Arabic handwriting in black grease pencil. The map was a single page that folded in half, covering Vatican City. He unfolded it. In the center of the city, at Saint Peter's Basilica, a rectangle had been carefully drawn in grease pencil. Another square was drawn around another area of nearby and to the southwest that appeared to be primarily residential. Unable to read Arabic, he wondered what all of it meant, but he heard alarm bells resonating in his head.

Where had the map come from?

Why was it here?

What were these markings, and who made them?

To see Cyrillic or Roman letters on such a map would not be out of the ordinary because both were scripts of the local language, but Arabic script on such a map was plainly worrisome. The last place he'd seen anything in Arabic was at Bocinja, and given what he'd seen there, he felt certain that this map and these papers were somehow linked to that bloody event. He struggled with the decision of whether to take the folder with him or to leave it on the desk. He hadn't brought a camera with him, so he couldn't photograph the map and documents. And yet, he knew that if he did take them, they would certainly be missed by the Cardinal and his people.

He scanned the office and the crystal chandelier hanging from the plasterwork ceiling. In the far left corner of the room he saw the fax machine. He walked over and placed the stack of papers in the tray, pulled out his wallet and found the business card for General Jon Thorpe, Commander, United States Joint Special Operations Command.

He pulled out a blank sheet of paper and quickly scrawled out a coversheet:

Personal For: General John Thorpe

From: Mark Lyons – EYES ONLY

He placed the coversheet on top of the stack of papers and the map, dialed the fax number by adding the country code for the United States: 001.

He pressed the SEND button and heard the dial tone, then the machine slowly dialing the number. Finally, there was the sound of the fax connection. He exhaled. The papers were drawn into the machine in rapid succession. As they were spat out, he took them one-by-one and placed them back inside the folder and on the desk as the fax machine continued to send.

He realized he'd spent too much time inside the residence, and knew he had to leave soon before the Cardinal returned. He quickly scanned the room, replaced the chair under the desk—where it was when he entered, shut off the desk lamp, and walked out of the study toward the front door. Just as he was about to open the door, the fax machine let out an extended beep and he heard the sound of a page being drawn into the machine and then released. A confirmation page.... Quickly, he walked back into the study, picked the paper out of the machine's tray and returned to open the door. It was only then that he heard the sound of a car door open and shut...and then the sound of voices speaking in Serbo-Croatian. The voices were unrecognizable; only one voice, the same rough, gravel-laced intonation he'd heard at the sermon—was unmistakably Papa Voyo's:

"God Bless, you."

"Papa! We are coming to the ceremony on Saturday!"

"Yes, yes! It will be our day!"

He walked quickly down the hallway, through the living room, past the kitchenette, knowing he had only seconds to spare before the front door to the Residence opened. At the end of the hallway, he found a locked door. He fumbled for a lever and instead found a switch that he was able to turn, releasing the lock as he heard the front door open, followed by steps down the hallway and a light.

The door led into another room...a vestuary...with dim light still on. The vestuary stored liturgical vestments worn by priests: habits and chasubles, embroidered in violet, pink, red, green, gold and white. He nearly passed by a half-open closet door, but the gold silk ropes and robes crafted in various colors and designs were what initially caught his eye. They were vaguely familiar even from a distance, but as he drew closer, he knew that they were the same embroidered white vestments he'd seen on the bodies of the soldiers in Stolac, with the same Latin inscription:

Sigillum Militum Xρisti

Through the door, the soft echo of steps approached.

He took one of the vestments and shoved it into his jacket pocket. He opened the vestuary door that led out onto the altar of the cathedral and shut it gently. The inside of the cathedral was illuminated by the flickering of a large red sanctuary lamp, a multitude of white votive candles, and the ambient light from outside the luminous stained glass windows. He passed by a tomb with the body of a cardinal on display. Drawing closer, he realized that it was a mannequin…and underneath it in an enclosed stone crypt was the body of Cardinal Alojzije Stepinac. He continued along the side of the church, along the wooden pews and past another crypt and three stone life-size statues. The creak of the vestuary door reverberated just as he reached the main entrance way. For a moment, in the shadows, he glanced back and saw the Cardinal who called himself "Papa Voyo."

Now was not the time to confront him.

As Voyo came into view, he unlocked the door and walked outside to the cobblestone plaza.

He took in the fresh cool air as he walked into an adjoining cobblestone alley and then stopped mid-stride.

The cat! It was a Siamese…. The same breed of cat Sandy had been looking for in Kate's apartment….

He leaned up against a stone wall and it was then that the realization set in.

…Celo was right.

Now he was certain of it.

He pulled out his cell phone and found the speed dial for John Thorpe. At the moment the call went through he heard John's voice, and the bells of Saint Stephen's Cathedral began their deafening clamor.

CHAPTER 66

SANDY EVENSON DECIDED to change her airplane ticket's destination to Belfast, Ireland at the moment she arrived at the Burlington International Airport.

After their telephone conversation, she felt as though she were about to disintegrate...a feeling of unease that grew with the realization her that she had a very limited understanding of Mark Lyons...who he was, what made him tick.

And that's what made her change her ticket. She remembered that he'd spoken to her about his Aunt Maja—Celo's mother—who had raised him in Belfast after fleeing from Yugoslavia...that Celo had remained in Yugoslavia because of the injuries he sustained. Throughout that discussion, she remembered that the only time he'd really smiled was when he talked about his aunt. He avoided talking to her about the events surrounding his wife's murder.

Perhaps the best view of Mark Lyons came from John Thorpe. In the brief conversation with him that morning at the Holiday Inn in Sarajevo, he'd calmly told her over his cup of coffee, *"Mark Lyons has never forgiven himself for what happened to Annalisa...and that's a helluva burden to bear."*

Mark's words kept returning to her. *"...Don't you see? We can't be worrying about one another now...."*

They echoed, as she sat flying over the Atlantic, but his voice was unsteady and oddly detached. She now regretted the abrupt way she'd hung up on him. What she wanted so desperately was an explanation...from him...from anyone...so she could understand what was going through his head. Most of all, to talk to him and understand him.

The explanation, she finally decided, was to be found somewhere between Bosnia and Northern Ireland. Seeing his interaction with Celo and his outright avoidance of any conversation about his wife convinced her of it. If she were ever to understand him, she decided that she had to meet the one person who knew him…who knew about the whole of his life, rather than only parts and pieces of it.

Maja Mescic Lyons…

She studied the faxed copy of CIA stationary that Jim Goodwin had given her with the name, address and telephone number for Mark Lyons' aunt. It had taken only a bit of cajoling at the airport, and a two minute conversation between Goodwin and someone back at his Langley Headquarters to get it.

Mark's aunt was the only one she knew of who could lend the kind of perspective she so desperately needed…of the man she now knew she was falling in love with. She studied Maja Lyons' address and an internet-generated map she'd run off at the airport's business center as she waited for the evening flight.

Maja Lyons lived in Antrim…at the northern tip of Ireland's coast.

FEBRUARY 13: ZAGREB, CROATIA

Major Savo Heleta watched as Mark Lyons spoke on his cell phone in the sculpture park in front of the Zagreb Police Station. Sitting in his black Audi across the street, hidden from view by police cars parked on the curb, Heleta observed Mark with interest through darkly tinted windows. Here was the man who had managed to inject himself in the mission for which he was responsible. He matched the family film footage at the Archbishop's Palace after Papa Voyo had asked him to investigate the break-in. And now he was here, visiting with the police.

Heleta had been notified by his own men in the police department of Lyons' visit there. The photograph they'd taken of him at Saint Francis Church in Stolac matched perfectly. Mark Lyons, he now knew, was the same one who had flown in an American Air Force helicopter to the church where his men had been slaughtered. He was also the same one in the photos carrying the bags with their operational fund from the church.

He had little real information about this man, Mark Lyons. His contacts at the United Nations Headquarters in Sarajevo had told him about the position he'd just assumed as Assistant Commissioner of the European Union Police Mission…he was from Ireland, they said, but he spoke fluent

Serbo-Croatian...and was hand-picked by the United Nations High Commissioner, Roman Polko.

He studied Lyons closely through a small spotting scope. Lyons didn't look like a policeman or the typical UN bureaucrat. His hair was too long, and in lieu of a uniform, he wore a navy blue polo shirt, blue jeans, grey suede military boots. His lean, muscular physique betrayed the fact that he was obviously very fit. His eyes routinely canvassed his surroundings—effortlessly and skillfully. Heleta switched to his camera, periodically taking photographs through the Leica zoom lens. He observed as Lyons dialed his cell phone and carried on a brief conversation.

Heleta saw a pattern in Lyons' actions that indicated that Mark Lyons was no ordinary policeman. After Voyo's frantic call he knew that Lyons had broken into the Archbishop's Palace without a warrant...his men had kept him under surveillance as he met Celo at the church in Stolac arriving on a U.S. military helicopter just as the church was demolished with explosives, and from his contacts in the police he knew that Lyons had flown on a UN helicopter at the site of their raid in Bocinja—all of it ran counter to the expected behavior of a policeman, or a soldier for that matter. Heleta entertained the thought that he could be a spy...for the CIA or MI6 or the Mossad.

But his instincts told him otherwise.

Mark Lyons, he suspected, had a mission of his own, independent from his UN duties and from the direction of any superior. After speaking with Papa Voyo the last evening, Heleta had come to the conclusion that Lyons had at least a general knowledge of their activities, and of the Islamic nuclear threat that triggered the activation of his Gabriel Team.

Because of what had happened in Stolac, coupled with the missing vestment—the "orphrey" as Voyo called it—he had to assume that Lyons knew about the Gabriel Team as well.

From a distance, Heleta admired Mark Lyons for his perseverance and luck, if not his bold investigative skills. Lyons had stumbled upon far more than anyone else to date—more than the CIA Station Chief that he'd buried outside the church, and more than the woman reporter whom he'd suspected of having CIA ties after examining her email messages. Papa Voyo had insisted on dealing with both of them personally. It was that admiration which saddened Heleta—saddened because someone whom he had begun to perceive as an equal...a peer, had chosen to inject himself into an operation that was far more complex than he could ever know. Lyons' interference could not be tolerated.

He sensed that if he were given the opportunity, Mark Lyons would be a formidable adversary. The imperative remained: to eliminate him as a threat to the mission and recover the funds stolen from the Gabriel Team.

CHAPTER 67

MARK LYONS ENDED his call with John Thorpe as he sat down at the café. In the wake of the call, and in hearing Thorpe's vague, yet alarming message about the Pakistani tanker and an additional unspecified threat to the Vatican, he struggled to make sense of the many disparate events and facts that were now confronting him.

At the police station, armed with test results from the FBI lab in Quantico, he'd been able to confirm for the homicide investigators that Kate Kamrath had indeed been poisoned. He also inquired about the unique chemical substance that had been found on her forehead and lips during the autopsy. He'd pulled out his notes and shown them to the detective:

...trace residue of Olea Europaea (olive oil), Cinnamomum Zeylanicum (cinnamon), Acorus Calamus (calamus), Cassia Angustifolia (cassia) on forehead, lips and chest regions.

What he'd initially regarded as a typical ladies' evening skin lotion had suddenly taken on much greater significance when he realized that these organic oils and herbs were also used by the Catholic Church in the issuance of the Last Rites...the Sacrament for the Sick and Dying. He'd gone to the police station to present them with this evidence and his theory that Cardinal Vojislav Pijadje had murdered Kate Kamrath and Robert Childs. With everything that he presented to them, even the location where he believed Robert Childs had been buried, he found the Zagreb Police Detectives skeptical, if not overtly hostile. He'd received a rebuke from one of the detectives who he'd thought was actually listening to him.

"Our priests are not murderers, Commissioner...."

Rather than continue to fight with the detectives, he'd gotten up and left.

He sat in the park and scanned the front page of the Herald Tribune. He found the story there, below the fold:

A Controversial and Potentially Violent Sainthood
New York Times News Service

In five days, a controversial Croatian icon and World War II-era Roman Catholic Cardinal, Alojzije Stepinac, will be canonized into Sainthood by Pope Vincent at the site of the last miracle attributed to him, in Medjugorje, Bosnia and Herzegovina. In what is normally a quiet tourist town, more than 3,000 EUFOR troops and 1,000 local police are deployed in and around Medjugorje for the first time, where celebrants and protestors are expected to converge in the coming days. Water cannons now line the streets in Medjugorje in preparation for this large-scale event. Additional surveillance teams and cameras are mounted on churches, hotels and guesthouses.

The unprecedented measures have been attributed to the newly appointed Commissioner of the European Union Police Mission, Mark Lyons. In a press statement, Lyons said, "We are particularly concerned for the safety of the celebrants, the police and EUFOR troops, as well as for the protestors this weekend. We will take all necessary measures to ensure the ceremony is able to be conducted safely and with minimal disruption." Lyons is well-known in the European Union for the dramatic and often violent policing efforts he implemented in Northern Ireland that led to the latest cease-fire there.

General Ian Rose, Commander of the European Force in the Balkans, responded to concerns over potential clashes between Bosnian Serb and Muslim-controlled Federation forces and Croatian militias in and around Medjugorje by pointing to the planned heavy ground and air EUFOR presence in the area, saying, "Those who doubt our resolve and ability to maintain a peaceful and secure environment will see that we have the capability to deal with any eventuality."

Vojislav Cardinal Pijadje, the Archbishop of Zagreb and widely known as "Papa Voyo" has championed Croatia's advocacy of Cardinal Stepinac's canonization. In his Sunday homily, Pijadje dismissed the threat of violence in Medjugorje by announcing, "They can not intimidate us from honoring this holiest of men who prayed for all of us…and for who prayed for peace." When pressed further on the possibility of delaying the ceremony until hostilities in Ravno cease, he pointed to the inevitability of Stepinac's sainthood as "God's will." Cardinal Pijadje has come under increasing criticism for his advocacy of using Medjugorje as the site for the Stepinac canonization and for the timing of the ceremony, given the growing crisis in Ravno that is rapidly spreading throughout Bosnia and Herzegovina.

A senior official in the U.S. State Department confirmed that White House attempts to convince officials in the Vatican to change the venue of the Stepinac Canonization in view of the ongoing crisis in Ravno had thus far failed.

Pijadje's most vocal critic is a Roman Catholic priest, Friar Nicola Milesevic, the Provincial Minister for southern Croatia and prelate for the Franciscan Monastery on the island of Orebic. "It is a foolish decision," Milesevic says, shaking his head slowly, "the Archbishop [Pijadje] is attempting to spread the war, when the rest of us are doing our best to stop it. It's reprehensible."

He hadn't expected to see himself quoted in the *Herald Tribune*. He winced when he saw the quote from General Rose. But it was the last paragraph that caught his attention, mentioning Papa Voyo's critic, Brother Nicola Milesevic.

He pulled the yellowed newspaper clipping he'd been given in Mass only three days ago out of his jacket pocket that described Papa Voyo's early years as a priest.

"Pijadje was ordained in the Franciscan Order and has been assigned to the diocese of Medjugorje, Bosnia and Herzegovina...."

John Thorpe had just confirmed over the phone that the documents he'd faxed from the Residence to be al-Qaida targeting files consistent with others found by Delta Force operatives at the warehouse at Bocinja. He'd also verified that the silk vestment he'd found on the bodies of the soldiers at the church in Stolac were estimated to be between four and six hundred years old.

The possibility that one man...a Catholic Cardinal...was responsible for all of the violence that had started at Oborci was way beyond the pale. He really couldn't blame the Zagreb detectives for their skepticism or hostility.

He glanced back down at the newspaper to reread the last paragraph of the article.

"The Cardinal is attempting to spread the war, when the rest of us are doing our best to stop it. It is reprehensible."

He redialed the number on his cell phone. As it rang, he noticed the black Lexus idling alongside the curb about seventy yards away. The dark tinted windows were a prime indicator that it was occupied by Croatian Ministry of the Interior people, probably dispatched, he thought, to watch him after his confrontation with their homicide detectives.

After a single ring, he heard General Thorpe's voice on the other end.

"John, your hunch was right...," he glanced toward the Lexus as it suddenly drove off. "It *is* all connected, and if you'll meet me, I think I can prove it...."

CHAPTER 68

GENERAL JOHN THORPE studied the satellite photos of the tanker sailing in the Mediterranean, fifty nautical miles south of Neum, Bosnia, on a southeast heading toward the Suez Canal. Most of the black and white photos were grainy, and depicted the cargo ship overhead and at various angles. One of the photos showed the name of the ship, printed on its hull:

MADHUMATI II

Outwardly, there was no indication that the ship's intent was hostile. None of the crew members that he could see in the photos was armed. All seemed to be performing their standard duties. Aside from some isolated incidents with crew members in port, there was nothing but the documents that Mark Lyons had faxed to him to bring the ship under suspicion. He needed more information...a cargo manifest, a crew manifest, radio intercepts, reports of crew activity...currently, he had nothing, and he was painfully aware that boarding a ship in international waters was no small affair. Such an action would certainly impact the U.S. relationship with Pakistan whether they found a nuclear device or not. He needed answers, and quickly. He was receiving incessant calls from the Secretary of Defense, the National Director for Intelligence and the National Security Advisor. After several hours of consultations and reviews of diplomatic and military options, he retreated to an isolated office space his people had created for him at a nondescript CIA safehouse on the outskirts of Sarajevo to consider how to preempt an imminent and potentially catastrophic chain of events.

He looked at his watch. It was 10:34 A.M., six hours ahead of Washington, D.C. and Norfolk, Virginia. He picked up the secure "Red Switch" telephone and dialed the number for the U.S. Special Operations Command Operations Center in Tampa and requested a conference call with the Commander of the Naval Special Warfare Command in Norfolk, the Chairman of the Joint Chiefs at the Pentagon, and Jim Goodwin at the CIA.

CHAPTER 69

"YOUR EMINENCE, they are cousins, I'm sure of it."

Papa Voyo listened incredulously to Savo Heleta's report on Mark Lyons. He'd watched Heleta place two 8x10 photographs on the table in front of him. He had only wanted a simple report on Mark. Now, he was hearing about a family tie between Lyons and Celo Mescic. Not only was it unexpected, it seemed preposterous. And yet, he was well-aware of Heleta's precision when he'd been assigned a task. He had, after all, trained him — and so he was privately unsettled by the revelation.

Voyo leaned back in his chair and laughed, feigning amusement. "Savo, I give you a mission to watch a single wolf, and you return to me with a report on the entire pack!"

Heleta maintained a serious expression, and shook his head slightly. He reached into his briefcase and placed a sheaf of papers, yellowed with age, on the table beside the photos without comment.

"What are these?" Voyo asked, concealing his growing uneasiness.

"Records of release from the Marshal Tito Orphanage, here in Zagreb. I found them in the municipal archives. They're nearly forty years old."

"For whom?"

Heleta pointed at the name on the top of the form. "Marko Mescic, adopted by Milan Mescic and Maja Mescic on August 3, 1976.

Voyo shook his head insistently. "This proves nothing!"

Heleta leaned over and pulled a portable DVD player from his briefcase and opened it so the screen faced Voyo. "Eminence, they are in fact first cousins. I took this video of both of them at Saint Francis Church in Stolac, *our tactical headquarters*, before it was destroyed."

Heleta pressed the "play" button and watched the footage of Mark Lyons meeting Celo at the church…inspecting the bodies of the Gabriel Team that Celo's militia had killed there…and of Mark taking the bag of money from Celo.

Voyo was silent. He pushed the DVD away and stood up. His jaw had started to ache and begin to tighten. It was a familiar feeling that he dreaded. He pulled the bottle of *schlivovitz* from his pocket, hurriedly opened it and popped several of the pills into his mouth. Heleta passed him a glass of water to chase them down. He quickly drank from it.

He remembered both names vividly from that fateful night. He could still hear both boys calling out to one another in terror…their names meant nothing to him when spoken alone, but in unison they revealed themselves in full.

…Marko…Celo….

They had eluded him all these years. He recalled that he'd killed men in retribution for what both boys had done to him…for the way they had disfigured his face, and for the tortuous pain they had forced him to endure in the three and a half decades since.

"Eminence?" Heleta finally asked.

After a long silence, Voyo looked back at Heleta with eyes that burned black and grey. He seemed to awake from a trance. He was stroking his beard obsessively.

"Where is this man, Mark Lyons, now?"

"We followed him to the airport where he parked his car. Our attempt to eliminate him there, upon his return, failed."

"And then he came here?" Voyo spat furiously. "Why? Why did you fail?"

Heleta's voice remained calm as he leaned back and glared at Voyo with resentment. "I do not know, Eminence, but I believe he was warned."

"By whom?" Voyo asked acidly.

Heleta shrugged. "Someone called him on his cell phone as he approached his car."

"Then you were being watched yourself."

Heleta nodded. "Perhaps."

Voyo slammed his fist down on the table, his face suffused with rage. "No! Not perhaps! Don't patronize me, Savo! I may be an old man, but I'm not daft!" He walked over to the window and looked out with his arms folded tightly against his chest. When he spoke again, his voice was low and even. "Someone was watching you. It is the only explanation. They know about you. They know about us."

Voyo walked back to the table and pulled out the surveillance photo of Mark and Celo standing together at the church in Stolac. "Celo killed your men there. He knows about you. He is your problem."

Heleta was silent.

Voyo handed him the photograph. "As for this fellow, Mark Lyons—he is my problem."

CHAPTER 70

FLYING LOW along the Dalmatian coastline, Mark Lyons looked down on the mountains running parallel to the sea, sparsely dotted with trees and shrubs, serene archipelagos and rocky beaches. The air was cool and crisp and the sky was cloudless. After only an hour of flying in the U.S. Air Force Pave Low Helicopter, the evidence of war appeared abruptly when they reached the sliver of land that was Bosnia's only coastal village. Rubble lay on cinder block foundations where homes and shops once stood. Burned vehicles lay on the sides of the roads. Artillery pieces were positioned intermittently in wood-lines along the hillsides and in the blasted-out shells of buildings.

The same Flight Engineer that accompanied him on his flight to Stolac pointed outside.

"That's Neum, below," the Flight Engineer shouted above the rotor and engine noise.

Mark nodded, and as he gazed into the once beautiful coastal town, he realized that there were no people visible below them.

The flight engineer pointed further out at a neighboring village that had been devastated. "And that's Ravno."

The livestock that populated every Balkan town and village—the cows, chickens, goats, even the stray dogs—were also missing. The entire village was gutted and devoid of life…a carcass. Bluish fog and smoke wafted through the shattered, bullet-ridden remains of homes.

At the edge of the village, he saw the corpses. Pile after pile of them, dumped into trenches in grotesque heaps, some impaled on industrial "I" beams and rebar and decapitated; and as they flew on, still more dead bodies were left decomposing on roadsides amidst the burned out wreckage of trucks, bicycles, carts and automobiles.

The helicopter flew back over the shell-damaged city of Neum and banked sharply over the Adriatic. He saw the other Pave Low helicopter in trail and below them, the mountains of the Peljesac Peninsula jutting out from the mainland. Vineyards and fruit trees occupied its mountain slopes. The whitewashed homes and villas that dotted the valleys still had their distinctively orange-tiled rooftops intact, all of them left untouched by the war. He remembered that these homes were Croat-owned. The "Ravno Crisis" had begun here in the former Croatian controlled "Herzeg-Bosna" corridor, and yet he was less certain whether it would end here.

He welcomed the warm air of the Adriatic rushing inside the cabin as the helicopter began to circle. Off the ramp to the rear of the Pave Low, the Franciscan Monastery came into view. It was larger than he'd expected. The church was its centerpiece. The steeple towered above like a beacon overlooking the channel between the peninsula and the mainland. A patchwork of vineyards, gardens and orchards surrounded the monastery. A monk, dressed in a dark brown habit was waving from a tractor, directing them to a rectangular landing zone freshly cut in a field beside a grove of tamarisk and pine trees. An old limestone wall separated the landing zone from the monastery.

The helicopter touched down and the trail helicopter landed adjacent to them. The second helicopter had departed from Sarajevo with John Thorpe on board, and rendezvoused with them mid-flight. He had given Thorpe only scant details for his urgent request to meet him here. He knew Cardinal Vojislav Pijadje, aka "Papa Voyo," was responsible for the ambush of the American delegation at Oborci, and the raid at Bocinja. He also believed that Voyo was responsible for the murders of Robert Childs and Kate Kamrath.

The coincidence of finding this man after so many years as a Cardinal in the Catholic Church was still too much for him to fully reconcile, professionally or personally. He still did not know "Papa Voyo," or the precise plans he harbored. There was no guarantee he would find those answers here, but he also knew Friar Nicola Milesevic was his last best hope.

The helicopters shut their engines down and he walked briskly toward John Thorpe with his head slightly ducked. He was encouraged by John Thorpe's willingness to fly down to meet him. At least someone was listening…and cared. Nonetheless, he still found himself struggling with how much he should tell Thorpe about the ostensible linkages between this enigma of a man, Vojislav Pijadje, and about his own distant past.

SANDY EVENSON KNOCKED on the door to the villa set under a grey canopy of fog.

Embedded in the forest, with a long, winding driveway from the country road, the house was larger, more isolated than she imagined it would be.

The lady who answered the door was tall and elegant, with white-grey hair and worry lines around her eyes. She wore a light blue cashmere sweater and black stirrup pants.

"Maja Lyons?" Sandy asked.

The lady nodded and smiled back at her. Sandy felt her heart racing, and anxiety was tightening her shoulders. She wished that she had called in advance.

"I am a friend of your sons'…in Bosnia," Sandy said in Serbo-Croatian, in a gesture of respect.

"Marko?" She uttered softly, drawing back. Her surprise quickly transitioned to concern, and hearing Sandy's American accent, she switched to English. "Is he okay?"

Sandy waved her hand and smiled to reassure her. "He's just fine." She paused for a moment, searching the woman's kind eyes. They were welcoming and conveyed kindness, but wisdom borne from experience. "And so is Celo."

Maja Lyons raised her hands to her heart. Looking back at Sandy, her eyes were wide and her voice came as a faint whisper. She reached out and grasped her hand holding it tightly—insistently. "You've seen him? He and Marko…are they together?"

Her English was flawless, with only the trace of an accent to betray her Yugoslav origins.

Sandy nodded, unsure how best to respond. "They are. They're together, Mrs. Lyons—they're both fine." She paused again, unsure what to say next. "That's…why I came."

A fleeting look of relief came over Maja Lyons. Sandy saw her tears.

"I'm sorry. You have surprised me." Maja said, motioning her inside. "Please, come in. I'll put on a kettle."

OREBIC, CROATIA

FRIAR NICOLA MILESEVIC greeted Mark Lyons and General John Thorpe at the entrance to the monastery. Milesevic was short and stocky, almost square, with a large balding head, thick neck, and serious, sober eyes, like an old bulldog's and a face like worn asphalt, fissured and cracked. He wore the Franciscan brown habit, hooded on the back, with a white knotted rope around his waist, and a wooden cross hung on his chest.

Both men followed the monk through the whitewashed stucco hallways of the cloister to his office, passing other monks in brown habits sweeping the floors. It was well-lit, organized and spacious—furnished with handmade Scandinavian hardwoods…a large desk and chairs, tables, and several bookshelves. Enlarged color photos of Pope John Paul II's visit to Dalmatia over two decades ago hung on the wall. One photo depicted a vast open-air Mass. Another showed the Pope greeting well-wishers, smiling and shaking hands.

Milesevic gathered up his habit under his arm and invited them to sit in a black leather sofa positioned beside an exposed brick wall near a large handmade crucifix. The lifelike reproduction of Christ showed every muscle and bone carved into the wood, precisely to scale. It produced the illusion of an additional presence in the room.

"It's magnificent, isn't it?" Milesevic asked proudly, noticing their interest in the crucifix. "It was hand-carved and donated to us by one of the world's greatest sculptors of wood in Oberammergau, Germany. Every seven years, Oberammergau hosts the Passion Play, you know, and our monastery has always participated in it, even during the days of the Cold War." Milesevic touched the cross reverently. "This was their gift to us."

"It's beautiful," Mark said.

"An extraordinary piece," Thorpe commented.

Milesevic held his hand up and pointed upwards. "Anything that brings us closer to God, such as this, deserves our admiration." He lowered his arms, walked in front of his desk, and leaned against it. For a moment, he was silent. His expression was pensive, if not sad. "You are here, I think, because of the situation with Cardinal Pijadje?"

Mark nodded at the wizened old monk. "There are some significant issues that relate to him—yes, Father."

Milesevic shook his head thoughtfully. His voice was solemn. "I am sad to say, he has caused many problems for us down here. In my opinion, he is the main cause of the recent fighting. If there is anyone to blame, it is Voyo."

Thorpe looked up and shifted in his seat. He'd obviously not expected the accusation and although Mark had already established Vojislav Pijadje as a threat, he hadn't anticipated it from Milesevic. Thorpe leaned forward with his hand outstretched. "Father, please pardon me, but could you explain? How is Zagreb's Archbishop a cause for this crisis?"

"He is an 'Archbishop Cardinal' in name alone, General," Milesevic replied, shaking his head. He reached for the fruit basket on the table and pulled out an orange. He rotated it in his hand, contemplatively. Finally, he looked directly at both men, and held up the orange. "When you see this, you see an orange, yes?"

They nodded.

"And it is, just that...an orange," Milesevic answered himself professorially, "It may look appealing, but we can never know its true quality until we peel it or cut it open. When we do, we may find it to be too dry or even rotten to consume."

Mark was reminded how people in the Balkans, especially the elderly, liked to speak in clever metaphors and allegories. He saw Milesevic as an Aristotelian personality who also seemed to enjoy extending the images he constructed.

"May God forgive me...," Milesevic began reluctantly. "Vojislav Pijadje, like the orange, is rotten inside. I have known him many years. We attended the Seminary together. Only one year separated us. I was the elder of us. I'm afraid my impression of him then is the same as it is now. He is the worst kind of priest—a priest with political designs and a very dark soul. He used his position as Minister General of the Franciscan Order to become the Archbishop of Zagreb. And he has used Croatia's own Catholicism as a subterfuge to fuel Croatian nationalism...*and* expansionism. The politicians and media have encouraged him. The people have been like lemmings. It's despicable. *Despicable*." He nearly spat the last word.

Thorpe shifted uncomfortably in his seat and leaned toward Milesevic. "To gain any traction, he'd need the Vatican's support. Are you saying they're complicit?"

"Complicit?" Milesevic repeated with a choked laugh. "It depends on how you measure complicity. Certainly one is complicit if he conspires, but is he complicit if he has knowledge of an immoral act and does nothing to intervene? It is a military as well as a moral code, is it not, General?" He shrugged. "Everyone is to blame. No one is innocent." Milesevic stood up. He walked over to his desk and pulled out a large, oversized magazine that had been folded in half. He walked back to Mark and handed it to him, still folded. "Our Archbishop...," Milesevic said sternly, handing it Mark. "He walks with the Devil."

It was Croatia's most popular current events magazine, dated a year ago, and it had a close-up photograph of a bearded Cardinal Vojislav Pijadje on the cover, dressed in a shiny gold and red robe, holding an infant in front of a church, surrounded by a group of smiling people. He towered above them. The caption in large, bold red Serbo-Croatian read:

Ravno's Saviour!

Mark quickly flipped through the magazine and found the cover story with the expanded headline:

Zagreb Archbishop stops Muslim Plan to Demolish Ravno Church: Condemns Islamic Fundamentalism as "Gathering Threat" to Croats in Bosnia and Herzegovina

"You see! It's simply preposterous. All theater," Milesevic said, exasperated. "He brought the reporters from Zagreb with him. And buses filled with people from out of town. What this awful article does not say is that the church--Saint Damian's--was to be demolished for severe structural problems. We had plans to rebuild it! He knew that, but ignored everything we told him—he refused to talk to us. It was as if everything had been scripted." He shook his head and looked up toward the ceiling, and then at John Thorpe, continuing. "And unbelievably, do you know, he had EUFOR soldiers providing security for this spectacle? Somehow, he convinced your General Rose of the need for EUFOR protection! He said Mass inside and...."

Milesevic's voice trailed off for a moment, and again he was shaking his head. "He brought the bones of Alojzije Stepinac from Saint Stephen's with him! He paraded them through the streets, through Serb and Muslim neighborhoods and before we knew what was happening, Voyo's mob was setting fire to their homes and businesses, as EUFOR watched! They did nothing to stop them. It was outrageous…outrageous and disgraceful."

"All of the other accounts blame the Serbs for attacking the Croats," Thorpe said.

Milesevic shook his head. His hands were folded together on his lap. "Voyo provided the spark that ignited everything." He pointed at the magazine in Mark's hand. "Since that day, there was retribution throughout Bosnia against Croats living in towns dominated by the Serbs and Muslims…churches were destroyed, priests killed, nuns raped, the house burnings began and all of the refugees, thousands of them. It was awful."

"And Medjugorje?" Mark asked. "We understand he arranged for the Stepinac canonization there."

Milesevic collapsed in his seat. "It is more of the same…I have counseled, urged and warned the Vatican. *I warned him of the consequences!* But he laughed and told me I should 'have faith' and that it was 'God's will.'" The old monk was showing exhaustion. "I warned them…I told the Vatican of the violence that would erupt all over Bosnia and Croatia, but they would not listen to me. As the high commissioner, Roman Polko has the ability to stop this, but he says he will not. Now, all of this has taken on a life of its own. I can do no more."

For a moment, no one spoke. A tractor's engine hummed outside, the scent of freshly mown grass filled the room, mixing with the tobacco smoke.

Finally, Mark stood and walked over to Milesevic, pulling the folded vestment out of his pocket. Mark handed it to him. "Father, can you tell me what this is?"

Milesevic's expression seemed to dissolve, his face turning pale as he stared at it disbelievingly. Lifting his shoulders, he quickly handed it back. "Where…?" he demanded. "Where did you find this?"

"On the bodies of Croatian paramilitary killed outside Stolac," Mark answered quietly, still standing.

Milesevic shook his head nervously, like a half-mad prisoner about to be led away to the asylum. The blood drained from his face. He stood abruptly and walked to his desk with a series of throat-clearing rasps. Finally, he said bluntly, "I cannot help you. I'm very sorry."

"Father, it's why we came here to see you."

"You came to ask me about Voyo Pijadje, not this!"

"This vestment was also found in Voyo's vestuary, Father." Mark countered evenly. He hadn't expected this kind of reaction from the old priest. He was intrigued.

At first Milesevic stared at him; then rubbing the back of his neck, walked back to his chair and sat down, looking both men over with an air of frank appraisal. After a moment, he began to shake his head and repeat to himself, "After so many years...we were told they were disbanded. Never to return. But they still exist. Even today." He whispered the words to himself as surprised lament.

Mark and Thorpe exchanged glances. Thorpe's eyes were wide with curiosity and his brows were raised.

"What, Father? Please tell us," Mark urged.

Milesevic leaned back in his chair, again looking up at the ceiling, shaking his head. His mouth tightened.

"The orphrey you hold belongs to a group that was only whispered about since I have been a priest. It has been the subject of late night discussions in abbeys and monasteries where speculation is rampant and rumors abound about DaVinci Codes, Knights Templar and secret societies...we have called it "God's Left Hand." During the Cold War, they worked in the shadows, but I thought the group was done away with. So we were told...."

"Well, it's not nonsense, Father. During the past several weeks, many people have been murdered, Top Secret documents have been stolen, two American ambassadors were assassinated for those documents, and I fear that unless we act now something far worse will happen," Mark said, standing over him. "We need your help."

Milesevic looked at both men, still shaking his head. His disbelief seemed to be transitioning to panic. "What can I do? There is nothing I can do for you!"

"You can tell us what you know about this organization...about this," Thorpe replied, pointing at the vestment in Mark's hands.

"What I can tell you is that I believe you are in grave danger now, having this orphrey in your possession. Having touched it, they will not allow you to live. They cannot."

"Who are *they*?" Thorpe asked.

Milesevic's thick brows drew down. "They are said to wield the sword of the Archangel Gabriel. They are protectors of the church, commissioned by

356

the Holy See itself. They have revealed themselves publicly only once, in 1982 when the Turkish assassin Mehmet Ali Agca attempted to kill Pope John Paul II in Rome. There were nearly a dozen of them that swarmed the area within seconds. They disappeared as quickly as they arrived."

"Are you certain?" Mark asked.

Milesevic stood and walked over to a file cabinet, opened it, and pulled a file. He handed it to him. "Judge for yourself."

Mark opened the manila folder and found a stack of 8x10 color photos. They depicted men in dark suits and sunglasses with the Pope in the aftermath of the shooting, pistols and submachine guns drawn in full view. As he flipped through them, one of the bodyguards' suit jackets was opened, revealing the orphrey in full view—with exactly the same embroidered design as the one he now held. Mark passed the photo...and another to Thorpe.

Milesevic continued. "Many thought that Agca acted alone—"

"It was a Bulgarian-run plot, as I recall," Thorpe interrupted.

Milesevic nodded slowly, and walked over to Mark. "We know the Bulgarians planned the assassination attempt, but the KGB directed it. The photos you see now show the aftermath."

Mark looked up at the priest. "The aftermath?"

"Of the Gabriel Execution Squads."

The next photographs he saw were grotesque black and white images of men obviously shot dead, partially and fully clothed, riddled with bullets to their heads and torsos. Some of the photos were taken outdoors, and displayed the victims slumped over on park benches, lying in ditches and in driveways. Others depicted bloodied bodies in cars, in hotel rooms and their homes.

Mark handed each photo to Thorpe as he viewed them. He now saw clearly in each image what the old priest was trying to convey to them.

Thorpe was placing the photos on the table in front of him, side-by-side. He looked up at Milesevic. "Father, these could be mafia or organized crime murders, couldn't they? I'm not sure I see them as the result of a Vatican-run assassination program."

Milesevic shook his head, conveying both sadness and genuine fear. "General, you must look more closely."

Thorpe held the photos and began to view them again. Mark leaned over and pointed at the white embroidered orphrey in each photo, in every instance placed on the victim's feet. Thorpe looked silently over at Mark, his eyes wide. His lips tightened and thinned. "My God."

Milesevic returned to his desk drawer. "All the victims in those photos were of Bulgarian nationality, each of the murders happened between 1982 and 1984." He pulled another large envelope out and handed it to Mark. "But these were different."

Mark opened the envelope and sat beside Thorpe. These were color photographs. They depicted the bodies of five men, each apparently in their homes. Some were dressed in street clothes, others in their underwear, and in bed. There was no blood in these. No gunshot wounds, but in each, the orphrey was there, at the feet of their victims.

"These victims are Russian," Milesevic said. "All but one of them were active KGB agents believed to be involved in planning the Pope's assassination."

"There are no gunshot wounds, Father," Mark said.

"Indeed," Milesevic replied sitting down again. "These victims were poisoned."

Mark's heart was pounding with the mention of the second common thread to these executions…first the orphrey and now the method of poison as a murder weapon.

"You said all but one were active KGB agents?" Thorpe asked.

Milesevic nodded and pointed to the remaining photo in Thorpe's hands. "This one…this one was retired KGB."

Mark looked over Thorpe's shoulder at the photo, and saw a photo of an elderly man collapsed on the floor dressed in pajamas. An embroidered white orphrey was at his feet.

Mark pointed at the orphrey. "That is the vestment—"

"It was a reproduction of the original orphreys," Milesevic interrupted.

"Who's the dead guy?" Thorpe asked.

Milesevic's voice was solemn and quiet, almost a whisper. "He retired as head of the KGB—Secretary General of the Soviet Union, Yuri Andropov."

Chapter 71

United Airlines Flight One-Seven-Four with service to Boston will now begin boarding passengers seated in rows fifteen to ten....

SITTING IN THE WINE BAR in the Belfast International Airport's Departure Terminal, Sandy Evenson tried to ignore the boarding announcement. Her passport and airplane ticket lay on the table in front of her. They seemed to levitate, rising and falling with each breath. She placed her hand on the ticket to stop the illusion. Her shoulders slumped. The ticket brought her home, but did nothing to resolve her dilemma for what to do next. Getting on the plane was perhaps the prudent thing to do, but she could not shake the rather sickening feeling that by going home she was also plainly giving up.

She recalled Maja Lyons' confiding hand in hers and her words that still resonated with her:

"Everything is close to the surface for Marko.... It's good that he and Celo are together again after all this time. So they can talk...and try to make sense of what happened to them. Neither of them has ever come to terms with what happened.... They must talk... accept what separated all of us. In the meantime, I am sorry to say there is nothing you can do."

Although they had been spoken with kindness, they had come suddenly and with certain finality.

"There is nothing you can do..."

The intimacy of the encounter, the comfort of Maja's voice...someone who knew Mark so well had given credence to what she had suspected about his past and how it had so profoundly affected him. And yet, her words hung around her like a dense haze. She already felt light-headed from the wine, which only served to amplify the conflicting voice within her...calling her back to the Balkans. Throughout her years living there, feeling helpless had never been an option—because she'd never allowed it to be. She had always been able to brazen her way through anything.

That didn't explain why she'd stayed in the Balkans when all of her other compatriots had long ago left—and even after her family had begged her to come home.

Maybe she was a Don Quixote after all. How wholly typical it was of her life to be chasing Balkan windmills! She'd done all the analysis...searched for the reasons before, but the truth was, she didn't know why she'd stayed, except that in Bosnia the cause had a face.

She took another long sip of the Merlot, quickly emptying the glass. She studied the ticket again. Her seat was 2C—it had been called long ago for boarding. In the departure gate across from her, the few remaining passengers were handing their tickets to the agent at the door.

She ran her fingers through her hair and closed her eyes to fight off a dull, emerging headache. She opened her eyes when she heard the final boarding call for the flight to Boston. A female voice with an Irish accent then paged her by name. She was reaching for her purse when she heard the reporter's voice reporting on the Ravno Crisis in Bosnia.

She glanced around looking for the television and found it above the bar, turned to the BBC. The volume was nearly inaudible.

"The ongoing conflict in Ravno...risks being further escalated by the Croatian pilgrimage to Medjugorje for the Canonization of Archbishop Alojzije Stepinac tomorrow afternoon..."

She stood and felt the wine momentarily unbalance her on the way to the bar. She leaned forward to listen more closely, watching the images of an overturned bus in flames flashed on the screen. She struggled to hear the reporter's voiceover that was drowned out by yet another departure announcement, followed by the sounds of the bartender scrubbing glasses at the sink.

"...Serb Militias destroyed a Catholic Church in the neighboring town of Stolac two days ago..."

"Excuse me!" Sandy looked at the bartender and pointed at the television. "This is important. Could you turn up the volume?"

"...The first buses have been greeted by mobs of angry Bosnian Serb protestors...by all accounts, EUFOR military units have been slow to respond, and

have struggled to stem the violence at this early stage..."

The bartender dried his hands and reached for the television remote. He pointed it at the television set and the reporter's voice became louder, clearer.

"...more buses are departing Croatia in scores, and are anticipated to pass through ethnic Serb and Muslim regions of Bosnia. Roadblocks manned by armed Serb militias have already been reported and have been declared illegal by EUFOR Commanding General Ian Rose. United Nations High Commissioner Roman Polko is expressing grave concern to the Vatican that unless the canonization ceremony is moved to a separate venue or rescheduled, widespread riots and further loss of life will result. The Vatican has so far refused. The Archbishop of Zagreb, Croatian Cardinal Vojislav Pijadje dismisses these concerns...

The image appeared of a tall older man wearing black and a clerical collar. Part of his face was disfigured—a concave pattern of grey whiskers filled in where his cheekbone and jaw once were. His English was very good, yet thickly accented.

"...The church will not be intimidated. Archbishop Stepinac is Croatia's saint and nothing can prevent us from having this day, at the site of his final miracle. ...The Pope is expected to arrive in Sarajevo tomorrow by jet. He will then be flown by his official helicopter here, to Medjugorje. Security for this event has been described by one Vatican official as 'unprecedented.' This is Xenia Dormandy with the BBC, reporting live from Medjugorje, Bosnia."

Suddenly, with rising fear and realization, her conversation with Kate Kamrath in the Irish pub in Sarajevo rushed back to her. Kate had told her she was investigating a possible linkage between Medjugorje and the disappearance of Bob Childs.

The female voice on the loudspeaker again paged her by name, more insistently this time.

She dug into her purse and found a fifty pound note and tossed it on the table. She picked up her coat from the chair and rushed to the departure gate while digging out her cell phone from her coat pocket. She reached the departure gate and handed her ticket over to the attendant.

"*I'm* Sandy Evenson," she inhaled anxiously. "I can't get on this flight."

CHAPTER 72

SANDY EVENSON HEARD Jon Schauer's voice answer just before she knew his voicemail would pick up.

"Jon, I'm getting on a flight to Zagreb. Can you pick me up at 8:30 tonight?"

There was an extended pause on the other end. "Where *are* you?" Schauer's voice was incredulous.

"In Belfast."

"Northern Ireland? Why—?"

"I don't have time to explain, Schauer." She heard her voice rise. "I'm getting on the plane *now*. Can you pick me up or not?" Her voice was now calm and measured.

"Are you sure you want to do this?" Schauer replied simply.

"This is the only thing I'm sure of at this moment, Schauer," she answered. "And we need to drive down to Medjugorje."

He did not immediately respond.

"Jon?"

"I heard you," Schauer replied, pausing. "Sandy? ...is this about Mark or is it about Ravno?"

She felt her head rush as she stood at the Croatian Airways departure gate. She sat down to steady herself. She was in no position to drive. Her head was spinning from the combined effects of exhaustion, stress and wine. "It's about both. I can get a rental car—just tell me if you can't pick me up."

"Of course I'll pick you up," Schauer answered quietly. "See you at 8:30 then."

She thanked him and a wave of relief passed over her. She folded her cell phone and proceeded to hand her ticket to the Croatian Airways attendant at the gate.

CHAPTER 73

MARK LYONS HANDED a beer to John Thorpe and turned the television on to the BBC as soon as they'd arrived at Jon Schauer's apartment. Schauer told Mark, when he called, that he had several errands to do, and would set a key aside for them.

The focus of the news was on the worsening crisis in Ravno. It transitioned quickly to another related story that caused Mark to set his bottle of beer down and turn up the volume.

...This afternoon in the embattled town of Stolac, the Bosnian Serb leader Celo Mescic placed five captured British SAS commandos on display in the town center who he alleged were in the midst of an effort to arrest him and deliver him to The Hague.

"Today, we fight for our existence, and at every turn the world has opposed us! Our homes are destroyed! Our land has been taken from us! They accuse us—they accuse me—of war crimes! I have told the United Nations and NATO that I will gladly turn myself in to them and even stand before a trial if they would only ask me...I have told them not to attempt to arrest me or to launch a special operation to capture me. But they have done that! Not once, but twice! And twice I have defeated them without violence. I am through negotiating. The next time, we will defend ourselves, and these commandos will pay the price with their lives!"

The European Force Commander, General Ian Rose, reacted to the images of the captured SAS soldiers: "Celo Mescic is wanted by The Hague for war crimes committed in the first Balkan War, and now again during the crisis in Ravno. He is responsible for many serious violations of international law, to include the wanton destruction of Saint Francis Catholic Church in Stolac just two days ago. The methods he has adopted to shock and intimidate are appalling, and they are reprehensible. We have demanded that he release these soldiers immediately and surrender himself to authorities...."

Mark turned down the volume. Thorpe was sitting on the sofa.

"I told Ian not to do this…that I would handle Celo…that I could convince him to surrender to the Tribunal, but he didn't listen, and now it's led to this!"

"Was that the church that blew after my crew flew you in?"

He nodded. "He did it as I was boarding the helicopter. I had no idea that was his plan…I didn't even see the charges, but it was perfectly timed. Meant as a message for me, I suspect."

"Well, I don't have to tell you—he's not helping himself…or his cause."

"No, he isn't," Mark began. He paused for a moment and leaned forward on the edge of the sofa. "But he's the best source of information we've got. If he's arrested, the well goes dry."

Thorpe cast a thoughtful glance at him. "All right, I need you to tell me, objectively…is any of this influenced by the fact that you two are cousins?"

He attempted to gather his thoughts. The depth of Thorpe's awareness surprised him. He'd never told Thorpe about Celo, and although he hadn't sought to cover it up, he hadn't publicized it either. "I'm sorry, John. I should have told you myself rather than let you find out from some intel report."

"I didn't get it from an intel report. Annalisa told me long before she died, Mark."

He nodded.

Of course. Annalisa was the only one whom he'd ever told—but even she didn't have the full story. Only she and his Aunt knew about the event at the dam and his forced emigration to Ireland. Others only knew bits and pieces. He preferred it that way.

Mark motioned toward the muted television set. "My relation to Celo doesn't have anything to do with—"

"I'll talk to Ian Rose about Celo, Mark, but he's going to have to release those SAS troopers," Thorpe replied quietly. "He can't hold on to them or deliver any more ultimatums to EUFOR or NATO."

There was a moment of silence between both men.

Thorpe took a sip of beer and leaned back into the sofa. "In our business, we have a term for guys like Celo."

"What would that be?"

"NAFOD."

"Nayfod?" Mark repeated.

"No Apparent Fear Of Death," Thorpe explained.

Mark smiled and nodded his understanding. Before he could answer, his cell phone rang. He heard Celo's distinctive deep inflection in Serbo-Croatian on the other end.

"Marko, I need to talk to you."

He looked at Thorpe, responding in Serbo-Croatian. "I'm listening."

"No, I need to talk to you in private. It's very important. Where are you?"

"Zagreb. Where are you?"

"Mostar. Are you with anyone?"

"General Thorpe."

"The American Special Forces General?"

"That's him."

He heard Celo laugh. "Does he want to arrest me?"

"No, but he wants you to give up the British soldiers you've taken hostage." He paused. "And so do I."

"They tried to arrest me again," Celo growled. "I told you...I told *them* there would be consequences...now maybe they will believe me!"

"You have to let them go, Celo."

There was an extended silence before Celo replied. "Meet me in Mostar tomorrow night, at 7:00...at the Restaurant Taurus on the Ustashe side of the Stari Most. Bring the General along. I have a deal I will make."

"Will you release the soldiers?"

"We will discuss this."

He heard the line go dead, then looked at Thorpe. "Speak of the devil...."

"Is he going to release those soldiers?"

"I told him to let them go," Mark answered. "He wants to talk tomorrow night in Mostar, and he wants you to come along. He said he'd 'make a deal'...I don't know, John, but I think there's something else he wants to tell us."

Thorpe nodded thoughtfully and looked back at Mark. "Okay. Let's go then...what do you want to do about the cardinal?"

"Voyo?"

"Yeah," Thorpe answered. "Him."

"I'll deal with'im," Mark answered simply.

"And Celo?" Thorpe leaned forward. "Christ, Mark, now we're having *dinner* with him."

"I'm not making any excuses for Celo, but this Gabriel Team...," he held up the orphrey and set it back on the table. "...is something more than a paramilitary group or militia. They're the greater threat, and Voyo appears to be directing it."

"Well," Thorpe said slowly, "what would you say they are then?"

"You saw Milesevic's photos. They're an assassination squad. All of the evidence points to them being responsible for the Fulbright ambush and the raid at Bocinja."

"If that's true, that would mean they also may have a nuclear device in their possession," Thorpe said.

He nodded. "Those papers I faxed to you came from Voyo's office. And this vestment was one of about twelve that were in the vestuary at the Cathedral—"

"What, then, was their motive for Oborci and Bocinja?" Thorpe asked. "A preemptive strike?"

He nodded and pointed at Thorpe's briefcase. "The Vatican is an al-Qaida target—the report from Bob Childs that was in their possession indicates they knew it."

"Before we did."

Thorpe nodded, pulling the faxed papers out, reviewing them. "They also point to Medjugorje as a potential target."

"The canonization ceremony is on Sunday at Medjugorje."

Thorpe looked up from the papers. "The Pope will be officiating the Mass...."

"The question is where those devices are now?" Mark replied quietly. "You have to assume the Pope is a viable target."

Thorpe nodded. "For any device to be fully effective, it would need to be targeted against a government, an event, or a population center. And you have to consider the obvious—that it has to be moved, and there are three ways to do it—by air, land or sea."

"We have a good idea of al-Qaida's targeting, but what about this Gabriel Team? If they have a device, would they use it?"

"We can only hope they wouldn't," Thorpe replied. "But I'm not sure they'd give it up either. It would beg the question of how and where they got it."

"John, you told me years ago something I've never forgotten: 'Hope—"

"...is not a method." Thorpe finished. "I know. Somehow we have to determine their capabilities and plans…and the Cardinal seems to be the linchpin to all of it. He's already demonstrated that he'll kill to defend the church."

"It's why we need Celo—without him, we've blinded ourselves," Mark replied with quiet urgency.

Thorpe nodded. "I'll talk to some folks and see if they'll grant him a reprieve, but he needs to know it's temporary—there's not a lot of room left for deal making. Ultimately, he's gonna have to turn himself in."

Mark nodded, hesitating for several seconds. "John?"

Thorpe looked up from the photos.

"There's something else I need to tell you about Cardinal Vojislav Pijadje…."

ZAGREB, CROATIA

Papa Voyo watched the two men depart the Danish photographer's apartment. It had been the second time he'd seen this man from the church there, and he sensed that they were using it as a base from which to plan and launch their operations. Everything pointed to it, the activity that occurred there after he'd killed the reporter, after the raid in Bocinja, and after the attack on his men and the destruction of Saint Francis Church in Stolac.

Savo Heleta had given him the address, and the identity of this man who he'd seen at Mass on Sunday in the front pew…Mark Lyons, Commissioner of the European Union Police Mission.

Cousin to Celo.

It was this man Mark Lyons, then, who along with the Serb, Celo Mescic, had killed his men and taken the operational funds meant to counter the gathering Islamic threat.

It was Mark Lyons then…Marko… who had nearly killed him so long ago, that night at the dam.

Another troublesome thought occurred to him: who Lyons could be affiliated with…which intelligence agency?

He did not know, but eliminating both men was now his highest priority.

PART V

REDEMPTION

CHAPTER 74

SANDY EVENSON WEAVED through the crowds in the Zagreb airport and emerged from the Customs area to see Jon Schauer waiting with a wry smile. She kissed him hurriedly on both cheeks and surrendered her bag to him.

"I know you think I'm crazy, Schauer."

Schauer laughed out loud. "Crazy? No, absolutely not," He countered. "Madly in love? Yes. Indeed."

"Please don't start, okay? I've got a hangover, and I'm already feeling emotionally weak and pathetic as it is."

Schauer grinned silently. He was visibly amused, but he knew not to push her too much more. They emerged from the arrivals terminal and he pointed toward his car parked in the first row of the parking area. The air was crisp and cold, with a slight breeze.

"You know they were at my flat until a few hours ago...."

She stopped in midstride. "Who's at your flat?"

"Mark and General Thorpe," Schauer replied. "They said they were flying down to Mostar."

"You didn't tell them I was flying in, did you?"

He shook his head. "No, but I don't see why I shouldn't have."

"Because you're a friend, and because I asked you not to."

Schauer shrugged. "Maybe you should tell me your plan, then, Sandy. Because I'm feeling more and more like an observer than an active participant."

She paused. "First, we need to go to the Archbishop's Palace and see the Cardinal."

He opened the trunk of his car and loaded her suitcase. His expression was incredulous as he closed the trunk. "I see...we're just going to drop in on the Archbishop of Zagreb?"

She climbed into the car and sat in the passenger seat. A moment later, Schauer opened his door and sat down beside her.

"Well?"

"Well, what?"

"Why are we going to see the Archbishop?"

She leaned her head back and exhaled. "Because I was reading Kate's notebook," she said, pulling out the notebook and flipping to the page she'd marked with a 'post-it'. "Look—." She handed him the notebook. "It's the last location I can place her before she went home. And this 'ABPAL' must be her shorthand for 'Archbishop's Palace'...it's the only logical explanation."

"What do you think it means?"

"I don't know, but what's really strange about it is...according to Kate's notes...." She flipped through the preceding several pages of the notebook. "'ABPAL' was also the last place Bob was before he turned up missing." She dropped the notebook into her lap. "Too much of a coincidence?"

Schauer's eyes widened in a sudden realization, and then nodded his agreement. He turned the car's ignition and as if it were an afterthought, passed her a box containing a stack of 8x10 photos. "Those are the photos I printed from Kate's camera chip," Schauer said.

Among them were the images of Bob Childs' house, his wife Renee, and Saint Stephen's Cathedral. There was another zoomed shot, taken from the inside of a car, of a tall priest, with a grossly disfigured face wearing a pectoral cross and a red cap. "So perhaps we should pay the Archbishop a visit!"

"I'm not sure that's a good idea, Sandy."

She shook her head. "Nonsense. Strength in numbers, Schauer...."

VANGA ISLAND, CROATIA

SITTING IN HIS SMALL room in the monastery, Major Savo Heleta had been ignoring the Croatian News Broadcast, until he overheard the live report on the Bosnian Serb activities in and around Medjugorje. He glanced up and saw the image of Celo Mescic, standing on a stone wall with an AK-47 in one hand, and gesturing wildly to a large Serb mob with the other.

Heleta turned up the volume on his television set. Celo's angry mob had stopped seven buses and had surrounded them. The mob was rocking one of the buses until it tipped over…filled with people. Heleta heart beat heavily.

The reporter was a woman standing on the periphery of the mob. Heleta could see she was frightened, and trying desperately to maintain her composure on camera. After only another thirty seconds of footage, she hurriedly stated her name to conclude her broadcast…a Croatian name he thought…she was reporting from Mostar. Only thirty minutes from Medjugorje.

So, he's in Mostar.

He knew Celo. He'd met him once during the previous war in Bosnia in Mostar. He'd gained legendary status then, and a cult-like following among the Serbs which he used fully to his advantage. He'd earned their respect on the battlefield and managed to transform it into political capital. During the Bosnian war, he had fought heroically. He was a natural leader and also a ruthless killer. He had read several accounts of how Celo had nearly been mortally wounded. He had been shot in the chest and the bullet had missed his heart by a hair's breadth, but he recovered miraculously and continued to fight.

Heleta did not fear Celo, but he did respect him. He knew he would be a formidable adversary.

He picked up the phone near his bed and dialed it. "Prepare a helicopter… have it ready to depart in thirty minutes. Have a car standing by to meet us in Mostar."

ZAGREB, CROATIA

MARK LYONS and John Thorpe arrived at the Zagreb airport and the blades of the Pave Low Helicopters were already turning. The static electricity from their rotors had created a spectacular light show of flashing orange, yellow and red luminous hues.

The wind from the helicopters' rotor blades initially whipped hard against them. They ducked their heads and held their jackets close to their bodies as they walked briskly to the back ramp of the lead helicopter. Once inside, both men sat on the webbed seating and buckled their seatbelts. Mark heard the helicopter's blades begin to wail as they changed pitch, biting into the air to create lift. A moment later, the aircraft lifted up dramatically and then banked to the right where the lights of Zagreb came fully into view.

Thorpe handed Mark a shoulder holster with a Browning High Power 9mm pistol and four magazines fully loaded with ammunition. Mark hesitated at first to take them, but Thorpe's intense gaze conveyed that he had no choice.

CHAPTER 75

SANDY EVENSON and Jon Schauer rang the bell to the Archbishop's Palace, and when no one answered, Sandy rang again. After the second ring she whispered to Schauer that she could hear movement inside.

When the door opened, there was a priest, wearing a black cassock and a white rope around his waist. Sandy announced herself with her ICTY credentials and asked to speak to Cardinal Pijadje. Before he could answer her, another tall elderly man in a black Cossack with a pectoral cross and red cap appeared behind him.

"Can I help you?"

She was initially taken aback by Papa Voyo's appearance...his face was an oval, partially covered by dark grey and white whiskers, but not enough to conceal the deep cavity on the left side of his face that she'd seen in Kate's photographs. Everything about him stood in stark contrast to his clerical attire. His eyes were most intimidating and saturnine: large, black, liquid in hollow sockets that seemed to exude coldness and an innate suspicion. An uneasy feeling came over her and she resisted her initial urge to walk away while she could. Reflexively, she slipped her arm into Schauer's.

"Cardinal Pijadje?"

Voyo nodded. "Yes? I am Papa Voyo. Can I help you?"

She handed him one of her cards and introduced herself as a special prosecutor for the War Crimes Tribunal.

Voyo nodded his recognition, but his face was impassive. He remained in the doorway as if his intention was to block it. His voice was deep and his tone was brusque and patronizing. "I must apologize, you see, we're departing now for Medjugorje—you know our greatest Cardinal, Alojzije Stepinac, will finally be made a Saint on Saturday. And so I'm afraid we are in a great hurry—"

Sandy felt her adrenalin surge without warning, taking her by surprise. Her instincts were screaming like claxons. Something was out of place—not quite right.

She knew that this would probably be her last chance to talk to him...unannounced, when he wasn't prepared. She released Schauer's arm and waved her hands apologetically. "Not at all, Your Eminence! We're going down there too! We won't take much of your time, but we do need to ask you some questions."

"Questions?" Voyo asked.

Sandy nodded and forced a smile, staring past him at the open closet. "The first question, and I'm terribly sorry, Your Eminence, but *where is your bathroom*?" she asked guilelessly. "I'm desperate. Just flew in from a funeral, you know...."

Voyo shook his head, asymmetric in astonishment. "No, you must understand, I am in a great rush—"

Schauer nodded and then shook his head apologetically. "Sorry, Eminence...small bladder."

Before Voyo could respond, she removed her coat and hung it in the open closet at the entrance, stepping around Voyo. "When you gotta go, you gotta go. I'm sure you understand!"

She felt her heart beating wildly not sure if her maneuver would work. The residence reeked of pipe tobacco, the air was stale...and as she walked down the darkened hallway, the internal alarm bells in her head became louder, and she found herself wanting to run, not walk back outside. She was relieved to hear Schauer's voice follow behind her over Voyo's protests.

"The WC is on the left, Miss Evenson," Voyo called to her, clearly exasperated. The priest who answered the door rushed behind to show her.

She saw two doors exuding sunlight. She turned into one and found herself in the office filled with books on shelves that lined the walls from floor to ceiling.

"No," Voyo called. "The water closet is the next door down."

She stepped out and turned back to Schauer. "John, you have *got* to see these books! Come see!"

On cue, Schauer stepped past Voyo and into the hallway. "You're a collector of books, Your Eminence?"

"Please! Why have you come here?" Voyo replied irritably.

"Be with you in just a moment!" she called out from the bathroom, standing by the door. Outside, she could hear Voyo's strident protests.

She flushed the toilet and opened the door. Voyo was outside his office, alternately watching Schauer and glancing down the hall to see her emerge from the bathroom.

"We're hoping you can help us find out more about the murder of our friends Kate Kamrath and the disappearance of Robert Childs, Father."

Voyo shook his head insistently. "What?"

She drew closer to Voyo. Schauer was now in the doorway of the office. "In each of their cases, we've been able to conclude that this was their last stop."

"This is a surprise to me," Voyo shrugged. "But perhaps it would be logical for them to come here, to church, would it not?"

"Maybe, but they also came to see you, specifically, Your Eminence," Sandy responded, holding up Kate's notebook. "You see, Kate Kamrath's notes are what brought us here."

Voyo glared at the notebook possessively. After a moment, he nodded somberly. "Yes, of course. I do remember her. She came to ask me about Cardinal Stepinac's canonization. She was writing a story on it, so she came to interview me. We spoke."

"Kate also came to talk to you about Bob Childs' disappearance, didn't she?" Sandy flipped through the notebook as she spoke. "That's what her notes say."

"Robert was a friend of mine. He came here quite often, you know. His disappearance has been vexing to all of us," Voyo shook his head slowly and walked into the library, maintaining an anodyne, ecclesiastical innocence. "A great tragedy."

Sandy followed Voyo into the library. At once, something permeated the air and made her shudder. She felt faint. Sunlight poured through a crack in the dark curtains. "It seems like a great coincidence, also, doesn't it? For both to have come here before they died?"

Voyo spun around and faced her. His pleasant voice suddenly went cold. "Madame, please excuse me. I do not know you. I cannot explain these events to you!"

"Did Kate Kamrath talk to you about Bob Childs?" she continued.

Voyo shrugged. "I cannot remember…perhaps she did, but I could not provide any information to her, simply because I had none to offer."

Sandy nodded. He was lying, and now she was certain of it. The potted plants by the stained glass windows caught her attention. The leaves were long and lance-shaped, thick and leathery, but the clusters of white flowers caught her attention. She walked over and knelt beside them. "I understand,

Your Eminence."

Voyo checked his watch. "Please, I must get to the airport if I'm to be on time for my flight. I'm sorry, if you will please excuse me."

She rose up from one of the larger plants. From the next windowsill a cat jumped down and bolted out of the room...*it was a Siamese.*

Suddenly, she felt a cold chill run through her and it was difficult for her to breathe. His face had tightened and he was staring at her with barely undisguised hostility. She swallowed hard, attempting to hide her reaction, but she was, undeniably, spooked. "Of course. I'm so sorry. Thank-you so much for your time." She glanced over at Schauer and began to walk down the hallway.

Voyo was rubbing the side of his face as he trailed behind them. "I do not mean to be inhospitable...."

She pulled out her coat and saw the tan overcoat that was hanging beside it. Her heart began racing again. She'd seen the style before, frequently...at the U.S. embassy in Sarajevo. In a swift, nearly imperceptible movement, she pulled the overcoat from the hangar and folded it under her own coat and turned around to Voyo.

"Your Eminence, good luck with the ceremony — maybe we'll see you in Medjugorje?"

Voyo nodded and leaned forward to open the door. "Yes, I hope so. Goodbye, Madame."

Voyo offered his hand to Sandy. His grip was loose and cold. His hand rough.

They stepped outside. The door shut abruptly behind them.

They walked down the cobblestone parking lot without speaking. Schauer broke their silence as they turned the corner where the car was parked.

"Now tell me why we just stole an overcoat from Zagreb's Archbishop?"

"Because it's not his," she replied flatly, looking straight ahead. "Did you see the cat?"

Schauer shook his head. "No...what cat?"

"There was a cat!" she exclaimed. "And it was a Siamese! I'm sure of it!"

Schauer shrugged. "So?"

"Kate had a Siamese, 'Buster,' and it was missing from her apartment when Mark and I went there!"

"And the coat?" Schauer unlocked the doors to his car remotely. "If it's not his whose might it be?"

"It's a State Department-issue overcoat, Schauer. When was the last time you saw a Cardinal or a priest dressed like a jar head?"

Schauer opened her door. "Are you saying that belongs to Bob Childs?"

She dug into the pockets and pulled out an opened roll of breath mints, tissue paper, and a set of keys. She studied them. "Not unless the Cardinal drives a BMW...."

She climbed into the passenger seat. Schauer shut her door and she saw him shaking his head toward the ground as he walked around to the driver's side.

"So you're theory is that he killed them both, is that it?"

She handed him the leaf. "I pulled this from one of the plants in his library. I'm not an expert on flora and fauna, but my mother had oleander plants in her garden and my guess is that's what this is."

"What's so significant about Oleander?" Schauer asked.

"It's the source for the poison digitoxin. I found that out when our cat died from eating its leaves."

Schauer was shaking his head. "Are you serious?"

"Dead," she answered with finality. "It's the only logical explanation when you consider the details of Kate's notes and how she was killed. On top of that, the guy's a creep and only a creep would grow a poison...let alone poison someone."

"He had a lot of other plants in the hallway," Schauer offered, turning the ignition. "God knows what those were."

"Goddammit, Schauer, who would do something like that?"

"Not the priestly type," Schauer said, agreeing with her. "Now what?"

"Now...," she was paging through Kate Kamrath's notebook and finally stopped at one of the pages that provided an address.

"Now, we go see Bob Childs' wife."

AT THE MOMENT he closed the door, Voyo found himself pacing in the darkened hallway with her business card in one hand, holding his jaw with the other. The tingling in his jaw and cheekbone had begun to ache and his vision was now blurry. He knew instinctively what was coming. He willed it away, but it never helped.

Why had they come here? Why now?

He continued to pace, from one end of the hall to the other.

What had led them here?

He felt panic begin to build and staggered into his office and sat down at his desk. He recognized the woman as the one who had accompanied the police commissioner into the reporter's apartment.

It proves nothing!

Could it?

He dialed Major Heleta's cell number. It rang twice before he heard Heleta's voice on the other end. "Your Eminence?"

"Where are you, Savo?"

"In Mostar. I've found Celo Mescic."

Voyo did not respond. He massaged the side of his head as the pain worsened, radiating to the back of his head in spasms. He bowed his head stiffly.

Heleta continued. "I will see him in several hours, face to face. I—"

"We must eliminate these people who are interfering with our sacred mission, Savo. No matter what the cost, and we must do so now…before it is too late."

CHAPTER 76

MARK LYONS FOLLOWED John Thorpe into the Restaurant Taurus and at their request a waiter led them past the fireplace out onto the patio. The terrace overlooked the *Kriva Cuprija* Bridge—a smaller, older version of the famous *Stari Most*. They sat under the fading sky beside a stone wall overlooking two waterfalls discharging into the aqua green foam of the Neretva River. The air was cool, but comfortable.

Thorpe pulled out one of the cigars from his case. A Leonard Cohen song was playing in the background. The waiter returned with their beer and asked if they were ready to order. Mark told him in Serbo-Croatian that they were waiting for someone.

"John, do you have any cargo planes...empty ones...that are scheduled to come over here in the next month or so?"

Thorpe nodded. "We have a fleet of 'em. The MC-130s make routine runs from Hurlburt Air Force Base through Ramstein in Germany. They're not always empty though—why do you ask?"

"Hurlburt is in Florida, isn't it?"

Thorpe nodded and drank from his glass. "On the panhandle."

He paused and turned his glass several times on the table. "Hypothetically, if there were some supplies delivered to Hurlburt, would they be able to bring them here?"

Thorpe cast a sidelong glance at him. "What kind of supplies?"

"The humanitarian kind."

"Well, then, I'd say they'd qualify."

He took a folded piece of paper out of his shirt pocket and passed it to Thorpe across the table. "You don't need to look at it now, but whenever you get the chance."

Thorpe's attention was diverted momentarily. He nodded toward the double doors leading onto the patio. "Isn't that him?"

He looked over and saw Celo surveying the patio and locate their table with a single, well-practiced sweep of his eyes. The chains and necklaces were gone—he was wearing new Calvin Klein jeans and a white button-down shirt that left the top three buttons unbuttoned to reveal his tanned, muscular frame. Over one arm, he carried a black leather jacket. Mark waved and caught his attention unsure how he would be received, given their last confrontation at the church in Stolac. He approached with his characteristic long strides and extended his hand to Thorpe. Mark was surprised to hear him introduce himself in English and then quickly resume in Serbo-Croatian.

"General, I am Celo. *Dobar vecer.*"

Thorpe stood and shook Celo's hand. *"Dobra vecer,* Celo." Thorpe motioned toward the seat beside him at the wall.

As he sat, Celo reached over and slapped Mark on the shoulder affectionately. "There are better ways to see Bosnia than this, cousin."

"You always make it interesting, Celo," Mark answered. He turned to Thorpe and translated their exchange.

"I am sorry, General, for my English. It is very bad and so you may not understand me," Celo said in halting English, repositioning his jacket on the empty chair beside him and pushing his long, thick hair from his face. He turned to Mark. "Marko will have to translate for me—okay, Marko, you will do this?"

Mark nodded without saying a word, studying Thorpe for his reaction. He was relieved that he'd told Thorpe about his boyhood experience with Celo. But he still hadn't mentioned his birth name to him. Celo's use of it now was disarming, but Thorpe did not appear to be surprised or affected by it in any way.

"Have you ordered yet?" Celo asked, pointing to the menu and their glasses.

Mark shook his head. "Only beer."

"Good! I will order for us then!" Celo exclaimed, picking up the menu. "The calamari is excellent here. You like calamari?"

Mark smiled and translated for Thorpe. "Calamari is fine."

"Only for an appetizer," Celo announced. "For dinner, I recommend the *Dulbastija.*"

"Dulbastija?" Mark asked inquisitively.

Celo nodded. "Beefsteak, covered with avjar—roasted red pepper spread—and onions...excellent! The veal cutlet is also superb."

The waiter returned to take Celo's drink order. Celo ordered a mineral water. Mark heard his voice falter when he said he'd return to take their dinner order and saw that he recognized Celo. *How could he not?*

Mark looked at Thorpe. He also saw the sudden change in his demeanor. Two tables away, he saw a group of businessmen whispering to one another and staring at them.

"I think you've been discovered," Mark said quietly, taking a sip of beer.

Celo laughed dismissively. "It's funny that they think only the Ustashe can come here." He leaned back, rested his arm casually on the chair beside him and shrugged. "It's a free country now...at least until they arrest you and take you to The Hague!"

Mark looked at Thorpe. He was sitting patiently, with an impassive expression that reflected a basic understanding of their conversation. Mark summarized their exchange and Thorpe nodded.

"Will you agree to release the Brits, Celo?" Thorpe asked quietly. Mark translated.

Celo smiled broadly as the waiter delivered his drink. "It's being done now, while we eat. I didn't want to do this, you know, but they gave me no choice. I was fishing with my son. Every Sunday, we go to the lake and fish. And they were there, in the woods, waiting for me." Celo shook his head slowly as Mark continued to translate for Thorpe. He suddenly switched to English. His tone was matter-of-fact, unapologetic. "They were very stupid to think I would not know they were there. Because, like every Sunday, I bring my son to fish, but this time!" He held up his index finger triumphantly. "This time I bring many more men to fish for *them!*" He laughed and appeared genuinely amused. "They give me no choice...but because you ask me, not the other General...who is he? Rose? ...Because you ask me, *not him*, I released the British commandos. They are free now."

"You said you wanted to make a deal?" Mark asked.

Celo took a gulp of his mineral water and nodded, returning to Serbo-Croatian. His body was composed, but his eyes were restive and sharp, sweeping the patio. "I will turn myself in to you now, but not to that other General...the British one...Rose."

Mark looked at Thorpe, and turned to Celo. "Why now, Celo? In exchange for what?"

"In exchange for nothing," Celo answered leaning back. He pointed at the Old Bridge in front of them, the churning waters flowing underneath. "You know, they blamed us for blowing up that fucking bridge...the big one over there," he said, pointing. "Down the river...the *Stari Most*. They blamed me for giving the order. I read they heard me give the order over the radio! This is why they want to arrest me!" He laughed, shaking his head and taking another drink. Mark translated for Thorpe simultaneously. "But it was not us. It was the Ustashe—do you know why they blew up this fucking bridge?"

Mark shook his head slightly.

"Because the Turks were using it to transport ammunition across the river and using it against their own future allies, the Ustashe! They were fighting *each other* then. The Ustashe were running low on ammunition and could do nothing to stop them. We heard the Ustashe on the radio talk about this. We were glad they were fighting one another because both were our enemies. As long as they were fighting one another, they would not fight us! ...So! I had an idea."

A waiter approached to take their dinner order. Celo confirmed that they wanted the beefsteak. He quickly ordered a dish of calamari and *Dulbastija* for them.

Celo collected the menus and returned them to the waiter. "We delivered artillery and mortar shells to the Ustashe. *For that I'm guilty!* But *they* blew that bridge up. Not me!"

As Mark translated for Thorpe, he watched his eyebrows slowly rise.

"No ethical issues there," Mark commented to Thorpe in English.

"It's war!" Celo exclaimed in response. "The Turks and Ustashe were being trained by American mercenaries to fight against us! They were killing my men! I didn't give a damn whether they destroyed the bridge or not—I just wanted them to kill one another, so my men would not bleed. So—" He leaned toward them and unfolded his hands, as if unwrapping a gift. "If I'm to blame for war crimes, others are also to blame, are they not?"

"That would be for the Tribunal to decide," Thorpe answered, looking directly at Celo.

Celo stared at Thorpe for several seconds in silence. Neither man averted his gaze. Finally, Celo laughed.

"I look forward to seeing these judges and telling them about the war, just as I am telling you."

"That would be your right," Thorpe answered.

"When will you arrest me?"

"We can arrange a flight for you, Celo," Thorpe said. "You should wrap things up with your family first."

"My family does not understand any of this," Celo said quietly, his eyes averted and focused on the bridge. "All they know is that I fought for our people, and now I'm called a war criminal." He turned back to Thorpe. "I think maybe you should wait until after this fiasco in Medjugorje tomorrow before you arrest me." Celo said conclusively.

"Is there something we need to know?" Mark asked.

Celo shrugged. "You did not believe me when I warned you about the Ustashe. Did they not try to kill you at the airport with a car bomb?"

"How do you know about that?" Mark asked sharply.

"I make it my business to know these things, cousin," Celo said. "Why didn't they succeed?"

"Someone warned me," Mark answered. "…Someone who calls himself Lazarus. Honestly, I thought it was you. Now, I can't help but think you installed the bomb too."

Celo howled. "Me? You give me too much credit! I only learned of it after it was defused and detonated. Who is this Lazarus?"

"I don't know," Mark said evenly. He turned to Thorpe and summarized their on-going conversation in English. Thorpe nodded.

"He knew about our families…your father and mine…about what happened at Brnisi Dam," Mark said.

"Ahhh, *could it be?*" Celo asked, obviously intrigued. "Could it be the man you dragged from the grave that night?"

"I never told you about him, Celo," Mark answered. At this moment, he didn't trust Celo. He stared at him appraisingly. "It seems too much of a coincidence that you would know about him now," he shot back.

"Okay," Celo shrugged his apathy. "I'll gladly take credit then, if that's what you want."

"What I want is the truth," Mark answered flatly. "Unvarnished."

Celo did not respond at first. He looked down at the river raging below and leaned back in his chair. His tone was suddenly different…more subdued, serious. "You want the truth?"

Celo spoke, almost in a whisper. He struggled to hear.

"I watched you drag that man from the grave from the hilltop. I saw everything. I've known for the past thirty-five years that the priest was the officer who tried to kill us…that he killed my father. I saw it happen in front of me. I could *never* forget!"

"You knew?" Mark asked in disbelief, suddenly angry.

Celo nodded. "I was going to kill him for it long ago, but I saw him up close—his face—what you did to him. Living with that every day, I decided, was punishment enough until I could get to him and kill him myself. And now he is their Archbishop! *It's a joke!*"

Celo continued. "It is *all* a joke! Over on the opposite end of the bridge are the Turks. These are the scum you protected during the last war! Look how they repay you! They hijack airplanes and fly them into your buildings and kill you by the thousands! *That is the truth!*" Celo pounded the table with his fist, silencing the conversation at the tables beside them. "And…they are not finished with you," he concluded quietly.

"What do you mean?" Thorpe asked with an edge to his voice that betrayed his mounting impatience. Mark translated the question. "If you know something, you should tell us."

"I am not involved in this fight," Celo said.

"You wouldn't know it, watching you on television," Mark answered.

"*That* is *my* fight! Those are my people! When they try to kill us or drive us from our homes, they give us no choice. I make no apologies for it," Celo said matter-of-factly. "What they are planning now, is not my fight. It's yours I think."

"What are they planning?" Mark asked.

Celo shrugged his thickly muscled shoulders, and pulled out a digital 35mm Nikon. He turned the power on and handed it to Thorpe. He showed him the button to advance through the stored photographs. He whispered conspiratorially, like a half-mad prisoner: "We see things…things that cause us suspicion, like brand new Mercedes sedans that carry seven Mujahideen to the mosques over there and to the home of the head Imam." Celo pointed across the river at the skyline of orange-lit towers, disks and spires. "For seven days they meet with him. And then, you see the photo of the truck that comes to the mosque?"

Thorpe pushed the advance button until the image of a white panel truck appeared, parked in a sheltered gateway near a fruit market beside the mosque. Thorpe nodded to Celo.

"It came two days ago, at night. They guard it closely, but we don't know what is inside that they guard. Five of the Muj have been at the mosque for 28 hours, maybe more."

"Five?" Mark asked. "You said there were seven."

Celo pointed to the camera in Thorpe's hands. "You will see the photos.

They left the mosque yesterday. We followed them."

Thorpe leaned over to show Mark the digital photos that were stored in the camera. Several of them were nondescript...they showed two men getting into the black Mercedes, and departing the mosque, driving along a two lane road. Most of them were slightly out of focus, and he could see that they'd all been taken through the windshield of another car. But the next photos were different. These were taken outdoors, and were clear and in-focus. The Mercedes was parked on the side of a city street near a large Catholic church.

"Medjugorje?" Mark asked.

Celo nodded.

The last photo was a close-up of the two men as they emerged from the church. They had olive skin and short black hair.

"Who are they?" Thorpe asked.

"Turks...you must find out their identities for yourself," Celo answered. "Is it not strange for Turks to be in a Ustashe church?"

"Did they return to the mosque?" Mark asked.

"One of them stayed behind at a pension across the—"

Before he could answer, Mark saw Celo focus beyond him and Thorpe, toward the doorway. He caught a sudden flicker of movement, then in a kinetic burst of activity, everything erupted.

Celo's movements were fluid and swift. He reached into his jacket with one hand and pulled out a nickel plated Smith and Wesson .357 Magnum.

He turned and saw a man with cropped hair wearing a black leather jacket and the waiter moving toward their table at a brisk walk. It could have been the restaurant's manager accompanying the waiter with their meals, were it not for their quick and purposeful gate.

Celo shot first. Two shots exploded in quick succession.

It took only an instant for him to see in their hands what Celo had anticipated—the man in the black leather coat carried an Ingram MAC-10 and another waiter, a Mini-Uzi—both compact submachine guns, now being leveled in their direction. One of them had been hit in the shoulder by Celo's .357, but he continued to advance.

Screams and shouts erupted from the adjacent table. Bullets splintered through the wood overhang.

In a well-practiced reflex, Mark pulled the Browning High Power pistol from his shoulder holster. A cacophony of gunfire burst over the roar of the

Neretva River raging below. John Thorpe was already kneeling beside his chair, arms outstretched with his pistol gripped in both hands. He fired two quick, well-aimed shots into the waiter's torso, causing him to drop heavily in front of them on the floor.

Celo was still standing up in full view, aiming and firing—the shots from his Smith and Wesson resounded like cannons against the staccato automatic fire from the MAC-10. With every shot, a flame flew out of the barrel. The sound of shattering glass, ricocheting bullets and crashing furniture filled the patio and echoed against the opposite bank, adding to the noise. Sparks and large splinters from the wood beam roof flew around them.

Mark canvassed the terrace, but could not see his target until he spotted movement behind a corner of the stone building. There was a clanking of hollow steel falling to the ground. He felt the hot draught of a bullet passing by his cheek.

Celo was moving toward the sound, calmly reloading his Smith and Wesson with a circular speed loader. He walked around the tables, benches and chairs that were strewn about, calmly opening the cylinder and dumping the empty cartridges onto the ground.

A black image emerged from around the corner, and Mark saw the MAC-10 aimed at Celo. He fired three shots in rapid succession at the man, but the bullets impacted just above his head, narrowly missing him. The rattle of two more bursts from the MAC-10 were answered by the loud, slow and sustained volleys from Celo's Smith and Wesson.

The sounds of broken glass and crockery continued unabated.

Mark and Thorpe fired their pistols again in unison. The assassin with the MAC-10 dropped—into the bicycle and patio furniture. An eerie silence followed, and the rush of the river was all that remained. Mark quickly ejected the empty magazine and slapped a fresh magazine into the grip. With one round still in the chamber, he scanned for more targets and slipped on the thumb safety.

It was over.

Thorpe rose from his kneeling position, still holding his pistol at the ready, and was inspecting the waiter's body. Celo, once standing to his front, was no longer there. Mark rose. Behind the upended tables, overturned chairs and wooden benches, Celo was sprawled face-up on the stone floor of the terrace. His eyelids were flickering. His giant hand covered a bright crimson stain on his white shirt.

Mark holstered the High Power and tore off the buttons, exposing a single wound in the center of his chest at the sternum—above his scar from his last gunshot wound he'd sustained over a decade ago. With each breath, blood swelled out in a thick crimson foam. He took a cloth napkin and held it tightly against his chest. Thorpe called for an ambulance. Celo's chest rose and fell; his breathing was labored. He struggled to speak

"Marko.... I'm cold...."

He applied pressure to Celo's wound. "Save your energy, Celo...."

A smile emerged from Celo's lips. "No...it's over, Cousin. My fight is over.... Tell my Mother I'm sorry... I never stopped loving her."

He nodded and a feeling of desperation overcame him. "I will."

Celo swallowed, his eyes were focused on him. "I always knew...."

Celo started to cough up blood and he placed his arm under his cousin's neck and cradled his head.

"I knew she was fine because you were with her...."

"Celo, *stop.* You're going to be okay. An ambulance is on the way."

"After Pa was killed I couldn't leave here...I was responsible."

He shook his head and realized he was now sobbing. "No, Celo, I was responsible. Not you...."

"No," Celo responded. He suddenly appeared entirely lucid. His eyes were like blue match flames, wide open and intense. "Pa told me not to return to the house after what happened at the dam, but I did anyway. He came to find me and they were there...waiting. I stayed in the woods. When he drove up to the house looking for me, they took him...they executed him."

There was more blood coming from Celo's wound, the stain now larger than his hand. He felt his own tears well from within. Celo's voice was low and hoarse.

"It was my fault...for going down to the grave. I'm sorry...I've never stopped thinking about it."

Celo attempted to laugh but could only cough. "It's past, Marko," he said thickly. "You were right to go there. Your own father...could have been there."

He began to cough again. "Take care...of my family...."

Mark felt Celo convulse and held on to him tightly.

"So cold..."

"Shhh...quiet," Mark repeated over and over to his cousin.

Celo struggled to speak. When he did, it was a hoarse whisper that he could barely hear over the raging river, but there was a sudden fleeting, shade of lightness in his eyes. "May the god's accept me...."

His eyes shut tightly and then flickered open again. His coughing stopped abruptly. His body seized, then went limp. His eyes were staring blindly upward, the rictus of agony in his face now fully dissolved.

Mark leaned over his cousin and held his body tightly, trembling. He covered Celo's face with his hand and the inertia of grief passed through him in what seemed a tidal wave, swallowed by the roar of the Neretva River beside him...awash with the memories of their boyhood. A dark shadow seemed to fall suddenly over him. For the first time since his wife had died, Mark Lyons cried, realizing that for Celo the horror of that day at Brnisi Dam was over at last.

CHAPTER 77

MARK LYONS LOOKED up, his face tight with anguish. John Thorpe was standing above him, his pistol still in his hand. Mark gently shifted Celo's head from his lap to the ground.

"He's gone, John," he said, blinking hard.

Thorpe knelt beside him. "I'm sorry, Mark," Thorpe answered simply.

Mark stood and nodded. Looking down, he realized that he was covered with Celo's blood. The monotonous blare of police sirens came over the sound of the river in the distance. Furniture was scattered across the empty terrace. The air, dense with smoke, carried the still sharp tang of burnt gunpowder. Thorpe took a tablecloth off the ground and covered Celo's head and torso.

He looked up at Thorpe, whose eyes were filled with pain.

Thorpe pointed to the bodies of the men who attacked them. "Both dead." He led Mark over to the waiter's body and pulled the shirt apart to reveal a white silk orphrey. "The other one over there in the leather is wearing the same thing."

The wailing of sirens drew closer and louder. Thorpe held up the digital photographs that Celo had shown them. "If what Celo told us is true, I'm not sure we have the time to deal with them."

"Did you find anything else on them? Papers? Anything?"

"No. They're clean."

"Okay. I'll handle the police," Mark answered, his tone urgent. "You better go, John. Look for their car outside...if they have one, it'll likely have Croatian plates. I'll call you."

Thorpe looked down at Celo's body and hesitated. "Are you sure? I don't want to leave—"

He nodded. "I'm sure. Absolutely. Go on."

He reached into Celo's pant pocket and pulled out the oil cloth he'd shown him at the discothèque. Inside were the shotgun shell, small caliber bullet casing, and Serb Orthodox cross. As the sirens grew louder, he placed the oil cloth in his own pocket.

ROUTE 5, NEAR JAJCE, BOSNIA AND HERZEGOVINA

SANDY EVENSON RECOGNIZED the telephone number on the Caller ID as an official line from the UN Headquarters in Sarajevo. As Jon Schauer drove, she wondered aloud who it could be. Answering it, she immediately recognized Mike McCallister's voice.

"Mike?" Sandy spoke into the phone. "What is it?"

"Sandy, General Thorpe asked me to call you…he wanted you to know that Celo was killed about an hour ago in Mostar. Mark and General Thorpe were with him. They're fine—"

She took in a deep breath. She felt as if the wind had been knocked out of her. After a moment, she forced herself to speak. "What happened?"

She listened to McCallister relate what he knew about the incident based on local police reports and that he and Vladimir were flying down to Medjugorje to meet Mark. He wanted her to know….

For a moment, she felt as if she were in a free fall. She lowered the cell phone. Her worst fears were being realized…they'd killed Bob and Kate, and now Celo…but Mark was still alive.

Vaguely, she heard McCallister repeating her name from the cell phone on her lap.

Sandy lifted her cell phone back to her ear and brushed her hair away from her face. Her tone was resolute. "We're an hour or so away from Sarajevo now—we're coming with you. Wait for us."

MOSTAR, BOSNIA AND HERZEGOVINA

JOHN THORPE WALKED out of the Restaurant Taurus just as the convoy of police cars was pulling up to the entrance—sirens blaring. Thorpe looked up the narrow maze of cobblestone streets. Curious onlookers were beginning to congregate outside the restaurant. He walked into an approaching crowd of teenage boys who were rushing to the scene, rapidly forming their own mob. He weaved between the stampeding gaggle, and looked down the walkway. A black Audi with Croatian plates was parked on the curb where the road stopped and the walkway began.

He walked toward the car and a boy stumbled into him, nearly knocking him over. The boy apologized absently in Serbo-Croatian. Drawing closer to the Audi, he saw the Zagreb city designation on the license plate. Because it was parked in the shadows of the alleyway, he could not tell if there was a passenger still inside. Moving cautiously, he felt for the Browning High Power seated in the shoulder holster and withdrew it, holding it down and close to his side. Through the tinted glass, he saw that the car was unoccupied. Walking to the front of the car, he peered through the windshield and saw a briefcase lying flat on the rear seat.

The racket of sirens and excited shouting of bystanders had grown louder. He holstered the pistol, looked around and found a loose brick lying along a cobblestone driveway under construction. He picked it up and walked over to the rear passenger side window and hurled it inside with a hard sidearm pitch, shattering the glass. The car alarm blared, blending with the onslaught of police and ambulance sirens.

Thorpe leaned his arm inside, grasped the briefcase handle and pulled it out in a quick, seamless motion. He leaned inside to the front passenger seat, and quickly opened the door. Repositioning himself, he pulled on the glove compartment latch. It fell open to reveal a .45 Colt automatic pistol, a stack of euro bills and two Croatian passports. He scooped them up and pressed the button to unlock the trunk. He walked around to the rear of the Audi and lifted the trunk-door. The light came on, illuminating what he immediately recognized as a Barrett .50 Caliber Sniper Rifle—one of the most lethal long-range weapons made—with several boxes of armor piercing .50 Caliber ammunition, and an M4 Automatic Carbine equipped with custom grips, laser sights and magazines filled with 5.56 Caliber ammunition.

He closed the trunk of the Audi and walked down the alleyway, now certain that this was the assassins' vehicle. He pulled the cell phone from his inside jacket pocket and pressed the speed dial for the line to Jim Goodwin at the CIA Headquarters in Langley, Virginia.

CHAPTER 78

MARK LYONS FELT a bitter, cold isolation, as if he'd been thrust into the same recurring nightmare from which there was no visible escape. The night was now cold and everything seemed to be collapsing around him. Everyone, it seemed, was made to pay the price for knowing him…and in the most perverse twist of all, he was left to survive them. On these occasions, he found himself wanting to die too…so the dream would end. Time and again, he would tell himself it was only a dream…an insidious, horrific dream. But nothing ever changed.

He'd agreed to come to the police station to fill out the necessary reports, answer questions and confirm Celo's identity at the morgue. His head was pounding, and he was drained--emotionally and physically. Now Celo, too, was dead and he was alive.

He rubbed the exhaustion from his eyes. Nothing seemed real to him any more.

His cell phone rang as he stepped out of the Mostar police headquarters.

He lifted the cell phone to his ear, and answered but there was no immediate response. He was about to end the call when he heard the same calm, abstracted, yet distinctly scrambled voice that he now recognized as "Lazarus."

"I am sorry about Celo, Marko. It is tragic…a terrible loss for his family…for you and your aunt for Celo's family…."

"How did you know?" He shuddered, feeling a visceral rage coursing through his veins. *"How the fuck did you know? Who are you?"* He realized he was screaming into the phone in front of the police station. Several policemen were staring at him.

"You know who I am," Lazarus replied calmly, mechanically, seemingly unaffected by his outburst. Although the voice was altered electronically, the resoluteness of his answer was enough. "You must know by now."

He inhaled deeply and lowered his voice. "I know who you say you are…but I don't deal well with ghosts. How is it that you always know so much?" he asked, walking toward the street.

"I am afraid I don't know enough. I could not save Ms. Kamrath, Robert Childs, and now, Celo. I could not save your father or your uncle...and so, in many ways, I've failed."

"Failed?" Mark asked incredulously. "At what?"

"Repaying my debt to you...my covenant."

Mark laughed, but it was thick with sarcasm and disdain. "You can consider it bloody well paid now, you fucking lunatic! You've done enough already...Celo's dead...now leave me the hell alone!"

There was no response, but the connection held.

"Did you hear me?" He repeated into the telephone. "Leave!"

"The violence must stop, Marko. And you are the only one who can stop it."

"No, understand me! I'm not doing this. Not with you...not with anyone!"

"You must understand. It is not my desire to harass you, but I fear what will happen if Voyo is not stopped. No one else understands what he is capable of...."

"Well, he's not bloody special in that regard. There are plenty of others out there who are just as guilty. Probably you among them!"

"He's started this war again, but, in his mind, it is not enough. He will not stop until Islam has been dealt a mortal blow."

He laughed dismissively. "The destruction of Islam...that's a rather lofty goal, I reckon."

"After the massacre at Bocinja, would you question his capabilities?" Lazarus asked.

Mark was stunned at his mention of Bocinja and could not immediately respond. "How do you know about —?"

"It is not important how I know," Lazarus replied. "It only matters that you know and understand Vojislav Pijadje as I do."

"Thanks to you, I know what he's done to my family," he answered impulsively. He considered Lazarus' motives and laughed. "Is this it? After all these years, you want me to kill the Archbishop of Zagreb for you?"

"You know the name, Gavrilo Princip?"

He paused. "Archduke Francis Ferdinand's assassin...started the First World War in Sarajevo...."

"Yes, it was about a hundred years ago. Then, it took only a single fanatic with a pistol to pit empire against empire."

He realized Lazarus was now lecturing him.

"The fanaticism we see today is far more ominous, Marko...it is the religious fanaticism that will start a third world war, more devastating than the others of the last century combined."

"A warning of the coming apocalypse. That's bloody wonderful! Thanks for all your help," he said, his exasperation mounting.

"If the Islamists target the Vatican, where do you think the Vatican would seek to retaliate?"

"The Vatican? Retaliate? You're bloody unhinged."

"You are dealing with an enemy who is cold and implacable...ruthless," Lazarus answered. "You of all people should know this by now."

"It's madness," he exclaimed. "My friends and family are dead or dying, and I have a certified fucking lunatic calling me to 'help,' pardon me if I don't reciprocate."

"If that is so incomprehensible to you, Marko, I suggest you search the tankers preparing to sail through the Suez Canal in the direction of Mecca."

"How—?" he stopped mid-stride. "How could you know that?"

"It is not important how I know."

Mark heard the line go dead. From where he stood on the ledge of the concrete stairway, he caught sight of several men gathered near an SUV in the distance. He pushed the speed-dial for John Thorpe as he descended the steps.

Thorpe answered.

"John! ...Christ! It's Mecca...their bloody target is Mecca!"

Thorpe paused for a moment. "Where are you, Mark?"

"Leaving the police station," he said absently. "Did you hear me?"

"I heard you," Thorpe answered. "We're on it. Your report confirms what we found in the documents I took from their getaway car near the restaurant—that was a good call to look for it. Just as you predicted, there was a briefcase in the backseat with loads of documents. We're sifting through them now."

"And?"

"And a Turkish bulk cargo tanker, called the *MADHUMATI II* was chartered four days ago in Neum using funds from a Swiss bank account, loaded with construction materials."

"Turkish?" Mark repeated dubiously.

"It's a flag-of-convenience ship. Her crew is Pakistani and Yemeni."

"Are you saying the device they took is on board that tanker?"

"It looks like both hired guns who attacked us in the restaurant were with the tanker when it was loaded. The manifest lists Jeddah, Saudi Arabia, as the destination...." He heard Thorpe consulting with someone in the background. After a moment, he spoke again. "Jeddah is only 50 miles or so from Mecca. Jesus... Mark?"

Mark drew a deep breath. "Yeah?"

"I called Mike McCallister in Sarajevo. He should be there to meet you. Do you see him?"

He looked through the fog over at the SUV, and saw Mike McCallister standing beside it with Vladimir and Jon Schauer.

"I see them," Mark answered.

"They'll take you to the UN compound. We're moving on the information Celo gave us now—"

Mark heard Thorpe again consulting with his staff, catching references to "CSG" and "High Interest Vessel" in the context of commands. When he returned to their telephone conversation, his tone was solemn.

"I've got a call waiting from Washington, Mark. I'll call you."

Mark signed off with Thorpe, knowing it was going to be a very long night.

He reached the bottom stair and glanced over in the opposite direction to see Sandy Evenson across the street facing him—wearing a full length dress coat, grasping her arms together tightly.

Chapter 79

FOR ONE HUSHED MOMENT, Mark Lyons and Sandy Evenson regarded each other in awkward silence from across the street. He searched her face, and with a fleeting shift of her gaze away from him he saw her own shock, mingled with sadness and self-doubt.

"Sandy?" He spoke her name softly, crossing the street. "I thought you were –"

"You know me," she said dryly, but smiling ruefully. "Balkans junkie. I just can't stay away from this place."

He smiled faintly. "I never expected you could."

She shook her head as she approached him. "Mark, I'm *so* sorry about Celo."

She stopped in front of him and looked into his eyes with something like a plea.

Mark looked down at the ground and then away from her, inhaling the cold night air. He stood there, just gazing down the street in silence. After a moment, he met her with half-drowned eyes. Caught up in the chaos that swirled around him, she was here, and all he knew was that her presence gave him a distinct sense of relief.

She began, haltingly, to explain how McCallister had phoned her, but he shook his head and pulled her close, holding the back of her neck softly.

After a moment, he drew back and looked into her eyes. "Sandy, I need to find John Thorpe. Now."

She stepped back and took hold of both of his arms. "Listen to me, you need to sleep—or you won't be any good to anyone!"

He shook his head, now feeling dizzy with exhaustion. "We can rest on the roadside. All hell's gonna break loose in a little over an hour."

"Stubborn man," she sighed, taking in a deep breath. "Never a dull moment with you is there?"

"Not tonight." He felt her arm around his waist as they walked toward the car where the others were waiting. He stopped abruptly. "Sandy?"

She looked up at him in silence. He was searching her eyes. He started to speak, but he hesitated for a moment.

"I didn't mean what I said to you on the telephone. I'm sorry, I—"

"Are you kidding?" she replied, pulling him closer to her. "You couldn't have kept me away, Mark Lyons."

CHAPTER 80

MARK LYONS PULLED the SUV to the side of the road. He reached back and removed the black nylon backpack from the back seat and stepped outside. He set the pack down and unzipped it. They were on the edge of a vineyard bordering the Neretva River. Sandy walked to the back of the vehicle where Mark was fiddling with a miniature butane burner—the kind used for camping, and set it down beside a stone wall on the ground. He pointed down the road. "There's the road that leads into Mostar and the Karadzozbeg Mosque."

"As dark as it is, I can't see a thing," she said.

He smiled thoughtfully. "When it's dark enough, you can see the stars."

"Ralph Waldo Emerson," she said matter-of-factly. "I'm impressed."

"*He* said that?" Mark said, genuinely surprised.

Sandy nodded. "I studied Emerson in college. He said it," she replied casually but conclusively.

He was silent, suddenly lost in his own thoughts.

After a moment, she knelt beside him. "Who did you think said it?"

"My father...he used to say it to me at bedtime, right after he would read me a passage from *Idylls of a King*...about King Arthur and the Knights of the Round Table."

"Mixing Tennyson and Emerson. Your father was quite the renaissance man," she replied sincerely. "He was a poet?"

He looked at her, and in the darkness could only discern the lines of her profile. "He was a professor of literature at the University of Belgrade." He lit the butane burner with a cigar lighter, illuminating them both.

"What are you doing?" she asked, noticeably distracted.

He looked up at her and smiled. "And so...it's tea time."

"*Tea time?*" she asked, eyes raised. "Do we have time for this?"

He nodded. "Our work will begin in due time. Without something to drink and eat, we'll be famished." He switched to a contrived Irish brogue. "And it's a wee bit cold...so a nice spot of tea is in order."

MOSTAR AIRPORT, BOSNIA AND HERZEGOVINA

INFRA-RED AND LIME-GREEN Starlight scope images from cameras clandestinely emplaced around the areas of tactical interest, and from aircraft flying above were being downloaded live via satellite to the plasma screens lined up along the hangar wall. John Thorpe studied the images that depicted the Karadzozbeg Mosque at different angles and distances to show not only the mosque, but the avenues of approach leading to it. Thorpe reviewed the target folder. The Karadzozbeg Mosque had been constructed of stone and mortar during the mid-16th century. The mosque was surrounded by a high stone wall, with wrought-iron gates set on the sides and an enormous beech tree with low descending branches. Cobblestone streets surrounded the mosque. An ancient cemetery, fountains and large trees occupied the mosque grounds.

Inside the hangar, the lights were dimmed and the air was cold and stale. The Satellite Communications, or SATCOM, radio transmissions echoed against the wall as if they were in a cave. The transmissions were between Delta Force reconnaissance and support teams located in various positions around the mosque and the assault teams that were preparing to lift off in helicopters from the blacked out flight line just outside the hangar.

Outside, the whir of rotor blades on the flight line intensified into a roar, as if pressing Thorpe for his decision. He quickly scanned the bank of digital clocks arranged overhead with time zones: 0304 hours local time...1004 hours in Washington and Fort Bragg, North Carolina.

Just then, Thorpe got word that the reconnaissance element identified the same truck Celo had shown him in the digital photos at the Restaurant Taurus. The helicopters would lift off from the tarmac of the Mostar airfield in ten minutes and the raid on the mosque would commence in 21 minutes.

An Army major in camouflage fatigues and a "Special Forces" tab on his shoulder approached him. "Sir, as requested, we have the EUFOR Commander...General Rose on the Red Line for you."

Thorpe nodded. He walked over to the secure Red Line telephone that sat amidst a bank of other telephones and radios. A large pilot's map of Bosnia covered in Plexiglas hung on the wall in front of the secure telephone. An orange square was drawn around Mostar. Photographs of the mosque, taken from different angles were posted around the map.

Thorpe picked up the telephone's receiver and squeezed the handle to speak. "Ian?"

"John? It's bloody early. What can I do for you?" General Ian Rose's voice conveyed the confusion and grogginess that came from a deep sleep that had been interrupted. As the commander of all European forces in the Balkans, Rose was owed the courtesy of an eleventh-hour notification, but given the circumstances, nothing more. The speed at which events were now transpiring precluded anything else. Because this was deemed a "No-Fail Mission," details of the operation were strictly compartmented to those with a direct need-to-know. Despite his rank and position, Rose did not technically "need" to know.

"Ian, I need to inform you of a high value target we're about to light up down here in Mostar...."

CHAPTER 81

THORPE WATCHED the helicopters lift off and disappear into the deep night sky. The beat of their rotors faded away. Walking back into the hangar, his steps echoed on the cement floor. He looked at the digital chart on the wall denoting radio call signs for the raid's key maneuver units:

Champion Zero-One: Commanding General (Mostar Airport)
Champion Zero-Three: Operations Officer (Mostar Airport)
Tango One-One: Troop Commander (Raid Commander)
Tango Alpha One: Support Team Leader (East of Target)
Tango Bravo One: Support Team Leader (Blocking Force North of Target)
Tango Charlie One: Assault Team Leader
Hotel Alpha One: Support Team Leader (West of Target)
Hotel Bravo One: Reconnaissance Team Leader
Archangel Two-Zero: AC-130 Gunship (Aerial Fire Support)
Comanche Six: NEST Team Leader (Nuclear Emergency Search Team)

Thorpe poured a cup of coffee. He was impressed by how quickly his staff and the delta force troop had spun up the operation, but he wondered if it would all be for naught. Even for the seasoned commandos, finding a nuclear bomb in the hands of terrorists was as difficult a proposition as they came....

MOSTAR, BOSNIA AND HERZEGOVINA

MARK LYONS POURED the tea into a stainless steel cup and handed it to Sandy Evenson. She was sitting against the stone wall, watching his tea brewing skills with some measure of fascination.

"Here you go," he said. "Be careful, it's hot."

She smiled. "I'm impressed!"

"With what?

"That you can make tea in the midst of a crisis."

He laughed and shook his head. "You Americans just don't understand! If we don't make tea, *that's* the crisis!"

She blew her tea, looked at him. "That settles it then."

"Settles what?" he replied with a confused expression.

"You may have been born here, but you're definitely Irish, through and through."

"Hmm," he looked over his cup at her. "Actually, it'll help keep us awake, but I'll take that point under advisement, Counselor."

She sipped from her cup and smiled back at him. "Good tea, Commissioner."

"We Irish are good for that, you know."

"I met your aunt," Sandy Evenson announced abruptly in the darkness. "I stopped by to see her in Antrim...on my way back from Kate's funeral."

He took a deep breath, drew himself up a bit, and continued to drink his tea. "I know."

They both sat for a while in silence, aware of each other's slightest movement.

"I understand if you're upset," she said tentatively. "Maybe I shouldn't have gone, but after I called you, I—"

"I'm not upset," he answered. "Her apple cakes are excellent, eh?"

"After we talked on the phone," she continued. "I just needed to understand why—"

Mark waited for a moment to answer. "Now ye're no-doubt thinkin' it's a wonder I ever grew up, eh?"

She shrugged a little in the moonlight and smiled.

"I'm glad you went to see her," he said finally. "And I'm glad you came back."

She eyed him dubiously. "You are?"

"After all that's happened... I just couldn't accept the thought of you being hurt because of me."

"I had a feeling that might have been behind it," she said, sipping her tea. "How many other women do you know who'd be crazy enough to live here for so long?"

He pulled back and smiled. "Not many."

"Your aunt wanted me to tell Celo that she loved him," Sandy said solemnly. And then she looked back into his eyes. "But I was too late."

Mark shook his head. "No...you weren't," he replied softly. "I told him. He knew."

A long silence followed. Finally he asked, "What else did she tell you?"

She held her cup with both hands. "She told me about what happened to you at the dam, with Celo."

Mark nodded.

She continued. "She said she thinks that it continues to haunt you. That, along with what happened to your wife."

He lifted up the pot and walked over to pour more tea into her cup. "Maybe she's right," he said simply. It occurred to him that he'd never talked to anyone about how any of those incidents had affected him. "I just try not to think about it too much...nothing good ever comes of it."

"'Never look back,' is that it?"

He looked at her thoughtfully. "Something like that."

"Nothing good comes from avoiding one's past either," she answered quietly.

He leaned against a tree opposite her. "I'm not avoiding it. I think about it every day...at night, I dream about it. I wake up in a cold sweat because--"

He stopped mid-sentence.

"Because...why?" she asked.

He looked away from her, toward Medjugorje. The sun was emerging on the horizon. "...Because every time...in every dream, I can't save them."

She did not immediately respond. "I think you've placed an unfair burden on yourself."

"Unfair?" He shook his head resolutely. "I'm the one who's still alive...my father, my uncle...and now Celo...*they're all* dead because one man was trying to kill me, and I couldn't save them. Is that fair?"

"Of course not. None of it is," she answered quietly. "But you didn't kill the people you loved. Someone else did."

Mark stood. "Well, now I *know* who it was that did it."

"You mean...." She looked up at him searchingly. "But how?"

"Because he had the photos taken himself...as he killed them."

"What?" She looked startled.

He passed her a small flashlight, pulled the black and white photographs from his coat pocket and handed them to her.

Several of them dropped to the ground. She picked them up slowly, looking at each of them closely. "These photographs...they're your family?"

Mark picked up the remaining photograph off the ground and handed it to her. "My father and my uncle."

Sandy pointed at the executioner in the first photo. "And this is the man who killed them?"

He nodded. "Papa Voyo."

"They don't look like the same person...his face...."

Mark pointed at the photo of the man kneeling in front of a trench. "I believe that's my father, it was taken before Celo and I ran into Papa Voyo at the dam...before he was ever a priest." He pointed at the second photograph. "This is my uncle...Celo's father."

Sandy turned to him. "The executioner's face—it's bandaged."

"That's the wound he received at the dam after he tried to kill us...he should look familiar to you."

"Oh my God—" Sandy gasped.

He shook his head and waved his hand. "I've been through this, Sandy. Time and again, I've been through it...and I've denied it, chalking it all up to coincidence—but I keep coming back to the same conclusion every time. It's the only explanation." He pulled out the newspaper article from his jacket and handed it to her. "He was an officer in Tito's army and then went off to the seminary and became a monk. John Thorpe and I went down to the Franciscan monastery in Orebic and spoke to one of his fellow seminarians, and he had nothing positive to say about Cardinal Vojislav Pijadje."

She flipped through the stack of photos and reread the newspaper article. "How did you get these?"

"Some sod who I may've pulled from the site of the execution twenty-five years ago, who has his own vendetta against him...," he answered. "Now that I'm back here he seems to think that he's my bloody guardian angel."

"Or surrogate...," she suggested. "Have you considered that?"

"Aye," Mark said, nodding. "But quite honestly, I haven't a clue what his motivations could be."

"And you don't know who he is?"

He shook his head. "He calls himself Lazarus."

She shook his head and said dryly, "Not his real name, I assume?"

He turned off the flame to the burner. "No, I think not."

"Mark, I'm pretty certain the Cardinal killed Bob Childs and Kate. His residence is filled with poisonous plants."

He looked up at her with a surprised expression. *"You went there?"*

She nodded. "With Jon. I found Bob's coat hanging in his closet."

"Well, I believe I found where they buried him," he said.

Her eyes were wide with surprise. "Where?"

"At a church cemetery outside Stolac."

She crossed her arms, but did not immediately respond. "So far away?"

"It was Voyo's headquarters. Celo found his grave."

"So who is Papa Voyo? A serial killer? Or an assassin?

"I don't know what you'd call him or what he's about. Serial killers kill for themselves, but it seems he's killing for the church."

"And the Vatican? They can't be supporting him, can they?"

"We'll sort that out when we have the time."

"After tea time?" she said, holding her cup up. "Let God sort them out, is that what you mean?"

Mark shrugged. "It means that I'm none too worried, and I'll do whatever's necessary to stop 'im."

She was quiet as she considered his response.

"You don't approve?" he asked, scrutinizing her expression.

"I think what you just said has a lot of implications...a lot of meanings."

"It means I don't much care how Vojislav Pijadje ends up—dead or alive. Simple, really."

She pushed herself off the boulder and brushed herself off. "Its simplicity depends on who you are."

He looked up at her. "No, metaphysics aside, it doesn't much matter, does it?"

"It matters," she answered. She looked out toward the lights of the town as she considered her response.

"Whatever my moral shortcomings, I'm no murderer."

She shrugged contemplatively. "During the last war here, my language assistant was killed by the Serbs in Srebrenica, right beside me...one second she was alive, the next second she was dead, bleeding in my lap. Just like that." She paused. "Afterward, all I felt was anger. All I wanted was revenge for what they did, but a Dutch Army chaplain who was there came up to me and told me that in war, you face two enemies. The first and easiest, he said, is the one you face on the battlefield...the one who's actually trying to kill *you*. But the most formidable...the most dangerous enemy of all is the one within...the one you face every day in the mirror."

He stood up and shook his head. His tone was clipped, matter-of-fact. "Perhaps easier to consider when you aren't facing someone who's killed your own family, eh?"

"In a strict moral sense," she said, "there's a thin line between judge, jury and executioner."

"Mark?" Sandy asked after a moment of silence.

He looked up at her expectantly.

"You know you're not alone ...."

Mark nodded tentatively, glancing up at her with a look of understanding. The sounds of the helicopters' rotor blades were becoming louder. He poured out the rest of the tea and knelt down to repack the gear into his backpack, meticulously, as if to restore order.

She handed him her cup. "Have you considered that Lazarus and the Cardinal might be one-in-the-same person?"

He shook his head as he continued to repack. "Quite honestly, I haven't a blistering clue who he is."

The sounds of automatic rifle fire erupted, echoing against the hillsides. Mike McCallister had already pulled his vehicle across to block the road.

He pointed at the headlights fast approaching. "It's show time."

MOSTAR AIRPORT: MOSTAR, BOSNIA AND HERZEGOVINA

THE DIGITAL MOVING MAP on the plasma screen depicted the MH-60 Blackhawk helicopters' course to the mosque. Along the way, the troop commander and Nuclear Emergency Search Team leader —known as NEST, call sign "Comanche Six"—would be receiving last minute updates from the support and reconnaissance teams on the ground. Thorpe sat in front of the radio station and adjusted his headset. Another plasma screen beside him depicted a live-broadcast image of the target area around the mosque in the lime green hue of the reconnaissance team's night-vision optics.

Thorpe saw the darkened silhouettes of four men emerging from the mosque just before he heard the reconnaissance team's report over the radio. All of them were armed with AK-47 assault rifles and were walking toward the truck.

The reconnaissance leader's voice came over the radio. "Tango One-One, this is Hotel Bravo One, we've identified four sentries inside the wall on the south end of the mosque, armed with assault rifles, walking toward the target, now engaging."

"Hotel Bravo One, this is Tango Alpha One. Roger...copy," the Troop Commander answered calmly, his voice shaking with the vibration of the helicopter's rotors. "Estimate we're one minute out."

"Tango Bravo, Hotel Alpha One. WILCO," the reconnaissance team leader replied with the military acronym for "Will Comply." "We hear your approach. Engaging now."

Several seconds later, he watched all four men drop to the ground simultaneously, shot at long range by the Support Team snipers who were occupying the surrounding rooftops.

He took a long sip of black coffee, his third cup in the last hour.

The operation had begun. He'd approved it, but now everything was in the hands of his men on the ground. It was always like this: the reluctance to let go...the concern about his men, faith in their instincts and training...and the struggle to control the adrenalin rush that inevitably accompanied it all.

The form of another armed sentry emerged from the mosque and ran up to the bodies of the four that had just been killed. Just as he reached them, he too was collapsed from the precision .308 caliber bullet to his chest. "Target five, one enemy KIA, Tango One-One."

"Roger that," the troop commander responded from the air, "The Comanche element will remain airborne."

Comanche—or NEST—was a national support asset trained to disarm nuclear weapons. They were technicians, not soldiers, and were therefore only lightly armed with pistols. The Delta Force operatives were there to protect them, as front-line tackles would protect their star quarterback. If NEST technicians were shooting, something had gone terribly wrong. As a team, Comanche would remain on call and land only if a radiological or nuclear device was found, and only after the target site had been fully secured by the assault team.

Thorpe looked behind him and saw his personal staff staring at the screen. He removed his earphones and flipped the switch to "speaker."

"Okay. Here we go, gentlemen...."

At once, the screen was lit up by the approaching helicopters' infrared spotlight. Two helicopters hovered above and inside the wall on both ends of the mosque. Two other Blackhawks were landing on each side of the compound, outside the walls.

The landing had been fast and violent.

Two more Blackhawks could be seen on several of the plasma screens circling the mosque like birds of prey. Each of the American assault force members was clearly identified by patches of reflective glint tape on the tops of their helmets and on their sleeves in the infra-red light. Muzzle flashes and flames came out the ends of the machine guns, but the sound came only sporadically over the radio when the assault force transmitted.

The radio speaker cackled with the voice of the support team leader on a road just east of the mosque. "Tango One-One, Tango Alpha One, outside perimeter secure. Five Enemy KIA. No friendly casualties."

"Roger that," the troop commander answered. "Tango Alpha One, your status, over?"

"All secure. Five Enemy KIA. No friendly casualties. Alpha Team is up."

"Roger. Tango Charlie One, status?"

"Target Secure, Charlie Team up," the assault team leader answered. "Target secured. We're at the truck. It's locked tight—we're breaching the doors now, over."

"Roger that," the troop leader acknowledged. "Standing by."

Thorpe pushed the "Perspective" button on the remote, and the image shifted to the full view angle of the truck. Two assault team members, their glint tape shining like a powerful flashlight, were at the rear of the truck's trailer, cutting through the door's lock and hinges with a Quickie Cut-Off Saw.

A voice came over the radio as the breaching team announced the door had been breached.

Thorpe switched to a different angle in time to see four assault team members storming the back of the trailer.

"Tango One-One, this is Tango Charlie One," the voice announced, brittle with static. "We have something here... stand by."

"Roger," the troop commander answered. "I copy. Standing by."

Thorpe leaned back and threw his Styrofoam cup into the trash can. And waited.

We have something here.

The implications of the statement were terrifying. If it was a nuclear or radiological dispersal device could the NEST team defuse it without setting it off?

Another voice came over the radio. "Tango One-One, this is Archangel Two-Zero...." It was the AC-130 Gunship flying overhead. "Be advised, you have what appears to be a convoy of police cars inbound fast on a high-speed avenue a mile to your North."

Thorpe turned to his operations officer and up at the digital panel that defined the call signs.

He nodded. "Okay. Someone needs to deal with that."

The assault team leader responded immediately, as if on cue. "Roger, I copy. Break. Hotel Alpha One, this is Tango One-One, are you able to intercept that convoy?"

"WILCO," the support team leader answered. "Lethal or non-lethal means, Tango One-One?"

The assault team leader paused. Before he could answer, Thorpe keyed his microphone. It was a trump card he employed only on rare occasions and this would be one of them. "Tango One-One, this is Champion Zero-One, start with non-lethal and escalate as required. They gotta be stopped though—whatever it takes."

There was another pause. "Champion Zero-One, Tango One-One. WILCO."

Thorpe turned to the technician standing behind him. "All right, let's get that situation on a screen, now."

The technician pointed toward a plasma screen two screens down the line, in the corner of the room. "Archangel 20's camera is over here, sir. They've got a million candle IR spotlight on the area. "

"Okay, what've we got?"

The plasma screen depicted a vertical view from the airplane overhead, zoomed in. "Looks like five cars...lights flashing," the operations officer replied, studying the screen. "At their rate of speed, they'll arrive at the target in three...maybe four minutes."

"Where's the Support Team located?" Thorpe asked.

The operations officer moved to the map. Thorpe looked over to where he was pointing. "They have an element positioned here, sir...half a mile down the road."

He nodded. "Okay." He turned to the support team's liaison officer. "Give 'em whatever they need."

Another voice from the radio echoed in the hangar. "Tango One-One, PC Secure" The support team leader at the truck exclaimed. "This looks like the real deal. We'll need Comanche down here right away. It's encased...lead and glass maybe. Inside it looks like what could be a gun-type device. Long, cylindrical in shape."

"Roger, I copy that, Tango Alpha One," the troop leader answered. "Break. Comanche One, this is Tango One-One. Prepare to land. Hotel Alpha One, mark a landing zone for the Comanche element at the fruit stand outside the mosque."

"This is Hotel Alpha One. WILCO, we're on the way."

The troop leader called to the support team leader. "Tango Bravo One, this is Tango One-One. Pull in, form an inner perimeter around the target. Respond when you're in position."

The operations officer tapped Thorpe on the shoulder as he watched the scene unfold before him. "Sir, you might want to see this...."

He looked up and stood, following his operations officer to the screen that depicted the AC-130's vantage point overhead. "It's the damndest thing, sir. That convoy of police cars is at a full stop."

"The support team was successful?"

The operations officer shook his head and pointed a half mile to the south at the support team's position across the road. There were six people with two SUV's in a road block formation—the team members and vehicles clearly marked with glint tape. "No, sir. It wasn't the support team. They're here. Someone...something else stopped them all the way up here...."

At that moment, Thorpe's cell phone vibrated and rang simultaneously. He answered, and immediately recognized Mark Lyons' voice. "John! We've managed to slow the local police down a bit—Sandy, the lads and I have. They're bloody beside themselves, but Sandy's telling them you're from The Hague in the middle of arresting a big-time war criminal...."

Thorpe smiled. "Thanks, Mark. That'll be fine. It's good to hear your voice. I appreciate your help. Keep 'em there if you can." He ended the call, shaking his head slightly as he sat back in front of the plasma screen that showed the truck in full view.

As he sat watching, the images of two MH-47 Cargo Helicopters appeared near the fruit stands, lifting an enormous cloud of dirt and debris into the air as they landed. When the dust settled, part of the NEST team could be seen running toward the truck escorted by members of the assault team.

"Tango Alpha One, this is Comanche One. Be advised, this *is* a live one. Fully viable gun-type Whiskey forty-two thermonuclear device, lead-encased…that explains why we weren't detecting anything during our aerial surveys. Judging from our initial tests…radiation emissions point to a plutonium core. Whoever constructed it knew what the hell they were doing."

"Roger, Comanche," the troop commander answered. "Understand. How would you recommend we proceed?"

"I can't vouch for its stability, Tango One-One. Recommend we defuse it on-site and prepare it for movement."

"How much time do you need?" The troop commander asked.

The NEST team leader did not immediately answer. A burst of static came over the radio. The troop commander repeated the question.

"This is Comanche One. We estimate twenty minutes to prepare it for air movement. It'll fit in the cargo bay of our helo."

There was another extended silence and then the assault leader responded. "Roger, copy that. You have twenty minutes, Comanche. We'll keep the barbarians at the gate. Break. All Tango and Hotel elements, this is Tango One-One. This is going to take a while. Get those choppers in the air until I call for them. Archangel Two-Zero, what do you see?"

"Tango One-One, this is Archangel Two-Zero," the AC-130 Gunship responded. "The police convoy is at a full stop up the road to your north. Not sure why…."

He pulled out his encrypted cell phone and dialed Lyon's number, also encrypted. He heard Mark answer. There was a female voice shouting in the background. Thorpe recognized the voice as Sandy Evenson's…loud, aggressive and relentless.

"Mark, we found a device in the truck at the mosque, just as Celo told us. We have about twenty minutes left on the ground before we can disarm it. Anything you can do?"

"Got it. We'll find a way to keep them occupied here."

Thorpe turned to his operations officer. "I need to get over there. Get a helicopter for me."

"There's an MH-60L standing by on the flight line, sir."

Thorpe knew the MH-60 "L" model well—a special operations equipped Blackhawk helicopter, with sophisticated communications and optics making it ideally suited as a command and control helicopter and because it is armed with a variety of weapon systems like Hellfire missiles, miniguns, rockets and an automatic cannon, is also used extensively for close-air support of special operations units.

"Okay. Call the White House Situation Room and National Military Command Center. Tell them what's happening. I'll stay airborne."

The operations officer gave Thorpe a "thumbs up" sign and picked up the Red Switch that would connect him to the SITROOM and NMCC.

Outside the hangar Thorpe found the MH-60L Blackhawk waiting for him, blades spinning. He ran to it and climbed aboard, sitting directly beside the pilot who handed him a helmet. Thorpe quickly strapped himself in and donned the helmet that offered him full audio of the situation at the mosque. The small black-and-white television screens in front of him provided him a similar visual link like he had in the hangar, albeit on a smaller scale.

In seconds, the helo was airborne and flying at high speed over Mostar. In the distance, he saw the shadow of the four other helicopters flying over the mosque.

The radio traffic was slow, limited to the troop leader's status checks of his assault, support and reconnaissance teams. Thorpe checked his watch. Seven minutes had elapsed since the NEST team leader had given his time estimate to render the device safe for transport. Thirteen minutes to go.

"Tango One-One, this is Tango Charlie One. Be advised...we're taking small arms fire here at the truck. They're shooting at us."

"Roger. I copy," the troop commander answered. "Archangel Two-Zero, can you see any muzzle flashes inside the target compound?"

"Negative," the AC-130 Gunship responded after a brief pause. "We can't see any from here."

Thorpe listened to this latest exchange on the radio. They were only thirty seconds away from the mosque. "Tango One-One, this is Champion Zero-One, we're flying above your location now. We'll take a look."

He directed the pilot to fly around the perimeter of the mosque compound. Over the radio, he heard another call from the Assault Team Leader. His voice was stressed and winded.

"Tango One-One, Tango Charlie One," the assault team leader barked into the radio. "We have a man down...need a MEDEVAC now...where's the shooting coming from?"

The pilot pointed down at the mosque. "There, Sir. It's coming from the minaret. There's a sniper shooting from inside that tower...that's why they couldn't see him." Thorpe looked down at the minaret. He caught the image of a man aiming a rifle down at the truck.

"Can you engage him?" he asked the pilot.

He felt the small helicopter accelerate and zoom forward. "Tango Charlie One, this is Champion Zero-One. Your sniper is in the minaret. We'll handle him. Break...."

At that moment the MH-60L rocketed dangerously close to the top of the minaret, forcing the sniper to duck inside. The door gunner let loose a long burst from his mini-gun, blasting out chunks of concrete from the minaret. Thorpe knew the effect could very well only be temporary.

Thorpe called to the AC-130 Gunship, flying well above them. "...Archangel, can you hit the minaret with your cannon?"

"Affirmative. We'll need you out of the area though."

He looked at the pilot who nodded and gave him a thumbs-up sign. "Roger, we're repositioning now."

"Tango One-One, this is Archangel Two-Zero. Advise your elements to back well away from the minaret before we engage."

"That's done, Archangel Two-Zero. Commence firing!"

"WILCO, Tango One-One. Firing now, danger close!"

Thorpe looked over at the minaret. A quick volley of red streaks came down from the sky, like lightning bolts being hurled to the Earth. In an instant, the minaret was vaporized in a cloud of smoke.

"Thanks, Archangel, that'll do it," the assault team leader acknowledged. "Tango Alpha One, I need that MEDEVAC *now!*"

"Roger," the troop leader replied. "It's on its way in to you now. Mark your position with an IR strobe."

Through Thorpe's night vision goggles, he could clearly see the assault team leader's infra-red strobe flashing near the front of the truck. The Blackhawk MEDEVAC helicopter appeared as a grey blur, swooping down in the direction of the strobe. Two medics were frantically tending to the wounded soldier. Thorpe keyed his radio to communicate with his headquarters at the hangar.

"Champion Zero-Three, this is Champion Zero-One, Over."

Thorpe heard his operations officer acknowledge his call, and he keyed his microphone again.

"Stand by for a casualty. He's in critical condition. Shot in the neck. I want the C-17 prepared to take him and our docs on board, ready to fly him to Landstuhl as soon as the MEDEVAC bird gets there...." He watched the Blackhawk land and the soldier being carried by two members of the assault team. "Arrival should be ten minutes from now."

Landstuhl was the Army Trauma Center in Central Germany—a one hour flight by jet. The massive C-17, pre-configured for In-flight medical care, was waiting on the tarmac, engines running. "WILCO, they'll be standing by. Champion Zero-Three, Out."

He redirected his attention to the troop commander. "Tango One-One, Champion Zero-One. Status on the PC?"

"PC" was the technical acronym used to refer to the nuclear device. Translated literally, it stood for "Precious Cargo."

"They're drilling into the casing now," the troop leader answered. "They're telling me it'll be ready in five minutes, Over."

Thorpe acknowledged and directed his pilot to fly to where the police convoy had been stopped.

More police cars had arrived at Mark Lyons' road block. Thorpe counted twelve cars in all. The four Delta Force soldiers had moved their vehicles up to augment Mark's makeshift roadblock. They were standing with their M4 automatic rifles at the ready. He directed the pilot to reduce their altitude. He could see Mark with Sandy Evenson by his side, waving her arms and pointing her finger into the chest of one of the policemen.

Thorpe pulled his cell phone out and pressed the speed dial and heard Mark answer. Sandy Evenson's voice was strident and clear in the background. "Mark, how are we doing down there?"

Mark looked up at the Little Bird and waved. "We're just fine, John, but as you can no doubt hear, the natives are restless. I'm not sure how much longer we'll be able to hold them here."

"I need five minutes. Can you do that?"

"I'm not sure. The police chief here is insisting that they have a right to respond since we didn't consult with them. They're not being...cooperative, shall we say."

Thorpe paused for a few seconds. "Okay. Let me speak to the team leader there with you—he'll go by 'Hotel Alpha One'."

Thorpe watched Mark turn to the Delta Force commando behind him, and overheard him ask, "Are you Hotel Alpha One?"

After a moment, the support team leader answered.

Thorpe identified himself and issued a simple order to the team leader. When the team leader acknowledged, he asked to speak to Mark Lyons again.

"Mark, get into your vehicle now and drive to the northeast end of the Mostar Airport. You can't miss our hangar. It looks like Cape Canaveral. Leave now. I'll see you there."

"Okay, John. We're outta here then."

He thanked Mark and watched the scene unfold rapidly from above. Mark and Sandy and the others quickly climbed into their UN-marked SUV's and drove off. The Delta Force Support Team spread out, approaching each police car, and started to fire their pistols at the tires. At first the police watched them, stunned. After the second car's tires were shot, furious protestations erupted from the police officers who were forced to stand by and watch them...dumbfounded.

"Okay, that should buy us some time then," he said to his pilot. "Ian Rose can deal with them in the morning. Let's get back to the mosque."

As they flew back to the mosque, he heard the call from the troop commander. "Champion Zero-One, Comanche reports the PC has been seized and rendered safe, preparing for air transport now, Over."

"Well done," Thorpe acknowledged. He knew the device was now being loaded into the MH-47 and would be flown to the Mostar Airport to be prepared for final shipment back to the United States when it would be analyzed and destroyed.

By the time the troop commander had acknowledged his directives, the Pave Lows were landing. Within two minutes, the Karadzozbeg Mosque and the surrounding area had been fully evacuated.

"Champion Zero One, this is Tango One-One. All elements have cleared the target area."

Thorpe acknowledged the troop commander's transmission. It was quickly followed up by another from the NEST Team Leader.

"Champion Zero-One, be advised, it's a preliminary analysis on our part, but that's a fully operational weapon. Probably ten or fifteen kilotons, at first glance. Maybe more. Whoever put that together knew what the hell they were doing. MIT couldn't have done it better. I hope there aren't any others like it."

A distinct feeling of dread came over Thorpe with the NEST Team Leader's call. He didn't immediately respond.

"Wait for me at the hangar, Comanche Six," Thorpe finally answered, his voice was solemn and subdued. "We may have one more out there."

CHAPTER 82

ZRACNA LUKA
AIRPORT MOSTAR
"S prijateljima preko Beca u cijeli svijet
"Daily via Vienna to the wide world"
  <   <   <   <   <
Tyrolean Austrian Airlines

MARK LYONS POINTED at the blue and yellow sign that announced their arrival at the Mostar Airport. "Feel like escaping to Vienna?"

"That would depend on whether you'd be coming along, Commissioner," Sandy answered coyly...absently, with her road map in hand. "Wait! ...There—" She pointed at a side road directly in front of them. "That should lead to the hangars...this road we're on will take us to the main terminal."

Mark quickly turned their Toyota 4Runner onto the service road.

"I dare say, those aren't part of the Tyrolean Airline fleet," Mike McCallister commented from the back seat.

In the distance, Mark saw what he was referring to. The lights on the tarmac...and the distinct silhouette of a C-17 cargo jet dominated the tarmac, dwarfing the three Pave Low helicopters at its side. Several other different models were parked near a lone hangar, their rotor blades still turning. From inside the vehicle, they could hear the roar of the helicopter blades cutting through the steady hum of jet engines.

He drove along the service road that circled the runway. The ride was bumpy and He swerved to avoid the potholes...sometimes succeeding, sometimes not. They turned the far corner of the runway and saw the group of hangars behind another fence. The gate was heavily guarded. It became obvious as they approached that the guards were not dressed or equipped like conventional guards or soldiers...but more like members of an elite SWAT team. One of the patches on their shoulders was an American flag sewn with subdued black and brown thread.

"This must be the place," Schauer commented dryly.

Mark turned to Sandy. "They'll need our identification cards—if you could collect them up."

She retrieved I.D. cards from everyone and handed them to Mark.

Mark rolled down his window and passed them to the guard, who checked each of their I.D.s and peered into the vehicle to verify each of their identities.

The guard signaled a second guard standing in front of their vehicle with an M4 Carbine at the ready while another guard inspected the car's undercarriage and trunk. When the inspection was complete, the guard stepped aside and the gate was pulled open.

"General Thorpe is expecting you, Boss," the guard said, pointing at the hangar to their front. "He's waiting for you in the first hangar, over there."

He drove through and parked the 4Runner on the side of the hangar. When the doors opened, they were greeted with engine noise from helicopters and other cargo aircraft. A figure of a man emerged around the corner of the building, who he recognized as John Thorpe.

Thorpe's imposing presence was enhanced by the light green flight suit he was wearing. Three black stars were affixed to each of his shoulders. His name and the designation "Lieutenant General, U.S. Army" were printed in silver on a black leather tag on the front of the flight suit.

Thorpe slapped his back. "You okay?"

He nodded. "I'm fine. I hope we didn't get in the way back there."

Thorpe shook his head and smiled.

Sandy followed with the others, and Thorpe shook their hands. "Your help was critical," he bellowed over the engines. "You bought us some time we desperately needed. We're preparing to fly this cargo out, as they tie it down, I wanted to show you what we found." Thorpe dug into his pockets and pulled out sets of disposable foam earplugs. "Here...you'll need these."

Mark walked beside Thorpe to the flight-line where the aircraft were parked. "So Celo's information was accurate, I take it?"

Thorpe nodded somberly. "Dead-on." They walked up to the ramp of the C-17 and were met by a blast of hot air from the jets. A team of Delta commandos were positioned at each of the aircraft doors and at its ramp.

When the others caught up with them, Thorpe led the group up the ramp and into the cargo jet's cavernous gangway. Inside, a long rectangular, dark grey, steel cargo container was strapped down to the floor of the aircraft, pre-positioned for moving a nuclear device. It was nearly twice the average height of a man, and several times that in depth. There were no markings on it except the ominous universal warning symbol for hazardous radiation material, stenciled in red spray paint on all sides.

Thorpe nodded at a man and woman dressed in civilian clothes with identification badges hanging from their necks reading "SANDIA NATIONAL LABORATORIES." They unlocked the cipher to the heavy door, prompting it to open slowly with the power generated by its built-in hydraulic system. Mark heard the vacuum seal release and a bright fluorescent glow emerged from inside the container. The female civilian technician led them inside along a narrow walkway that bordered a raised, fully illuminated glass-encased island. Inside the glass, a long, shiny metallic cylinder was fastened with nylon straps to large steel eyelets. A variety of gauges with western and Arabic script were built into the cylinder. As Mark studied them, he realized that the western script and terminology was in French.

Mark turned to the technician beside him. "Is this safe to transport?"

The technician nodded and pointed toward the drill holes on both sides. "It was rendered safe on site. The detonators were neutralized here." She walked to the far end of the device. "…And we flooded the central processing unit with a specialized form of silicon that causes anything electrical—to include electrical detonators or blasting caps—to be rendered fully inoperative. It also seals any radiation leakage…so with the exception of the plutonium and the explosives stored inside, it's essentially dead. The glass is lead-based Pyrex…nearly a foot thick. Another shield to protect from radiation leakage." The technician pointed at the ground. "And this container we're standing in is a lead alloy steel."

Mark looked at the others standing beside him. They were all quiet—uncharacteristically so. Several other technicians were monitoring the device with Geiger counters and radiacmeters.

Thorpe stood on the opposite side the island. "We estimate it's a 10 Kiloton device. Almost as powerful as the one that took out Hiroshima, but less than half its physical size."

"The target?" Mark asked.

"From the papers we found in the truck, we think they were aiming to use it in Medjugorje tomorrow. There were photos of a lot where they were planning to park it, only ten or twelve blocks from the site where the Pope's ceremony is planned."

"Good Lord," Sandy responded.

Thorpe nodded. He led them out of the container.

Mark turned to Thorpe as they emerged back into the gangway. "What about the other one?"

"It was taken from the warehouse in Bocinja," Thorpe answered. "Based on the information we've gotten from your source and from the briefcase in the car, we're tracking this tanker in the Adriatic right now that was referenced in the papers we found in Bocinja—the *MADHUMATI II*. We've classified it as a high interest vessel. It's under a Turkish flag, and manifested for Italy, but it turned around and is now headed toward the Suez."

"The Suez...," Mark said thoughtfully, linking the cryptic conversation he'd had with Lazarus. This seemed to confirm it. "Jeddah and Mecca are on the other side—"

Thorpe nodded slowly. "And The Haj starts a few weeks from now."

Mark stared at the container, the full scope of the threat suddenly clear. "A nuclear detonation there...."

"Would cause a clash of civilizations like we've never seen before," Thorpe finished. His expression was serious, resolute. "The Navy has positive control of it and the tanker. I expect we'll be boarding it in several hours." He paused and appeared to be considering his next words. "I'm flying out to our carrier in the Mediterranean now, *USS ENTERPRISE* ...you're all welcome to come along."

Mark looked at Sandy and the others. He turned back to Thorpe and shook his head. "Thanks, but we have some unfinished business to take care of down the road in Medjugorje, John."

Thorpe nodded his understanding. "All right, let's meet back up...whenever we can." He turned to face Sandy and smiled. "I'll leave the restaurant up to you."

Sandy smiled. "We may just eat in. Good luck, General."

Thorpe looked down at the ground thoughtfully and then back up at them. "And to *you*."

CHAPTER 83

"THEY WERE MY BEST MEN!" Savo Heleta screamed, his face fierce and contorted, suffused with dark blood. "Even if you did not know them, they were *your* best men. And you act as if they were disposable—like garbage!"

Papa Voyo sat behind the large, carved mahogany desk, staring at Heleta with a composed, if not slightly amused expression. Outside the rectory, he could hear the throngs of people, buses and automobiles passing by...all arriving for the canonization ceremony.

"Savo, they were soldiers," Voyo said, rising slowly, almost floating. "And now they are martyrs. They are the fortunate ones."

"They were my men!" Heleta shouted. "I was responsible for them! Because you would not allow us to plan adequately, they are dead."

Voyo grasped Heleta's shoulders. "They live through the Church they have saved. There is nothing else we can expect of them. Only through the blood of our men can we eradicate these demons from the earth. Our victory *demands* their sacrifice!"

Heleta shook his head insistently. He drew away from Voyo and slammed the wall with his open hand. "It was never to be like this! These people who are now fighting us are *not* our enemies!"

Voyo approached him slowly and spoke softly in a conversational, almost solicitous tone. "Savo, you know our covenant. We must eliminate those who seek to destroy the church—and oppose all those who seek to obstruct us."

Heleta twisted his mouth in derision and looked away from Voyo, out the window. "Are you blind? *They know who we are!* Most of my men have already been slaughtered 'saving the church' as you say." He scoffed. "There will soon be none of us left!"

Voyo's face was impassive and his tone indifferent. "You must have faith. We have more to do tonight...tomorrow. As we speak, the apocalypse approaches if we fail. You know this."

"If it comes, I fear you will cause it. I am through…finished."

Voyo shrugged and looked away. "You are indeed a foolish man, Savo," He sighed heavily, receding momentarily into a shadow in the corner of the room. "And so tonight, you have chosen the moment of your salvation."

Heleta turned and faced Voyo, puzzled at his remark. For a split second, Voyo caused him to lose his ice-cold presence of mind. The atmosphere in the room seemed to change. He was not prepared to see Voyo eyes smoldering, with his arm outstretched, holding a pistol with a long, black silencer attached to the muzzle.

"Eminence? What—"

Voyo pulled the trigger twice in quick succession. The thuds resonated in the rectory, sounding as if some books had fallen flat to the floor. Voyo stood in place calmly, knowing no one else was present to hear the shots in the monastery.

The bullets struck Heleta in the center of his chest. He reached up reflexively with both hands, struggling to comprehend what had just happened. He looked at Voyo with an astonished expression.

"Why?" was his last utterance…a bare whisper before crashing to the floor in a heap.

Voyo lowered the pistol and walked over to Heleta's lifeless body and knelt reverently beside him. Voyo untied the silk cords around his neck and removed the orphrey. He carefully placed it on Heleta's chest, over his wounds.

"And now, my son, you too shall rise in martyrdom to join our Savior at the right hand of his Father…."

Voyo watched the orphrey's white silk gradually turn a deep crimson as the blood from Heleta's wounds soaked through the delicate strands.

Behind the orphrey, attached to a chain around Heleta's neck, was the card with half of the permissive action link codes required to activate the device now positioned on the *MADHUMATI II*. It was no larger than a credit card, and encased in a brittle plastic sheath that was pink in color. Voyo removed the card and then his own card, identical in size and format, but with a ceramic sheath that was light blue in color. He cracked both cards open forcefully on the side of the nearby table. Together, they completed an alpha-numeric equation. Prompted by the required tones over the telephone line, he dialed the combined set of codes on his cell phone. Through the secure digital activation system, the device had been activated.

He placed his left hand on Heleta's forehead and crossed him with his right hand with consecrated oil for anointing of the sick. In a series of low-pitched, well-practiced utterances, Voyo commenced to deliver the Sacrament of Last Rites to Savo Heleta.

Chapter 84

AS HE DROVE along the steep mountain road toward Medjugorje, Mark Lyons pointed toward the group of Mercedes and BMWs parked on the side of the road near two long-bed trucks filled with lumber. Men wearing suits and leather dress shoes were glaring at them as they passed by.

"What in the world—?" Sandy remarked from the passenger seat. "Something tells me they aren't in the lumbering business...."

"No, you're right. They bloody well aren't," he answered. He turned to Sandy. "Dial up EUFOR Headquarters, would you? Ask for General Rose."

Anticipating her request, Mike McCallister dug in his pocket and passed up a laminated card with key EUFOR and UN telephone numbers from the back seat. She dialed the number. Mark listened in as it took her several minutes to navigate the various gatekeepers at the headquarters before Rose himself answered. She briefly introduced herself, and then handed Mark her cell phone.

"Ian, it's Mark Lyons," he said a little hoarsely. "We're down here in Medjugorje, just about to enter the town. We just passed a group of rather unsavory looking characters in suits with chain saws and a lumber truck. They're letting everyone in, but my guess is that they'll release their load over all the major routes so no one can get out of town—and so no help can get in."

He heard only Rose's breathing on the other end. "Ian?"

"I heard you, Lyons," Rose answered. "What is it that you need from me?"

Mark felt his frustration building, and took a deep breath. "I'd recommend you get armored buses down here with EUFOR clearing and riot teams. My guess is that we have about a five hour window before they've organized and by that time it'll be too late."

"Who are the suits?" Rose asked.

"They're Serbs," Mark replied matter-of-factly. "No surprise since they're the most unhappy about the ceremony, and they're just now hearing the news about Celo's murder—so I'd imagine they feel they've a score to settle."

"All right then, I'll take care of it.... Mark?"

Before he could answer, Rose continued. For the first time, his tone was subdued...and sincere. "I'm sorry about Celo. That's not the way we wanted it. You know that?"

Mark paused, knowing that Rose could not yet have any idea of how critical Celo's cooperation was to them in Mostar, which made his expression of sympathy that much more meaningful. "I know. Thanks, Ian."

USS ENTERPRISE (CVN 65) EXPEDITIONARY STRIKE FORCE

JOHN THORPE LOOKED out at the Mediterranean Sea from the bridge of the aircraft carrier, *USS ENTERPRISE*. Its vastness was humbling, and the ship seemed to have the ability to harness the energy and power of the sea through its sheer size. Watching the crew, listening to the helm's terse, antiphonal reports he could not help but be impressed with this seaborne behemoth and the monumental human effort that sustained it.

He watched the *MADHUMATI II* on the ship's monitor. Fifteen miles away at an elevation of 25,000 feet, a P-3 Orion Maritime Patrol Airborne Early Warning radar aircraft had been shadowing the vessel 24/7 using their Inverted Synthetic Aperture Radar.

Rear Admiral Bill Janis, the grey-headed commander of the *ENTERPRISE* Strike Group, wore a quiet confidence and a reputation throughout the Navy for his intellectual prowess and personable style with his sailors. He pointed out the window of the flag bridge. It offered an unobstructed view of the flight deck. Two F/A-18 Super Hornet strike fighters were preparing to launch over calm seas and into cloudless skies. The sky was still dark, with the sun rising in thirty minutes. As the first Super Hornet roared off *ENTERPRISE'S* deck, Janis turned to Thorpe, standing beside him in a camouflage battle dress uniform—three large black stars on a Velcro patch in the center of his Gortex field jacket.

"Sir, they'll go into a holding pattern over the target until you give the order to execute. The SEAL Team is in an Advanced SEAL Delivery System submerged off the tanker's port quarter. Their Delivery Vehicle was attached to the sub. It released about thirty minutes ago. The team is commanded by Lieutenant Tom Olson—he's a good man."

Thorpe had been involved in the development of the Advanced SEAL Delivery System, or ASDS, years ago when it was first considered as an undersea means of infiltration—it was, in fact, a mini submarine capable of delivering the underwater commandos close to a target, from behind, undetected, where a full-size submarine could safely not go. More than a decade later, it was fully operational.

He nodded. "What else do we know about the ship and crew?"

"We have the ship's manifest here." Janis pulled out a sheaf of papers that had been stapled together. "The ship is Turkish and the crew is mostly Pakistani. The names alone are cause for suspicion, but—"

He leaned in to hear Janis above the noise from the flight deck as the second Super Hornet took off. He was intrigued. "But what?"

"Well, it's strange any way you cut it." Janis walked over to the map board, shaking his head. Operating areas, warning zones, and territorial boundaries were outlined in prismatic lines. He took a one-meter ruler and placed it on one of the lines that cut across the Adriatic and Mediterranean Seas, leading to Italy. "You see, they were heading to the port of Civitavecchia in Italy, on this westerly track, two eight six degrees." Janis drew a line with a black grease pencil and glanced back at Thorpe. Civitavecchia was the closest port to the Vatican. "They say they had no cargo and claimed they were going there to pick up a hundred eighty-five tons of wheat and barley. That changed a day ago, when they returned to a port near Dubrovnik. "Now, look at this…." He adjusted the ruler and drew another line, this one in dark blue. "Instead, they abruptly turned around here, seventy-five nautical miles from shore and took up an easterly heading of two eight three degrees and returned before steaming off again southwest here…changing their course."

"Toward the Suez." Thorpe commented.

Janis nodded, looking back at him with a concerned expression. "And Saudi Arabia. Their destination is now filed as Jeddah."

"All right," Thorpe said in a resolute tone. "Get the Situation Room on the line. Have them connect me to the National Security Advisor."

He watched as ENTERPRISE's Captain, standing across from him, pressed a button on his secure "Red Switch" telephone. He spoke briefly and then handed the receiver to Thorpe. "The SITROOM is on the line, sir. They're connecting now. They've asked you to stand by."

Thorpe looked at his watch. It was 9 p.m. in Washington...seven hours behind them. After a brief delay, he heard Jim Goodwin's voice come over the line, announcing that the National Security Advisor, Chairman of the Joint Chiefs of Staff, and Secretary of Defense were present with him.

"Good Evening. I'm on board *ENTERPRISE* with Admiral Bill Janis. I believe we've established probable cause to board the *MADHUMATI II*. We have fighters overhead and a direct action force prepared to board the ship upon the President's approval."

There was a pause in the conversation. The tension was heightened by the silence on the bridge. "No overt indicators yet that they have a radiological or nuclear device on board, but we have good intelligence and a NEST Team here as part of our task force that helped us defuse the last one at the mosque in Mostar. Our first step will be to immobilize the ship, by force if necessary, and then conduct a non-compliant boarding."

"Okay," Rachel Cook replied. "I'll brief POTUS and get back to you with his answer."

"Yes, ma'am," Thorpe replied. "We're standing by."

CHAPTER 85

AS MARK NEGOTIATED a curve in the road, the traffic came to a full and sudden stop.

Buses, cars, and horse-drawn carts filled the road, creating lanes where there were none and blocking the oncoming lane and each of the shoulders. Horns were blaring and black exhaust erupted from tailpipes of the buses to their front. A full panorama of humanity descended locust-like into the valley leading into Medjugorje—cars and buses decorated with lights, crucifixes and artists renditions of the Virgin Mary and photos of Cardinal Alojzije Stepinac. Banners were strung across buses with messages in elaborate decorative script that read:

SAINT ALOJZIJE STEPINAC PRAY FOR US!

STEPINAC! PATRON SAINT OF CROATIA!

"We're not in Kansas anymore, Toto," Sandy deadpanned.

USS ENTERPRISE (CVN 65) EXPEDITIONARY STRIKE FORCE

THORPE LEANED AGAINST the ship's railing and looked out the window at the sea's hypnotic boil. Through the indigo night sky, the stars reflected violet-white against the sea like thousands of chips and scratches on an old onyx slate. In the distance, he saw the other ships that made up the *ENTERPRISE* Strike Group—orbiting in formation around her: guided missile cruisers, Zumwalt-class destroyers, cruisers, frigates and Fast Combat Support Ships sailed through the night.

As the Commanding General of the Joint Special Operations Command, or "JSOC," John Thorpe's presence on-board *ENTERPRISE* was somewhat of an anomaly. In any other circumstance, Rear Admiral Janis would be responsible for the operation in its entirety, but because it was a nuclear weapons search and SEAL Team Six was one of his elite counterterrorism units, Thorpe had assumed the role of "incident commander."

The mission of SEAL Team Six was to board the ship, search it and, accompanied by NEST, neutralize any threats they found on-board.

The ship's Captain approached Thorpe and Janis. "Gentlemen, we have National Command Authority approval to conduct Visit, Board, Search and Seizure of the *MADHUMATI II*."

The sea heaved below. Thorpe nodded and turned to Janis. "Okay, Bill. It's your show."

Moving back to the Bridge, Janis nodded and turned to the Captain and gave the order: "Illuminate and challenge."

CHAPTER 86

HORNS WERE BLARING and black exhaust erupted from the tailpipes of the buses to their front. Mark found himself privately chastising himself for being so naïve as to believe the trip to Medjugorje would be an easy, unimpeded one given the impending Vatican ceremony.

"Well, it's hard to imagine that we'll be moving any time soon," Sandy Evenson said, observing the ensnarled traffic in front and around them. She leaned her head on the door, using her coat that she'd folded up as a makeshift pillow.

"Okay...," Mark uttered. He released his seatbelt and then turning to Mike McCallister in the back seat. "Mike, would you take the wheel?"

"Are you leaving us?" Sandy asked, unable to conceal her surprise.

Mark turned to her, with a wry smile. "Can't miss church, can we?"

McCallister smiled broadly. "Oh no, that would be a sin, I reckon!"

"Hopefully it's not mined," Schauer called out.

"Is it?" Mark asked, turning to Sandy.

"Not here," she answered after a moment. "There hasn't been any fighting here in this or the last war...."

"Not yet," Schauer replied.

"That's right," she repeated, looking at Mark. "Yet."

Mark opened his door and moved to the back of the SUV and opened the hatch. The other doors opened. He pulled a backpack out, strapped it on and walked over and looked inside the driver's-side window at the three. Jon Schauer was left in the back seat checking his cameras and Vladimir took the passenger seat. As Mike McCallister was getting situated in the driver's seat, Mark poked his head in. "You gents okay with this?"

"No worries," McCallister answered cheerfully. "We'll find you when we get through all of this mess,"

He extended his hand and Mark shook it, thanking the three men before joining Sandy Evenson on the jagged pathway into Medjugorje.

USS ENTERPRISE (CVN 65) EXPEDITIONARY STRIKE FORCE

STANDING ON the *ENTERPRISE* Bridge, Admiral Bill Janis picked up the radio receiver and listened as the Officer of the Deck hailed the tanker over the commercial maritime hailing frequency. "*MADHUMATI II*, this is the United States *ENTERPRISE* Strike Group, I repeat, you are detained. Stop your ship immediately and prepare to be boarded by United States forces."

The order was repeated three times with no reply.

"No response from them, sir. We've also sent orders recorded in Serbo-Croatian, Turkish, Urdu and Arabic. No response to those either."

"Okay, tell the Super Cobras I want them to strafe the bridge of the ship's control room and to launch two Hellfires into the rudder, on my command.... That should stop 'em."

"Aye, sir," the Captain responded

Janis pointed toward the flight deck where two grey AH-1Z Super Cobra attack helicopters were taking off in tandem.

"We'll see the fireworks out there in a few minutes," Janis said, pointing toward the shadow of the *MADHUMATI II* on the horizon. "The lesson here...never bring a knife to a gunfight...." The comment was a subtle yet prescient message to both men that this would not be a typical boarding operation.

Janis switched to a satellite radio link to the submarine at periscope depth.

"Brightstar One, this is Charlie One-One Actual. Cobras are cleared hot with Hellfires. Tell the SEAL Delivery Vehicle to standby for boarding after impact," he ordered, referring to the mini-submarine that would "deliver" the SEALS to the tanker.

Janis turned to the Marine Corps brigadier general commander of the Expeditionary Strike Group. "Steve, let's get both Forty-Sixes' in the air and in a holding pattern. If we need your Marines on that tanker they'll be going in after the SEALS."

The Marine general nodded and gave Janis a quiet "thumbs-up." Moments later, Thorpe saw two grey CH-46 cargo helicopters taking off in sequence from the flight deck.

"Sir, the SEAL Delivery Vehicle is in position," the Captain reported.

"Very well," Janis replied. "Launch the Hellfires now. Autonomous double-round engagement."

Seconds later, the visual display from the P-3s lit up.

Thorpe heard the Super Hornets flying overhead.

"Irongate One, this is Charlie One-One Actual. You're cleared hot. Gunfighter, Execute."

"Roger...missiles away."

"Okay," Janis said to Thorpe, pointing to the flight control center. "Our best vantage point is going to be this screen with the infra-red illumination."

"Direct hits to the control room and rudder, as ordered, Charlie One-One," the Super Hornet Commander reported.

The screen depicted a bright glow coming from where the tanker's control room once was. The infra-red view was much like watching a movie in orange, red and yellow negative format. Two bright yellow streaks flashed across both ends of the ship from opposite directions. A second later, he heard two back-to-back sonic booms that sounded like explosions.

"Those are the F-18s," Janis explained to Thorpe. "...A diversion to assist the boarding party—here—" he pointed at the screen. "You can see the SEALS boarding on the tanker's port side."

The screen showed glowing green images of men climbing two rope ladders on the tanker's hull, with short, compact submachine guns. Janis pointed at the thermal images of several crew members armed with assault rifles scattering after the Super Hornet flyover, and then regrouping in disciplined movements like ants on an anthill. When they started to approach the boarding party, the SEAL Commander picked up the microphone to speak to the SEAL platoon leader.

"Saber Six, be advised you have enemy approaching your position on the starboard side behind a container to your front, danger close."

A hiss of static, and a beep. "Charlie One-One, Roger. Thanks...we'll handle 'em. Out." It came as a near whisper.

A moment later, and in quick succession, each of the enemy fell silently to the deck, like figures in a video game. A group of SEAL's approached with their submachine guns glued to their cheeks in a rapid, synchronized movement.

The next transmission came from the SEAL platoon.

"Saber Three, Saber Six. Five enemy confirmed kills, Over."

Over the speaker in the flag bridge, a clear voice announced, "Charlie One-One, this is Saber Six." It was the SEAL platoon leader. "We're all on-board. Five enemy kills. Commencing search, Over."

The SEAL Commander acknowledged his transmission. Janis shifted his attention to the screen.

The bright orange silhouettes of the Super Cobra Gunships flying like wasps around the tanker, providing close air support to the SEAL platoon as they canvassed the deck with devastating effect. Smoke and flames were pouring out of the tanker's control room, occasionally obscuring the overhead view with black cloud-like puffs. The tanker turned uncontrollably to starboard as it slowed, rudders out.

"Saber Six, this is Irongate One. We spot four hostile personnel in the open, vicinity targets near the control room. Will engage, Over."

The SEAL Platoon leader acknowledged the Super Cobra Commander's transmission.

Janis pointed at the four figures carrying weapons emerging through a door near the smoke of the control room. An instant later, the Cobra Gunships fired a burst from their .20 millimeter gattling guns and they too fell in unison to the deck.

"Saber Six, this is Irongate One, four enemy down."

"Roger, Irongate. Thanks—"

There was an extended pause interrupted more than a minute later by a rush of static and the voice of the SEAL Platoon leader. "Saber Six, I'm not sure if it means anything, but our measurements tell us we may have a false transversal bulkhead…three feet out from where it's supposed to be…."

"Roger, can you breach it?" the SEAL Commander asked.

"Roger that…stand by," the platoon leader responded. Aside from the static and some occasional chatter on the other radios from the jets and helicopters in a defensive pattern above, dead silence…

Breaking the silence, Janis turned to his Operations Officer. "Give me an attack solution for the tanker quickly."

Seconds later, the excited voice of the platoon leader broke the static: *"Holy Mary, Mother of God! What the—"*

Janis' eyes narrowed with concern. He signaled to the SEAL Commander who reached for the hand-mike for the radio from the console in front of him. "Saber Six, this is Charlie One-One Actual. What is your situation, Over?"

There was no immediate response. Only static. The SEAL Commander calmly repeated his request for a situation report several times until the SEAL platoon commander's response finally came in a breathless, urgent tone.

"Charlie One-One Actual, there are bodies stacked up down there like cordwood...they've been summarily executed. And we've located what appears to be a device in one of the cargo-holds with a false bulkhead...it's booby trapped in several locations...as near as we can tell, it could be an implosion device...approximately four by five feet...but it looks like they've gotten to it first and started the clock on it. It's set to detonate 91 minutes from now...and counting...Charlie One Actual...." The SEAL Platoon Leader paused, attempting to suppress the panic in his voice. "Sir, the device has a permissive action link and all of its electronics are encased in Titanium and glass...in order to get to the physics package that controls the device we have to be able to penetrate its casing, but we can't even get within arms reach of it the way it's been set up. We can only look at it. We could attempt an Emergency Destruct, but there's no guarantee we won't detonate it in the process...."

Janis felt a chill go through him. A permissive action link was a sophisticated heat and time-sensitive locking system that was extremely difficult to defeat under the *best* of circumstances. But the situation they now faced fit squarely in the "worst case" category.

The Captain spoke. "Sir, a nuclear yield appears imminent unless we have the permissive action link codes. Since we don't, recommend we sink her...the water and pressure may interrupt the firing sequence...we're looking at a high magnitude nuclear event either way, but an underwater detonation would be more contained than one on the surface."

Janis exchanged a look of alarm with Thorpe. "Who would have those PAL Codes, Sir? Any idea?"

It was a last desperate attempt to disarm the device in the time they had left remaining...90 minutes and counting.

Thorpe took out his Satellite telephone and pressed the speed dial for Mark Lyons' cell phone. He looked at Janis. "I may."

CHAPTER 87

SANDY EVENSON POINTED to the hill enshrouded in fog on the horizon. "That's Mount Krizevac...Cross Hill, where they say the children stood to see the image of the Virgin Mary appear to them over there at the smaller hilltop that they call Apparition Hill."

"Do you believe it?" Mark asked.

She shrugged. "The Franciscans at the time built that church, Saint James...," she said pointing. "They were in a clash with the Bishop of Mostar to stay independent...and their 'miracle' here gave them their independence. That seems to be the real miracle if you put it all in context." She walked with Mark through the crowds, weaving between pilgrims. "The concrete cross on Mount Krizevac is said to have a piece of the true cross embedded inside. Frankly, I don't know what I believe anymore."

"Careful," Mark said, glancing back. "Yer startin' to sound like me."

"Heaven forbid," Sandy answered, trailing behind him.

They walked along in silence. Mark felt his cell phone vibrate and then heard its ring. It was Thorpe.

He sounded distant, as if he were in a tunnel, underwater. "Mark, I'm on *ENTERPRISE*. We've got a situation—we've found another device, more sophisticated than the last. This one's been armed remotely and looks like it's timed to go off in about an hour and a half...89 minutes from now...unless we can find the permissive action link code sequence. Given everything we've learned, I believe there's only one person who would have those."

"The Cardinal," Mark answered.

"Yeah."

"I can try to find him here, John, but it's a bloody mess with the crowds. We're on foot just outside Medjugorje...how much time can you give us?"

Mark waited as Thorpe consulted on the other end of the line. After a few seconds, he came back. "I can give you an hour," Thorpe answered. "No more."

CHAPTER 88

THE FOG BURNED off in the sunlight and the street opened up to reveal the courtyard around Saint James Church. Road blocks had been placed around each of the roads leading to the church, severely constricting traffic. Groups of children were washing the windshields of cars with bottles of dirty water, demanding payments the drivers had not agreed upon. Souvenir hawkers were selling statuettes and portraits of the Virgin Mary and many varieties of colorfully beaded rosaries. Throngs of people were gathering around the church. In the back of the church entrance, a large white gazebo and altar were entirely surrounded by bulletproof glass. Security agents, Federation police and EUFOR soldiers and armored tactical troop carriers had formed a perimeter around the courtyard of Saint James Church.

"Is this your first canonization?" Mark asked absently, doing his best to not appear stressed after Thorpe's call.

"No, no…," Sandy remarked, having seen his demeanor noticeably change. "I always wait until they come out on DVD." She pulled out the plastic identification card holder inside her coat and hung it around her neck. "Between your credentials and mine, we should be able to get into the church, don't you think?"

He pulled his badge out so that it too was hanging in the center of his chest, in full view. He nodded toward the church where two black Mercedes were pulling into the controlled security area. "Who do ye suppose that is?"

"Do you have your binoculars in that pack… or is that only for tea?" she asked, smiling.

He was already digging into the pack. "You Americans are sometimes too preoccupied with function, you know." He pulled out the set of Zeiss Binoculars and raised them to his eyes in time to see the Mercedes come to a stop in front of the church. A cardinal, dressed in a scarlet simar emerged from the church to greet the party. The doors opened and a group, all dressed in business attire, stepped out.

"Who are they?" Sandy asked.

He shrugged. "All suits…with bodyguards. Looks like the Croatian Prime Minister and President of the Bosnian Federation. Roman Polko's with them."

"Forever the politician," Sandy said. "I can't imagine he'd miss this spectacle."

"I'm actually surprised he came."

"What?" Sandy said in mock disbelief. "Roman Polko—miss an audience with the Pope? I don't think so."

"He opposed the ceremony happening here."

"Yeah, but he didn't stop it," she answered. "And it was fully within his authority to if he wanted."

The sound of helicopter blades echoed against the hillsides. A loud murmur passed through the gathering crowd, followed by the eruption of excited shouts from people pointing at a white helicopter approaching in the distance. More police surged to the square and struggled to keep the crowd contained.

"Speaking of His Holiness …," she added.

"They're going to land him right there, in front of the church!" He continued to scan the area around the church with his binoculars. With the Pope's arrival, the official delegation emerged from the church doors and stood in front, waiting for the helicopter to land. Roman Polko was standing on the church steps in front of the square with the Archbishop of Sarajevo, along with the Presidents of Croatia and the Bosnian Federation.

CHAPTER 89

JANIS TURNED to the SEAL Commander. "I want them out of there in fifty minutes, not a second more."

The SEAL Commander repeated the command to the SEAL platoon.

Because it was booby trapped, it was unlikely that fifty minutes would allow the SEAL and technical teams the time they would need to penetrate the device casing and render it safe. In any other circumstance, they could also emplace heavy explosives on the ship, rigging it to sink—but in this case, there wasn't sufficient time.

Janis turned to his Operations Officer. "What's the range to the tanker?"

"Eight thousand five hundred meters, sir, bearing one eight five."

Janis turned to his Captain and began speaking in a calm, yet intense rapid fire tone. "Get those fifty-sixes in the air and have them ready to pick them up exactly fifty minutes from now. Vector that SEAL Delivery Vehicle and Sub out of the area now. If we don't get those codes and can't disarm that device, when they're clear of the tanker, we'll commence firing."

"WILCO, sir," the Captain replied.

The operations officer handed him a sheet of paper with the recommended ordnance to be directed at the *MADHUMATI II*, with the objective to sink her.

Janis nodded. "All right. Turn us around. Put as much distance between us and that tanker as possible. I want a minute-by-minute status report with the position of every ship and aircraft."

"Your sub would be able to survive this?" Thorpe asked.

Janis nodded, looking through his binoculars at the tanker. "Yes, sir. She's much faster underwater, and she'll stay deep. It'll be tight, but with the time we have, we should be able to put sufficient distance between us and the blast when it is scheduled to occur."

Thorpe nodded and looked around the bridge. "Okay. I need to get the SITROOM back on the line."

The Captain handed Thorpe the telephone receiver. "They're standing by now, sir."

Thorpe took the phone and asked the Situation Room communicator for the National Security Advisor. The sky was becoming lighter as sunrise approached. Seconds later, he heard Rachel Cook's distinctive voice on the line.

"Ma'am, I need to brief you on the situation we're facing now...."

MEDJUGORJE, BOSNIA AND HERZEGOVINA

MARK LYONS and Sandy Evenson flashed their UN credentials to the police at the barriers surrounding Saint James Church, and stepped through the cordon into the square where the Pope's giant white Sikorsky helicopter had just landed. Its rotors created a wind that pushed Sandy into Mark's side. He put his arms protectively around her shoulders as it lifted off.

"Voyo's gotta be on that helo," Mark said, struck by the air of excitement around them, bordering on frenzy. "He wouldn't miss this."

He'd seen the Pope, his entourage and welcoming party walk inside the church, but not Voyo. Flags of Croatia and the Vatican hung on the bell-towers of the church welcoming the Pope. As the helicopter landed, the crowd grew, clamoring for a view of the pontiff. Reporters, photographers and news vans occupied a section of the square closest to the church. Beside them, people of all ages were waving placards, flags and scarves with photographs and artists' renditions of Cardinal Alojzije Stepinac. Another group, on the opposite end of the square was chanting and carrying banners and signs with collaged photographs, swastikas, Maltese Crosses, and angry slogans in bold red and black print:

STEPINAC THE MURDERER!

NAZI COLLABORATOR!

USTASHE EXECUTIONER!

Sandy nodded in the direction of the protestors. "The loyal opposition?"

"Every canonization ceremony has one...." he commented dryly. He pointed at the door to the church.

"I'm gonna see the Pope looking like *this?*" she exclaimed, making a vain effort to arrange her hair.

"You look great," he answered.

"I don't look great—I'm a mess," she shot back. "I have no makeup on, my hair is in tangles from the goddamn helicopter and I'm wearing the same clothes I've been wearing for the last twenty-four hours for Christ's sake!"

Mark laughed. "I doubt seriously we'll even get to see the Pope. They usually keep him all cloistered up, isn't that what they call it?"

"You're a big help," Sandy answered, climbing the steps to the church. She dug in her pocket for a hairbrush and flashed her credentials again to the Vatican guards at the door.

Mark pushed the front door to the church open.

The doors swung closed, shutting out the cacophony behind them. Priests in various styles of religious dress...black and brown monk habits and clerical suits, were quietly bustling around the church carrying saffron and violet-colored silk vestments and conversing with one another in low, hushed tones.

"Mark, I'm the only woman here," Sandy whispered, walking down the aisle beside him.

"You can balance things out, then."

"I get the distinct feeling we're crashing their party."

He pointed. "Over there." The same group of men in suits they'd seen get out of the cars were standing beside the altar near a bank of lighted candles. Roman Polko was off to the side speaking on his cell phone, holding his finger to his ear. After a few moments, he spotted Mark and Sandy and signaled to them.

As they approached, Mark could detect grave concern and finally impatience in Polko's voice and in the single word questions he was asking of the caller on the other end of the line.

"When? ...Where? ..." Polko looked up and saw them. "I understand, General. They just arrived."

Polko lowered his cell phone and cast a grave look. "That was General Thorpe. He told me to expect both of you...and asked that I grant you unrestricted access to arrest a key dignitary for his responsibility in the Fulbright assassination? He said this person is in possession of codes that could prevent a nuclear detonation? He said you would provide the details."

"I can, sir."

"Well, then, perhaps you should tell me, now." Polko's tenor was impatient. *"Who—?"*

"Cardinal Vojislav Pijadje."

"He is responsible for the canonization, yes, but—"

"No," Mark replied, shaking his head slowly. "He is responsible for everything...for all the chaos that's happened here since I arrived. I'd suggest you ask him to explain," Mark replied evenly.

"He is the Archbishop of Zagreb—a Cardinal!" Polko exclaimed, in animated disbelief. "You are certain—?"

He nodded. "I am, sir...fully certain. Is he here?"

Polko nodded. "He and the Archbishop of Sarajevo may be preparing to brief the Pope on the ceremony now."

Mark inhaled deeply, looking around the church. "It's important that I talk to him now. Given the circumstances, I'd recommend that you postpone this ceremony until we get this sorted out."

Polko nodded silently and glanced back toward the vestuary with a sober expression. "And what will you do with him? Arrest him?"

Sandy nodded. "Sir...with your permission, I'd like to have him indicted for war crimes."

"You are absolutely *certain* he has done these things?" Polko asked again.

Mark nodded, glancing at his watch impatiently. "We are, sir, but we simply don't have time—"

"Yes...okay, then." Polko finally nodded. "I will approve that, but there are others who must—"

Sandy pulled out her cell phone. "I'll clear it with The Hague." She waved at Mark. "Go!"

Polko walked over to the Croatian Prime Minister. He pulled him away from the rest of the delegation and spoke to him quietly.

Mark saw the Prime Minister's initial smile transition to shock. He glanced over at them, and then nodded back at Polko before summoning one of his bodyguards.

"There, now you've done it, Commissioner," Sandy whispered.

"Done what?"

"Worked everyone up...."

Roman Polko walked back to them. "They will bring him to you."

"Why is it that I can't help but think they won't find him?" Sandy commented.

"Maybe we can help them with that," Mark replied.

Polko nodded and looked directly at him. His expression was authoritative and his tone was demanding. "I would like this done quietly. Is that understood?"

USS ENTERPRISE (CVN 65) EXPEDITIONARY STRIKE FORCE

"GET THE *CHAFEE* on the line," Janis ordered. "Tell 'em to prepare four Harpoons to launch into the hull of the tanker. And then I want the *CARTER* to launch two Mark 48's near-simultaneously, set to explode below the hull."

"Aye, sir. Harpoons make ready, all plans sent," he replied, understanding the physics behind Janis' order. The AGM-84 Harpoon missiles launched from the Destroyer, the *USS CHAFEE*, would flood the tanker's hull with water upon impact. That alone would be enough to sink the tanker, but to do it quickly Janis had taken the necessary second step by ordering the torpedoes from the *ENTERPRISE* Strike Group's submarine, *USS JIMMY CARTER*, to detonate underneath the hull of the tanker in order to create a vacuum, thereby breaking its back and splitting it in two. He picked up the receiver to the SATCOM radio.

"Four Harpoons and two Mark 48's...stand by for launch."

Janis turned to his navigator. "How deep is the water where that tanker's sitting?"

The navigator checked the charts in front of him and turned to Janis. "About 8000 feet, sir."

"Our speed?"

"32 knots."

Janis nodded and grasped his Captain's arm. "Get as many aircraft below deck or in the air now.... I want everything buttoned up. Keep all aircraft that are airborne in the air and tell 'em to find a place to land on shore." He looked up at the red digital clock display. "We have forty minutes. Do it now, but do it safely."

"Aye, sir," the Captain answered.

MARK STEPPED UP to the sanctuary and into the vestuary where there were more priests quietly dressing and preparing for the ceremony. He approached the priests with his identification badge.

"Cardinal Pijadje...Papa Voyo?"

Each shook his head until one of the Franciscan monks, dressed in his brown habit, nodded and smiled his recognition.

"Where is he?" Mark asked in English and then in Serbo-Croatian.

The monk pointed outside, and in a subdued voice indicated that he could find Papa Voyo in the tented annex attached to the back of the vestuary.

As he walked through the vestuary, a stir outside...doors slamming shut, orders shouted...and then two of the bodyguards coming back inside alerted him. He looked at them intently as they passed him...the one who the Prime Minister had spoken to...returned his gaze, and at that moment he realized what had just happened. He cursed.

Mark felt his body suddenly in full propulsion. Running through the tent, he pushed a priest aside. It was divided into compartments and fully furnished with sofas and tables and chairs on one side and an altar with pews on the other. He walked swiftly through the tent, past several priests, kneeling in prayer. One of them was the Archbishop of Sarajevo and the other, also kneeling, he recognized immediately from the white cap and white robe as the Pope. They looked up at him, and he bowed his head slightly and walked quickly to the rear entrance of the tent.

Outside, beside the exterior altar of the church where a church choir was practicing, Voyo, dressed in a white robe, was stepping into a black Mercedes.

"Hey!" Mark shouted. "Stop!"

As he sat in the driver's seat, Voyo looked calmly up at him for an instant and closed the car door.

Mark cursed again and ran toward the Mercedes.

The car's engine roared. He saw Voyo driving away in a cloud of flying gravel.

Outside, he found another black car idling, a BMW 750i, with a VIP chauffeur sitting inside. He opened the door and presented his UN identification card.

"Police!"

The man refused to move, and began shouting at him in Serbo-Croatian. Mark reached inside and grasped the man's white shirt with both hands and threw him forcefully out of the car onto the gravel.

Mark stepped inside the driver's seat and shoved the car into first gear. He squealed out of the private parking area in the direction he'd seen Voyo drive, he slammed his brakes, nearly hitting Sandy, who was running at full speed around the corner in the middle of the road. She hit the hood of the BMW with both hands and jumped back as it skidded to a stop. A moment later, she was opening the passenger door.

"I'm coming with you!" she yelled, climbing inside.

He threw the car back into first gear and rapidly accelerated, breaking and weaving through the sea of pedestrians.

"There!" Sandy shouted, pointing at the black Mercedes. It had climbed a sidewalk and was recklessly hitting the kiosks of souvenir vendors, causing them to crash into shop windows. People quickly fled its path, screaming and sheltering one another behind buildings.

He followed behind the Mercedes. They were closer now…and Voyo was in plain view, four cars ahead of them. His tires were screeching and it was fishtailing wildly down the street.

"Oh My God! Look!" Sandy shouted, pointing to her front. A single horse drawn cart brimming with something that appeared like dirty crimson-colored softballs was rolling into the next intersection. An elderly man and woman were driving the cart.

He sounded his horn just as the Mercedes plunged into the cart. A heavy cloud of dust and dirt erupted. The other cars came to a full stop, and Mark slammed on his brakes, narrowly missing the car to his front.

"Christ, he hit them!" Mark exclaimed under his breath. The Mercedes was stopped in front of them.

They both opened their doors and ran toward the Mercedes, weaving between the other cars and the crowd of people who were beginning to swarm to the accident site. The siren of a police car blared out in the distance.

"What was in the cart?" Sandy shouted.

At a glance he could see that the Mercedes had broadsided the cart, causing it to jackknife and tip over. "Beets," he replied, picking one of them up and throwing it back down.

Beets were scattered around in every direction. The horse was frantically whinnying and bucking off to the side. A man had taken hold of its harness and the driver of the cart was on the ground, alive but badly hurt. A younger man with a cell phone was trying to connect.

More sirens shrilled in a developing cacophony.

The young man with his ear to the cell phone announced that an ambulance was on the way.

"Mark!" Sandy was standing beside the driver's side door of the Mercedes. "Come here! Look!"

Mark stepped over the shattered cart and pushed aside the piles of whole beets.

The door was open. And empty.

Above the terrified whinnying of the horse, the surging crowd and excited shouting, Mark stood up and scanned the crowd, but could not find Voyo or anyone who vaguely resembled him. He climbed to the damaged hood of the Mercedes and searched the horizon.

The white habit was what first caught his attention…and then his height, relative to all the people. He was walking at a brisk, purposeful pace, and yet with a distinct limp against the flow of the rest of the crowd. Somehow he'd already managed to put a good distance between himself and the accident site. The road ended at a parking lot at the base of a hill…the same hill Sandy had pointed out as they were entering into the town.

Mount Krizevac…Cross Hill.

He looked down and found Sandy directly below him. "There he is over there—at the parking lot!"

The parking lot was filled with buses and cars and crowds of people of all ages, accompanied by priests, nuns…preparing to ascend and pray at the famous shrine before the canonization ceremony began.

He hopped down from the Mercedes and reached for Sandy's hand, leading her through the crowd, pushing onlookers aside. After clearing the mob of onlookers, Mark thought he caught a glimpse of Voyo's tall white figure standing between two buses, watching them. "There!"

As they ran toward Voyo, he withdrew into the shadows.

Inside the parking lot, Mark moved quickly, searching between and underneath the buses…with no trace of him.

"Are those buses unlocked?" he called out to Sandy.

She didn't answer him. He looked behind him where he last saw her, but she wasn't there. A distinct sensation of panic and dread overtook him. Somehow they'd become separated, and he chastised himself for allowing it to happen. It couldn't happen. Not here. He wouldn't allow it. He reached inside his coat and pulled out the Browning High Power pistol from his shoulder holster, took it off "safe" and chambered a round.

He called out her name again, this time louder, above the noise of engines and the crowd. He still could not find her in the sea of people gathering at the trailhead, beginning their ascent.

"Do you think you'll need that?" Sandy's voice came back. She was standing near a café at the start of the trail uphill.

Mark dropped the pistol to his side, and in the calmest, even tone he could muster, said, "You *can't* leave me like that."

She was about to answer with a counter-lecture but she stopped herself, seeing the concern in his eyes and said simply, "Okay."

At that precise moment, the gravel and rocks began to stream down the embankment above him. He looked up the hill and then at one another and they knew. Voyo was climbing Mt. Krizevac along with the throngs of other worshipers.

Crowds of people had gathered and were beginning their ascent.

Cursing, Mark holstered his pistol, and rushed into the wooded area, climbing frantically around boulders, grasping at saplings, stopping between the mass of rock outcroppings. He felt his ankle turn between one of them, and cursed quietly.

He saw the people above. As he continued to climb, he could hear them, quietly chanting and praying as he ran up the pathway. The sound of wooden walking sticks echoed around him.

The trail was littered with stones and rock outcroppings that had become smoothed over from the millions of others who had walked over them.

Voyo was taking long strides, maneuvering around the crowds of people. A large group of people were congregated around one of the stations of the cross.

Racing through the crowd and around one of the trail's switchbacks, they were stopped by a group of priests crowding the trail in a long procession that extended up the next turn—all of them dressed in long white, brown and black habits. Another group of pilgrims was congregated around an aid station. A priest with a megaphone was broadcasting a series of prayers. A women with a baby held loosely in her arms sat on the edge of the trail, begging for money.

Weaving through the procession, Mark reached out and took hold of the priest's arms...turning them toward him so he could look at their faces before releasing them.

He ran up the trail a short distance to the next switchback. The trail was clear, except for one very tall white figure walking with his hood covering his head like a ghost, cresting the hill up ahead. Sandy was ahead of him.

He took in a deep breath, watching Voyo disappear to the top of the hill.

Mark and Sandy ran up the trail, zigzagging between a group of tourists with walking sticks and more groups of worshipers praying in German, French and English.

USS ENTERPRISE (CVN 65) EXPEDITIONARY STRIKE FORCE

JOHN THORPE LOOKED outside and below the bridge to see a CH-46 helicopter landing on the deck of the aircraft carrier. It dumped out the contingent of SEALs, and then just as quickly lifted off again. Only two SEALs and two NEST Team members were left on the *MADHUMATI II*.

"Get the SEAL platoon commander up here on the bridge now," Janis ordered. "Right away."

"He's on his way up, sir," the SEAL Commander answered.

"Janis turned to Thorpe. "Sir, if the device detonates underwater, we're estimating that our ships will be at least twenty-five nautical miles away from it when it does...that's more than minimum survival distance, but we're not taking any chances."

Thorpe nodded. Beside him, a giant of a man in a black wet suit, camouflaged face, and holding an MP-5 submachine gun entered the bridge, filling the doorway.

"Lieutenant Olson reporting as ordered, sir."

Janis walked over to him. "Son, as quickly as you're able, I need to know what you saw on that tanker."

As Olson started to speak, Janis ushered him inside to the console of plasma screens.

He pulled out a digital camera and began to scroll through the photos he'd taken. "Sir, we found it inside one of the grain holds portside, bolted to these two tables. It had a stainless steel or titanium shell and it was shaped like an oversize pumpkin, all encased in a shell of what we assumed to be leaded glass. Our diagnostics indicated the core is probably plutonium, with enough gamma emissions to indicate a minimum 20 kiloton device."

Janis looked at Thorpe, clearly concerned.

Lieutenant Olson spoke again. "Gentlemen, there's something else we came across in that ship that I think you should see...."

MEDJUGORJE, BOSNIA AND HERZEGOVINA

MARK FELT HIS LEGS straining. As he crested the hill, he saw the massive cross that overlooked all of Medjugorje ahead of them. Steel posts with chains as an aisle way led up to the cross. It was windy and cold. A few people were milling about, but he could not find Voyo among them. He held his pistol at his side and walked along the perimeter of the hill frantically searching for him. Sandy followed.

There was a sudden explosion of motion. And then a cry in Serbo-Croatian, *"He has a gun!"* Pilgrims were pointing at him, scattering down the trail, excitedly repeating the warning to others who were ascending.

Mark raised his pistol and pointed it toward the cross as they proceeded to its opposite side.

Behind the cross, he saw a priest in a white habit kneeling at the base of the structure with his hood up and his large hands clasped together in prayer, chest heaving from exertion.

USS ENTERPRISE (CVN 65) EXPEDITIONARY STRIKE FORCE

"I'VE NEVER SEEN anything like that, sir...," Lieutenant Olson shook his head and pointed at the image of the deck where shoes, hats, gloves and other clothing items were strewn about. "We weren't prepared—" Olson stopped in mid-sentence.

"For what, Son?" Thorpe interjected.

"The crew…," Olson began again. "They were all dead…every last one of 'em. The men than were coming after us on deck were not the crew. They weren't even sailors"

"Who were they?" Janis repeated.

Thorpe could now see the underlying shock register in Lieutenant Olson's eyes, and sensed that he was struggling to maintain his composure in front of the one and three-star flag officers to whom he was reporting. He advanced to another photo of a steel doorway in the tanker.

"This is the galley," Olson said. "It's apparently the only room that would hold the entire crew." He advanced to the next image.

The bodies were stacked in grotesque heaps, randomly lying about on top of one another in various states of dress. They were all men with beards. Some wore shirts that had been badly torn; others rain jackets and thick wool sweaters. Many of them were missing their shoes and socks.

"That's the crew?" Thorpe asked.

Olson nodded. "Yes, sir." He backed up several images. "The clothing outside that you see here…on the decks…in the passage ways—it belonged to them. They were dragged and thrown inside."

"Dead or alive?" Thorpe asked.

Olson advanced the camera to the next image of a corpse's face, and then another. Each of them looked like a character in a horror movie, faces contorted, their heads cocked at unnatural angles, looking as if their faces were made up grotesquely in dark rouge. "Their eyes have been gouged out, so my guess is that they were already dead, or at least close to it."

"To disallow them of an afterlife," Thorpe concluded. "I'd say it was personal."

"The tanker was taken over without firing a shot," Thorpe answered matter-of-factly, looking intently over to Janis.

"So the terrorists on-board the tanker killed the entire crew and took it over…but who are they?" Janis asked.

"Janis pointed at the image on the camera. "*How* did they do this? I don't see any wounds, do you?"

Thorpe nodded. "If we had the opportunity to do autopsies, I think we'd find they were poisoned, Bill. We've seen this before, but on a much smaller scale."

He turned to Olson. "What else did you find, son?"

Olson looked toward the doorway to the Bridge and saw another SEAL in his wetsuit holding a black rubber bag. He walked over and took it from him. He reached inside the bag and pulled out a discolored white silk orphrey.

"This, sir," Olson said, handing vestment to Thorpe, who held it up critically. "We found one of these on each of the terrorists we killed."

MEDJUGORJE, BOSNIA AND HERZEGOVINA

MARK APPROACHED, stopping a short distance from Voyo, and raised his pistol at the old prelate. He could not see the Voyo's hand under the robe.

"Let me see your hands!"

Voyo looked at him contemptuously, his head beaded thick with sweat. He shook his head and laughed thickly.

Voyo held a hand up to the side of his face. "You are the boy, one who did this to me, are you not?"

"Give me the codes for the nuclear bomb on board that tanker *now*," Mark shouted above the wind, now aiming directly at Voyo's head.

"Marko Mescic...that was your name, I recall," Voyo answered slowly, ignoring Mark's demand. "I do remember you, Marko...it was so long ago. It has taken me a long time to put all of the pieces together...it is like a puzzle, is it not??"

Mark attempted to move around him, but Voyo countered by turning with him as he spoke: "I remember seeing you in your home when I arrested your father. I sent you to the orphanage in Zagreb where I could keep an eye on you."

"The Codes!" Mark's eyes darted around, his heart pounded furiously. *"NOW!"*

Voyo's voice was harsh and guttural. "You should have stayed there. And you would have been one of my commanders."

The memories of his father and his uncle came rushing back like a tidal wave, and made his head swim. He remembered the photos that Lazarus had left for him at the cathedral. He pulled them out of his coat with his free hand and threw them at him, but Voyo only glanced at the photos, making no effort to pick them up off the ground.

His cell phone rang. With his free hand he answered the phone while still aiming the pistol at Voyo.

"Mark, we've run out of time."

"I have the bastard in front of me, John."

"It's too late," Thorpe said. "We're going to have to sink her and hope for the best."

"Well, he did it. We have all the proof we need."

There was a pause on the other end. It seemed ominous. And Thorpe's voice, however altered by the satellite transmission, was subdued and distant. "I've gotta go. Be safe, Mark. I'll see you."

USS ENTERPRISE (CVN 65) EXPEDITIONARY STRIKE GROUP

"H MINUS SIX minutes, sir," the Captain called out.

"All right," Rear Admiral Janis answered. "Get those remaining SEALs off that tanker now."

Several seconds later they saw the infra-red image of a helicopter touching down on the tanker's deck and two figures running on-board.

"All friendly forces off the *MADHUMATI II*, sir," the Captain announced.

Thorpe understood that the situation already qualified as an international incident. Now circumstances and decisions—like this—would dictate its gravity. He knew there was no other rational decision. He nodded at Janis. His tone was clipped and resolute, devoid of any hesitation. "Okay, Bill. Sink her."

Janis nodded and pointed to his Captain. Giving the order, the Captain's voice was flat, emotionless: "*CHAFEE* and *CARTER*, this is Charlie one-one. Take Track five zero one seven. I say again, take track five zero one seven. Launch all weapons systems now."

The Captain transmitted the order and in a matter of seconds relayed the response back to Janis. "The *CARTER* reports 'Torpedoes Away.'"

"And the *CHAFEE*?" Janis asked.

"The Captain listened to the incoming call on his headset. "They're reporting 'Missiles Away' now, sir."

Janis turned to Thorpe and pointed at four streaks of light that suddenly appeared on the horizon. "Those are the Harpoons from our destroyer—the *CHAFEE.*"

A split second later, a series of explosions illuminated the sky where the tanker was sitting on the horizon. As each missile smashed into the *MADHUMATI's* hull in the distance, a separate fireball erupted. Thorpe had the impression he was watching another town's Fourth of July celebration. The rumble from the explosions resonated back to them like distant thunder.

"The torpedoes from the *CARTER* are next," Janis advised Thorpe.

In the distance, the fire onboard the *MADHUMATI II* suddenly flared. Its glow distended, and then just as quickly subsided.

"She's gone, Sir," the Captain reported.

Janis nodded. "Okay, tell the *CHAFEE* and *CARTER* to get the hell out of the area. Every one of our ships should be moving at flank speed. And I want to know their locations at regular intervals starting now." Janis turned to Thorpe. "Now we wait to see, if after all that, it can still detonate underwater."

Janis nodded, his face illuminated a dark red and blue from the screens on the bridge. "Give me an idea of what kind of waves we can expect."

The Captain led them to the Bridge's Plexiglas map board, illuminated with a dim blue light from the surrounding consoles. "Sir, we can expect two waves. Our best guess...," he pointed at the orange circle around the location where the *MADHUMATI II* had been sunk. "The first wave isn't the most dangerous." He pointed toward a larger blue circle drawn with a grease pencil around the orange one. "Here at surface zero, we can expect a surge of 40 feet or so, rushing outwards at a speed of over 55 knots." His hands created a steadily expanding circle. "So it's the second wave that we need to prepare for...80 to 100 feet high a kilometer away from 'surface zero'...the good news is that those waves rapidly weaken as they proceed outward to us." He pointed to a larger green circle, "Here, at 7 nautical miles, the waves will be 36 to 50 feet high. For us, here...twenty-five nautical miles away from surface zero," he continued, pointing to a black circle further out. "We'll turn bow on the blast site at H minus two. We can expect the waves to be anywhere from 23 to 30 feet high depending on the payload...enough to feel like a very bad roller coaster ride"

"H-3 Minutes, sir," another voice called out.

Janis turned to the Captain of *ENTERPRISE.* "All right, I want General Quarters with minimum manning at their stations. Get all nonessential personnel off this bridge now. Set MOPP Level Three. I want *everyone* off the decks and all doors and hatches shut tight! Bring us around so the tanker is straight off the bow."

"Aye, sir," the Captain answered as he ordered General Quarters, preparing the ship for battle and getting people in the proper gear for what was to come. A Bosuns Mate announced General Quarters over the ship's loudspeaker system—commonly called the "1MC."

MEDJUGORJE, BOSNIA AND HERZEGOVINA

"If you remember me," Mark began. "I can only wonder if you remember the others you murdered?" A rush of adrenalin surged through his veins. "My father, my uncle...my cousin! All of those you killed? My family?"

Voyo remained kneeling. There was no reply and he could see the old priest's jaw compress.

The pistol was shaking in his hand. "Why? Tell me why!"

Voyo turned his head without looking directly at him and pointed at the giant white cross overlooking Medjugorje. "...You should not have come back," Voyo answered, his voice pitiless and acidic. "You should have stayed in Ireland with your aunt. All of the killing...all of this death—it was all so..." His voice, graveled and sonorous in its delivery, drifted off.

"So what?" Mark shouted in English, shaking his head. "So *what*? You fucking animal! So *what*?"

"So...unnecessary," Voyo replied with surprised amusement, pressing his hands together.

"You bloody well deserve to die," Mark answered, his stomach twisting with rage. "And I may just do you that favor."

As his face darkened and the grip on the pistol tightened, Mark felt Sandy's hand on his shoulder. "Mark, please! Please...don't let him do this to you...."

Voyo laughed and lifted his tall frame slowly, facing away from them. "You should listen to her, Marko," he taunted.

Sandy was taken aback by Voyo's response, but then stepped forward. "Shut up, you *fuck*! You sick bastard! How can you live with yourself? You call yourself a *priest*? *A Cardinal?"* She screamed back at him. "You killed Kate! And all the others...Jack Fulbright...Bob Childs! I found his coat in your goddamned closet! You're not a priest, you're the goddamned Anti-Christ! You *do* deserve to die!" She wheeled back to Mark. "Go ahead! Go ahead and kill him!"

Mark glanced over at her in disbelief.

Voyo shook his head slowly, and walked toward the side of the hill overlooking Medjugorje.

"Let me see your hands!" Mark directed in English and then in Serbo-Croatian.

Voyo continued facing out and remained motionless, chanting: "What was hidden from mankind for centuries is being revealed to save the world from its certain destruction...they will not stop until they annihilate the church...until they know we will respond in kind...until we baptize them in their own blood."

"You've failed, Your Eminence," Mark shouted above the wind. "We intercepted the tanker in the Mediterranean Sea--quite far from Mecca really. If it explodes it will be a dramatic display for our navy and it'll kill quite a few fish, no one else...."

Voyo answered with a scowl of indignation. "You have no idea what you've done." His tone betrayed a heated rage, an unrestrained animality accustomed to dominance.

"Oh, I think I do!" Mark answered forcefully. "We prevented you all from starting a nuclear holocaust. And we found the other one at a mosque in Mostar."

"You are a fool! All of you are fools!" Voyo shouted maniacally, furiously. "I was protecting you!"

"By killing millions of innocent people?" Mark responded, shouting over the wind. "Is that how you were protecting us? Is that what the Catholic Church wants to do?"

His face boiled with rage, his nostrils flared and his voice took on a dark, menacing tone. "God will punish Islam."

Mark shook his head. "Yeah, well, not this time. Get up!"

Voyo shook his head slowly, as if in denial, abandoning any attempt at civil discourse. "You do not understand...*we are the hand of God!"*

"Somehow I don't think the Pope would agree with you on that."

Voyo cast a contemptuous glare. "It does not matter if the Holy Father approves or not…he is irrelevant—he has no authority over me…God's Covenant absolves us, and I am faithful only to its calling…."

"Executing you here would be the humane thing to do."

"*Thou shalt not kill*, Marko, do you not remember God's Commandment that *I* taught to you?" It came as a laugh, dripping in sarcasm.

He felt momentarily paralyzed. He remembered Voyo-the-Lieutenant quoting the same commandment to him thirty-five years ago on the hill at Brnisi Dam. "Of course I remember. I remember you trying to kill two innocent boys because they saw too much."

He heard Voyo's rasping laugh. "*No one* is innocent! We are all lambs to the slaughter…all of us! When we die for the church we are *ourselves* martyred!"

Mark paused for a moment, looking over at Sandy. Her arms were crossed. "But you see there's this small matter, you see, of trying you for war crimes at The Hague. They have a cage waiting for you there."

"War crimes? No…," Voyo said, turning around to face Mark, his bloodshot eyes blazoned into his. His hands were clasped together. "These are not crimes we have done, they are God's will. And *you*…." He took a step toward him. "Had you stayed home that day, everyone…your family…they would all be alive today."

His heart pounded as he stared into the eyes of his father's executioner. They were venomous eyes, dull, enameled, and seething with malice. Here was the one who had changed his life forever…who had taken away those closest to him, with no remorse or hesitation.

"You killed them after we met at the dam, didn't you? My father was alive when I was at the orphanage…." Mark knelt and picked up the photographs of both executions…of his uncle and his father. "After what happened at the dam, you killed them both!"

"How could I let them live after what you had done, Marko?" Voyo answered, coughing roughly. "After all the damage you had done? We all must atone for our sins. We must execute the defiant…your father and uncle among them."

His words came over him like a cold sweat, but he kept his pistol trained at Voyo, doing his best to keep his hand from trembling. "Let me see your hands, Your Eminence, now, or I'll have no choice."

Voyo laughed heavily. "You always had a choice, Marko. That is precisely the point! All of them died for *your* sins. Were it not for you, they would still be here."

His heart thundered inside his chest. A wave of horror and despair ran through him. At once, he felt stricken. "In God's name! *You bloody animal!"*

Voyo looked away and shrugged. "Do what you have come for...."

The statement caught him off-guard—it was disarming. In that fleeting second of confusion, he had not seen Voyo's right hand disappear into his vestments to reveal a pistol in his hand.

Sandy shouted his name, and he reacted quickly, aiming his Browning High Power at Voyo. But it had already happened—a loud, distinctive *THUH WUUP!* ...Too fast for either he or Sandy to understand fully what had just occurred. Mark jerked involuntarily. Behind him, he heard Sandy draw her breath in sharply.

Abruptly Voyo had dropped the pistol, just as he'd begun to raise it. Both arms fell to his side and his hood blew off his head in the strong breeze. His head and body were still, but his face had an expression of profound bewilderment. A small stream of blood trickled from his mouth onto the white habit. He looked down at the ground and then over to Mark and Sandy. For a fleeting moment, he smiled...an empty, vacuous smile with pitiless, glassy eyes.

"The blood of Christ shall drown the damned...."

Voyo's voice was hoarse and choked, and the words came slow, but they were clear. As soon as he'd spoken to them, his eyes turned expressionless and he fell forward like a giant tree that had been cut down at its stump.

For a moment, there was a stunned silence. Only the sound of the wind.

"Mark!" Sandy rushed up to his back and held on to him.

He took hold of her hands, finding them surprisingly warm.

"Is he—?"

Mark nodded. "He's quite dead."

Voyo's body lay in front of them, face down on the ground. There was a large dark stain developing on his white habit in the center of his back. Mark kicked the pistol away and leaned down to check for Voyo's pulse, finding none, only his dead, staring eyes and bloodless lips. He checked his pockets and found two plastic credit cards...one pink and the other light blue...with digitized alpha numerics printed across.

The permissive action link codes.

Voyo could have stopped it all...but he'd refused.

"Indeed, you do walk with the devil, Father." Mark said under his breath to the corpse of Vojislav Pijadje.

"You shot him?" Sandy asked, behind him, eyes wide.

Mark shook his head numbly and looked around. "No. Someone else did."

USS ENTERPRISE (CVN 65) EXPEDITIONARY STRIKE FORCE

"GENERAL QUARTERS, GENERAL QUARTERS. Set Condition Zebra throughout the ship."

The captain didn't have to repeat the well-drilled order. Dictating the watertight condition of the ship, "Condition Zebra" was the tightest, because it dictated *all* hatches and windows be secured.

A claxon boomed and a procession of crew rushed passed them and proceeded downstairs. Only a few crewmembers remained. The Captain passed Janis and Thorpe some heavily tinted, oversized sun glasses. "Welder's glasses, gentlemen...."

Thorpe, Janis, the Captain of the *USS ENTERPRISE* and the Executive Officer watched the digital countdown on the Bridge. The numbers were displayed in a luminous red that indicated hours, minutes and seconds. When the display passed zero without incident, they were reminded that it was only an estimate derived from the SEAL team's earlier report. It was eerily quiet after Janis had evacuated the rest of the crew below deck. The fabric of the sea reflected blue and black against the moon and stars. But it was a calm that belied the potential destructive force they were facing seven nautical miles away. Thorpe wondered whether sinking the tanker had somehow prevented the detonation of the device.

The blast occurred just as Thorpe was starting to take the welder's glasses off at minus forty-six seconds...an electric blue...blinding, sudden, and unrestrained flash. Thorpe involuntarily squinted through the welder's glasses. He gripped a nearby rail tightly, with both hands. The predawn sky lit up around them, reflecting vibrant reds, oranges and yellows on the water's surface. Just as quickly, the fireball subsided to reveal an expanding cloud of spray, like a parachute suddenly opening in reverse. It, too, quickly receded to reveal the sea surging upward in a monumental white cone of water, capped by a darkened crown of debris from the sea floor. Next, spikes and plumes jutted out from the cone like a feral weed hybrid. It was all unfolding in complete silence...as if they were watching a drive-in movie with no audio. Just as quickly, the entire carrier began to vibrate and a sustained, earsplitting roar enveloped them like a locomotive barreling through a tunnel.

In only seconds, the cloud lifted like a screen, exposing the characteristic dark mushroom cloud with a white stem from the ascending water column.

The expanding cloud of spray at the base of the column moved outward, resembling a wall of foaming, boiling water and the predawn sky abruptly turned grey.

"Sir, thirty foot seas approaching!" The Captain announced.

Janis turned to Thorpe. "Hold on tight, Sir. We're in for a helluva shock."

With the initial wave of heat and compressed air, the windows to the bridge fogged around them, like a green house would in the dead of winter...with no warning...a seemingly endless sheet of water descended upon the massive carrier with enough sustained force to make the ship begin to list. Thorpe hunched his shoulders protectively. As the wave hit the hull of the carrier, it pitched the ship to its starboard side. All three men were thrown into the glass and into one another, gripping railings, instrument consoles and map boards trying desperately to regain their balance.

The concussion and thermal pulse seemed to envelop them, and Thorpe felt himself struggling...ravenous for each breath of air. Inside the bridge, the air conditioning and lights had cut off, and it was oppressively hot. The air was humid and his lungs burned. Through the fogged window of the bridge, he saw the second tidal wave, a foaming wall of water that took up the entire horizon.

"Dear God," Thorpe gasped.

Chapter 90

THE DOOR BELL to Jon Schauer's apartment rang. Mark Lyons walked to the door and opened it to find John Thorpe, dressed in a brown canvas jacket and khaki pants, standing with a bottle of champagne in one hand.

"I heard there was a party?" Thorpe asked, grinning broadly. With the exception of the area around his eyes, his face had a deep reddish tint—he looked as if he'd been badly sun-burnt on the ski slopes.

Mark broke out in a wide grin. "You're bloody right there is!" He reached out for Thorpe and embraced him. "I'm glad you're okay, John."

"Likewise," Thorpe answered. "It's all enough to make you realize your own mortality. Boggles the mind. I never thought I'd witness something like it in my lifetime."

"Yer okay?"

Thorpe nodded slowly. "The tidal wave knocked the *ENTERPRISE* over on her beam, but miraculously, she somehow managed to right herself."

"Were many hurt?"

Thorpe shook his head. "A few seriously, quite a few with minor injuries…it was a damn close-run thing for everyone."

"Thank God for small mercies." He invited him in.

"Are *you* okay?" Thorpe asked inside the entryway. "Sandy told me what happened over the phone."

"It's over." Mark answered. "Thirty-five years later, and it's finally over."

"Any idea who shot the cardinal?"

He shook his head. "Someone who could fire a 7.62 caliber rifle at long range…it could've been anyone. Lazarus, the Vatican, the Serbs…Christ if I know. It's the trouble with these matters. Seldom a clear read…but the rutting bastard's dead and I cain't say I mourn 'im."

Thorpe nodded his understanding as Sandy rushed up to him and hugged him, casting an eye at Mark.

"What are you two talking about? Get in here!"

Thorpe smiled warmly, and handed her the bottle of champagne. "This is for you. The bloody Irish can't appreciate good champagne."

"You're early, John," Sandy said. "We have plenty to celebrate, and we're just getting started!"

Jon Schauer was unwrapping trays of condiments and hors d'oeuvres and passing them to Mike McCallister to place on the dining room table. There was a general air of relief and celebration in the apartment.

Thorpe took off his jacket in the hallway and handed it to Mark, who placed hung it in the closet.

In the background Sandy was directing Vladimir to get the beer and soft drinks from the refrigerator as she was pulling crystal glasses from the cabinet. "And there should be a bottle of Merlot on the counter near the stove."

Thorpe handed Mark a copy of the *New York Times* in the hallway. "You might want to take a look at the front page."

Mark read it as he walked through the hallway into the living room.

Fulbright Death in Bosnia Not an Accident
By Chris Solomon
New York Times **News Service**
Sarajevo, Bosnia-Herzegovina, March 2—A New York Times investigation has revealed that Chief American envoy, Ambassador Jack Fulbright and his delegation were not killed in an accident in Bosnia as officially stated, but instead in a deliberate ambush by international terrorists. Authorities have not commented except to point to an FBI investigation of the incident that is still ongoing. A series of photographs obtained by the New York Times show the ambush in progress, conducted by militants of unknown origin, emplacing landmines under the wheels of the diplomatic convoy vehicles and firing weapons into them.

An anonymous European Union law enforcement official called it a "cold-blooded murder." Senate Majority Leader, Edward Gray, offering the photos into evidence, has called upon the Attorney General to appoint an independent prosecutor and grand jury to investigate the attack on the Fulbright delegation. He has asked President Sells for a full explanation for the erroneous report to Congress and the public. One senior administration official, speaking on condition of anonymity because the matter is classified, has called the misrepresentation "intentional, but necessary."

When asked about the matter, National Security Advisor Rachel Cook refused to comment.

461

Mark shook his head and looked up at Thorpe. "They're still not coming clean on any of this."

Thorpe nodded his understanding. "I warned them, but they wouldn't listen."

"Well, then they deserve what's coming to 'em."

Thorpe tossed the paper in the nearby waste basket. He accepted a bottle of Heineken from Schauer, and thanked him. He took a sip and turned back to Mark, changing the subject. "You asked a while back about moving some cargo over here?"

"I did. Is it still possible?" "I have a C-17 that will be taking off from Tampa by the end of the week...and right now it's empty."

Mark nodded at Thorpe. "I think I can fill it up, if you'll allow me to, John."

"It's all yours," Thorpe answered. "It's a waste to fly those massive jets empty. Can I ask you what kind of cargo the crew should be planning for?"

Mark nodded and smiled. "Tell them to plan for construction supplies...a variety of them, I'd say."

"There are two Merlots," Vladimir called out genially. "One's a 2004 vintage, and the other is older...much older—looks like a 1982! Which one?"

Both men looked into the apartment. Sandy was calling out from the dining room. "Open the '82! I'd say it's about time.... You don't have any objection, do you, Jon?"

Vladimir showed the bottle to Schauer, who shrugged. "I don't remember buying it, but I agree! It's time!"

Thorpe nodded at Mark and returned his smile. "I'll let them know then."

Mark stopped inside the kitchen as he watched Vladimir begin to unscrew the cork for the bottle of Merlot.

"...the other is older...much older—looks like a 1982!" Vladimir's statement returned to him, causing a sudden dissonance in the back of Mark's head. A tremor of unease passed through him. He closed his eyes for a split second, and the fragmented memory of Papa Voyo saying Mass at Saint Stephen's, uttering the Eucharistic Prayer, watching him in the front pew, flashed back to him.

...Take this all of you and drink from it: this is the cup of my blood, the blood of the new and everlasting covenant. It will be shed for you and for all so that sins may *be forgiven....*

In the same image, Voyo was pouring the wine into the chalice and drinking from it. And then, just as quickly...just as vividly, the image shifted to Voyo on top of Mount Krizevac standing before him in his white habit just after he'd been struck by the sniper's bullet.

"The blood of Christ shall drown the damned."

At the time, he'd discounted them as the final words of a certifiable madman and mass murderer, but now they resonated with the dissonance of a stray chord.

What did he mean?

His mind raced, searching for any hidden logic...or perverse meaning to those last words.

In the Catholic Eucharist, blood was symbolized by red wine....

A warning from the grave, meant to be heard...deciphered after the fact.

Voyo had poisoned the bottle of wine that killed Kate Kamrath, by smuggling it into her own apartment. *It too had also been bottled in 1982.*

He had plenty of experience with many other serial killers to know they all had their own preferred, often unique signature. *Could he have possibly done the same here...and broken in to Jon Schauer's apartment while he was in Zagreb?*

"Mark, are you okay?" Thorpe asked, hitting him on the shoulder.

Mark looked up at him and nodded absently.

We stayed here whenever we were in town during the last several weeks... he could easily have watched us....

"Let's get you a beer. You need one after all of this," Thorpe said reaching for a bottle McCallister was handing him.

He knew...he knew my name...everything about me...my family...what he'd done to them...

He knew!

He felt a tingle in the back of his head and his heart skipped a beat. In Voyo's mind, his victims...those he could reach and execute himself were "Martyrs." And in his twisted mind, those he could not were "The Damned."

Dear God.

Mark walked quickly over to Vladimir, who had just succeeded in pulling the cork from the old bottle of Merlot. In a quick motion, he reached for both bottles and slid the bottle of champagne that Thorpe had brought in, over to him. "Let's open this, Vlad. I'll take these, if you don't mind."

Vladimir cast a short confused glance at him and began opening the bottle of champagne.

Mark carried both bottles of Merlot into the bathroom. He closed the door and opened the small window to the alleyway.

The first bottle he released to the street was the unopened 2004. A moment later, the glass shattered in the street below. He turned the water on in the sink and poured the entire contents of the 1982 vintage down the drain before placing it, too, out the window and releasing it. The bottle had a hollow sound when it shattered on the cobblestone alleyway.

He emerged from the bathroom and Sandy was standing there at the door waiting for him with two pints of Guinness, with a wary expression. She handed him one of the pints.

"I take it we don't like Merlot either...."

"Life's too short to drink bad wine," he answered simply.

Epilogue

MARK LYONS SLEPT SOUNDLY, DREAMLESSLY. He had arrived at the park at dawn, well-prior to the dedication ceremony and concert. He sat on a large boulder near the open air stage and watched the crowds of people gathering for the dedication concert. As they waited, men and women were pushing infants in strollers around the well-equipped grounds as children of all ages ran around.

Surveying the park from his vantage point, he was struck by the permanence of the place. It had taken nine months to clear the land of the wreckage and rubble, landscape it, lay the asphalt jogging trails and construct the expansive playground from the equipment that had been flown into the Mostar airport with four separate sorties of C-17 cargo jets that John Thorpe had arranged for him. It was one of many immense construction efforts in rebuilding Ravno after the wholesale destruction wreaked upon it during the last year, but combined with the other two projects...rebuilding the Catholic Church in Stolac and repairing the Karadzozbeg Mosque in Mostar, it had quickly become the single largest development venture in Bosnia. He'd started it with the money Celo had handed to him at the church in Stolac. When he'd started, he thought 4 million euros would be more than enough. When that ran out, he was still six million euros short. Roman Polko filled the shortfall by arranging for United Nations development funds, and the Vatican had provided its own money for the project.

He'd never envisioned himself as a developer or construction foreman, but as he considered turning the seized money in to the UN or the Vatican, he was more and more convinced that turning the money in would only serve to pad an already burgeoning bank account somewhere far from Balkan shores, and be of no service to those who had suffered during the past year as a result of the crisis in Ravno.

His final decision to go forward with the projects came to him during Celo's funeral. Although he was certain these projects were certainly not the way Celo would have spent the money, it was ironically Celo, with all of his past transgressions and imperfections, who made it all possible. There were other influences too: Kate Kamrath, Ambassador Fulbright and his delegation, Robert Childs. All that remained in the wake of their sacrifice was their memory, and he would not allow for them to be forgotten. Roman Polko's impassioned requests that he focus on the children to prevent future Balkan wars, his own childhood memories of violence growing up here...all of these made his plan seem logical, if not altogether obvious.

Once begun, it had become his personal crusade to transform a monumental tragedy into an enduring legacy for those who had sacrificed their lives for peace.

With Sandy's help, he'd custom designed the playground in wood to resemble a castle, complete with a waterless moat, passageways, lookout towers; and in another section, a giant pirate's ship with covered slides, mazes, swings and ropes. The sun glistened on the vast winding man-made lake that he recalled had been stocked with ducks donated by the Sarajevo and Zagreb zoos. Sandy Evenson had arranged for a large children's garden to be donated by the New York Times. After months of waiting, thousands of trees from Western Europe had arrived by barge and had just recently been transplanted along the complex of winding trails.

Now, everything seemed possible. He felt the anger and resentment so firmly lodged in his past disappear—now, it truly was *"the past,"* and it would no longer define him.

On stage, technicians were conducting last-minute preparations, setting up instruments and conducting sound tests. The media vans had set up in an area behind the stage offset from the band's tour bus, emblazoned with their gold and black "CHIEFTAINS" logo on the sides. When he called the Dublin-based band leaders who he'd known for years, they immediately agreed to come down to play a benefit concert for the dedication of the park, and to help rebuild the schools of Ravno and the surrounding area.

"Are you planning to come down from that rock any time soon, Commissioner?" Amidst the cacophony of sounds from the stage and the crowds, he recognized the voice below him as Sandy Evenson's.

"That's 'Soon-to-Be Former Commissioner' to you, Counselor," Mark answered, smiling. "This is my last day, remember?"

Sandy gathered her hair in a coy gesture and lifted it, exposing the curve of her neck. *"And now that ye'v quit yer day job, have ya decided yet what's next for ye?"* She asked in the best Irish brogue she could muster.

He smiled and then laughed. It was an admirable attempt for someone from Connecticut. He responded in kind, "Aye, well ye see...I've a trip planned."

She eyed him narrowly. "A trip?"

"Aye." He nodded coyly. "Ye see, I was hopin' if I offered ye a suitable inducement, ye might be willin' to take a wee trip to the Antrim Coast with yers truly...."

Her eyes lit up and her American dialect returned. "You're kidding me, right?"

He smiled and shook his head, taking a package out of the backpack that was sitting beside him on the boulder. "That is, only if ye enjoy gardening, bike riding, milkin' the goats...." He continued with his brogue. *"So, I've the tickets right here...if yer willin' a'carse."*

She'd crossed her arms to contain herself, a sudden smile lighting her face. "Aye," she answered. "Well, if you'll have me, I suppose I'm willin'!" she answered coyly. "Now get down here! Besides, the *Chieftains* are summoning you...they're wondering where you've gone."

He slung his backpack over his shoulder and maneuvered down the massive boulder, hopping down to the smaller ones beside it, and then jumping to the ground in front of Sandy. She was grinning broadly, and he could see the remnants of tears in her eyes before she embraced him. At that moment, she was luminous.

Her long brown hair brushed against his cheek, its smell fresh and clean. Enfolding her in his arms, her body pressed tightly against his. He pressed his hands against the strong curve of her back. After a moment, he kissed her.

He embraced her and breathed in deeply.

It was over. The nightmare he'd been living was finally over. In the time he'd been in Bosnia, there was the realization—at once sudden and also comforting—that he'd surfaced from an abyss of terror, horror and death for which he never thought he would receive a reprieve.

"When do we leave?" she asked, pulling back yet still holding him tightly. Her eyes were gleaming, her smile radiant.

He stroked her cheek. "Late tonight. Several connections, but we'll be on the cliffs of Antrim by this time tomorrow."

"I never thought you'd ask."

"Well, you can blame it on my aunt," Mark answered. "You made quite an impression upon her, you know. She *demanded* that I bring you back so she could have another cup of tea with you."

She attached herself to his arm and walked with him toward the stage.

She pointed at a jungle gym set a short distance away where a young boy was playing. His mother stood below watching over him with a baby stroller. As they drew closer, she smiled and waved at them. It was Celo's widow, infant and now seven-year-old son.

When he'd gone to visit them after Celo's death, Mark learned that Celo had named his oldest son, "Marko." His wife had named their newborn son "Goran" with "Celo" as his nickname.

Beside the Chieftain's tour bus, Mike McCallister, Jon Schauer and Vladimir stood talking. They congratulated him as he passed, and in response he slapped them on their shoulders and shook their hands, telling them *they* were the ones who deserved to be congratulated. Each of them shared responsibility for the collective success of the reconstruction projects. He'd given Mike and Vlad responsibility for supervising the reconstruction of the church in Stolac, and Jon Schauer had taken on the reconstruction project for the mosque in Mostar.

Near the base of the backstage stairway, John Thorpe, Ian Rose and Roman Polko were conversing together with the Archbishop of Sarajevo and the Grand Mufti of Bosnia, who were both dressed in their full ceremonial religious regalia.

Mark and Sandy approached the group, welcoming them.

Mark looked at all four men as he shook their hands. He paused for a moment and looked into their eyes.

The Archbishop of Sarajevo introduced himself to Mark and shook his hand. "Commissioner, I would like to thank you for what you have done."

Mark was taken by surprise. "Your Eminence, I think it would be better if I *apologized* to you for all that's happened. I'm sorry we were not able to better contain it."

The Archbishop shook his head resolutely and his lips pursed in somber reflection. "No, your pursuit of Voyo was necessary…for us, for the church, it was for the best." He shook his head, glanced at Thorpe and Rose, and looked at Mark with serious eyes. "You know, it is the capricious hand of fate. Among us, even among the most powerful in our church, there are those who subvert it for their own purposes." The cardinal looked over at the gathering crowd. "You see, there are no angels among us, no innocents. All of us…we are all sinners."

"And now what will happen?" Mark asked.

"And now?" The cardinal smiled thoughtfully. "And now," he said after a thoughtful pause. "…We have Hope, do we not?"

He nodded. "Indeed, we do," he said, meaning it.

An announcer came over the loudspeaker system, speaking in Serbo-Croatian and then in English, requesting the audience to take their seats or positions on the lawn as the concert was about to begin.

Mark spoke to all five dignitaries. "Thank-you for making this park…all of this possible."

Polko smiled and spoke for the group. "Mark, it is *you* who made this possible. Not us."

Mark shook his head slowly and smiled. "The ones who are no longer with us…I think they made it possible. It's here to honor their memory."

The men nodded their agreement.

Ian Rose extended his hand. Mark met his handshake as he looked in his eyes. A brief smile transformed his face, conveying respect and gratitude. No words were necessary between either man and Mark was grateful, now, for his presence.

Sandy walked up to Mark and took his arm. "Celo's wife and boys will be in the front row."

Before Mark could respond, someone shouted his name out the backstage door.

"I think you're wanted backstage," Thorpe said.

Mark looked up at the Chieftain's lead singer who repeated his plea to join them. He nodded and waved, turning back to the group. "You all have front row seats too, you know…."

Roman Polko stepped forward and nodded to Sandy. "May I steal him from you for a moment, Sandy?"

"Of course," she answered, releasing her grip on Mark's arm and retreating to Thorpe's side.

As they approached the stairs, Polko stopped and turned to Mark. "Mark, I know you're leaving tonight. Before you do, I want to thank you, personally, for all you've done for us…for me. I have seen many things in my lifetime. I have seen a wall that divided us torn down, I have won medals in the Olympic Games, but what you have accomplished here…it is the finest thing I have ever seen."

He smiled at the elder statesman. He glanced up at the forested slopes around them, and at the mountains in the distance. A flock of doves took flight around them "It's for the children."

Polko nodded. "Yes, the park is magnificent, but that is not what I meant. I am thankful for what you have done as a man." He pointed at a group of children taking their seats. "You are an example to them."

He shook his head. "I hardly deserve any thanks, sir. My reward is to see them here together, playing, being children again." He smiled, motioning toward the mob of laughing children. "You were right all along. They decide the future, not us."

Polko was silent as he looked into Mark's eyes with a glint of memory that seemed to convey recognition and gratitude. After a moment, he pursed his lips. "Marko, how can I make you understand?" Polko said slowly, steadily, squeezing his arms with both of his hands. "*Hvala, Comchye*...thank you, neighbor."

Polko smiled silently, bowed his head and abruptly turned away.

When Mark looked back, Polko was gone. A stage hand called for him to step up to the crowded backstage area. Absently, he stepped up and Sandy handed him his violin and bow. It was his father's violin. He drew the bow across the strings and tightened them to fine-tune the instrument. Down from the stage, he saw the group he'd just left. All of them were sitting in the front row.

A loud voice came over the loudspeaker, accompanied by a melodic Celtic instrumental tune. Applause erupted from the audience. He walked on stage with the rest of the band, and as they began to play, the band's lead vocalist introduced him: *"Mark Lyons: Friend, Fellow Musician, Hero... Founder and Architect of Camelot Park."*

He was greeted with rapturous applause. As they played the ballad he'd written long ago in honor of his father, he closed his eyes and ran the bow delicately across the violin strings. For a long moment, he felt purged of the guilt and sorrow...the ghosts that for so long had haunted him.

He looked down at the seat Roman Polko had just been occupying. It was now empty. And in that instant he understood the meaning *and the intent* of Polko's message to him during their encounter, only minutes ago.

Crystalline images returned like a kaleidoscope flashing before him. With each draw of his bow, an intuitive, deep awareness emerged. He remembered their second meeting in his office, and the photograph of

Roman Polko winning the Bronze Medal for the Biathlon as a young man...the target rifle had been strapped to his back. He recalled Polko's silver voice and his words that day, describing the other photo taken after his attempted defection to the West:

"I was just released from three years as a political prisoner in Belgrade...."

He felt a shiver. His head was spinning. And then, something like an epiphany...a sudden, revelatory flash of certainty: Polko had used his childhood name, *Marko*, the first day he'd met him, more than eight months ago, but this time he'd called him *"Neighbor."* Only the man he'd helped at the grave that night three and a half decades ago had called him that.

Only him.

Only someone with specialized training could have successfully achieved the long-distance shot that killed Papa Voyo. Of all the people who could possess those skills, he realized, an Olympic Biathloner would certainly be one of them.

He'd known about Voyo all along....

Now, he recognized the face of the sniper who had shot Cardinal Vojislav Pijadje; and too, the cryptic voice of the man who had been calling him, guiding him in Voyo's direction all along—whom, as a boy, he once rescued from the grave.

Lazarus.

ABOUT THE AUTHOR

John Fenzel has served on the personal staffs of the Vice President of the United States, the Secretary of Defense, and the Director of The Office of Personnel Management, Janice Lachance. He served as the commander of an Army Special Forces battalion at Fort Bragg, NC and commanded an Army brigade at Fort Knox, KY. In the wake of the September 11th attacks, he was the Staff Director for Homeland Security Advisor, Tom Ridge and was the principal architect our nation's color-coded alert system. He has led Green Berets in peacetime and in war.

John lives with his wife and three children in Washington, D.C. *The Lazarus Covenant* is his first novel.